Abandon is an original publication of NCP. This work has never before appeared in book form. This work is a novel. Any similarity to actual persons or events is purely coincidental.

New Concepts Publishing, Inc.
5202 Humphreys Rd.
Lake Park, GA 31636

ISBN 1-58608-724-x
© Kaitlyn O'Connor
Cover art (c) copyright 2006 Dan Skinner & Kat Richards

All rights reserved, which includes the right to reproduce this book or portions thereof in any form whatsoever except as provided by the U.S. Copyright Law.

If you purchased this book without a cover you should be aware this book is stolen property.

NCP books are available at special quantity discounts for bulk purchases for sales promotions, premiums, fund raising, or educational use. For details, write, email, or phone New Concepts Publishing, Inc., 5202 Humphreys Rd., Lake Park, GA 31636; Ph. 229-257-0367, Fax 229-219-1097; orders@newconceptspublishing.com.

First NCP Trade Paperback Printing: June 2006

D0880589

OTHER TRADE PAPERBACKS FROM NEW
CONCEPTS PUBLISHING BY KAITLYN O'CONNOR:

Clone Wars: ARMAGEDDON

GUARDIANS

ABIOGENESIS

CYBORG

WHEN NIGHT FALLS

THE LION'S WOMAN

ABANDON

By

Kaitlyn O'Connor

Futuristic Romance

New Concepts   Georgia

Be sure to check out our website for the very best in fiction at fantastic prices!

When you visit our webpage, you can:
* Read excerpts of currently available books
* View cover art of upcoming books and current releases
* Find out more about the talented artists who capture the magic of the writer's imagination on the covers
* Order books from our backlist
* Find out the latest NCP and author news--including any upcoming book signings by your favorite NCP author
* Read author bios and reviews of our books
* Get NCP submission guidelines
* And so much more!

We offer a 20% discount on all new Trade Paperback releases ordered from our website!

Be sure to visit our webpage to find the best deals in e-books and paperbacks! To find out about our new releases as soon as they are available, please be sure to sign up for our newsletter (http://www.newconceptspublishing.com/newsletter.htm) or join our reader group (http://groups.yahoo.com/group/new_concepts_pub/join)!

The newsletter is available by double opt in only and our customer information is *never* shared!

Visit our webpage at:
www.newconceptspublishing.com

BELOW

Chapter One

It might almost have been Earth. The globe below them was awash with ocean--80 percent to be precise--but the glow from the red sun that sliced through its atmosphere gave the waters below the eerie look of blood....

"An ocean of blood."

Victoria glanced sharply at Captain Huggins. Seated before her at the console, his back was to her as he divided his attention between the viewing screen and the readout from the vessel's probes.

After a moment, she realized he wasn't telepathic. It was only a coincidence that he'd voiced her own thoughts. An involuntary shiver skated along her spine as she returned her attention to the viewing screen.

"Creepy, eh, Tory?"

It took an effort to keep her upper lip from curling in distaste, but Victoria Anderson was a firm believer in self discipline. She kept her expression impassive. She didn't turn to the speaker. There was no sense in encouraging the man. Not that he could be discouraged.

"Chilled," she lied succinctly. However much she would've liked to dispute it, even to herself, she found the prospect below them unnerving.

"Right. Takes a bit to get the blood pumping after such a long hyber-sleep. I could warm you up a bit, if you'd like."

This time Victoria didn't bother to hide her distaste. "Do you mind?"

"Eh?" Jim Roach's look was hopeful.

She gave him a plastic smile. "I'd like to hear the report." She moved away from him, closer to the console, where the captain was pulling up a report from the computer. "What's it look like?"

He frowned, but didn't turn. "A bit more than tolerable, I'd say."

Victoria's lips flattened. She could see enough of the report to tell that barely tolerable might be an understatement. "They said the conditions were acceptable."

Captain Huggins threw her a quick glance before returning his attention to the report. "It's livable, if not hospitable. The construction crew seemed to deal with the conditions without any problems. Anyway, you knew the information the company had was sketchy."

A flash of anger, quickly quelled, went through Victoria. He was right. She'd accepted the assignment, knowing how the company was, knowing they hadn't seen much beyond the find of the century. The crew's survival was important to them, but only in terms of whether or not they survived long enough to mine the precious mineral that resided a scant 50 feet below that deceptively threatening surface.

It *was* deceptive, she told herself. Granted, this tiny system was at the very edge of the outer rim, light years from the beaten path. But several probes had been diverted to the planet to gather as much information as possible before the first landers were dispatched.

"You pick up on the beacon yet?" 'Hugs' Huggins asked his communications officer, Leigh Grant.

"Nothing ... too much interference. Wait."

"You got something?"

"Yeah. Faint. There's ... yes. Definitely. Looks like about 60 degrees starboard. Maybe 50 clicks. Good job, Hugs! You sat us down practically on top of it."

'Hugs' looked anything but huggable, Victoria thought wryly. He was built in the general shape of a water bug--a pear shaped torso, arms and legs like skeletal remains, no doubt from 40 years of shuttling around the galaxy and doing little beyond moving from his console to the hyber-chamber and back again. He'd probably spent two thirds of his life in hyber-sleep, which no doubt accounted for his youthful appearance. He didn't look half his 68 years.

One would've thought the compliment would've pleased him, but he didn't show it. In fact, he looked faintly alarmed.

Victoria felt another prickle of uneasiness as he glanced over his shoulder at the ground crew assembled behind him. His gaze finally settled on her. "You heard Grant. We'll be docking shortly. Maybe you'd like to get your gear together."

No way was Victoria going anywhere, but she could see his point.

"Roach. Get the crew below and ready the equipment for off loading."

For a moment, he looked as if he would argue. Finally, he shrugged and gestured the crew out. He stopped as he reached the portal. "What about the tadpoles?"

Victoria's lips tightened. Her eyes narrowed. "The what?"

He grinned, showing two rows of teeth in serious need of good hygiene ... or maybe they were beyond that. "You know. The slugs. Fish."

She strode over to him. "That's not only distasteful, it's stupid," she said, keeping her voice low. "They're human beings."

"Half," he corrected, obviously unrepentant.

Victoria gritted her teeth and counted to ten. "Genetically altered."

Again he cut her off. "To be half fish."

Victoria counted to twenty. "We have to work as a team, Roach, or this isn't going to work at all. Once this crew leaves, we're on our own, and we'll need everybody, EVERYBODY, to work together if we're going to survive. I don't give a damn what your personal opinion is of the project, or genetics in general. They're telepathic, you fool. So you put that shit out of your head right now, and go down and tell the deep water mining CREW that we're about to dock. You got that?"

"Yes, sir, chief! I mean, ma'am! " He gave her a mocking salute and marched out.

Victoria glared at his back as he left. Where the hell the company had dug him up from was a mystery to her. If he had any kind of specialty at all, it was in being a royal pain in the ass.

It was hell trying to work with morons. There were half a dozen surface crew members, including her and Roach, almost four times that number of genetically engineered deep water mining crew who--despite the company's reassurances about their psychological stability--were an unknown quantity, they were about to be dropped on a rock that was virtually uncharted, were a bare minimum of three months from any rescue team, and Roach was hell bent on stirring up trouble before they'd even been dropped.

She'd been assigned to oversee the work, not baby sit, and certainly not referee. Six month's duty began to seem like a long, long assignment.

Dismissing it, Victoria turned her attention to the more immediate problem, returning to her observation position. She knew they must be getting close to the rig by now. "Any response to the hail?"

Leigh shot a look at the captain. A silent communication passed between them. "Nothing yet," she responded finally.

The by-play between them set Victoria's teeth on edge. "I'm in charge of the mission. Do me the courtesy of responding directly to my questions."

Again the silent communication between the two at the console. Apparently, they'd been flying together so long, telepathy wasn't necessary.

"Dead air," Captain Huggins replied shortly.

"Could they all be down below?"

"Not likely. There's supposed to be a surface crew on duty at all times, unless a storm forces them under. The sky's clear though."

Victoria studied the sky skeptically. The atmosphere looked like mud from where she was standing. Dimly, in the distance, she caught a glimpse of shining metal. "There!"

Captain Huggins glanced at her and then followed the direction of her pointing finger. He frowned. "Looks like debris. Maybe they had a blow?"

They'd dropped low enough, skimming little more than a few meters above the waves. Victoria saw now that there was an alarming amount of debris bobbing in the water. She focused her gaze on the horizon. "That's it! Jesus Christ!"

The habitat/mining rig had been under construction for over a year. The construction was to have been completed months ago. The last she'd heard, it had been reported 95% complete. Even from this distance, she could see it was a hell of a long way from that. Briefly, she wondered if somebody had just hedged on the numbers, or if it was even the main habitat she was looking at, but she realized fairly quickly that the size alone was evidence it could be nothing else.

It was the main rig all right, but something had battered the hell out of it.

Leigh shot a panicked glance at the captain. "Hurricane, you think?"

He shook his head. "Can't tell at this distance."

"They didn't report anything?" Victoria demanded.

"We haven't heard from the ground crew since mid-way," Captain Huggins said reluctantly.

"Between Kay and Zeta Station?"

He looked uncomfortable. "Earth."

Victoria fought a round with her temper. "You're saying we haven't heard from anyone on the rig in six months and you didn't think it was important enough to wake me up and tell me about it?"

Huggins spared a moment to glare at her. "It was reported to the company. The company checked it out and gave me a go."

"Where's the report?" she asked tightly.

"In your quarters."

Victoria strode from the cockpit and down the corridor to her cabin. A ten minute search unearthed the one page report--make that one paragraph. 'Communications tower down. Proceed. Report repairs.'

Victoria wadded the report into a ball. They didn't have a damned clue of what they were walking in to.

The company had already sunk billions into the project and had yet to pull the first ton of ore. It wasn't likely they were going to pull the plug for something that could easily be explained away as equipment malfunction. She should have known that.

They could've diverted a damned probe, though. If they'd bothered to, they would've seen it was a hell of a lot more than equipment failure. The communications tower wasn't just down. It was gone.

Feeling a fluctuation in speed, Victoria took a deep breath and dismissed her frustration. Purposefulness took its place. They were going to be caught up in repairs for months. If there was any money to be made, she was going to have to get the crew into high gear the moment they off-loaded.

And there would be money. She was determined on that. With her pay plus the bonus they'd been offered for every ton she brought in over quota, she'd be able to retire from the company within two years if she could make it through two tours here. Six on, six off and then another six on. After that, if she lived through it, she'd be able to pursue her dream, find a quiet little homestead on the back side of nowhere and concentrate on perfecting her skills as an artist--particularly sculpting.

She'd had no confidence she had the talent to become a successful artist, which was why she'd accepted that she'd have to earn a living and consider art no more than a hobby until she could afford to do otherwise. The upside to putting it on hold and building a nest egg first was that it wouldn't matter whether she was talented enough to make a living at it or not. She could do it for the sheer joy of it. If she sold anything, fine. If she didn't, she was still going to be OK.

It had seemed worth it to take high risk work that would ensure she could launch her career in art while she was still young enough to dream, but it was a goal she'd shared with no one. Even the mention of 'retiring' before thirty, to pursue a career as an artist of all things, would have landed her in the company shrink's office for a psych evaluation. She might just as well claim she wanted to marry and stay at home to rear children. She wouldn't be considered any more maladjusted.

As far as she was concerned, however, it was not only crazy to consider a full fifty with the company, it was downright suicidal. Whatever they might think, she had no intention of being stuck working for the damned company until they managed to get her killed on one of their low budget, high yield enterprises.

As usual, her focus on her ultimate goal brought her boiling frustration under control. Leaving her quarters, she made her way down to the lower deck to check the crew's progress.

As she strode along the upper corridor, something skated through her mind, almost as if someone had caressed her.

Victoria paused, looking around, certain at first that someone actually had touched her. She was alone though.

Except in her mind.

Raphael.

Irritation surfaced. With an effort, she closed her mind to his inquisitive probing. He had no right to intrude on her private thoughts, but he was beginning to do it with increasing frequency. She wondered if that meant he was growing stronger, or....

She dismissed the thought before it had time to fully form.

The project had hinged on a revolutionary genetic experiment. Genetic manipulation was almost as old as space mining and colonization. It was the most practical way to go about both mining and terraforming. A 'perfect' world was one in a million, or maybe a billion. Most of the worlds they'd found were fairly close to useable, but certainly not prime real estate. Genetic manipulation allowed the companies to 'acclimatize' miners and terraformers to the conditions, which minimized the danger to the workers and, purely coincidentally, also lowered the company's expenses, since they didn't have to supply the workers with environmental suits. It also enabled workers to produce better since they weren't hampered by bulky suits and oxygen tanks, another plus on the side of the company, who seemed to suffer no moral or ethical qualms about the fact that the workers that underwent the genetic manipulations were generally doomed to live out the remainder of their lives on the planet they were designed for, since very few ever earned enough money to pay to be acclimatized to Earth's conditions once more.

KAY2581, or Kay as they called the planet they were about to mine, had posed a unique challenge. The ore they'd discovered was only to be found beneath the planet's oceans. That in itself was not the only problem, or even the main one. The planet was so far out it would've been economically unfeasible to mine due to the cost and time involved in getting workers and equipment to the planet.

Someone in the company had hatched the brilliant plan of developing the deep sea crew in vitro, en route. They'd accelerated the growth beyond anything ever attempted before, and arranged to 'install' education and behavioral modification via computer through minute chips implanted in the embryos' brain stems.

Victoria was appalled. They might be genetically enhanced, but they were still human beings. It was just plain wrong to grow them completely in a tube, without any human contact whatsoever, without even the opportunity to 'grow up'--no childhood, no family, no friends--no life experiences. They might have been nothing more than androids for all the consideration that was paid to their innate humanity and the rights they should have been able to expect.

Six months into the trip, they were to be turned out to learn to interact--but only with each other. She and the crew would still be in stasis.

How could they be expected to be able to interact with humans that had not been genetically altered as they had, or even relate to them, under such circumstances?

Their psychological profiles were to be carefully monitored, but that had given her little comfort. She'd insisted her chamber be set to wake her periodically so that she could observe their progress herself, but she was a long way from being convinced that the company's decision had been a wise one.

Her first few attempts to communicate with them had been stonewalled. They were supposed to be able to communicate with each other and the ground crew via telepathy, but she'd come to the conclusion that that little part of the experiment had been a complete bust ... until she'd noticed Raphael.

It was hard not to notice Raphael. That wasn't his 'real' name. The company, obviously deficit in the imagination department, had merely numbered the workers. But the moment she'd seen him she'd been captivated by the sheer beauty and symmetry he represented--on a purely artistic level naturally. The master, Raphael, one of the greatest creators of beauty of all time, had come instantly to mind and from that moment on she had thought of him only as Raphael.

His perfection made it difficult to actually look directly at him, however, without going into a trance-like state of admiration.

He'd noticed she had trouble looking directly at him. Unfortunately, he seemed to have completely misinterpreted the reason for her discomfort. Somehow, she suspected that was one of the reasons he made no effort to hide his interest in her. He enjoyed making her squirm and, eventually, his preoccupation with her had led her to realize that the deep water crew was perfectly capable of communicating via telepathy. They simply had no interest in communicating with the two-legged, air breathing humans.

As she reached the lower deck, Victoria's gaze went automatically to the tank that took up the majority of the space. Glass surrounded most of the holding tank where more than half her crew had been packed in like sardines in a can. She stopped abruptly at the thought, realizing it was a poor choice of metaphor under the circumstances.

It's the right metaphor, said an amused voice in her head.

Her heart seemed to trip over itself. Raphael.

He glided to the glass, his lips curled faintly.

It took an effort to block his telepathic probing, but she had found that she could, so long as she was warned ahead of time that he would intrude. And, if he was looking at her, he was almost certainly probing her thoughts.

Victoria allowed herself a brief glimpse of him before she focused her gaze on a spot below his chin. She couldn't help but wonder where they'd gotten his root stock. She had never in her life seen a man so perfectly, flawlessly be the persona of male beauty. His facial features were lean, sharply detailed, almost angular, from the classic lines of his nose, to his high, prominent cheek bones, to the clean line of his jaw. The one, tiny imperfection was a noticeable cleft in his chin, but even that seemed to enhance his disturbing good looks.

His arms and torso were magnificent. He'd been designed for strength and stamina underwater and there was little doubt in her mind that he was muscular enough to handle pretty much any situation he was likely to encounter.

His male member was just as masterful and just as disturbing, if not more so, but Victoria didn't delude herself that it was in any artistic sense. She couldn't help but wonder if it was by accident, or design, that the coloration that covered his lower body, almost like an elaborate, intricately detailed tattoo, dipped under his phallus, almost seeming to frame it. Certainly, the effect made it impossible to ignore his endowment.

It might be a fluke, but she had a sneaking suspicion that somebody in the genetics lab had a warped sense of humor.... Someone gay, or someone female.

The females hadn't been designed in such a way--their breasts and their sex were 'tattooed', only the males were, apparently, designed for their shock value.

She'd never really found the other males quite so ... disturbing, perhaps because they weren't quite so well endowed?

The strangest thing about her discomfort, however, was that she didn't recall ever finding herself in a situation where nudity disturbed her. Privacy was only for high pay officers in the company. The grunts who started at the entry level positions more often than not shared group quarters, which did not allow for excessive modesty. By year two, pretty much everyone had grown accustomed to bathing and showering with, or within view of, everyone else.

Nor was she without sexual experience. She had never really found a partner that inspired a lot of interest in sex for her, but the company required employees to share sexual favors, not necessarily as recreation, but to cut down on emotional stress and mating competitiveness. She had made it a point to participate at least often enough to keep her name off of the antisocial list--a determination to go up in the pay ranks in the company required a willingness to sacrifice individuality for conformity.

Unable to come up with a comfortable conclusion, she dismissed it, prodding her memory for the reason she'd decided to confront Raphael. Her irritation returned with the memory.

"You were probing my thoughts," she said accusingly.

He gave her a look of innocence, but his eyes gleamed with amusement. *Not I. One of the others, perhaps?*

"I know it was you. I ... uh...."

The amused gleam was replaced by another emotion, one Victoria was at pains to ignore. *Recognize my touch?*

To her surprise and discomfort, a blush mounted her cheeks. "It's hardly a touch," she said sharply.

True. It's far more intimate than a touch, he countered.

The comment made her careless. *How would you know?*

A slow smile curled his lips. *You could always prove me wrong....*

Chapter Two

"In your wildest dreams," Victoria responded tartly.

They're pretty wild. Would you like me to show you?

The blush that had barely begun to fade, turned fiery. Self-consciously, Victoria glanced quickly around to see who might have observed the interchange between the two of them. To her relief, most of the crew members were occupied. Roach, however, was dividing a speculative look between her and Raphael.

She was on the point of striding over to him and demanding to know if he was under the mistaken impression that he held a special position on the crew that allowed him to sit on his ass while everyone else worked, but Raphael caught her attention once more.

Why do you call me Raphael? It's not the ... name I was given.

Victoria's head snapped around. For a moment, their gazes locked. With an effort she broke the contact, gazing over his shoulder at the other crew members, who'd congregated at the opposite end of the tank. She wasn't about to tell him how she'd arrived at the name, however. "Names are easier to remember than numbers," she said flatly.

But that's not the reason, is it?

Victoria looked at him a moment before her gaze wandered to the others once more as it occurred to her to wonder if they could 'hear' the conversation between her and Raphael.

They're not listening. It wouldn't be polite.

Irritation surfaced again. "You don't seem to have a problem listening to my private thoughts."

His brows rose. *I thought we were conversing.*

Victoria gave him a look. They both knew he'd been under no such misapprehension, but it seemed childish to bicker about it. "I gave everyone names because ... it's part of who a person is and how they identify themselves."

He studied her consideringly. *This is why you don't like it when Roach over there calls you Tory. It's too ... intimate. Victoria is less approachable, isn't it?*

Caught off guard, Victoria allowed him to capture her gaze once more. To her relief, however, Huggins announced on the inner com at that moment that they were about to dock. "We're docking. You'll have to excuse me."

* * * *

It looked far worse up close than it had from the viewing screen, and she'd thought it looked like hell from several miles out. Victoria stood on the gangplank, surveying the landing platform and the area immediately around it.

Most of the damage appeared to be the ravages of severe weather, but there were at least two scorched areas Victoria was almost certain were from laser fire. She held up one hand as crew members began to crowd onto the gang plank behind her.

"Hold! Roach, get the weapons out."

Nobody moved and after a moment Victoria turned around and looked at them. "Today, people!"

They scattered, moving to the cases that held the lasers. Victoria stepped back up the gangplank until she reached the inner com. "Huggins?"

"What is it, Anderson?"

"Looks like we might have had some laser fire here. You might as well settle in for a game of cards."

"Laser fire?"

"Could be lightening strike, but I'm going to take the crew in to check it out before we begin off loading."

"Keep in touch."

"Will do." She looked up. "Roach, issue everybody a com unit too. We're going to take this by twos. Roach, you and Kichens. Brown, you can go with Tuttle. Clancy, you're with me."

Trouble?

Victoria frowned. *Could be. I'm not certain yet, but you'd think someone would've come up to greet us, wouldn't you? I'd just rather be safe than sorry.*

We should check the mine area.

Right. Hang on a minute.

She followed her surface crew members down the gang plank. "Spread out and check the immediate area. I don't want anyone going down yet, though." She moved to the edge of the platform and looked down, calculating the distance to the surface of the water. *Looks like about 20 to 30 feet, Raphael. Hold for now. We'll check the main structure. When we get done, I'll have the tank lowered and your crew can go in and check out the mines.*

We could make the dive.

No. It's too risky.

It could be more risky to leave three quarters of your team caged and unable to come to your aid.

That's an asinine thing to say, Raphael.

But true.

It's completely unjust and you damn well know it! The containment's for the water, not the crew.... Have it your way! She stalked up the gangplank to the inner com. "Huggins. I need you to lower the tank. The deep sea crew is going in to check out the mines." She released the button. "Clancy, give me a hand lowering a case of munitions for the crew. If they do run into trouble, I want them armed."

When they'd removed the munitions case, the gangplank was raised and Huggins moved the ship just off side the habitat. Hovering a few meters above the water, he lowered the containment and released it as Clancy and Victoria watched from the flight deck.

As soon as she saw they'd safely off-loaded, she and Clancy secured the munitions case, wrenched it up over the top of the railing and began lowering it over the side.

The railing wobbled as Clancy climbed up on it to steady the guide wire. Victoria looked at it in alarm. "Get down, Clancy."

He glanced at her. "We need to hold the case free of the structure and make sure it doesn't get tangled on the way down. It's got a little wobble to it, but it's safe enough."

Victoria was checking the railing as the first pair of crew members returned to report in. "Tuttle, find something we can use to steady the munitions case while we lower it. Clancy, get off the damned rail. It's unstable."

Tuttle returned with a bar, Roach and Brown trailing behind her. The bar had a right angle on one end she used to catch the guide wire. Roach set his laser down and went to the railing, leaning over it to peer down.

"Get off...." Victoria broke off as the railing leaned outward with the grinding shriek of metal. "Grab him. Somebody grab him!" she yelled as Clancy, who'd already begun to climb down, teetered when the railing shifted.

Time seemed to hold its breath, slowing almost to a standstill. She released her hold on the guide wire, leaping forward with one hand outstretched. She managed to grasp a handful of Clancy's clothing, but it was snatched from her grip as he went over with the railing.

"Head's up!" she yelled to the crew below as she watched one whole section of railing break loose and begin to fall, watched

Clancy twist, grabbing frantically for a handhold. He caught the edge of the platform. She hit the deck, almost skidding off the edge of the platform herself, trying to stop her slide and grab Clancy's hand at the same time.

One of the crew members grabbed her legs, anchoring her to the deck. Brown grabbed a handful of Clancy's sleeve. He slipped from both their grasps, following the broken railing over the side.

Numbly, she watched as he seemed to fall in slow motion, endlessly. Below, the crate of munitions crashed into the sea. The railing struck the water only seconds behind it. The crew below had scattered to a safe distance when the first shouts went up. She caught a glimpse of their upturned faces and bare shoulders, bobbing above the water, but she couldn't seem to tear her gaze from Clancy as he continued to fall on and on, his face screwed up as he yelled something she couldn't seem to hear, his body twisting.

He was almost halfway down when something shot from the water like a projectile from a cannon. She realized it was one of the sea crew as he met the falling man midair. The smacking sound of colliding bodies was like a thunder clap. They seemed to struggle for several moments and then Raphael gripped Clancy tightly against him and executed a mid-air back flip. They seemed almost to hover for several heartbeats before slicing head first through the water.

Victoria held her breath, waiting, watching for them to emerge, fearing they'd struck some of the debris below and it had injured both of them.

After what seemed a very long time, two heads bobbed up.

"Is he alive?" she shouted.

He's breathing. I don't know how long.

Victoria leapt to her feet and raced toward the ship. It took her ten minutes to prep a pod. Tuttle burst through the hatch and scrambled into the jump seat before she could lift off. Victoria nodded at the medic and punched the button to open the bay door, launching the pod almost simultaneously.

Within seconds, they were skimming just above the reach of the waves. Tuttle threw her restraints off and opened the hatch as they drew alongside the two men. Clancy, Victoria saw as she twisted around for a quick look, was bleeding from the mouth and nose. Raphael was bloody, as well, but she couldn't tell if it was from his own injuries or if it was Clancy's blood.

"Get in, Raphael. We need to check you out, too."

He shook his head. "I'm all right."

"Damn it, Raphael! Get in the frigging pod!"

A slightly crooked smile curled his lips. "I do love a woman with fire," he murmured. In the next second, he'd disappeared beneath the waves.

Victoria was still gaping at the space he'd so lately occupied when Tuttle sealed the hatch. Briefly, their gazes collided. Victoria turned away, shooting skyward once more with the pod the moment Tuttle announced that she and Clancy were secured.

Clancy was barely breathing when they managed to get him onto an examination table in sick bay. Working together, they were able to get him stabilized after about an hour. They could find no evidence of internal bleeding from his organs. He was suffering from a concussion and several breaks, however, including his collar bone, several cracked ribs and two breaks on his left arm. When they'd set the breaks and stabilized the arm, they bound his ribs and realigned his collar bone, binding him to keep it from shifting again.

Finally, Victoria left Tuttle to keep a watch on him and returned to the deck. Brown and Kichens met her at the end of the gangplank. "Is Clancy going to make it?

Victoria drew in a deep breath. "Looks like it." She scanned the area. Roach was sitting on the deck, tossing coins at the wall. It was patently obvious that he was completely unmoved by everything that had just happened, despite the fact that he could hardly have failed to know that it was his added weight on the railing that had caused the accident. Victoria saw blood. She strode over to him and decked him with her fist on the side of his jaw. He fell sideways. Before she could swing at him again, Brown and Kichens seized her.

"You damn near got two men killed! Endangered the crew members below. You step out of line one more time, Roach, and you'll be spending the next six months in the brig!"

He rubbed his jaw, grinning up at her, but there was malice in his eyes. "Damn, Tory! That almost hurt!"

Victoria tried to pull free, but Brown and Kichens had a firm grip on each of her arms. "Tell me you understand what I just told you, Roach!"

He shrugged. "I heard you say Clancy was OK."

"He's NOT OK! He'll probably live, but he's not OK. And he wouldn't even be in that good a shape if Raphael hadn't risked his life to save him!"

Roach looked at her blankly a moment, then smiled snidely. "You mean lead tadpole?"

Brown released her, but before Victoria could react, he'd slugged Roach so hard his eyes rolled back in his head.

Victoria glared at the semi-conscious man. "Lock him in the brig, Brown. When you're done, check on Clancy. If it's safe enough to leave him for a little while, bring Tuttle back with you. If not ... I guess it'll just be the three of us making the sweep."

* * * *

Brown and Tuttle had discovered during their sweep of the upper deck that the power station had been blown, which meant neither the lights nor the lift were working. After collecting miner's helmets, Victoria led the way down the stairs.

The upper deck was supported above main operations by a web of steel girders. Victoria examined them as they descended, but could see no obvious signs of damage. She paused as they reached the lower deck, looking out over the railing at the sea below them. She'd heard nothing from the deep sea crew since they'd gone under to retrieve the munitions. She'd tried reaching Raphael telepathically several times, but he either wasn't responding or he wasn't able to 'hear' her over such a distance. The underwater com units didn't appear to work--not really surprising since the ones they were using didn't work worth shit either. She didn't know whether to put it down to the planet's conditions, or sorry equipment--neither of which would have surprised her.

It made her uneasy that she hadn't heard from the crew, however. She had no way of telling if they'd managed to retrieve their weapons, or if they'd encountered a threat below.

She glanced at Brown and Kichens. "This could be nothing more than weather damage, so watch it with the lasers. We don't want to shoot any of the good guys."

Kichens and Brown exchanged a look, but it was Kichens who spoke. "You think there's a chance there's still somebody alive down there?"

It was the question everyone had been avoiding, but they all knew it was doubtful. Both communications and the power were out. If there'd been anyone left, there would have been signs that attempts had been made to restore the power at least. Beyond that, they had made no attempt at a stealthy arrival. Even if the entire ground crew was huddled below for some reason, they must have heard the arrival of the relief crew.

But it was inconceivable to Victoria that all sixty crew members had been killed.

It would almost have been easier to believe pirates had raided the place except for the fact that there were no obvious signs of an attack, two possible laser blasts, and possibly not--no signs of blood--no bodies. And they'd found a good bit of expensive equipment. It seemed doubtful pirates would've overlooked it.

"We have to assume there are some survivors," she responded finally. "If there are, they could be armed, so watch yourselves."

The door, they discovered, was locked.

Victoria and Kichens stood back while Brown hit it with a blast of laser fire, then kicked it open before stepping back. Victoria stood away from the direct line of fire. "Replacement crew!" she yelled. "Is anybody hurt down there?"

Her voice echoed eerily down the stairwell. She waited several minutes, listening intently. "This is Victoria Anderson. I'm the mission supervisor with NCO! We're coming down!"

Again, her voice echoed hollowly, as if she'd shouted into a metal can. After waiting for a response and receiving none, she entered the stairwell, keeping as close to the wall as possible. They made their way down to the first level. The door opened out onto the stairwell, but it was steel, at least, and would protect whoever opened it from fire in the event someone was waiting for them.

She and Brown flattened themselves against the wall by the opening and she nodded for Kichens to open it. Kichens grasped the handle and gave it a yank. The door didn't budge. The three of them exchanged a look. "They sealed themselves in," Victoria muttered. It began to look like an attack after all.

There was just one problem.

If someone had attacked the rig, the bolted doors might have slowed them down, but they wouldn't have held off a determined attack. They should have found that the doors had been blasted open. There should have seen signs of a fire fight.

Kichens blew a hole in the lock. Grasping the handle again, she jerked the door open. Brown hailed this time.

When moments passed and they received no response, Victoria eased up to the edge of the door, took her helmet off and flashed the light around the room beyond, expecting any moment that it would be shot out of her hand. Nothing but the same eerie silence greeted them. Finally, Victoria braced herself and dove into the room beyond, rolling to a stop behind a low wall. After a moment, Kichens and Brown followed her.

"Brown, watch the door. Kichens, you take that side. I'll take this one."

Unlike the upper deck, the operations floor looked untouched. It was deserted, however. She met up with Kichens and Brown again.

"I found the auxiliary power supply. Looked to me like it ought to be operational."

Victoria frowned. "I don't see how it could be. If it was working, it would be on, right?"

Kichens shrugged. "Maybe they didn't get the chance to turn it on. Or maybe they left it off for a reason."

"Give it a try. I don't see stumbling around in the dark if there's a chance of getting the lights on."

To everyone's surprise and relief, the power supply kicked on, flooding the operations room with light. They discovered, however, that the lift still wasn't working.

Shutting off the lights on their helmets, they moved back into the stairwell and down to the next level. The second level contained the living quarters of the supervisory level employees, the dining hall and kitchen, and the media and recreational rooms. It, too, was deserted, seemingly untouched. The third level was primarily living quarters for the crew and also contained the sickbay. Below that level there were three warehousing levels. The ore processing plant was below the warehouse levels. The eighth and final level was about twenty feet above the sea floor and designed for crew access in and out of the rig and for bringing up the raw ore.

It took hours to search the rig from top to bottom. The door on every single level was bolted from the inside. Every level was seemingly untouched. They found no blood, no bodies, no signs of a struggle of any kind ... and no crew members. The lift, they discovered, had been deliberately sabotaged.

Victoria had fully expected to find the remains of the crew on the eighth level. She didn't know whether to be relieved or further unnerved when they discovered that the final level was as devoid of any signs of life--or death--as all the others. There were, however, signs of a battle.

The pressurized access pool had been covered over and barricaded. It was obvious, though, that the barricade had not held.

Chapter Three

"They fled up. What ever wiped them out came from below."

Victoria glanced at Kichens sharply. "Maybe. But it doesn't make any sense."

"How you figure?" Brown asked.

Victoria frowned, trying to add up what they'd found. "Why come in this way when it would've been easier to come in from the landing level?"

Kichens shrugged. "Element of surprise, maybe?"

"They weren't surprised. They had time to build a barricade," Victoria pointed out flatly.

"Maybe the attack did come from topside and the crew evacuated from here?" Brown suggested.

Victoria shook her head. "Evacuate to where? Anyway, you can see it's burst inward. Whoever attacked them broke through the barrier they'd built, and it looks like it must have been a pretty solid barrier."

"Explosives," Brown said, nodding.

"A battering ram, maybe, but they didn't use explosives," Victoria said. "There's no shrapnel. If they'd used explosives to blow it, there'd be a lot more debris scattered around here, and signs of fire-- there's not even an odor of smoke--."

"What bothers me the most is that there are no bodies." Kichens said, shivering as she glanced around anxiously.

Victoria glanced around, as well. "What bothers me the most is that there's no blood."

Kichens and Brown stared at her. Kichens was the first to grasp the implications. "They're alive then!"

"Not if whoever it was dumped the bodies in the sea," Brown put in.

"The problem with that, Brown, is that there's no damn blood. They would've been fighting for their lives, wouldn't you think? I can't picture sixty people simply standing by and watching their fellow crew members being tossed into the sea to drown one by one without making a push at the least to save themselves. But except for this room and the flight deck, there's no sign of any kind of struggle at all, nothing that could be interpreted as hand to hand combat, and no blood evidence of it."

The debris littering the access pool abruptly heaved upward. Kichens and Brown brought their weapons up instantly, trained on the moving debris.

"Hold your fire, damn it!" Victoria ordered.

"There's something down there," Kichens snapped.

"We've got crew members outside," Victoria reminded her sharply. "Hold your fire."

They moved back, keeping their weapons trained on the debris in the pool as it continued to shift and heave. After a few moments, whatever it was managed to create an opening and a dark head emerged. Victoria knocked Kichens' weapon aside when she heard the click of the trigger. The laser blast cut a two inch hole in one of the support columns. They were just fortunate it struck the column instead of the bulkheads. Otherwise the habitat might have depressurized, despite the shielding that had been built into the structure that was supposedly insurance against such 'accidents'.

"Damn it, Kichens! I told you to hold your fire! He's one of ours!"

She turned in time to see Raphael's head break the surface once more. He was glaring at them. Not that Victoria could blame him. She'd have been pissed, too, if somebody had just fired a laser at her.

"You OK?"

Shoving some of the debris aside, he emerged from the pool, lifting himself onto the raised edge. He was followed a moment later by several other crew members. He didn't look at her when she spoke, but rather continued to glare at Kichens, who was staring at him open mouthed.

"Fine."

His voice was deep, melodious and as smooth and rich as aged cognac. It sent a shiver of sensation chasing along Victoria's spine, as tangible as a caress. He stood up at just that moment and strode toward her, however, driving all other thought from her mind.

Victoria gaped at his legs.

They were legs.

"They are."

The words jerked her head up as if it had been attached by a string. It took her a few seconds to realize that she'd been too surprised to block her thoughts from him. "You're not...."

"Fuck me!" Brown exclaimed.

One of the mermaids--female deep water crew members--looked him over and smiled coldly. "Not in this life time."

He gaped at her as if she'd grown two heads.

After a moment, Victoria realized she should not have been so stunned. Galactic law prohibited genetic manipulation that created undue hardship for the recipient and/or irreversible 'abnormalities'. Companies like NCO could create four armed--or four legged--human beings, if they had sufficient data supporting the decision, but they also had to prove that the 'improved' or altered human could be rehabilitated when they'd completed their assignment to blend naturally with the race--they didn't have to prove these humans could afford to pay for normalization, or fund it themselves, only that it was possible.

She'd known the 'mermen' and 'mermaids' did not have gills. A specialized organ had been added to their internal physiology that pulled oxygen from water for them, as gills did for sea creatures--they 'breathed' water--and it was extra--they also had lungs for when the time came to discard the internal gills. Because of her position, she'd been fitted with a prosthesis similar to their 'natural' organ, so that she would be able to oversee the mining operations whenever necessary.

Their legs had appeared to be fused, however, and she'd assumed this would require a surgical reversal to allow the lower part of their body, which functioned in the same manner as a fish tail underwater, to function as legs when they no longer needed them for underwater maneuvering.

Obviously, she'd been wrong.

Raphael nodded abruptly. Victoria wasn't certain whether that was an affirmation of her mental dialogue, or a greeting of some sort.

"The mine shafts were collapsed about twenty feet down. Most of the equipment looks operational, though. There's probably two tons of ore, just sitting on the ocean floor--They mined it, but they never got it up. No bodies--at least not so far. Looks like what ever happened here, they managed to make it inside the rig. I've got some people working on clearing the mine shaft."

"No bodies here either," Victoria said grimly.

His dark brows rose. "Any theories?"

She shook her head.

"What do we do now?" the female crew member Victoria had named Sylvia asked.

Everyone turned to look at Victoria. "The structure seems sound enough. My guess is we'll be ordered to proceed as planned. I'll have to report what we've found to headquarters." She shrugged. "For now, we cool our heels and wait."

"What kind of down time are we talking here?" Brown demanded.

"Shit!" Kichens exclaimed. "Does that mean we won't get our bonus?"

Victoria held up her hand as everybody started talking at once. "Believe me when I say I'm as anxious to get started as the rest of you. We don't get paid for sitting on our asses. In the meanwhile, until we've got some idea of what the hell happened here, I want everyone on alert. Keep a weapon nearby at all times. Stay close. Preferably inside the habitat. No exploring.

"Right now, I want a crew in here to get this mess cleaned up and operational. Until you hear otherwise directly from me, make sure at least two people out of every work crew are stationed on watch at all times."

She turned to Raphael. "Can you spare some of your crew to help in here?"

He nodded and turned to Sylvia. She studied him a moment, nodded, and returned to the pool. Diving in, she disappeared from sight.

"I told her to pull a half a dozen people off the mines and bring them to help clear up the debris below that's blocking docking access to the pool. When they're done, they're to come in and help finish up in here."

"Good." She allowed her gaze to move over him fleetingly. "Remind them of the company dress code. While working outside or in the mines, you may do as you please. Anyone working within the habitat is expected to conform to company policy regarding dress. They can find uniforms in the commissary, either here in the habitat or on the ship." She turned to Brown and Kichens. "You two go ahead and get started here. Just do whatever you can till you have some more help. Stay alert, but watch your itchy trigger fingers. I don't want any more accidents. We've already got one crew member down. With the ground crew we were supposed to join missing, we're short handed enough as it is."

Brown and Kichens exchanged a look, but turned and began half-heartedly shifting the debris around. After a couple of moments, the two deep water crew members who'd emerged from the pool with

Raphael and Sylvia began helping them sift through the debris and sort 'recoverable' from 'unusable'.

Raphael studied them for several moments. "Robert--Jeremy, you heard the boss. Uniforms first. Commissary's on level six. Grab some for the rest of the crew while you're there."

Victoria glanced at Raphael. "I need you to come with me. It'll be best, I think, if you give your report on the mines directly. They'll want details."

Raphael gestured toward the elevator. "After you."

"The elevator's out. We discovered it was blocked on the second level. We'll have to take the stairs," she said, starting back toward the stairwell.

Robert and Jeremy proceeded them, jogging up the stairs at an astonishing pace. Despite that, their bare feet pounding against the treads produced surprisingly little noise.

"They didn't tell you."

Victoria glanced back at him over her shoulder as she started up the stairs. His gaze, she discovered, was resting upon her rear. He glanced up at her face as she turned. To her surprise, he neither gave her a suggestive look, nor appeared the least discomfited that she'd caught him in the act. "They didn't know. Communications have been out for several months, apparently. We'll have to transmit from the ship."

"I meant about us."

"Oh." Self conscious now, certain she could feel his gaze upon her ass, she tried to ignore it, resisted the urge to brush the seat of her trousers to see if she'd sat in anything. "They have a way of leaving out important little details like that."

"Does it make you uncomfortable?"

"Not nearly as uncomfortable as your preoccupation with my ass." She glanced back at him again as she reached the first landing. Despite the sarcasm in her voice, one corner of his lips curled up faintly.

"Was I--preoccupied?"

"Weren't you?"

"Yes."

She paused, looked back at him challengingly. "What? Have I got something on the seat of my pants?"

He frowned, leaned forward, lifted a hand, then slid it lightly, slowly over her rump. It was, unmistakably, a caress, not a brush. After that leisurely examination, he dropped his hand to his side once more. The frown vanished. His eyes glinted. "No."

She felt a blush that was only partially irritation, and immediately returned her attention to the stairs she was climbing.

No. Just like that. No pretense that it was anything beyond an interest in her ass. He'd initiated 'the ritual'. She could take it up--or not. She decided to ignore the opening he'd provided.

"I suppose, if I'd given it any thought, I would have wondered at their reasoning," she continued with the previous subject after an uncomfortable pause. "It's certainly helpful having a deep water mining crew, but they only chose six topside crew members--not nearly enough to man the station once the occupying ground crew departed. I'd wondered how they expected us to process the ore with three miners to every one processor. Is it uncomfortable for you?"

"In what way?"

Victoria shrugged. "The transition, from water to air--the difference in pressure."

"It takes a little while to acclimatize."

Victoria sent him a wry smile over her shoulder. "I've got a feeling that's an understatement. I was fitted with a prosthesis similar to what you use to extract oxygen from water--to make it easier for me to keep an eye on the mining operations. It works, but I found 'acclimatizing' to breathing underwater a singularly unpleasant experience."

His gaze, she saw when she glanced back, was once more on her ass. She misjudged the distance to the next tread and almost tripped. It wasn't a stumble. She barely scraped the bottom of her shoe, but it was a close enough call to make her heart skip a couple of beats and to cause a color fluctuation in her cheeks. She wondered uncomfortably if he'd noticed. Her hair was closer to brown than red, but her complexion was very fair. When she blushed, it was hideously noticeable and the back of her neck felt hot. She'd twisted her hair into a knot low on the back of her head, however. Surely between that and the collar he hadn't noticed from his position below her?

"Careful. Watch your step."

"It's easier coming down than going back up," she responded a little stiffly.

"You sound a little winded."

She gritted her teeth, suspecting he knew very well that the climb was only part of the problem. She glanced upward. "Only a few more levels. I think I can make it."

They met Robert and Jeremy coming down again when they reached level six. Jeremy tossed Raphael a uniform from the stack Robert was carrying. Victoria continued the climb while he stopped to dress. He caught up with her again before she'd reached the next level, however, and proceeded to follow her the rest of the way up.

She'd thought she wouldn't feel quite as uncomfortable once he was dressed.

She'd thought wrong. It didn't raise her comfort level at all, particularly when she was almost certain he continued to study her backside all the way up.

Captain Huggins met them on the gang plank. "What's the prognosis?"

"Not good. The ground crew's gone," Victoria said grimly.

Huggins came upright, paling. "Dead? All of them? What the hell happened here?"

"Probably ... missing, presumed dead, at any rate. We found nothing. No survivors, no bodies, no sign of a fight. They've just vanished. And so far we haven't found much in the way of clues that might help us figure it out." Victoria strode past him.

"The company's not going to like this," Huggins commented, following Victoria and Raphael up the gangplank and into the ship.

Victoria's lips tightened. "I feel sure the missing ground crew wasn't too happy about it either."

"Any ideas? Theories?"

"None, unfortunately. It's not likely, considering it looks as if everyone must have barricaded themselves into the lowest level when they were attacked, but I suppose it's possible we might find some clues in the work log, assuming we can find it."

"They're not going to like that either."

Victoria sent him an impatient glance over her shoulder, but she knew he was right. The company didn't give a damn about facts, or even logic when disaster struck. They just wanted somebody to blame. They were not going to be happy she wasn't prepared to hand them some names.

They were not going to be pleased that they had no one to come down on, and no one to use as scapegoat when the media got wind of it.

They couldn't just brush it under the rug, however. Most of those who were missing had had friends, family. It was going to be one hell of a mess.

Huggins parted company with them when they reached the control deck.

"See if Grant can get me a secure channel, will you? And have her patch it through to my quarters."

Huggins nodded.

Victoria hadn't realized, until Raphael followed her into her quarters, just how cramped the space was. She looked around and finally gestured toward her bunk. "Sorry. Only one chair. Have a seat."

Raphael glanced at the bunk and then gave Victoria an inscrutable look. "I'm fine."

"Would you feel more comfortable with the chair?"

He shook his head infinitesimally, leaned against the door frame and crossed his arms over his chest.

She shrugged. "Suit yourself. It might take a while. If Grant can even get through to them. Kay's atmosphere is like soup--in case you didn't notice during the climb up."

After a brief inner debate, she chose the bunk herself. She'd spent months in hyber-sleep. Racing around the habitat with a gun, to say nothing of pounding up and down that many flights of stairs, was more of a workout than she'd anticipated immediately after debarkation. Propping her pillow against the bulkhead, she sat at the head of her bed, pushed her shoes off and stretched her legs out on the bed before her.

Raphael studied her for several moments, then stood away from the door frame and began to prowl the cramped quarters restlessly, examining her few personal belongings with his gaze, though he touched nothing.

"Any thoughts?"

His brows rose, but he didn't mistake the comment as an invitation. "Whoever did this clearly wasn't after the ore. Otherwise, we'd have had a reception committee when we arrived."

Victoria drew her legs up and began massaging her aching feet absently. "That's the biggest--or one of the biggest problems I have with the situation. No apparent motive. There's some damage, but nothing, except the crew, taken."

"Slavers?"

"I can't believe slavers would be ballsy enough to attack a company facility. Particularly not one so well guarded, or populated ... And that's another thing. As precious as that ore is, I know they had to have had a full company of security officers on the habitat. So why are there virtually no signs of a struggle? Except for a couple of laser burns on the flight deck, we saw nothing else."

"It happened too fast for them to get the chance to fight?"

"But not so fast that--some of them at least--didn't have the chance to bolt every access door on the way down, block the elevator, and pile everything they could get their hands on over the access pool?"

"So, if we eliminate pirates, slavers and competitors, what have we got left?"

Victoria thought on it for some moments before anything occurred to her. "Something indigenous?"

Chapter Four

Without invitation, Raphael joined her on the bed. Taking up a position about halfway down, he propped his back against the adjoining bulkhead. Victoria was still staring at him in surprise when he reached over and grasped one of her feet. After a brief tug of war for possession, he settled her foot in his lap and began massaging it.

The pressure of his hands on her throbbing feet was almost unbearably pleasurable. Caught by surprise, a moan escaped her before she could prevent it. She made a self-conscious effort to pretend she'd been clearing her throat. "I'd prefer you didn't do that."

He studied her a long moment. "No you wouldn't."

Victoria would have liked to argue the point, but he was right. If he was of a mind to do it, she was certainly of a mind to allow it. She knew she shouldn't. It was far too intimate, and despite company policies regarding sexual intercourse between crew members, she'd found that participating in it herself had a way of creating discipline problems for her. Men tended to think sexual favors should extend beyond the bedroom to special consideration regarding work, time off, and bonuses.

The best way to avoid complications that might have unpleasant repercussions on her work record was simply to refuse to take a lover at all except on those few, rare, occasions where she was assigned to a duty where there were officers of equal or higher rank than herself.

She placed her other foot in his lap, hopeful he wouldn't just stop at massaging one.

A faint smile curled his lips.

No doubt he considered this a triumph of some kind--a battle of wills? Annoyance touched her, but she decided it was worth allowing him a small sense of victory to get her feet rubbed.

She found, however, that she was having trouble redirecting her thoughts to the previous subject. "According to the reports compiled from the probes, Kay has no indigenous life forms to speak of, certainly none that are intelligent. In fact, nothing much above multi-celled micro-organisms."

Raphael shrugged. "Which means nothing. A couple of probes could have missed far more than they recorded."

"It took over a year to construct the habitat and set up mining operations. You'd think, in all that time, if there was anything dangerous here somebody would have seen it and reported it to the company."

Raphael gave her a look. "And, if they did, and they had, and it put the operation in jeopardy, do you think it would've appeared in the reports?"

Victoria's heart skipped a beat. Anger surged through her as it occurred to her that he was right. Before she could say anything else however, the com unit let out a burst of static. Snatching her feet from his lap, Victoria leapt from the bed and moved around the desk. Leigh Grant's transparent image appeared above the holo-port. "Did you get through?"

Leigh shrugged. "I've got a connection. There's a lot of interference, though. I don't know how long I'll be able to hold onto it."

"Patch me through."

A wavering image of Wilhem Marks, Chief of Domestic Operations for NCO replaced Grant's image. "Anderson? ....that you?"

"Anderson here," Victoria responded. "The habitat's in pretty rough shape, Marks. The ground crew's missing. No clue what happened here, but whatever it was, it was big."

" ....hear you ... crew missing?"

Unconsciously, Victoria raised her voice. If she'd thought about it, she would have realized the absurdity of trying to yell at a man all the way across the galaxy. "The whole damned ground crew's vanished, presumed dead. There's damage. Mostly on the flight deck and the lower level. Nothing that can't be fixed--I think--but we'll have to delay operations until we can investigate the incident thoroughly--Raphael's here to report what he found at the mine."

She moved aside and allowed Raphael to take her place. He'd no sooner begun speaking, however, than the connection was lost.

Victoria stared at the speaker in consternation, then glanced at Raphael. After a moment, she moved around him once more. In the tight space, particularly since Raphael was a large man, passage became an intimate dance of brushing bodies and hands groping for balance. Victoria was more than a little flustered by the time they'd negotiated the second pass.

"Grant?"

"Lost it. Sorry."

"Shit!"

"I'll keep trying."

"When you get them again--if you do--tell them I need to get my crew off this damned rock until there's been a thorough investigation of what happened here."

Grant's eyes widened. "They're not going to go for that."

"Tell them anyway. It's worth a try." It was a useless gesture and she knew it. God only knew how much the trip out had cost the company, but if it was more than five credits, they weren't going to listen to any appeals to remove the crew before the crew had earned that five credits back a thousand million times over.

Still, it was possible they would consider the risk of losing another crew versus losing more money--not that human life had a lot of value to them, but the potential for lawsuits by family members would multiply substantially if the new crew disappeared as well.

After a moment, she shook her dark thoughts off. Raphael, she saw, hadn't moved. He'd lifted his arms over his head, propping against one of the exposed beams that crisscrossed the overhead of her compartment and was staring at the dead com unit as if deep in thought. Realizing he had no intention of moving out of her way, she brushed past him again.

"What now?" he asked when she was chest to chest with him.

When he spoke, she looked up at him automatically and directly into his eyes. It was a mistake. Her mind went perfectly blank, caught up in the zen meditation that tended to seize hold of her whenever she looked directly at him. It was almost as if he had the ability to mesmerize.

This time her reaction was more pronounced than usual, however. She was far closer to him than she'd ever been before, unprotected by a glass wall, and mere inches separated them. Her heart pounded suffocatingly against her chest wall as his body heat and scent invaded her senses. With a mental shake, she brushed past him, putting some distance between them.

Her mouth and throat were as dry as dust. It took an effort to gather moisture and swallow. "As I said before, we wait."

Before she could say anything else, the com unit erupted once more. This time it was Captain Huggins. "You going to get some crew up here to start off loading?"

"Not until I hear back from NCO about the situation here."

"You know they're going to expect you to proceed as planned."

"I don't know that. And you don't know that, either. We've got a serious situation here, Huggins. I don't want to be stranded here until we have some answers. And there'll be hell to pay if we off load and leave all the supplies behind--which we might have to if we're forced to evacuate quickly."

There was a slight pause. "You've been working for the company long enough to know they're not going to whistle this much money down the tubes, Anderson. They're going to expect you and your crew to pull this together for them."

"If they leave us here and whatever happened to the previous crew happens to us, they're going to be losing a lot more money," Victoria snapped.

"You might have been able to convince them of that--in person--if they'd found out before they launched the newest mission. You're already here now. I'm telling you, they're going to expect you to go forward."

"It's going to go down as a matter of record, however, that it was not my decision to endanger my crew!" Victoria snapped. "No way am I going to be a scapegoat for them."

She switched the unit off before he could think up another argument. "I'm going down. Maybe I can find something in the work logs. You should go check the crew's progress."

Raphael followed her out of her cabin. "You said no one was to be left alone. I'll go with you to check the logs."

Victoria glanced at him, tempted to countermand, but he was right. Until they knew what was going on here on Kay, they needed to stick to working in groups. Instead of heading out immediately, however, she turned her steps toward the brig.

"You're going to release Roach?"

His voice was carefully neutral. Nevertheless, Victoria suspected there was more than a hint of censure in the comment. She nodded grimly. "I see no reason to allow him to sit on his ass--in safety-- while everyone else has to work--at risk. Do you?"

"I can't argue with that reasoning. On the other hand, he strikes me as a fairly useless human being, and one prone to creating problems besides."

"My assessment exactly, but I didn't pick the crew. I was assigned, just like everybody else. Any way you look at it, we're stuck with him now, and as much as I'd like to keep him locked up, I couldn't hold him more than twelve hours for insubordination anyway without the union coming down on me *and* the company."

"We're a little out of their reach at the moment," Raphael pointed out dryly.

"I'd like to go home someday, though. Besides, he's not worth the credits I'd have to pay out in fines," Victoria responded with a tight smile.

Roach was sprawled on the bunk in the cell, apparently asleep, when they reached the brig. He didn't so much as twitch when Victoria opened the cell door. She stalked across the room and kicked the metal railing of the bunk. "Up! Beauty sleep's over, Roach. You're needed down on the underwater access level to help with clean up."

Roach rolled to a sitting position. He didn't look like someone who'd just been awakened. Victoria's eyes narrowed.

He grinned at her. "Sure you don't want to join me here for a little recreation first?" he asked, patting the bunk beside him suggestively.

"As tempting as that is," Victoria said dryly. "We've got problems at the moment. Get below. Now."

He favored Raphael with a challenging glance before he swaggered out.

Raphael's expression was stony as he followed her out of the cell.

* * * *

Victoria heard Roach clattering down the stairs ahead of them as she and Raphael started down the stairs toward main operations. He made more noise than both of Raphael's men put together. The heavy issue, steel toed boots might have had something to do with it, but Victoria was inclined to think it was a little more than that-- grace for one thing. Then, too, the deep water crew had been developed in pressurized water tanks. It seemed to follow that their muscles were accustomed to more resistance than air.

"Just what is Roach's specialty--besides being a pain in the ass?"

A sense of deja vu went through Victoria. She glanced back at Raphael as she recalled thinking much the same thing about Roach. There was nothing in his expression, however, to indicate that he was being deliberately provocative. Perhaps it was only coincidence that he'd voiced her earlier thoughts? Or, just maybe, it wasn't too difficult for any number of people to reach a similar assessment?

"His records show a good deal of off world experience-- acceptable job foreman skills. Between the two of us, I think he was just fortunate enough to be born in the right family."

"He was placed?"

Victoria shrugged. "You and I both know it happens. The government can legislate as many fairness laws as they want, but they'll never eliminate corruption altogether. People in positions of power are going to use their power whenever they feel it's necessary--and my feeling is that someone was anxious to get Roach as far away as possible."

"Lucky us."

"Exactly."

They'd reached the main operations deck. Victoria hesitated once she'd gained the main corridor, glanced to the right and left and finally strode toward the first door along the corridor. The accounting office might have been the best place to start, but Victoria was more interested in the most recent logs and it seemed to her that the chances were good that those had never made it to accounting.

They found Pittman's--the man she was to have replaced--office without too much trouble. They encountered an unexpected problem, however. The password she'd been issued failed to open the files.

Raphael had remained by the door. He was propped causally enough against the door frame, but he was alert. "It would require voice id, wouldn't it?" he asked over his shoulder, sparing a glance at her.

"Unfortunately, Pittman didn't get the chance to turn it over to me. It was supposed to be set up when I got here, though. So, either the chip was corrupted when it arrived, it never arrived, or Pittman never got the chance to install it. The computer's not accepting the override either."

"They would keep physical copies, though, right? In case of equipment failure?"

Victoria shrugged. "Maybe. It's standard procedure on this kind of operation. Too many chances of equipment failure. But a lot more personnel ignore that little rule than follow it." She gnawed her fingertip thoughtfully for several moments. "Let's have a look, shall we? We might be able to break in, but I'd rather not. The company's going to want whatever's still in the computer's memory."

"I could probably bypass the security, if you want me to give it a try."

Victoria shook her head. "You know the company. They have eyes...." She broke off. "The security records!"

It wasn't that difficult to find the office of the head of security. Raphael had memorized the layout of the habitat far better than Victoria had and took her straight to it. The problem arose in trying to discover where the records had been hidden.

Apparently, the company had decided it would work best if no one other than the head of security actually knew about the security records. That way, no one would be able to tamper with them.

They were supposed to be tamper proof, of course, but everyone knew there had never been a device invented for the purpose of security that someone hadn't managed to crack, and these were typically generous souls who liked to share their knowledge.

They found a stack of records locked in the head of security's filing cabinet.

They had better luck accessing the security officer's computer. Apparently, he had a tendency toward memory lapses. He'd taped his password inside the filing cabinet.

The discovery humanized the missing man as nothing else and Victoria felt a touch of humor and her first true pang of loss. Up until that moment, she'd merely been stunned by the magnitude of the situation. She hadn't, personally, known any of those missing. She'd been shocked, horrified and frightened, but she hadn't felt any sense of loss. Staring at the carefully formed letters, hand written by someone who had vanished without a trace or explanation, Victoria felt a lump of sorrow tighten her throat.

It was a struggle to dismiss it, to step back once more to an emotional distance that would allow her to feel less and think more, but she was able to push it from her mind presently and focus on the immediate problem.

The records, they discovered, were either of poor quality, or had become corrupted by the conditions--or possibly both. Between blips of static, they caught glimpses of the crew going about their lives from various view points around the station, but, as bad as the video was, the audio was even worse and it was impossible to really tell anything about what was happening. The dates indicated that the recordings went all the way back to the current--or what should have been the current occupants'--arrival. There were none that were recent. The last one appeared to be several weeks before the last known communication with the crew.

To Victoria, there seemed to be an air of agitation in the mannerisms of the crew members on the last record, but she couldn't tell whether it was an assessment prejudiced by her knowledge of the disaster that had followed, or it the crew had already been aware of a problem. "Raphael, take a look at this and tell me what you think."

She made an aborted attempt to rise and give him her seat, but he placed a hand on her shoulder, leaning over her. More disturbed than she liked by his proximity, she did her best to ignore it and told the computer to replay the final log.

"They look scared, jumpy, on edge," Raphael commented.

Victoria glanced up at him.

"There! Replay that."

Victoria's head whipped back toward the image. She backed it up, staring hard at the crew members displayed. It was a man and a woman, standing in the corridor near the lift, but she couldn't tell which level they were on. They were talking in low voices, but even if they hadn't been, she doubted she could have understood what they were talking about from the blips of static interlacing the audio.

"Look at his lips. Five missing."

Victoria's heart skipped a beat. She reversed the record and played it several more times. "It could be," she said finally. "But even if that is what the guy said, it doesn't necessarily follow that he was talking about crew members. It might be anything."

"He looks a little too agitated to be talking about socks," Raphael said dryly.

Victoria frowned, irritated by the sarcasm in his voice. "I can see they're both upset about something, and it seems probable you've picked up on part of the conversation, but it still isn't much to go on. He could be talking about tools that went missing ... personal items that were stolen. The fact is we don't know what he's talking about and we can't just jump to the conclusion that it has to do with the missing crew members. We need the work logs."

A sound at the door of the office drew their attention. Roach was standing in the doorway. There was something about the way he was looking at her that set off alarm bells. Irritated at the intrusion, she frowned at him. "They can't have finished the clean up this quickly. What is it, Roach?"

He glanced at Raphael, his expression antagonistic. "I just wanted to put in my request before we settled on room mates."

Victoria felt her stomach clench. She'd hoped to avoid this confrontation all together, or at least put it off for a while in view of their current situation. It seemed useless, however, to point out to him that she felt like demanding a sexual partner now, when their situation was so precarious, was in poor taste, to say the least. Roach obviously didn't feel the least uncomfortable or disturbed about the missing crew members. Doubtless, if she mentioned it, he'd merely point out that the stress of the situation was all the more reason to settle on a partner to assure sexual release from tension. "This isn't the time. We'll discuss this later."

He frowned. "I figured if I waited till a more convenient time, you might come to an agreement with somebody else. I want it as a matter of record that I requested the first two weeks," he said, stubbornly refusing to leave without an answer.

Since there seemed no other way to avoid it, Victoria was on the point of telling him she wouldn't be choosing a room mate for a while--if at all--when Raphael spoke.

"She'll be rooming with me."

Chapter Five

Caught completely off guard, Victoria couldn't hide her stunned surprise at the announcement that the two of them had already reached an agreement. Fortunately, Raphael's comment distracted Roach, as well. Otherwise, he'd have known immediately that Raphael was lying and that could've made the situation even worse.

"Like hell!" Roach yelled furiously. "Stick to your own kind!"

Raphael stiffened almost imperceptibly. His eyes narrowed. "What kind is that?"

Victoria jumped up abruptly, knowing Roach was just hot headed enough, and stupid enough, to provoke a physical interchange. Nor had it escaped her notice that Raphael, who normally seemed very cool headed, was showing alarming indications that he was more than willing to take Roach up on his challenge. "Stop it!" Victoria snapped.

Both men ignored her.

Roach spat on the floor as if he tasted something bad. "You ain't figured it out yet? Cold blooded with cold blooded ... warm blooded with warm blood. They paired us up before we left, fishman."

"I said can it, Roach!"

Roach glanced at her then, his look assessing. "You got an agreement with him?"

Victoria's lips tightened in anger--at both men. Now she had to choose. It was no contest really. And, yet, she'd hoped to avoid a confrontation with Roach, had intended to express no interest in taking a partner at all at this time, so that she could avoid having to turn Roach down in the future. She didn't want Roach--at any time. But if she chose Raphael now, that would mean she'd either have to agree to Roach when her time was up with Raphael, or risk having--creating--just the sort of incident the company most disliked, battles between males, or females, over sexual favors. "Yes," she finally answered.

Roach's eyes narrowed. "In that case, I withdraw my offer. I'm not certain I could stomach taking the fish's leavings."

Insulting as it was--to both of them--Victoria couldn't prevent the leap of hope that entered her chest. She didn't have time to examine it, however. She had to jump between the two men to prevent them from coming to blows, for the words had no sooner left Roach's mouth than Raphael surged forward, his face a mask of barely leashed rage. Grasping Raphael's arm, she put her back to him and faced Roach. "At the rate you're going, Roach, you're going to be spending most of your time in the brig. Get back down below and get to work!"

His lips curled in a sneer. "Yes ma'am."

When he'd left, Victoria turned on Raphael. "What did you do that for? You know damn well we never discussed such a thing, much less arrived at an agreement."

"You didn't want him."

"No, I didn't, damn it! But I'd have liked to handle it myself. As it stands, you've put me in the position of playing favorites--or accepting him down the line. And neither damn one of those positions are acceptable to me."

He studied her a long moment, his face taut with anger. Then, to Victoria's shock, he snatched her up against him, hard, grasped the back of her head in one hand and lowered his mouth to hers before she could do more than gasp in stunned surprise. The moment his mouth covered hers in a kiss that was warm, moist and both hungry and possessive, something hot and liquid flowed through her, setting her flesh on fire, pulling the strength from her limbs so that she collapsed weakly against him. The arm he'd slid around her waist tightened. Unaware of anything beyond the feel of his mouth and tongue and the havoc they wreaked with her senses, Victoria weakly sought purchase to prevent herself from falling, grasping his shoulders, then slipping her arms around his neck, tangling her fingers in his dark hair as she responded to his kiss with fervor.

When he released her mouth at last, Victoria's head fell back weakly, lolling against his shoulder. She found she could not catch her breath. It sawed painfully in and out of her chest, her lungs struggling to keep up with the rapid, pounding beat of her heart.

He caught her face in one hand, tipping her head back so that he could look down at her. "Am I too cold for you, Victoria?"

With an effort, Victoria opened her eyes and looked at him blankly. "Wha...?"

A faint smile of triumph curled his lips, gleaming in his eyes, but before Victoria could even decide what it meant or how she felt about it, he lowered his lips to hers once more. This kiss was far less punishing, but just as possessive, and just as devastating to her already overloaded senses. She felt as weak and insubstantial as water.

"You are mine. I will not share you with another," he murmured when he lifted his lips at last.

Victoria stared at him blankly as his words slowly sank into her mind, slowly began to make sense to her. She stiffened, tried to pull away. He released her. It took an effort to stand upright without his support. "The by-laws prohibit...."

"I don't give a damn about the by-laws," he said grimly.

"Officers of the company are not allowed...."

"I did not choose my position."

"I did!" Victoria snapped. "I've worked too hard and too long to jeopardize my plans because of a ... a testosterone battle between you and Roach!"

His eyes narrowed. "You think that's what this is about?"

"Isn't it always?" Victoria said bitterly. She'd been in much the same position before. It had almost destroyed her budding career, and the worst of it was that neither man had really cared for her. The contest had been between them. They'd become so immersed in trying to outdo one another and claim her as their 'prize' that they'd either not seen, or not cared, that the rivalry between them was wrecking her chances of advancement with the company.

"Choosing a life mate is still acceptable, even in the fucked up universe we live in these days," Raphael said tightly.

Victoria gaped at him in surprise and unconsciously took a step back. "Life...,"she said faintly. "Among terraformers, colonists and the like, certainly, where a partnership is considered desirable and even necessary, but...."

"Isn't that our ultimate goal?"

The comment totally threw Victoria. "Our? How did you...?" But she knew how. Obviously, she hadn't guarded her thoughts from him as well as she'd believed. "Damn it, Raphael! You had no right to ... to...."

"You chose to meld minds with me."

Victoria stared at him uncomprehendingly. "I don't even understand what you're talking about! How could I choose?"

His lips tightened. Something curiously akin to pain flickered in his eyes. "Nevertheless."

Victoria looked away, feeling drained suddenly. "I can't deal with this right now. We have a dangerous situation. I need to keep my mind on keeping us all alive."

Raphael was silent for several moments. "Let's have a look for the work logs, then."

Relieved that he'd allowed the subject to drop so readily, Victoria nodded and they left the security chief's office and began a room by room search to find the logs. By the time they located them, however, Victoria discovered that she'd missed her window of opportunity insofar as using them as leverage to protect herself and her crew.

Tuttle came pounding into the control room, bellowing her name.

Victoria and Raphael exchanged a startled glance, dropped the records and raced into the main operations room with weapons drawn. "What is it?" Victoria demanded.

Tuttle was gasping for breath. "The shuttle--Captain Huggins took off without us!"

It took several moments for that information to sink in ... and Victoria still couldn't believe it. Without a word, she pushed past Tuttle and raced up the stairs. The landing pad, when she finally reached the flight deck, was empty except for the crates of supplies, which Captain Huggins and Grant had obviously off loaded hastily before their departure. She was still staring at the vacant spot the shuttle had occupied in shocked disbelief when Raphael and Tuttle joined her.

"What happened?" she demanded as she turned to Tuttle.

Tuttle shrugged. "He called me in sick bay and told me I needed to deliver a message to you. Said they'd heard back from the company and the orders were to proceed as planned and send a report on the investigation when it was completed. Clancy seemed to be doing OK, so I didn't argue. I had just started down the stairs when I heard the gang plank being retracted. When I turned around and ran back up, the shuttle was already leaving the pad."

"Son of a bitch!" Victoria yelled. "God damn those bastards to hell!"

Tuttle, she saw when she finally turned to look at her, was staring at her wide eyed. "Are we in trouble?"

It took a supreme effort to fight her temper down to a manageable level. "We don't know." Victoria gnawed her lower lip a moment. "Go below. The crew's working on cleaning up the access level. Tell them to knock off for today and get these supplies stowed, then they can choose quarters and settle in. And tell the cooks to get busy and see what they can come up with to feed the crew."

Tuttle nodded and turned to go.

"Tuttle."

She stopped and turned back. "I'll discuss the situation with the crew after dinner. That's all they need to know right now."

Again, Tuttle nodded and left Victoria and Raphael.

"At least he left the supplies," Raphael said when Tuttle was out of ear shot.

Victoria glanced at him. "I'd have felt better if he hadn't. At least then we'd know he was coming back."

Raphael's expression was grim. "Not necessarily--he could have taken off with our supplies and still had no intention of returning-- but I see your point. If we had the communications tower up, we might have had a chance of calling him back. As it stands...." He shrugged.

Victoria shook her head. "He'd ignore any order I gave him, even if we could communicate with the ship. He's been ordered back. He wouldn't have taken off otherwise. Huggins is a company man, through and through. He would not have made this decision on his own. And, unfortunately for us, it would never occur to him to argue with any decision they made."

"So ... what do we do now?"

Victoria turned to look at him. "Try to stay alive."

Chapter Six

The cooks had apparently decided that the desperate situation called for extraordinary efforts on their part. They'd put together a veritable feast for the crew members who presently trooped into the dining hall, tired and anxious, but freshly scrubbed and apparently hungry.

Victoria couldn't help but notice the crew members segregated themselves. Except for Raphael, everyone else that seated themselves at her table were top side crew members. The deep sea crew sat together, separated from her group by several empty tables.

It made Victoria uneasy. They had problems enough without being divided among themselves.

The situation between her, Roach, and Raphael was certainly not going to help matters. Roach was almost universally disliked, but it didn't necessarily follow that that meant the top side crew members would ignore his grievance and, in any case, Roach was the sort to extend his anger to encompass the entire deep sea crew, simply because he had a personal beef with Raphael. It was highly likely that he would be picking fights with any one of them that had the misfortune to come within 'firing' range of his temper. And she had no doubt that he would do his utmost to incite the other 'human' crew members to treat the deep water crew with prejudice.

Victoria found she had little appetite.

She wished suddenly that she'd left Roach in the brig. Perhaps then Captain Huggins would have taken off with him, as he had Clancy, and that would have eliminated at least one of her problems.

A useless thought, but she couldn't help but wonder if it would transpire that Clancy would actually be the luckiest of them all.

When everyone had finished eating, she stood and addressed them.

"I hope that everyone has settled in OK."

"Does that mean we're staying?" Brown asked.

"It does. The company has ... uh ... expressed their confidence in our ability to handle our current situation."

"Meaning they've abandoned us to sink or swim," Roach muttered in a perfectly audible voice.

Victoria pretended she hadn't heard him. "Our investigation into the situation we found when we arrived is ongoing."

"Which means they haven't a fucking clue what happened here," Roach said a little louder.

Victoria glared at him.

"Is that true? You still don't know what happened?"

"Yes. We still don't know. Which means I want everybody to stay alert and the orders I gave earlier stand. No one works alone. No one goes off alone. No crew works without at least two lookouts when outside the habitat. Tomorrow, the mining crew will concentrate on opening up the mine shaft. Top crew will test the processing plant and make sure its operational. Once we're sure we have a go there, we'll concentrate on the access pool. Raphael says there's several tons of ore mined and ready to process. I expect us to be fully operational within the week, but we're going to have to hump it if we want to see any bonuses.

"Our focus is going to be on getting the mine and processing plant operational so that we can begin making some money, people. Anything non-essential to our project here can wait until we get around to it, or wait for the next crew."

"What about the communications tower?" someone near the back asked.

Briefly, a sense of satisfaction touched her. At least they were willing to participate in group discussions. It was more important than ever that they work as a group. Their survival might depend upon it. "That's essential. I'll have the schedule posted in the morning. Check it and see who's been assigned to what duties. I'll be assigning a rotating crew to go topside and evaluate the situation with the tower and get to work on repairs. We need that operational as soon as possible."

Everyone seemed to take that as a dismissal. They began a general exodus from the dining hall and into the rec room.

Victoria glanced at Raphael. "I need to get the schedules worked out," she muttered, half to herself.

Raphael nodded. "I'll show you our room."

The words sent a shock wave of sensations and emotions through Victoria, but she resolutely ignored it. "I don't suppose Huggins had the grace to leave any of my personal effects while he and Grant were busy pitching our supplies out on the deck?"

"Oh, he was a thorough son-of-a-bitch. I'm just surprised he didn't park Clancy on the tarp before take-off," Raphael replied, rising. Sliding a hand beneath one of her elbows, he urged her toward the door.

Uncomfortable with the 'escort', Victoria straightened her arm abruptly, whereupon Raphael simply slid his hand along the back of her arm and grasped her hand. Victoria frowned. "Public displays...."

Raphael nodded. "Are forbidden."

He released her hand and grasped her arm just above the wrist.

The urge to remove her arm from his grasp was strong, but Victoria decided after a very little thought that that was likely to attract more attention than pretending she was unaware of his touch. Sharing sexual favors freely was encouraged. Emotional attachments were not. Emotional attachments were prone to create ripples of discord throughout a group and the company was against anything that might interfere with work.

"This is considered a show of affection?"

Victoria took a deep breath and decided to ignore the fact that he was reading her thoughts, as well. "Any touch that's more than casual can be construed as a display of affection."

"This is more than casual?"

Victoria's lips tightened. There was amusement in his voice. If she'd doubted before that he was being deliberately obtuse, she no longer did. "Since I'm perfectly capable of walking without assistance, yes."

"Good."

Victoria glanced at him quickly, but since they had entered the rec room and were in full view of everyone who'd remained to look for a little entertainment before retiring for the night, she said nothing, merely quickening her step purposefully. For all that, she didn't manage to 'out run' him. He matched her step for step, guiding her toward the room he'd chosen for them. It was no great distance, being situated about half way down one side of the rec room, but Victoria found her nerves were jumping long before they reached the privacy of the room.

Raphael, Victoria saw when she flicked a glance at him, was studying her with a mixture of amusement and barely concealed heat. Feeling the blood rise in her cheeks, Victoria looked away quickly and made her way to the desk in one corner of the room.

"There's no need to be so nervous," Raphael said quietly.

Victoria didn't turn to look at him. She was busy searching the drawers for pen and paper. "I'm not," she lied.

"You are."

Victoria drew in a deep, sustaining breath, trying to calm her jitters. "If I am, it's because of our situation," she said tightly.

"Partly."

Victoria set the materials down and turned in her chair to look at him. She was more than a little disconcerted to see that he'd sprawled out on the bed and was lying with his head propped on one hand, studying her. "Don't be shy," she said dryly. "Just tell me what's on your mind."

"You."

She hadn't expected him to be quite that forthcoming. Blood flooded her cheeks. She opened her mouth to speak but discovered she couldn't think of a thing to say. Turning away abruptly, she did her best to concentrate on the schedule, starting with a list of names. Her concentration was in shambles, however, and she discovered it was impossible to put names with faces, and abilities and specialties together with hardly any of the crew members.

"I could help."

She hadn't heard him cross the room. When he spoke, directly beside her, she jumped and dropped the pen from suddenly nerveless fingers. He knelt, picked up the pen and handed it to her, but he did not rise. Instead, he placed a hand on her knee. Victoria felt as if it was a firebrand, burning through the thin fabric of her uniform trousers.

"You're anxious, frightened. You've no need to be."

Victoria knew he wasn't referring to their precarious situation on Kay, but she wasn't ready to meet him head on on a personal level. "Of course, I'm anxious ... and scared. We've been abandoned on this God forsaken rock with no clue of what happened to the personnel that was here."

Raphael shook his head slowly from side to side. "You know that's not what I meant."

Victoria studied him, trying to decide how best to handle the situation she found herself in, but nothing came immediately to mind. She was accustomed to handling a variety of work related problems. She was even, somewhat, used to managing men and women seeking sexual favors. The latter created the least problems at all, for she had merely to point out that she was heterosexual and they usually gracefully withdrew. Men had rarely been a problem for her, as far as that went. In general, her demeanor alone was enough to keep them at a distance and even those who were attracted by the challenge of dominating a dominate female could be routed without a great deal of fuss simply by using her position in the hierarchy and assigning them to work as far away from her as possible.

"It won't work."

She discovered that Raphael was looking at her with amusement. "What?" she asked cautiously.

"Trying to avoid me."

Victoria sighed. "It carries no weight with you at all that I've expressly forbidden you to read my mind, does it?"

He frowned slightly. "I find it difficult not to. We are mind melded, you and I."

It was Victoria's turn to frown. "You said that before. I still don't understand."

His look was wry. "You are not telepathic. We should not have been able to meld at all."

Irritation surfaced. "That explains it so much better."

He chuckled. "You have a quick temper."

"I am perfectly even tempered," Victoria said stiffly.

His eyes gleamed with suppressed amusement, but in a moment, he leaned toward her. Victoria knew he meant to kiss her. She put a restraining hand on his chest, leaning away. "Don't do that! I'll become a mindless mass of quivering jelly and I won't get anything done!"

Instead of looking insulted that she'd pulled away, Raphael laughed outright. "That's what I've always loved about you, Victoria. There is no subterfuge in you."

Conflicting emotions collided inside of her--doubt, pleasure and confusion--and Victoria felt her face turning red. "This is your way of saying, I suppose, that I'm not a woman of mystery."

"You are a complex woman, but you and I are linked--we melded when I emerged from the incubation chamber. No matter where you are, how far away, I know what you are feeling. I feel what you are feeling." His expression became wry. "I don't always understand it, or why you feel as you do, but I feel when you are distressed, angry--everything that you feel."

Victoria wasn't certain she liked the sound of that. It sounded almost as if he was saying they were fused into one being. She found it hard to accept as a possibility. She found it even more difficult to accept in the sense of losing her individuality. Outwardly, she was a conformist, because she knew that was expected, and because advancement hinged on conformity. Secretly, she preferred to think of herself as completely unique. She wasn't at all certain she could share her inner self. She was pretty certain, though, that she didn't want to.

Raphael frowned. After a moment, he rose and moved away, pacing the room. "Quinton and Albert are programmed machinists. They would probably be best suited to work on the communications tower."

Victoria blinked. It took her a moment to realize he'd changed the subject completely. Finally, she nodded and turned to the schedule, writing their names down. "Any others?"

"None specifically programmed to work on communications, but Caroline and Barbara both know electronics and Xavier is an electrician."

Victoria added the names to her list, then frowned, set her pen down and flipped through the files on her crew. "We're hopelessly understaffed without the crew that we were supposed to be joining, but I've worked with Brown and Tuttle before. They know their way around a processor. It shouldn't take them long to figure out the setup here. We'll need some welders to repair the access cover ... and I'd like to beef it up. I think we're going to have to assume that whatever happened here, it's something we're going to have to contend with, as well."

* * * *

Working on the schedules reminded Victoria that, although they had finally found the work logs, she had left them on the upper level when she discovered that Huggins had departed without them.

Once she'd posted the schedules, she decided to go up to retrieve them so that she could study them. Without a word, Raphael fell into step beside her. Oddly enough, she found it comforting, rather than irritating. Distracted as she was, she would have gone up alone, even knowing that it was not safe for anyone to move about the habitat alone until they knew more about what had happened. Even if she hadn't been distracted, she would not have liked to demand an escort. It was all very well to point out that, logically, every man and woman was at risk. It still smacked of fear to ask, which translated to weakness, which was something she could not afford if she was to retain control of the situation on Kay.

She didn't notice Roach until he spoke.

"And there goes Ms. Tory with her faithful watchdog," he muttered as she and Raphael passed on their way to the stairwell. Victoria stiffened. She would have stopped and confronted him except that Raphael urged her onward.

"Why did you do that?" she snapped as they started up the stairs.

"It'll be best to ignore him."

"If you think that, then you've no understanding at all of the type of creature he is," she responded tartly.

"No, I don't. Enlighten me."

Victoria felt her irritation vanish. It was difficult to get used to the idea that Raphael had so few experiences to fall back on. "He's a bully. Ignoring him, or trying to, isn't going to do any good. He's spoiling for a fight. He's not going to be satisfied until he gets one."

Raphael frowned. "Bullies are generally cowards."

"Bullies are *always* cowards," Victoria responded. "But no two people handle fear the same way, any more than they handle any other emotion the same way. My instincts tell me Roach isn't going to be satisfied until he's convinced his fears aren't unfounded."

"And what do you perceive as his fears?"

There was a touch of amusement in his voice now. They'd reached the landing on the next level and Victoria paused, turning to look at him. "He's not certain he's man enough to control me, but he's determined to have a try."

All traces of amusement vanished from Raphael's expression. His eyes narrowed. "I won't share you," he said flatly.

Victoria was taken aback. It was on the tip of her tongue to inform him that it wasn't his decision to make. Instead, after wrestling with her temper for several moments, she merely shrugged. "Under the circumstances, there seems to be a very good chance that it'll never be an issue."

It was obvious from his expression that her comment was neither expected, nor welcome. He frowned. "That's not an answer."

"I wasn't aware that you'd asked a question. You said 'I won't'. You didn't ask me how I felt about it," Victoria said shortly and pulled the door open, heading for the office where she'd left the documents she sought.

"Because I know you have no desire to go to him."

"No, I don't, but that's beside the point. I make my own decisions, for my own reasons."

"So--decide."

Despite her irritation, Victoria felt amusement surface. Having reached the office, she stopped in the doorway. "You are bossy. You know that? Why do I get the feeling that as long as my decision coincides with yours, you'll allow it?"

His brows rose, but she could see his anger had vanished and amusement once more took its place. "Because it's true?"

She shook her head and set about retrieving the papers. By the time she'd finished, her brief sense of amusement had completely vanished. "It may still be a moot point," she said grimly as she started back. "Unless we can figure out what happened here, and how to prevent it from happening to us, we may not be alive in two weeks to make any sort of decisions."

Chapter Seven

By the time they reached their level once more, the rec room had emptied. Apparently, the crew had primarily been waiting for the schedule to be posted before retiring for the night. The total silence of a complete absence of habitation greeted them the moment they opened the door on the third level.

It hadn't occurred to Victoria until that very moment that she and Raphael were the only personnel in a position to occupy this level. Immediately tense, Victoria did her best to ignore it and strode purposefully toward their quarters.

Raphael forestalled her intentions, removing the reports from her hands and dropping them on the desk. Victoria looked at him in surprise, but before she could object, he'd pulled her into his arms and lowered his head, brushing his lips lightly against hers.

A flush of warmth went through her. "I really should look at the reports."

"They're not going anywhere and neither are we."

He was right, of course, but it seemed wrong to put off anything so potentially vital to their survival.

"Is there anything you could do, at this very moment, besides study them?"

"I don't suppose so."

"Then it'll wait till morning."

Victoria looked down at her hands where they rested against his chest. "I'm nervous," she confessed.

"So am I."

Startled, Victoria looked up at him.

He smiled wryly. "It's my first time."

The comment threw Victoria into complete disorder. "Oh--Oh my God, Raphael! I'm so sorry. It was thoughtless of me."

Smiling faintly, he reached for her tunic, unfastening it. "Don't worry. I believe it'll come to me." Removing the top, he dropped it to the floor and pulled her against him again, waltzing her backward.

"Where are we going?" Victoria asked, uncertain whether to laugh with him, or cry for him. He was so incredibly sweet it made her heart ache. The thought of all that he'd missed out on, been deprived of, because of what the company had done to him hurt in a way she didn't entirely understand.

"To the bed. Unless you want to try it standing. I can't vouch for my prowess, but I'm wide open to suggestion."

The mattress caught the back of her knees and Victoria fell backward with a little yelp of surprise. Shedding his own tunic, Raphael followed her down, lying half atop her. They gazed at each other for a long moment and then Victoria lifted her arms and draped them around his neck, tilting her face up for his kiss. After a moment, he leaned down, brushing his lips against hers. Victoria gasped at the desire that enveloped her in a hot wave at his first touch, opening her mouth to him. When he did not immediately seize the opportunity she offered him, she thrust her tongue into his mouth, caressing his tongue with her own, tasting him.

Raphael settled closer, focusing completely on the feel and taste of her, fighting the urge to rush, to taste and explore and possess her completely. When she withdrew, he followed her, thrusting his tongue into her mouth to explore her as she had him. She surprised him when she closed her mouth around his tongue and sucked. The sensation sent such a fiery rush through him that his pulse pounded, making rational thought an impossibility. Feeling that he would explode at any moment, he broke the kiss, gasping hoarsely.

Victoria reached for the fastening of his trousers, gnawing a trail along the side of his throat with the edge of her teeth, kissing his shoulders as she fumbled with the resistant fastening. He pushed her hands away and unfastened it himself, then reached for her, searching for the key to removing her bra. Smiling faintly as she kissed her way down his chest, Victoria unsnapped it and shrugged it off, tossing it to the floor beside the bed.

He pushed her onto her back, grasped her trousers and tugged at the fastening. His fingers, clumsy with desire, he succeeded only in binding the closure fast. Victoria gasped when he ripped it open and peeled away her trousers and panties, throwing them to the floor. She was far too anxious herself, however, to spare more than a moment of concern for the ruined clothing and immediately turned her attention to helping him strip away the last of his own clothing.

She ran her hands over his chest when he settled beside her again, but he held her away when she would have moved against him, examining her body with his hands and his gaze. Noticing the contrast between her pale white skin and his darker skin, Victoria felt a little self-conscious, wondering if he found her as attractive as she found him. He glanced up at her, his eyes filled with hunger. "You are so beautiful to me, it makes me ache for you. Always."

He leaned toward her, kissed her long and lingeringly. Victoria felt a blinding rush of desire the moment his mouth covered hers, felt as if she was falling into a dark chasm. She reached for him, wrapping her fingers around his cock, spreading her thighs. Waiting might make it sweeter, but she found she didn't want to wait any longer. She was so hot, her sex wet and aching for his touch, she knew instinctively that this time she would find what had always eluded her before, fulfillment.

He moved between her thighs, thrusting his hips as she lifted hers and aligned his cock with her own body. A shudder went through him as he buried himself to the hilt inside of her. When Victoria looked up at him through half closed lids, she saw that he had squeezed his eyes tightly shut, as if he was in pain, his facial muscles taut. He opened his eyes and looked down at her. "My God! I didn't know it would feel this good to be inside of you...."

Heat suffused her, the muscles in her sex clenching in response to the desire his words evoked. Victoria moved her hips against him. He uttered a low, growling groan and began to move, slowly at first and then increasing the tempo, thrusting his cock inside of her and then pulling away in a rhythm that built the ache inside her to a fever pitch so that she was moaning incessantly, gasping, could feel her body hovering on the brink of release.

She wrapped her arms around his neck, pulling him down for a kiss, suckling hard on his tongue as he thrust it into her mouth. It was the impetus that sent them both over the edge into blissful ecstasy. Victoria broke the kiss, crying out as waves of intense pleasure pounded through her, feeling the muscles inside her contracting and releasing his cock.

Raphael groaned, shuddering, his hips jerking as his hot seed spilled inside of her.

Slowly, when the spasms finally abated, he withdrew, wincing as the movement sent fresh needles of sensation through him. With an effort, he dragged himself off of her and collapsed against the bed, staring up at the ceiling through half closed eyes. "I thought melding minds with you was the closest I would ever come to heaven--I was wrong," he murmured.

"Mmm. Mind boggling. I always wondered why everybody was so preoccupied with sex. Now I know."

Chuckling, Raphael rolled onto his side and propped his head on his bent arm, studying her. It might have made her uncomfortable under other circumstances, but she was too wiped out to care at the moment. The only two thoughts that drifted through her sluggish brain was whether or not she felt like getting up again and having a look at the work logs, or if she was too tired to try to make sense of them. After a moment, she decided she didn't and curled up on her side, putting her back to Raphael and felt around for cover.

She remembered then that they'd fell into the bed fully made and she was lying on top of the cover, wondered, briefly, if she felt like getting up and pulling it down and finally decided she didn't.

The thought had barely drifted through her mind when she felt a tug as Raphael pulled the cover back and grasped her around the waist. Pulling her against him, he spread the cover he tugged loose over both of them. Victoria snuggled her butt against his crotch and settled again as Raphael slid a heavy arm around her waist.

Something long and hard insinuated itself between her thighs. Victoria couldn't decide whether to be irritated or amused. "We have to get up early in the morning," she murmured.

She felt the warmth of Raphael's breath as he leaned over and kissed her shoulder. It sent a flock of goose bumps chasing down her arm and made her nipples stand erect. A hand the size of a dinner plate slid upward and covered one breast, pinching the erect nipple between two fingers. It sent currents of pleasure through her, but Victoria decided to ignore it.

"What are these for?" Raphael murmured in her ear.

A smile tugged at her lips. "Holding my tunic out in the front--not that they do much of a job of it."

He squeezed the breast he held experimentally. "I like the way it feels in my hand."

"If it fit your hand I'd have a hunchback," Victoria said tartly.

"Prickly," Raphael observed, nuzzling her neck. "They're perfect, just like the rest of you."

She felt the curve of his lips and knew he was smiling.

"What are they good for, besides holding your tunic out, and feeding our baby?"

Victoria shrugged sleepily. "Nobody does that...." Her eyes popped wide open and she twisted around to look at him. "What did you say?"

"Feeding our baby?"

Victoria stared at him blankly while her mind sorted a hundred conflicting thoughts, finally those uppermost emerged into coherence. "It was just sex ... very good sex, but we didn't make a baby. I'm on birth control. Besides, I don't have a permit."

Raphael frowned. "You have to have a permit?"

"Of course you have to have a permit! You can't spit without a permit!" Victoria relaxed again, yawning. "Anyway, I don't plan to have any."

Raphael was silent for some moments. Victoria might have gone to sleep except she could tell from the tension in his body that he was debating with himself over something. The 'something' that might pertain to made her uneasy. He'd spoken before about 'their' plans and she couldn't help but worry that he might be working on other plans for the two of them.

"Is it difficult to get a permit?"

Victoria shrugged. "I don't know. Probably. Nothing in this life is ever easy, or uncomplicated."

He pulled her over onto her back and brushed the hair back from her face, studied her a long moment and leaned down to kiss her lightly on the lips. "I love you, Victoria. Remember that," he murmured, then nuzzled her neck.

Victoria stiffened at his words, but before she could think of anything to say, his lips closed over one nipple and she descended once more into the ecstasy only he had ever given her.

* * * *

Raphael was on his feet the moment the catch was released on the door and striding toward it. He was within three feet of the door when it was snatched open and Roach stepped into the portal. His first instinct was to plant his fist in the man's face. He quelled it, instead placing a palm on Roach's chest and propelling him backwards out the door. "You have a reason for being here?" he asked grimly.

Roach gaped at him, so surprised it took him several moments to think up a response. "Tory hadn't shown today. Just checking to make sure she was all right."

"She is," Raphael responded and shut the door in Roach's face.

Victoria had been swimming upward toward consciousness in a lazy, unhurried manner until the abrupt movement beside her brought her fully awake. She sat up with a jerk as Raphael leapt from the bed, certain there was some threat.

Anger surged through her when she caught a glimpse of Roach trying to crane a look at the bed around Raphael's broad form, but it vanished at his words.

"Shit! I overslept!" she exclaimed, leaping from the bed as Raphael closed the door and turned to look at her.

A wave of dizziness assailed her at her abrupt movement, and she sat back, dropping her face into her hands. She'd only managed to catch a few hours of sleep in between bouts of the best sex she'd ever experienced in her life. At the time, it had seemed well worth the loss of sleep. In retrospect, it seemed criminally negligent and she wondered how she could have been tempted so far off the track of sane, logical, dependability as to have romped half the night when she should have been resting to face the challenges she knew were waiting come morning.

"You should try to sleep a few more hours."

Victoria shook her head. "I'll be fine once I've had a shower and gotten a gallon or so of caffeine into my system."

Rising more slowly, she staggered toward the bathroom and indulged herself in a long, hot shower, more than half expecting Raphael to join her. To her relief, he didn't.

Despite her optimism, she felt very little better after the shower and had to fight the urge to dry off and climb back into bed. Instead, she resolutely left the bathroom with the determination to dress and study the reports she'd put off the night before. Raphael was no where to be seen when she entered the room. She wondered at it, briefly, but shrugged it off and looked around, wondering where her clothes had been stowed.

Groggy as she was, she found them after only a half a dozen tries and had just finished dressing when the door opened and Raphael entered carrying two cups of coffee. He set both on the desk and went into the bathroom to shower without a word.

Victoria was almost as grateful for his silence as she was for the coffee. Years of getting up before first light had not done anything to adjust her natural sleep patterns. She had always had the inclination to stay awake long into the night, and sleep well into the morning and she was definitely not a 'morning' person. She was never more than partially functional until she'd been up at least two or three hours and drunk several cups of coffee. It was for that reason that she'd made it a habit to do her paperwork in the morning.

True, it was enough, in general, to put her right back to sleep, but by doing it first she had an excuse not to face the crew until she had her wits about her.

Which was one of the things that pissed her off about Roach's intrusion. Not for one moment did she believe it had been concern for her safety that had brought him up to check on her. It had been pure, unadulterated, nosiness and nothing else. They had never worked together, but he most certainly knew it wasn't his place to check on the boss to see if she was up yet.

She didn't know how she was going to do it, but she was going to have to come up with some way to avoid partnering with Roach when her two weeks with Raphael were up.

She would have preferred to stay with Raphael as long as he wanted to room with her, but that wasn't an option. It would be blatant favoritism. Roach was certain to file a grievance when they got back even if no one else did, and her whole career could go down the tubes. If it had only been a fine she would be facing, she would be willing to pay it. She wasn't ready to whistle her career away, though. She needed to hang on to it at least another year, two at the most, and then she could tell them all to go to hell. No matter what happened here on Kay--assuming she survived--she'd have enough to buy a homestead somewhere and a nice little nest egg besides.

Fortunately, her career choice hadn't led her to accustom herself to more than the basics, because luxury wasn't in the picture for her, whether she stayed with the company or not.

She supposed, after a little thought, that she might be able to bribe a bi-sexual or a lesbian to pretend to be her lover for a couple of weeks. She'd have to do a little investigating and see if any of the women on the mission fell into one or the other categories and seemed open to the possibility of earning a little money on the side.

She dismissed the thoughts as Raphael came out of the bathroom. His expression, she noticed when she glanced at him, was grim and she supposed he was feeling the aftereffects of little sleep as she was.

"I'm going below to check the progress of the crew in clearing the mine shaft. Would you like me to check on the situation with the communications tower and report back?"

Victoria shook her head. "They probably haven't really had time to assess the situation fully yet. I'll check with them later."

He nodded and left and Victoria turned her attention to the files at long last. She looked at the latest date first and her heart seemed to stop dead in her chest.

The security crew is searching for the five men who disappeared yesterday and to try to ascertain what happened to the others. All mining suspended until further notice.

Chapter Eight

It was late in the evening the third day after their arrival when Victoria went to check on the crew's progress on the communications tower. The crew members assigned to the task had planned a replacement tower around the scrap metal that had been gathered and Quinton and Albert had begun manufacturing parts. Caroline and Barbara had managed to scavenge what they needed in the way of electronics from operations, but they were weeks away from even reaching a point where they could begin testing the possible range of the makeshift tower.

Caroline placed their chances of being able to reach the closest outpost at practically nil. Unless she had miscalculated, their only hope even once the tower was operational was the possibility of reaching a ship cruising the outer rim.

The lift was still out and Victoria paused at the rail to catch her breath as she left the habitat, looking out over the churning waters of Kay's red ocean at the ball of fire settling into the sea. The fiery disk that was Kay's sun had already begun to dip below the horizon. It would be dark soon.

Dragging in a gulp of Kay's thick air with an effort, Victoria moved to the stairs. She was little more than half way between the upper and lower decks when, faintly, she heard a cry from above, almost like the cry of a seagull except that Kay had no birds of any description that she'd seen. It was cut off abruptly.

Adrenaline charged through her and Victoria raced up the remaining steps. When she reached the flight deck and looked around, Quinton and Albert were peering down over the side.

Kichens was no where in sight.

"What happened?" she shouted, dread filling her even as she ran toward the two crew members.

They turned, their faces pasty.

"Kichens went over the side."

Whirling, Victoria raced to the alarm and slammed her hand down on the button. Nothing happened. She hit it frantically several more times before realization coalesced in her panicked brain. It wasn't working. "God Damn it to hell!" she cursed furiously. "Does nothing on this piece of shit rig work?"

Racing toward the stairs once more, she charged down them as fast as she could, nearly falling twice before she reached the lower deck, snatched the door open and raced down to operations. Punching into main communications, she prayed the repairs had been made in the mining area. "Attention! Man down! Man down! Raphael--Anybody in the immediate area of the habitat. We have a man overboard. We need rescuers in the water STAT!"

Raphael responded almost instantly. "Most of the crew's in the mine shaft. I'll go myself."

"It's Kichens. She might have five minutes, tops."

He rang off without another word and Victoria leaned against the console weakly, wondering if there was any chance Kichens had even survived the fall. When she turned at last, she found that Quinton and Albert had followed her down.

"What happened?"

The two men exchanged a look. "I didn't see. I was bolting a couple of beams together. When I heard her cry out, I glanced in her direction, but she was already gone."

"What about you, Albert? Did you see anything?"

Albert frowned. "Not much more than Quinton. I was holding the beams steady. The last I saw, she'd gone over to grab up another short beam. Then, when I heard her, I looked up just as she went over the side, but I couldn't get to her in time to help."

"Did she surface, at all, after she hit the water?"

Quinton shook his head.

"Not that I saw," Albert said.

Victoria ran a shaky hand over her face. "Get back to work. There's nothing you can do."

Quinton turned immediately on his heel and departed. Albert frowned, looked as if he might say something and finally turned as well.

Victoria stopped him. "You saw something, didn't you?"

He shook his head. "Just what I told you. I just don't understand how she could have fallen. The railing's solid there and she wasn't that close to it anyway. She would almost ... well I can't see how she could have fallen at all. She would have had to be standing on the top rail, or climbing on it. I don't see how she could have fallen between the rails, even if she'd tripped."

Victoria nodded and dismissed him. The temptation to contact Raphael was strong, but she knew she wouldn't be able to. In any case, he would call when he had something to report. The wait was nerve wracking, however. She glanced at her watch, saw that five minutes had passed and began to pace.

Kichens had not been equipped with the prosthesis that would allow her to breathe underwater. If the fall had knocked her unconscious, her chances were slim to none that she'd survive until Raphael found her. She hadn't been in the water herself yet, but the crew members who had said that visibility was down to a few yards at most.

Her heart jerked painfully when the speaker came to life.

"Victoria?"

"Here. Did you get her?"

"No sign of her. I've pulled the crew from the mines. We're going back to search for her again."

Victoria didn't know whether she felt more like throwing up or crying.

"You there?"

"Yes. Do what you can to locate her." She left off 'body', unwilling and unable to think of the twenty two year old woman in terms of a corpse. She hadn't even been with the company five years.

Pushing the thought aside, Victoria made her way from the operations deck to her living quarters. She was still staring at the blank fatality report when Raphael returned several hours later.

She looked up at him questioningly when he closed the door behind him. He shook his head. "The currents are pretty strong here. They must have carried her ... off.

We brought out the lights, but it's just too dark to keep looking tonight."

Victoria nodded and dropped her head in her hands. "I've never lost a crew member before. I know I'm supposed to file a report, but I can't think of anything to put in it."

She didn't hear Raphael's approach, didn't realize he'd crossed the room until she felt his hands settle on her shoulders, kneading them. "It's not your fault."

"The safety of every crew member on this job is my responsibility," Victoria responded angrily, but she felt too drained for the tinder to catch fire. Almost the minute the words had left her, her anger died.

"We did everything we could. You did what you could."

"Which was nothing."

"Sometimes there's nothing anyone can do. I'm sorry I failed you."

Victoria glanced at him in surprise. "You've got nothing to apologize for! You responded as quickly as possible!"

"As you did."

Victoria looked away. Raphael squatted beside her. "Come. You need to eat."

"I don't think I could choke down anything to save my life."

"Try."

Thankfully, most of the crew members had already eaten and departed. A few had lingered in the rec room, although no one seemed inclined to seek entertainment. Conversations broke off as she and Raphael left her quarters.

"Any word about Kichens?"

Victoria turned toward the speaker. It was one of the miners, but she couldn't seem to think of the woman's name.

"Sylvia."

Victoria nodded. "Missing. Presumed dead. I'll need volunteers to go out tomorrow as soon as it's light enough and look for her. Just sign up on the schedule for search duty."

She managed to eat enough to pacify Raphael and finally pushed her plate away.

Raphael, she saw, had eaten little himself.

"Do you think it's related to the 'incident'?"

Victoria shrugged. "I don't know what to think. Neither of the men with her actually saw anything, but Albert said he didn't see how she could have fallen. She wasn't even near the railing and he vouched for the integrity of the railing at that point."

"But they were busy. I talked to them myself. They can't say for certain that she hadn't gone over to the railing for some reason. Maybe she heard something, leaned out to look?"

"Neither of the men mentioned hearing anything. Surely they would've said something if they had. And they were working pretty closely together, close enough to hear anything she had. Still, I suppose it's possible--doubtful in my opinion, but possible," Victoria said.

Raphael was silent for some moments. "The crew is going to wonder if there was any chance of foul play."

Victoria glanced at him in surprise but said nothing, replaying the images in her mind. Finally, she shook her head. "There was absolutely no indication of any kind of scuffle. You said you talked to the two men. Did you see any signs indicating an altercation?"

Raphael shrugged. "I wasn't looking for one. I assumed it was an accident."

"Me too. But I knew Kichens well enough to know that there's no way in hell either of those men, or even both of them together, could have managed to throw her over without her leaving a mark on them.

"Besides, we haven't even been here a week. I hardly think that's long enough to develop deadly animosity.

"And, before you suggest self destruction ... I can't buy that, either. She had a psych evaluation before we left planet. If she'd had any kind of emotional problems, they would've caught it. Besides, as I said, I knew her."

Raphael stared down at the cup in his hands. "All the same, the accident is just iffy enough to have the rest of the crew speculating on the possibility that she was thrown."

Victoria sent him a wry look. "Roach."

He nodded.

Victoria frowned. "Ordinarily I'd say a making a very public, very thorough investigation would satisfy everyone. But, if I call Quinton and Albert in for questioning, I'm afraid it'll only cause more talk, not less, maybe even arouse suspicions where there were none before. I think we're just going to have to play it by ear."

They called off the search after the third day. Victoria made it a point to call on members from both crews to help her check out the accident site, hoping it would forestall the problem Raphael foresaw, but it was impossible to ignore the fact that tensions were building.

Victoria decided overtime was in order. If they were too tired to do more than crawl into their bunks at night, they would also, hopefully, be too tired to stir up trouble.

That seemed to work, to a degree, until the day Roach went missing.

Chapter Nine

Victoria's personal problems should have been the least of her worries, should not have crowded her mind with unwanted thoughts and emotions. She'd lost a crew member--a well liked crew member, who had too many friends who wanted someone to blame for her death.

Beyond that, the habitat was crippled to the point that they had barely begun to limp along in mining and processing ore well into their second week on Kay, and topping that was the fact that they were scarcely a wit wiser as to what had happened to the previous crew.

Victoria had had to let up on the crew after little more than a week. The overtime wasn't making the crew too tired to fight. It was making them tired enough that paranoia was beginning to set in and tempers growing short.

She gave them a day off to rest and sent them back to a regular work schedule.

Overall, tensions seemed to ease up a little after that.

Unfortunately, Victoria's stress level only climbed several notches higher.

As accustomed as she was to shelving her personal considerations and concentrating on the job at hand, her intimacy with Raphael had brought out something she'd previously managed to ignore--a strong emotional attachment. That bond only made her situation with Roach even more difficult. Whereas, from the moment she'd noticed his interest she'd felt a combination of physical revulsion, and the suspicion that Roach's interest was predicated on a personal myth that he would be able to control her once they became intimate, she now had added to that a curious attachment to Raphael that made the possibility of having to bunk with Roach even more repellent.

And Roach was counting the days—publicly--despite his insulting remark about taking Raphael's leavings, he made certain that everyone knew he'd staked a claim on being next in line to bunk with her, and no one could remain ignorant of the day count.

His preoccupation not only unnerved her, it infuriated Raphael--a singular feat since Raphael was very difficult to ruffle under almost any other circumstance, creating just the situation that the Company had hoped to avoid when they'd established the rule of intimacy--territorial propriety.

Her stress leapt several notches higher when she discovered that her birth control had expired before she'd ever arrived on Kay. She discovered it the hard way when Tuttle finally got around to running the routine debarkation check on the crew. It made it worse that she'd had no prior inkling of the difficult situation she was about to find herself in. Though Tuttle's request to speak to her in private after the examination had immediately alerted her to trouble, it had not prepared her for the shock of her life.

"I just wanted to make you aware that your blood pressure is up--too much stress. You're going to have to make an effort to control your stress levels."

Victoria gave her a wry look. "Suggestions?"

Tuttle frowned. "I'd give you something to help, but ... I don't know if it would be safe in your condition. I'm just a medic, not a doctor."

Victoria stared at her blankly. "Tuttle, if there's something I should know, tell me."

"Your birth control implant expired six months ago."

A wave of shock went through Victoria. "Expired? But ... wasn't it checked before we left?"

Tuttle shrugged. "Apparently somebody overlooked it."

Victoria's lips tightened. "Or they discovered it at the last minute and decided it wasn't worth delaying launch. Shit! I don't suppose you were issued any since we weren't supposed to be here more than six months?"

Tuttle looked away. "No. But it wouldn't do you any good anyway."

A flash of heat washed over Victoria, followed almost instantly by a flash of cold that left dizziness in its wake. She swayed, looked for a place to sit down. It was the last thing she remembered. When she woke up, she was lying on the floor. Tuttle's concerned face swam into view. "What happened?"

"You ... uh ... fainted."

Victoria sat up with an effort, holding her head. It felt as if it might explode any moment. "Did you say what I thought you said?"

"You don't have a permit, do you?" Tuttle responded.

Anger surged in her. "Why would I have a damned permit?"

Tuttle sat back on her heels. "This is really bad."

Victoria laughed a little hysterically, but there was no humor in it. "Just let them *try* to penalize me for this, damn them! I'll sue them for incompetence!"

"What are you going to do?"

"Now? Is there anything I can do?"

Tuttle sighed. "Not that I know of. To be honest with you, I've never been around anyone who was ... uh ... gestating. It's completely beyond my training."

Victoria thought about their precarious situation on Kay. "You are not to mention this to anyone. We've got problems enough. I don't want everyone panicking because they don't know if they can rely on me. Do you understand?"

Tuttle nodded, her eyes wide now. "It's that bad?"

Victoria calmed herself with an effort and smiled wryly. "Our situation isn't great. I'll feel better when they get the communications tower up and running."

Tuttle helped her to her feet. "You think Kichen's death was connected to what happened here before?"

Victoria shook her head. "At this point, it doesn't seem likely, but it was a freak accident, there's no getting around that. I imagine everyone's feeling about the same way you are--worried that there might be a connection, anxious about what threats we might be facing. That's why it's important no one have the additional concern about my health."

Tuttle nodded, but she grasped Victoria's arm as she turned to leave. "I wouldn't have told anyone anyway."

Victoria smiled. "Thank you for that."

Victoria strode toward the door, anxious to remove herself from the clinic, uncertain of whether she most needed to put the potentially catastrophic information out of her mind, or if she needed to mull it over and look for a solution to her latest problem.

"Victoria?"

She stopped and turned, trying to keep the impatience from her expression.

"This isn't something you'll be able to keep secret for long."

Victoria smiled with an effort. "No, but hopefully long enough to resolve some of the other problems we're facing."

* * * *

The moment Victoria had been dreading was upon her. She stared down at the water in the access pool, trying to calm her jumping nerves.

"You don't have to come," Raphael said quietly.

Keenly aware of Roach, who was making his first excursion into the sea, as well, Victoria set her jaw and leapt in. "I have to check the situation myself," she said when she'd caught her breath from the abrupt immersion in the chilly water.

Raphael's brows rose, but all he said was, "Ready?"

"As ready as I'll ever be," Victoria responded. Controlling her chattering teeth with an effort, she dragged in a deep breath, ducked beneath the waves and swam in the direction of the lights that indicated the mine area. Instinctively, she held her breath as long as she possibly could. When she began to feel the urge to breathe, she stopped abruptly, panic washing through her. Raphael caught up to her, wrapping his arms around her.

Just breathe.

I can't. I can't do this. I have to go back.

You can. You've done it before.

I'm ... scared.

I know. It'll be all right.

Despite his soothing words, Victoria struggled against his hold, becoming more and more desperate to retreat to the habitat. Finally, when she found she couldn't shake his hold, and she couldn't hold her breath any longer, she breathed. The sensation was indescribable and her panic only escalated for several moments before she finally filtered enough air through her prosthesis that her panic began to subside. She clung to Raphael then, where before she'd fought to free herself from him, finding comfort as she slowly adjusted to the artificial gills.

Finally, she pulled away self-consciously and looked around.

The miners nearest where they were looked away, allowing her the comfort of some doubt as to whether or not they'd witnessed her display of weakness.

Embarrassed as she was, when she looked around and found that two of the miners were holding Roach down while he fought them like a madman, her discomfiture subsided fractionally with the knowledge that she wasn't the only one who'd had difficulty with the transition. Perhaps, she'd handled it a little better as well.

She saw that Raphael was smiling at her. *What?*

For an air breather, you handled it very well. I have to confess we felt more than a little panic when we found ourselves breathing air for the first time.

Victoria smiled back at him but shook her head. *I don't believe you. You're just saying that to make me feel better.*

I said it because it was true. I had to be manful about it because you were watching, otherwise....

Victoria burst out laughing. *Liar! You were so pissed off because Kichens fired on you, you forgot all about the transition.* The thought of Kichens sobered her, and she changed the subject abruptly. *Let's have a look at the mine shaft.*

Roach, she saw, had recovered sufficiently from his distress to assume the cockiness that was his trademark once more. They left him tallying the ore and complaining that there wasn't more of it, and swam toward the opening in the floor of the sea bed.

The mouth of the shaft was huge, perhaps thirty feet by twenty. It began to narrow, however, as they swam deeper, traveling straight down for almost forty feet before branching out in every direction into shafts that ran horizontal to the ocean bed. Long before they reached the branch, Victoria became aware of the fact that she was not equipped to handle the increase in pressure for any length of time. Her chest and head began to feel as if a band cinched them, tightening as she swam deeper.

This is where we found the obstruction.

Victoria treaded water and looked around. *Just above the branch tunnels?*

Yes. It's why I needed you to come out with me, to look at it yourself so you could get a better picture of the situation. And also because I didn't want to discuss this on the habitat where we might be overheard--it doesn't look like a cave in. It looks like they deliberately sealed the shafts.

Victoria glanced at him. *Any guesses as to why?*

He shrugged. *Just a feeling ... up until yesterday. Nothing to substantiate it, which is one reason I didn't mention it before.*

And the other was?

We didn't uncover anything that even looked like evidence until we finished clearing the last shaft late yesterday. Rubble had been piled in all four tunnels. These two, he pointed, *were obviously speculative ... no sign of the ore, and no indication that any had been pulled from either one. Most of the ore came from a vein we located in this shaft. The other, apparently, yielded some, but petered out. The blockages were specific to these shaft openings, however, after we got the main tunnel cleared enough to come in for a look. I thought at the time that it was a peculiar circumstance that all four tunnels managed to catch enough rubble to block them completely. When we found no bodies, I thought it was even more of a coincidence that none of the miners had been trapped--a welcome coincidence, but still odd. When we opened the last shaft, though, we found things in the rubble that shouldn't have been there if it was just a cave in ... refuse from the habitat, even some pieces of equipment. It looked like they'd run out of dirt and scavenged everything disposable off of the habitat.*

They deliberately sealed the shafts? It was a purely rhetorical question, however, as Victoria pursued the implications. *Jesus Christ! Whatever it was that killed them ... they must have uncovered it!*

But they were alive, some of them at least, when they sealed the shafts, Raphael pointed out.

Which means they were too late! Whatever it was ... is, is already free.

Raphael nodded. *We've searched every inch of the shafts. There's no sign of anything in them now.*

You're certain of that?

As certain as I can be considering I have no idea what it might be. You want us to seal the shafts again?

Victoria considered it for several moments and finally shook her head. *If we do, we'll have to explain why and panic is an ugly, dangerous thing. If whatever it was is already free, there wouldn't be any point in it anyway. And then we have to consider the possibility that we could let even more out if we sink another shaft. What we need to find out is what was down here to begin with.*

Raphael nodded. *The problem is, we haven't any marine biologists with us, nobody that would have at least a clue of what to look for.*

Victoria frowned. *I'm no biologist, but it occurs to me that whatever it is couldn't have been completely sealed off even before they sank the shafts. Otherwise, how would it get food? Unless it was in something like a hibernation state and had been trapped after it sought a safe place to hibernate.*

That's a pretty long stretch--underwater hibernators? But if it's a possibility, then we'd certainly not be any safer sealing the shafts-- obviously it didn't work for our predecessors.

Victoria shook her head. *You're thinking in terms of Earth creatures. One thing you can count on when you've been on as many worlds as I have is that there's never any telling what sort of creatures might have evolved. There might be similarities--there often are, but there are always vast, unpredictable differences too. I can't even begin to guess what sort of conditions might result in an underwater creature that would hibernate, but that doesn't mean there might not have been conditions on this planet that would have produced such a thing. Anyway, it's all guesswork. There haven't been enough studies done on Kay to give us even an educated guess.*

What we need to know, fast, is if, whatever it is, is still active? If it is, we've got a real situation on our hands--the weapons the other crew had were inadequate protection against it and we don't have anything different.

Until we figure something out, remind the crew as often as it takes to get their attention that they're to stay alert for trouble at all times. We can't afford to be lulled into a false sense of safety by the fact that it hasn't attacked us yet, Victoria finished, deciding it was time to head back. The place gave her the creeps. It would have if it had been nothing more than a hole. The fact that there was, or had been, some dangerous creature, or creatures, living in the caverns made it that much more creepy.

We also can't afford to assume this is the source of the threat, Raphael said thoughtfully as he followed her back up the mine shaft. *It looks like they thought so, but they might have been dead wrong. The crew was attacked from above, not just from below.*

Victoria paused as they neared the entrance once more. *You think we're looking for two different threats?*

Possibly.

Victoria thought it over. *It does seem like the most likely scenario. To attack from above, it would have to also have the ability to fly, or climb--besides being able to breathe air or water. It seems the possibility would be pretty remote that one creature would be capable of it. This planet is mostly water ... doesn't seem like there'd be a logical reason for it to evolve in such a way. On the other hand, it's also possible that they were attacked by some local wildlife, sent out a distress call and exposed themselves to predators of a different variety,"* she pointed out. *The survivors of the attack by the creature might have been taken by pirates, as we thought before.*

Raphael frowned thoughtfully, but finally shook is head. *I think the threat's here. And whatever it is it's either more tenacious than anything we've ever encountered before, or it's intelligent enough that it figured out a way in.*

Restraining a shiver with an effort, Victoria checked her watch. *See how much ore you can pull today. Tomorrow, before you send them down, put them on moving the ore up for processing. I want to have a closer look at the shaft and see if we can come up with some clue of what we're up against.*

They left the cavern then and headed back toward the habitat. Roach, Victoria saw with a good deal of irritation, was nowhere in sight. She frowned, looking around, more than half expecting to find him sitting somewhere, watching the miners work. She knew they hadn't been down in the mine shaft long enough for him to have finished his tally. He was nowhere in sight, however, and her irritation increased as it occurred to her that he'd obviously thought up an excuse to return to the habitat. If he spent half as much time working as he did thinking up excuses to get out of work, he would've been a senior supervisor by now instead of just a foreman.

Raphael stopped her as she reached the access pool. *Remember to expel the water before you surface.*

She nodded, expelled the fluid and surfaced. The first breath of air she dragged into her lungs burned like fire however, and she still retained enough water to bring on a spasm of coughing. Brown helped her from the pool. "Where's Roach?" she asked when she caught her breath at last.

His brows rose. "I haven't seen him since he went in with you."

Victoria's annoyance vanished abruptly. "You're sure he didn't come back?"

Brown shrugged. "I've been here ever since you left. I guess he might have come back without me noticing," he said doubtfully.

She turned to look at Raphael, who'd emerged directly behind her. "Check with the crew. See if anyone's seen him."

Raphael nodded and dove once more. Victoria stood a little shakily and moved to the inner com unit. "Roach, come back."

She waited several minutes and tried the com unit again. "Roach, if you're in the habitat, come back."

Raphael surfaced. "No sign of him. Taylor said the last he saw of him was when he left the area to relieve himself."

"That moron!" Victoria snapped furiously. "Find him, and when you do I want him in the brig for disobeying a direct order!"

Victoria paced the floor while she waited for word, checking her watch every few minutes. A half hour passed, and then an hour and anger finally gave way to concern. It began to look as if Roach wasn't shirking his duties this time.

Chapter Ten

It didn't take long for word to spread that Roach was missing. It was obviously the topic of conversation in the dining hall for the moment Victoria and Raphael entered, conversation ceased immediately.

"Any sign of Roach?" Brown asked Raphael.

"No," Victoria said, answering before Raphael could. "We'll have a search party out again first thing in the morning."

"Looks to me like the humans here are rapidly becoming extinct," he muttered, returning his attention to his plate.

Victoria didn't have to ask him what he was implying. "Roach, as usual, completely ignored a direct order not to go off alone ... for any reason. He's no rookie. He knows damn well we know next to nothing about Kay and that there could be any number of dangers just waiting for the unwary. Don't make more of this than there is," she said, looking at Brown but speaking loudly enough that everyone nearby could hear her.

"You think he's dead?" Tuttle asked.

Victoria shrugged. "He could be. He might also be injured. Might have fallen into a chasm ... might have run into some of the indigenous life. We won't know until we find him."

"*If* we find him," Brown muttered.

Victoria gave him a look. "If," she said flatly and went to collect a plate.

Brown waited until they sat before pursuing the matter. "I'm thinking it's a little strange, it being Roach."

Victoria eyed him for several moments. "Why?"

"It ain't no secret he was hot for you and the ... underwater foreman didn't like it. Then, he goes down with you and Raphael, and you two come back, but he doesn't."

"Don't beat around the bush, Brown, just spit it out," Victoria said tightly.

"I didn't stutter," Brown snapped. "I'm saying maybe Roach had help disappearing ... like maybe Kichens had a little help over the railing."

Chairs clattered as Quinton leapt to his feet, his face dark red with fury. Brown was on his feet at almost the same instant. Before the two men could come to blows, they were seized by other crew members.

Victoria glared at the two men. "Take both of them to the brig to cool down." When the two men had been escorted out, Victoria turned to face the remaining crew members. "Let's not make this any uglier than it has to be, people. We have two crew members missing. It's a risk every one of us faces every time we take a mission onto an uncharted world. You all know this. We can't afford to degenerate to name calling and in fighting. We've got a job to do here, and we've got enough to contend with without fighting among ourselves, or throwing around unfounded accusations."

She looked at them each in turn, waiting to see if anyone else had comments to make. When they remained silent, she sat down again and made an effort to eat, although her stomach was tied into knots. One by one the crew members finished their meals and left.

"It was bound to happen," Raphael said when they were alone.

"What?" Victoria said irritably. "Being accused of doing away with a fellow crew member?"

Raphael frowned. "We are not the same."

Victoria rolled her eyes. "Not you too."

Smiling faintly, Raphael caught her chin in his hand. "We were bred in tanks," he reminded her. "We can't ... interact with the others in the way they think of as 'normal'. We make them nervous. They distrust us."

Victoria studied him a long moment and finally smiled faintly in return. "I couldn't help but notice that I don't seem to fall into either category."

"You don't."

Victoria shook her head. "I'm like everyone else around here--scared. The only difference, if there is one, is that I've never seen that turning on everyone around me helps in any way." She frowned. "You know, I wouldn't put it past that asshole Roach to have gone off hoping it would cause problems."

"You're going to feel remorseful for that remark if it turns out he really is injured."

"No, I won't. It he's hurt, or dead, it's his own damned fault. He was told. The problem with Roach has always been that he's one of those people who think rules were made for everybody else and don't apply to him."

"What about you?"

"What about me?" Victoria echoed.

"Do you always follow the rules?"

Victoria shrugged. "Not always ... mostly ... but if I choose to disregard them, I prepare myself for the possible consequences. I don't expect exceptions to be made just for me ... hope for them, maybe, like anybody else that gets caught doing something they know they shouldn't have. Roach not only disregards every rule and every order, he is outraged when he's punished.

"I think that's the main thing that pissed me off about Brown's suggestion. He knows Roach, knows how he is and the truth is he detests Roach every bit as much as I do. If we were going just by dislike, practically everybody on the habitat would've had a motive to get rid of him."

Raphael shook his head. "No. The main reason you disliked the accusation was because it was pointed at me."

Victoria glanced at him sharply, then looked away. "That wasn't it."

"As he said, he didn't stutter. He was pretty pointed about accusing the merfolk of trying to do away with the humans. Quinton and Albert pitched Kichens over the side ... not sure what their motive was supposed to be, maybe just because she was an air breather. And I removed my rival."

"That's absurd!" Victoria got up abruptly, cleared her place and strode across the room to drop her dishes in the tub provided for them. Raphael followed suit, but stopped her when she would have brushed past him.

"It's not true, but I'm not sure it'll make a difference now that Brown has stated it so baldly. It's what all of them were thinking already--Tuttle, Brown, the kitchen crew. They're surrounded, and outnumbered, by freaks they fear and distrust ... and it doesn't help that the two that went missing were with my people when it happened."

Victoria punched him in the chest with her finger. "Don't ever say that to me again. I don't believe that. They don't believe that ... not really. Do you think we've never been around genetically manipulated humans before? I've got news for you, if you think you're freaky ... 'your people' as you call them, are beautiful. You should see some of the horrors the company has come up with in their efforts to design 'humans' for every little project. I've seen them with four arms, eight legs--no noses, or ears ... skin like frogs, or alligators--and most of them are doomed to live like that for the rest of their lives.

"I know that none of you really had any life experience, but maybe you should consider yourself lucky, after all. This is what we are--distrustful, unforgiving of anyone who's different. If you'd grown up like we did, you would've already had the luxury of fending off bullies and clawing your way up from lowest man on the totem pole to a position where only the biggest fish in the pond get a shot at you.

"I've worked with most of these people before. As people go, they're good people. When they're scared, they get mean and nasty. If it wasn't you and your crew, it would be somebody else, because they're always going to find somebody to take out their fear and frustrations on."

She pushed past him then, strode from the dining hall, through the rec room and into her living quarters, slamming the door behind her. Raphael followed at a more leisurely pace, bolting the door behind him.

Victoria turned to glare at him. "I've got work to do," she said stiffly, moving toward her desk. He intercepted her, forestalling her intention.

"Not tonight."

Some of the fight went out of her. "If I don't do it tonight, there'll only be more tomorrow."

He gave her a look and a reluctant smile tugged at her lips. "I know what you have in mind, but I'm too tense to have any interest in sex right now."

"I hadn't thought of it, but now that you mention it...."

"Right."

He cocked his head. "If it would help you to relax, I'd be glad to accommodate you."

Victoria laughed. Giving up the fight, she lifted her arms and draped them around his neck. "You are a selfless man."

His lips twitched. "I am," he murmured just before he kissed her. Victoria melted against him, feeling tingles all the way to her toes as he filled her senses with his essence; the lazy caress of his tongue; the silkiness of his hair beneath her fingers; his scent; his taste; his warmth; and the power in the muscles holding her, pressed so tightly against her length she could feel every ripple, could feel the nudge of his erection at the apex of her thighs. Reaching down, she stroked the length of his cock through his breeches.

When he broke the kiss at last, they undressed each other, caressing every inch of flesh they unveiled in the process with their hands, their mouths and tongues. Raphael lifted her up when they were both naked, guiding her legs around his waist and capturing the peak of one breast in his mouth. Victoria locked her ankles around him, moaning at the wonderful sensations that emanated from the suction of his mouth through her breast and down into her belly, making her sex pool with the moisture of anticipation. Tightening her arms around him, she moved restlessly against him as he fondled first one breast and then the other, the rough texture of his lower body sending sharp needles of pleasure through the damp petals of her sex as she undulated against him.

She became restless to feel him inside of her, to feel the slow glide of his hardened flesh against the quaking walls of her sex. Anticipation burgeoned inside of her as he moved to the bed at last, but, to her surprise, he settled her on the edge of the bed. When he knelt between her parted thighs, a rush of heat went through her. He spread her thighs wide, moved closer and pulled her to him for a deep kiss that left her weak and breathless before he moved down, suckling each tightened peak of her breast hard. Her heart accelerated as waves of pleasure washed through her, her breath catching in her chest until her lungs labored and her head spun.

She leaned back, propping on her arms as he moved lower, his lips and tongue producing pleasurable quakes inside of her as he made his way down her stomach to her belly, sending flurries of goose bumps racing across her flesh. When he reached her sex at last, he paused, scooped an arm beneath each knee, lifting her thighs, spreading them wider still, studying her, his eyes darkening with desire. He lifted his gaze to hers, lowered his head slowly and ran his tongue along her heated sex.

Victoria shuddered, her eyes sliding half closed as pleasure washed through her. She bit her lip to stifle a moan as his mouth opened over her heated flesh, but she couldn't contain it as he lathed her with his tongue, nudging the center of her pleasure in a way that had her gasping for breath, moaning as the pleasure built to exquisite torture. The muscles inside of her palpitated as the pleasure built to a crescendo, exploded into a flood of fire.

The strength went out of her arms as her climax hit her and she collapsed back against the bed, uttering sharp gasps that bordered on screams as he continued to lick and suckle, pushing her climax to the limits.

She was barely conscious as he moved up and over her, pulled her tightly against him and kissed her. She kissed him back, tasting herself on his lips. It sent a heady rush through her, sent throbbing echoes of remembered passion through her belly, reminding her that she had received but had not given.

She rolled on top of him. Breaking the kiss, she moved down over him in worshipful fashion, caressing his chest with her hands and her lips, tasting him with her tongue, nipping him playfully with her teeth as she worked her way over his body until she reached her goal. Taking his cock in her hand, she looked up at him as she ran her tongue up his cock from the root to the rounded head. He shuddered, gasped hoarsely with pleasure as she teased the ultra sensitive ridge around the head of his cock with her tongue and finally covered the head of his cock with her mouth, sucking.

He clutched her hair, his fingers tightening reflexively as she slowly covered his erection, taking him as deeply into her mouth as she could, then slowly lifted her head once more, allowing him to slip almost free, until only the head remained in her mouth. She suckled him again, feeling her belly clench with pleasure as he groaned under her caress, moving restlessly, clutching at the sheets.

When she had teased him until she felt he was hovering on the verge of coming, she began to stroke him harder and faster with her mouth, pushing him toward climax. Finally, with a hoarse cry, he caught her, flipped her onto her back and moved over her, sinking his cock to the hilt in her flesh. Holding himself off of her with one arm, he slipped the other beneath her hips, pounding into her again and again. Victoria lifted her legs and wrapped them around him as she felt her own pleasure building again with each stroke of his flesh against the quaking walls of her sex.

Gasping, she met each thrust with one of her own as her passion rose higher and higher, until she was hovering on the edge of fulfillment. When he cried out hoarsely as his climax took him over the edge, his cock jerking inside of her with his release, she fell over the edge herself, clinging to him as wave upon wave of pleasure rocked her to her core.

They collapsed in a tangle of arms and legs, weak in the aftermath, shaking, struggling for breath. Finally, Raphael rolled off of her, gathering her close. Victoria snuggled sleepily against him, drifting, wondering if she could find the energy to leave the bed and tackle the paperwork she'd neglected.

Raphael sighed, stroking her. "The only time I have your full attention is when I'm making you moan with pleasure.".

Victoria sent him a startled glance and then chuckled. "Serves you right. I told you to stay out of my head."

He stroked her cheek. "I'd rather have a morsel of your time than the undivided attention of a dozen others."

Intrigued, Victoria pushed herself up so that she could look down at him. "Really? Most men would far prefer the harem. Not that that archaic concept is allowed anywhere in the known universe."

Raphael grinned. "You are a harem all to yourself, shy one moment, aggressive the next. I never know which woman I'll find in my bed."

"My bed," Victoria corrected.

"My arms?" he amended meekly.

Victoria tweaked his nipple. She might have tugged a hair, except that his body was smooth and hairless, making it impossible. She skated a hand over his chest, enjoying the sleek feel of his flesh. "I hope you're not suggesting I have schizophrenic tendencies."

He chuckled. "No. Only that you are always a ... delightful surprise." His amusement vanished, and he studied her seriously. "Stay with me, Victoria."

Victoria found she couldn't hold his gaze. She looked away, shrugged. "It's not my choice. You know that."

He caught her cheek with his palm, made her look at him. "I want to know what you want."

She sighed. The problem was, she didn't really know what she wanted. At the moment, she couldn't think of anything she wanted more than to wrap herself up in Raphael and ignore the troubles of the world she found herself in, but she cared too much for him to toy with his emotions. He'd said he loved her. Perhaps he did, or maybe he didn't know any more than she did, but she couldn't bring herself to risk wounding him deeply.

He smiled faintly. "I'll accept that ... for now."

Victoria shook her head, but found she didn't give a damn about that particular rule. Raphael was the only one that offered her comfort and relief. She needed that if she was to have any chance of getting any of them through this alive. She'd deal with the consequences later. Leaning up, she kissed him briefly. "Sleep. God only knows what we'll find tomorrow."

When tomorrow came, they discovered something no one had noticed during the turmoil Brown and Quinton's near confrontation had caused. One of the searchers hadn't returned.

* * * *

Slowly, he became aware of his surroundings.
It was dark, but he knew he wasn't in his quarters.
He felt strangely detached, but he knew he wasn't sleeping.

As he pondered the curious circumstances, the waters lightened around him, showing him that he was in the sea ... drifting. He frowned, realizing that something wasn't quite as it should have been. He could see movement, but he couldn't feel it.

He realized then that he could feel nothing at all and fear surged through him. Why could he feel nothing? Why could he not lift his hand, his arms, his legs? He struggled for a while, willing his body to respond to his mind, trying to sit upright.

Slowly, inexorably, pain began to spread through him. At first, he was almost relieved. He thought it meant that the strange paralysis was wearing off, but he found he still couldn't move any part of his body. He couldn't move away from the pain that became steadily worse until he felt as if he was on fire with it.

When he felt that he couldn't bear it any longer and live, the pain ceased almost as abruptly as it had begun. A sense of peace flowed through him, and relief.

But darkness flowed in the wake of it and he found he was afraid of the dark. He struggled against it.

Abruptly, he felt his head lift up. He opened his eyes, tried to focus. Slowly, his sight cleared.

And then he screamed and kept on screaming, because he could see where his body should be, but it wasn't there.

Raphael cried out, coming awake with a jerk. His heart felt as if it was beating a hundred miles an hour and he clutched his chest, massaging it.

Victoria complained sleepily, but roused enough to notice that Raphael was sitting up in bed. "What is it?"

Raphael turned to look at her, but already the images were fading from his mind. "I dreamed I was someone else," he said slowly. "I was there, I could see, but it was as if I was looking through someone else's eyes."

Victoria sat up, looking at him in concern. "What did you see?"

Raphael shook his head, trying to remember. "I can't remember. Only that it was horrible."

Victoria lay down, pulling him with her and snuggling against him. "It was just a nightmare," she murmured, rubbing his chest.

"A nightmare?"

"Bad dream. They always seem scary at the time, but when you wake up you either can't remember what you dreamed, or it seems ridiculous that it scared you to start with."

Raphael shuddered. "I don't think it was a dream."

* * * *

The transition from air breathing to gills was a little easier to bear when Victoria joined Raphael the following morning, not much, but somewhat. They divided the miners into two groups, one to handle moving the ore, the rest they broke into three smaller groups and sent out to search for Roach.

Victoria stood at the opening to the mine shaft for several moments, looking down and finally glanced at Raphael. *Ready?*

He nodded, his expression grim. *If we run into trouble....*

Victoria shook her head, knowing what he'd been about to suggest. She held her weapon up. *We go in together. We come out together. No heroics.*

Raphael lifted his brows but neither agreed nor disagreed, merely stepping off the rim of the opening and allowing himself to drift downwards. Victoria dived head first, clutching her laser rifle at the ready and using only her feet to propel her forward. As she passed Raphael, he bent double, twisted and, with a flick of his tail fin, shot past her, leading the way. He settled on the lip of the tunnel, waiting until she caught up with him before he moved inside.

Lights had been secured into the ceiling of the shaft every ten feet or so. They bathed the walls with a dull yellow glow, chasing most of the shadows away. Victoria examined the walls in a cursory fashion as they made their way deeper into the tunnel, but could see nothing that seemed even a little irregular or out of place. They'd been traveling down the tunnel for nearly twenty minutes when Raphael stopped, looking around.

This is where they stopped excavating.

Victoria stopped, as well, glancing around at the ceiling, the walls, the floor of the man made cavern. *It just stopped abruptly here? Who was in here first?*

Me.

You didn't see any sign that they might have dug something other than ore from the walls?

He shook his head. *It looks like the same tools were used to excavate this part as the rest. I suppose they might have run the tunnel into an existing cavern, but if they did I don't see any sign of it. You didn't notice any mention of anything like that in the reports?*

Victoria flushed uncomfortably. *I haven't had the time to go through all of the reports. I decided to start with the last and work backwards, but I haven't gotten very far.*

Raphael nodded without comment *It doesn't look like we'll find anything here.*

Victoria looked around the cavern again and finally moved closer to one wall, reaching out to touch the surface. The pressure field that supported the tunnel against collapse yielded as she pushed against it until her hand was resting on the rock surface. She found a small, round hole about two inches in diameter. *What's this?*

Raphael moved closer, looked at the almost perfectly round hole with a frown. *I don't know. I hadn't noticed it before.*

None of the equipment would have made anything like this?

He shook his head. *Nothing we have. Nothing I've seen that the crew before us might have been using. Maybe they set up some kind of pole system to support the tunnel until they had the pressure system up and running?*

Victoria looked around and finally shook her head. *There'd be a fairly regular pattern if they'd done anything like that. I don't see any other holes like that around here.* Turning back in the direction from which they'd come, she scanned the tunnel as she moved through it slowly. *I counted almost a dozen,* she said as she reached the mouth of the tunnel once more.

You think it's significant?

Victoria shrugged. *I don't know. I didn't see anything else.*

Raphael frowned. *I can't imagine that anything small enough to fit through one of those holes would be much of a threat.*

Victoria glanced at him. *A fairly large sea snake? Something like an eel? Piranhas aren't large fish, but they can eat the flesh from a large man in minutes. Or, it might be nothing more than air holes for something much larger that burrows into the sea bed.*

This deep?

Unfortunately, we can't limit our thinking to what something on Earth might do.

As they stood considering the possibilities, the ground beneath their feet began to shake slightly. Victoria glanced back over her shoulder, noticing with more than a little alarm that the lights in the tunnel were flickering. *Quake!*

Launching herself from the tunnel, she swam for the mouth of the main shaft as fast as she could, fearing the quake would knock the power out. Without the pressure unit, the walls of the shaft might well collapse upon them.

Raphael caught her around the waist and shot through the tunnel at blurring speed. Behind them, Victoria could see the lights winking out, one by one. She blacked out as they shot out of the mine shaft.

Chapter Eleven

The next moment that Victoria was aware of, she was heaving water from her lungs, choking. When the spasms finally passed, she felt the warmth of Raphael's body as he pulled her tightly against him. He was trembling, as if he was freezing. Or maybe it was her? It filtered through her mind, finally, that they were on the floor of the lower level of the habitat beside the access pool. "What happened?"

"I pulled you out too quickly," Raphael said apologetically. "The pressure...."

Victoria nodded. Her head still felt as if it might explode. She discovered, to her embarrassment, that her nose was bleeding and pulled away from him. Leaning over the access pool, she bathed her face until the bleeding stopped. "Thanks," she finally said shakily.

"For almost killing you?" Raphael asked tightly.

She glanced at him. "For saving my life. Did the shaft collapse?"

Raphael shook his head. "I didn't take the time to assess the damage. A shock wave hit me as we came out of the shaft, though, so my guess is, yes."

"Guess that's what happened before, huh?" Brown asked.

Victoria glanced at him. She hadn't realized until he spoke that they had an audience. She looked away. "Maybe."

"I sent for Tuttle. She's coming down to have a look at you now," Brown said.

Victoria shook her head. "I'm all right."

"You'll let her examine you," Raphael said coolly.

Victoria looked at him in surprise. Before she could inform him that she didn't take orders from him, however, Brown spoke again.

"It's procedure."

"Fine!" she snapped irritably and lay down once more, massaging her pounding head.

When Tuttle arrived, she checked Victoria's vitals. "I need to get her up to sick bay to give her a thorough examination," she said, glancing from Brown to Raphael.

"I'll carry her," Raphael said.

Victoria looked at him as if he'd lost his mind. "Up four levels? I'll travel under my own steam, thank you. You need to go check the progress of the searchers and assess the damage to the mine."

He scooped her up. "As soon as I deliver you to sickbay."

Brown trailed after them. "I can help."

Raphael paused, studied him a long moment and finally nodded.

Fighting the darkness that threatened to descend once more, Victoria held her head up with an effort. "You're both crazy. You'll both end up in sickbay if you try to carry me all the way up!"

Brown and Raphael exchanged a grin and ignored her protest. Locking their arms beneath her, they formed a 'chair' between them. Each time they reached another level, Victoria informed them that she was better and thought she could walk the rest of the way. Brown was breathing noticeably heavier and sweating by the time they reached the fourth level, which contained the crew quarters and the sickbay. Dismissing him, Raphael took her the remainder of the way, shouldering his way into the room and settling her on a gurney.

"I am better," Victoria said, somewhat petulantly. "Thank you," she added stiffly.

"There's a difference between being strong and just plain bull headed," Raphael said coolly when she dismissed him again.

Victoria opened her mouth to give him a blast of temper, but Tuttle grabbed Raphael and pushed him toward the door, closing it behind them. "Wait here. I'll let you know how she is once I've run some tests."

Raphael nodded and Tuttle left him pacing the hall and went in again.

Pushing the gurney over to the examination chamber, she helped Victoria shift onto the padded table within, closed the clear panel, and punched the code for a thorough examination on the buttons on the antiquated piece of equipment. She frowned as the data began to spill across the screen, comparing the data to Victoria's healthy norm and finally concluded that Victoria was more shaken than anything else. She didn't appear to have any serious damage from the abrupt change in pressure.

When the computer concluded it's assessment, she helped Victoria from the chamber onto the gurney once more.

"Well?" Victoria asked as Tuttle moved to the supply cabinet and took a syringe from it.

Without a word, Tuttle moved back to her, jabbed the syringe into her upper arm and depressed the plunger. "You'll be fine. You just need a little rest."

"What'd you give me?" Victoria asked, feeling a strange lethargy creeping over her.

"Something to *make* you rest."

"Damn it, Tuttle! I don't have time for this!"

Tuttle smiled faintly. "Somehow I knew you'd say that. That's why I didn't ask."

As she started to move away, Victoria grabbed her wrist. Tuttle paused and glanced at her questioningly. Victoria bit her lip. "Am I ... did I ... abort?"

Tuttle gave her a reassuring squeeze. "I think it weathered the shock better than you did. It seems to have dug in with real determination."

Victoria smiled faintly at the comment, trying to decide whether or not she was relieved. She found, however, that she was far too tired to consider it at the moment.

Having reassured Victoria, Tuttle moved to the door, opened it, and ushered Raphael in. "She's fine. A little off the norm, but not dangerously so."

Raphael glanced at Victoria and then at Tuttle. "She's unconscious."

Tuttle smiled faintly. "Not yet, but she will be ... for several hours. I gave her something to make her rest."

A look of alarm crossed his features. Tuttle studied him a moment before realization dawned . "She told you?"

He shook his head, studying Victoria. "I knew."

"I keep forgetting you're telepathic." She smiled faintly. "It won't hurt her or the baby. I'm no doctor, and I know my limitations, especially since I'm completely unfamiliar with this particular situation, so I checked the medic files so I'd know what I could give her and what I couldn't."

Raphael nodded and moved to stand beside the gurney, caressing Victoria's cheek.

"Insubordination," Victoria muttered, her speech slurred by sleep. "Throw you all in the brig."

Grinning, Raphael glanced at Tuttle. "She's all right," they said in unison.

* * * *

Victoria woke sometime later to the clank of metal on metal. Opening her eyes with an effort, she saw that Raphael had set a tray of food on the metal cabinet next to the bed. She stared at it blankly for several moments and finally sat up. "What's this?"

"Dinner. You missed lunch."

Victoria stared at him, torn between irritation, amusement, and an odd sort of warmth at his thoughtfulness. "I'm not an invalid."

His smile was a little crooked. "No, but you had me worried for a little while."

"I did?" Victoria asked, warmed inexplicably by the admission.

He nodded and sat on the edge of the bed, taking her hand. "You're such a strong person, it hadn't occurred to me before that you were strong in spirit ... not necessarily physically."

Blood rushed into her cheeks. She made a rude noise. "I'm hardly delicate!"

Raphael smiled faintly. "You are exactly that. No one's ever noticed, though, have they?"

Victoria glanced away uncomfortably. "I'm starved. Have you eaten?"

"I thought I'd wait for you."

"Let's go into the dining hall, then."

"You're sure you don't want me to coddle you?" he asked pensively.

Victoria laughed. "I'm afraid I might get attached to it ... which would be a bad thing since you'd get tired of it in a hurry."

He rose, helping her from the bed. "You don't know me nearly as well as you think if you believe that. I have infinite patience."

"Do you?"

He nodded. "It comes from being part fish."

Victoria glanced at him sharply, but saw that he was teasing. "And fish are patient?"

"They have to be. They're on the hunt constantly for food."

"Single minded," Victoria said succinctly, picking up the tray he'd just deposited.

He took it from her. "That too."

She was taken aback when she reached the dining hall. All conversation ceased abruptly as everyone turned to look at her, but not nearly as disconcerted as when a cheer went up. Blushing profusely, she struggled against a strong urge to retreat to her room once more. Mastering it, she bowed to the assembly and thanked them before taking her seat.

To her relief, everyone returned their attention to their food.

What was that about?

Raphael glanced at her in surprise, but in a moment a look of pleasure crossed his features. *They're glad you're all right. They were worried, too.*

That pleases you? she asked him curiously.

Yes. But it pleases me more that you addressed me telepathically. Except for when we're in the sea, you hadn't done that since....

Since?

Since we became lovers.

She glanced at him, studied him for a long moment. *I can't help it. I need to keep at least a part of myself for me.*

I know.

Victoria studied the food on her plate for several moments and finally began to eat. "What happened while I was out of it?"

"I'll give you a full report as soon as we've eaten."

Victoria gave him an indignant look.

He shook his head slightly. *It'll be best if we're alone.*

The comment made her uneasy, but she could see his point. Everyone seemed far more relaxed than they had in a while. It didn't seem right to risk taking that away from them by discussing bad news where they might hear.

Mentally shrugging it off, she focused her attention on her food. When she'd finished, she cleared her place and headed for the room. Raphael followed her, closing the door firmly behind him.

"Now. Tell me what happened," Victoria said, facing him.

Raphael frowned. "I'm not sure that what we felt was a quake. Something showed up on the readings, but it didn't read like a quake."

"What then?"

"I wish I knew. We had a power spike, which shut the system down just long enough that we had several collapses along the shaft ... not as much damage as one would expect, but it'll set us back at least a day in the clean up."

"All right. What do you *think* it was?"

"I haven't got a damned clue. But I will tell you one thing, if that wasn't a quake, then that wasn't a shock wave that hit us as we emerged from the shaft. It was some*thing*."

"What did you see?"

"Nothing ... just like we've seen since we've been here. Not a thing!"

Victoria frowned. "A belch of gases, maybe? Some sort of sonic wave?"

Raphael began pacing. "It could have been anything, I suppose. I felt it, I know that. We both did. Did you see anything? Feel anything at all?"

Victoria thought back to her last moments of consciousness. "Heat. Or warmth anyway. I thought it was just the blood pressure surge, though. It might have been, for that matter. Internal, not external."

Dismissing it, she asked about the search for Roach.

Raphael shook his head. "Still no sign of him. We found his tablet, though."

"You think he could still be alive?"

"Your guess is as good as mine. I've no idea of what the limitations might be on the artificial gill."

Victoria frowned. "I should know, but I can't remember. It was only intended for limited use, assuming we would have to be in the water a few hours occasionally. Our skin's not like yours. Even with the wet suit, prolonged exposure of the unprotected skin areas would cause problems. Then, too, there's the pressure to consider, lack of food and water, exposure to temperatures below our norm.

"I'd have a better idea of his chances if I could get into the computer system. I think it's time I took you up on your offer to hack in."

* * * *

After several hours of trying to hack in, Victoria began to lose hope that he would actually accomplish it. She glanced at her watch. "I should get back down and take care of my paperwork. I'm a day behind already."

Raphael nodded. "I'll stay with this a while longer. If I can get in, I'll patch it through to the computer in your quarters."

Victoria shook her head. "The rule stands. No one goes off alone."

"I'll escort you down then."

She gave him a look. "That applies to you, too."

He studied her a long moment and finally shrugged. "In the morning, then."

Victoria supposed she should have been suspicious at how easily he gave in. Raphael was patient, and even tempered, but he was also stubborn.

He sprawled on the bed as she settled at her desk to work and appeared to be sound asleep when she finally joined him several hours later. He was gone when she awoke the following morning, but she thought little of it. He often rose before her in the morning.

Climbing from the bed, she showered, dressed and went down to the dining hall to grab a cup of coffee. It wasn't until she returned to her desk to finish up the work she'd left the previous night that she discovered the note he'd left her.

He'd hacked in.

Victoria stared at the note blankly, but even as groggy as she was the implications were clear--contrary to her specific orders, and despite the risk ignoring that particular order carried with it, Raphael had only waited until she'd gone to sleep and had gone back.

Anger surged through her. She should have known this would happen. The last time she'd been fool enough to allow a man prolonged intimacy he, too, had considered that gave him the right to ignore her commands. It was the main reason she had avoided it ever since, the main reason she'd been determined not to allow Roach to bunk with her, because she'd seen he would become a discipline problem if she allowed it. She would never have thought that Raphael would.

After a moment, she sat down at her desk, deciding she needed to drink her coffee and wait until she was more fully alert to decide how to handle the problem.

It couldn't be ignored. It was absolutely essential that she retain command at all times. If she allowed anyone to disregard her orders, they would all begin to question them, which could put everyone in danger as well as the project itself.

By the time she'd finished her paperwork and her coffee, it occurred to her that Raphael had at least been discreet. He'd gone up while she was sleeping. No one but the two of them could possibly know. It made her feel a little better.

It also occurred to her that she could pretend she had no idea he'd acted against her orders. If she didn't ask him, she wouldn't have to do anything about it, because it also occurred to her that there was only one thing, really, that she could do, and that was to ask him to remove himself to other quarters.

She found that she was very reluctant to do that. She was disturbed by how deeply reluctant she was.

Finally, she decided to dismiss it for the moment and concentrate on the work at hand. She needed to look at the files. She also needed to go over the physical files she'd collected from the security office. She'd spent hours doing paperwork the night before, however, and two additional hours since she'd gotten up. She decided to check on the projects in progress before tackling more paperwork.

When she arrived at the flight deck, she saw that Quinton and Albert had almost completed the erection of the new communications tower. "How long before it'll be operational?" she asked them as she reached them.

"We'll have the tower done by tomorrow at the latest," Albert responded, "but you'll need to ask Caroline about the transmitter."

She located Caroline and Barbara on the main operations level. They were still trying to scavenge some of the parts they needed, but expected to have the transmitter ready, if the parts could be located, by the time the tower was finished.

For the first time since they'd been stranded on Kay, Victoria felt a surge of hope for their chances of survival. She knew very well that the odds were against them being able to make contact with anyone, even if they succeeded in getting the transmitter operational, but a ray of hope was better than what they'd had before--none.

"Good," she said. "When you get it on-line I want you to begin transmitting a distress call, immediately. If you manage to get anyone, explain the situation we found on arrival and tell them we need immediate evacuation. If you can't pick anyone up, try alternating with SOS."

Caroline and Barbara exchanged a look.

"Are we in immediate danger?" Caroline asked.

Victoria studied her a moment. "I think the longer we're here the greater risk, and the less likely any of us are to leave. Stay with it."

She paused when she reached her level once more, feeling an unaccustomed indecisiveness. She'd left her quarters with the intention of checking all of the projects in progress. She wasn't particularly anxious to tackle more paperwork, but found she was also reluctant to check out the mines.

It occurred to her finally that her indecision arose from a reluctance to allow anything to dim the hope the news from the communications crew had given her.

Shaking it off, she made her way down to the access level, stopping in the locker room to don her wet suit. They were bringing up a load of ore as she arrived at the access pool. "Where do we stand, here, Brown?" she yelled above the noise of the machinery they were using to haul the baskets up through a pulley system to the warehousing levels above them for processing.

"We processed the last of the ore the previous crew pulled yesterday. This is the first load our crew's pulled. Sylvia said they were up to quota yesterday before the cave in. I don't know if they've pulled any today or not."

Victoria nodded, waited until the basket had cleared the pool and leapt in. It was a little easier adjusting than either previous attempt. It was not something Victoria foresaw as ever being easy, or natural seeming, but it gave her hope that she would learn to endure better as time went on.

If they remained on Kay for the duration.

She very much hoped they wouldn't. It was one thing to take a high risk, high yield job. It was another matter entirely to take on a job that had wiped out everyone who'd tried before. That wasn't risk. That was suicide.

She hoped the crew's projections were right and the communications tower was up and operational soon. She meant to have someone on the transmitter day and night sending out a distress call. No way was she staying on this rock any longer than it took to be picked up.

No one was in the operations shack when she arrived. Frowning, Victoria debated briefly and finally decided to go down for a look herself. When she reached the main shaft, she could see the miners below her, steadying a load of rubble. Stepping back from the opening, she waited until they'd reached the top.

Sylvia was among them.

Victoria swam to her. *Where's Raphael?*

Sylvia nodded toward the main shaft. *Overseeing the clean up in the tunnel. I could tell him you need to speak to him when I get back down.*

Victoria shook her head. *I'il go down.*

Sylvia stopped her. *Are you sure you should? So soon after the accident?*

The truth was, Victoria would have just as soon not gone down into the mines, ever, again whether it was a particular health risk for her or not, but she'd made it a policy never to ask anyone to do anything she wasn't willing to do herself. She smiled. *Tuttle would have told me if she'd thought there would be a problem.*

Sylvia shrugged and returned her attention to helping the others maneuver the cart to the area they were using to dump the rubble. After watching them for several moments, Victoria shook reluctance and dove into the tunnel. Raphael looked up as she made her way to the end of the tunnel. He frowned, but then looked away, concentrating on his task.

Victoria waited until the crew had finished up and started out of the tunnel. *You made quick work of the clean up. It must not have been too bad.*

Raphael shrugged. *Bad enough we've lost half a day's work. We should go up. They need to get the equipment in here and get started.*

Victoria frowned, grabbing his arm as he moved to pass her. *Is something wrong?*

He stopped, studying her a long moment, but finally shook his head. *Not that I know of.*

You seem ... distracted. He seemed remote, but she couldn't decide why she felt that way.

We're running way behind schedule, he said and turned away again.

After a moment, Victoria followed him out. She saw the miners were waiting just outside the tunnel opening with the equipment and hurried to catch up to Raphael and get out of their way.

I need to pull the rest of my crew off of search detail. We're not going to make quota this week if I don't, he said as they reached the main entrance once more.

Victoria studied him, but somehow she doubted that was why he was behaving so coolly. It was possible, but she didn't buy it. Before she could probe further, however, a telepathic shout interrupted them.

We found him! We found Roach.

On the heels of that telepathic call came a sound that Victoria felt certain she would never forget, the rumbling growl of the mine as the shaft collapsed.

Chapter Twelve

Cave in!

Victoria whirled, too stunned for several moments to do more than gape at the belch of silt that rose from the mouth of the mine shaft like smoke from a dragon's throat. Around her, miners raced toward the shaft and dove in. She followed them, appalled at the amount of rubble that blocked the entrance to the tunnel they'd so lately occupied.

Who was in there? She asked as she fell in beside them and began digging rocks from the rubble and piling them into a bucket someone had lowered.

Richard and Linda, someone said. *Samuel, Kevin and Melinda,* someone else supplied.

Shouldn't we get some heavy equipment in here to move this faster?

They might be under the rubble.

Victoria nodded and kept digging. It took them an hour to clear an area large enough for someone to squeeze through, if they were small. *I'm going in.*

Raphael grabbed her, dragging her back. *Wait until we clear it.*

They might not be able to wait that long, Victoria pointed out.

They wouldn't have breathed up the oxygen in the water this quickly.

Victoria glared at him, but quickly realized that they did not have time to argue the matter and returned to helping with the digging.

A few minutes later the first of the victims trapped behind the wall of debris, alive and relatively unscathed, climbed through and Victoria relaxed as the others followed behind him. *Is this everyone?* She asked Samuel, who was the last to climb through.

Samuel nodded. *There were only the five of us.*

You're certain of that?

He looked a little hesitant. *I think so ... unless someone was behind us. The five of us all went in together.*

Everybody outside for a quick head count.

Raphael counted them twice and finally frowned. *Liam's missing.*

Oh God! Victoria thought. *Has anyone seen Liam?*

He was with us when we went out to search for Roach, one of the searchers said.

Did he come back with anyone?

The searchers all looked at each other but none of them said anything.

When was the last time anyone saw him?

After some discussion, they arrived at the conclusion that Liam had not been seen since they'd gone to search for Roach the day before. Victoria didn't know whether to be relieved to discover that Liam couldn't possibly have been trapped beneath the rubble, or unnerved about the fact that the search party had recovered one man only to lose another.

She sent them out again to look for Liam.

* * * *

They had to fashion a makeshift gurney to carry Roach up to medical. He was muttering incoherently, as if he was delirious. Victoria waited until the computer had scanned him and Tuttle had analyzed the data it collected.

"What are his chances?"

"He seems to be stable, for the moment, at least. He broke his ankle when he fell into the ravine. He's dehydrated. I'll need to keep a close eye on him for at least twenty four hours, but I think he's going to recover."

Victoria nodded, her lips taut with anger. "When he's well enough to move him, put his ass in the brig."

Tuttle blinked at her in surprise. "I said he'd be out of danger. It's going to take him a while to recover."

"He can recover in lock up. He ignored a direct order. No one is to go off alone, ever, for any reason whatsoever. We've lost another man searching for his sorry ass. As soon as he's out of danger, lock him up."

Returning to her quarters, Victoria showered, changed and settled down to study the files. Since Roach had been found, it didn't seem imperative to look into the computer files at once, so she concentrated on the files she'd retrieved from security.

From what she could tell, there'd been no real problems until the arrival of the mining crew. The construction crew chief had reported several accidents, but only one fatality during their stint before the arrival of the miners.

There was nothing particularly unusual in the fact that an accident had claimed the life of one of the construction crew members, particularly on a project this size. Despite every effort to provide safety, statistically speaking, the company expected 1.5 deaths per three construction projects. Construction was dangerous work. Construction on an uncharted planet was hazardous beyond that because of the uncertainty of conditions. Nor could she tell from the report that the accident might have been other than an accident.

It had taken almost a month for the newly arrived crew to get all of the equipment set up and operational. The first crew member disappeared within two weeks after excavation began.

The security chief had suspected foul play. There'd been an 'incident' between the missing man and one of the other crew members shortly before the disappearance. The security chief hadn't been able to come up with anything more than a hunch, however, and had finally released the suspect.

There were four more disappearances over a two week period. Three crew members had decided to go off to do a little exploring on their day off and had not returned. A three day search had turned up nothing and they had finally been reported as missing, presumed dead. The fifth crew member to disappear was one of the searchers who'd failed to return.

Three months into the mission, the power failed and the main shaft collapsed, trapping the majority of the miners fifty feet below the surface. The construction crew had gone in to rescue them, but they were unfamiliar with the equipment. By the time they managed to dig the rubble out the miners had run out of air.

Victoria felt as if someone had punched her in the stomach. She set the report down, fighting a wave of nausea.

It explained why the company had launched into such a drastic genetic program, developing Raphael and his crew en-route to the project. It also made it clear that the company had known about the incident, even though it hadn't shown up on any of the reports.

There'd been no mention of any other problems, so she assumed the communications tower had been intact at that point and if it had been, then the accident would certainly have been reported.

The company had been well aware that she and her crew were flying into a disaster area. They might not have been aware of the full extent of it, but they'd certainly known her crew wasn't prepared for what they would be expected to handle.

She'd been with the company for nearly ten years. Nothing they did, or failed to do, surprised her any more, but it still pissed her off.

Dismissing the fruitless anger, she thought back over what the report had said about the power outage being responsible for the collapse. The power had failed when she and Raphael had been down in the mines. Was there a connection to what had ultimately happened to the crew on Kay? Or could it be nothing more than faulty equipment?

She made a mental note to tell Raphael to put together a power backup unit and to have someone monitoring both the main power and the backup at all times in case it wasn't the equipment at all, but some sort of electrical interference. She'd have felt better if they'd had some good, old fashioned bracing to put in the mines so that they weren't dependent entirely upon the electronic pressure system, but she doubted they had the materials to manage it even if they scavenged parts from the habitat.

That being the case, she thought it might be a good idea to rotate the workers so that the bare minimum were exposed at any one time. Raphael's crew was not in danger of running out of air as the previous crew had, but they could certainly be crushed to death if they had a major collapse.

Victoria realized quite suddenly that her head was pounding. She checked her watch and was surprised to discover it was mid-afternoon. She'd missed lunch. Rising, she stretched the kinks from her back and went in search of something to hold her until dinner. Grabbing a can of fruit and a bottle of water, she headed back to her quarters.

She stopped dead still on the threshold. Raphael had turned at the sound of her approach, his arms laden with his belongings. She stared at him without comprehension. "What are you doing?"

He focused his attention on what he'd been doing. "It's two weeks. I thought I'd move my belongings to my quarters."

Victoria was so stunned she couldn't even think. "Two weeks?" she repeated blankly.

He nodded without looking at her. "Company rules."

Moments passed before Victoria realized she was gaping at him like the village idiot. With an effort, she collected herself and moved back to her desk, doing her best to ignore the activity behind her. Thankfully, he did not linger long. When the door had closed behind him, she turned to stare at it, trying to comprehend what had just happened. It was useless, of course. Her brain simply could not put the puzzle pieces together.

Had she misunderstood him when he'd said he wanted to stay with her? She frowned, thinking, but try as she might she couldn't recall the exact conversation that had passed between them. Maybe they'd been speaking at cross purposes?

It still didn't seem to fit because she couldn't think of anything he could have said that would have made her believe he wanted to stay with her if that wasn't what he'd meant.

She wondered if it wasn't something else. Had she said, or done, something that had made him change his mind? What, she wondered, could she have possibly done to have brought about such a change in him?

It was almost as if he was a completely different person--one who looked like Raphael, and spoke in the same voice, but who was someone else entirely.

She realized quiet suddenly that she was shaking, that she had been holding herself and rocking mindlessly. It was the pain she was trying to comfort herself from, the pain that was so acute she had gone numb from the shock of it. Now that the shock had begun to wear off, it crept through her in slow, agonizing waves.

A sound erupted abruptly from her tight throat, shocking her so that she jumped, clamping a hand to her mouth. Fearing someone would overhear, she leapt from the chair and ran into the bathroom, turning the water wide open. The face in the mirror didn't even look like her own. It was pale, her eyes red and swollen from the tears streaming down her cheeks. Scooping up handfuls of cold water, she dashed it over her face, but it did no good. The tears continued to flow, on and on.

Why was she crying? She never cried. She couldn't even remember the last time she'd cried, certainly not since she'd been a child.

More importantly, why could she not make herself stop? She climbed into the shower finally, fully clothed, hoping the water would somehow soothe her, help her to regain her self control. She wept until the hot became warm and the warm became cold. Finally, exhausted, freezing, she climbed out again, peeled her wet clothing off, dried herself and found dry clothes.

She returned automatically to her desk, sat and picked up the reports. She could not make any sense of them, however. It was almost as if she'd forgotten how to read. Finally, she decided she was just too exhausted to think. Dragging herself from the chair, she dropped onto the bed and was almost instantly asleep.

She awoke several hours later to the sounds of movement outside and sat up with a jerk, listening. It was the crew, coming in for dinner. Scrambling from the bed, she rushed into the bathroom to check her appearance. To her horror, she saw her eyes were still red and swollen. She splashed cold water on her face again and finally, in desperation found a cloth, soaked it in cold water and held it to her eyes for several minutes. Unfortunately, it didn't seem to help. It only made her vision blur.

Giving up on it, she decided she'd just skip dinner. She wasn't particularly hungry anyway. Besides, she'd never eaten the fruit she'd gotten earlier. Looking around, she discovered she'd left the can on her desk.

She needed to finish going over the reports anyway.

Her heart skipped a beat when someone tapped on her door. "Yes?"

Brown opened the door and stuck his head in. "Just checking to make sure everything was all right."

Victoria threw him a quick, distracted smile over her shoulder. "Thanks. I'm fine. I just need to get through these reports."

"You're not coming to dinner?"

She held up her can of fruit without turning to face him.

When he finally closed the door again, she set the can down and covered her face with her hands. She was being ridiculous. She couldn't stay holed up in her room. Everyone was bound to begin imagining all sorts of things if she did. Besides, Raphael was her second. She couldn't avoid him. He would be sharing the same floor with her, even if not the same room, and she would have to discuss the job with him.

She didn't have to see him tonight, though, now, when she was afraid anyone who saw her face would know immediately that she'd spent hours crying like a wounded child.

Returning her attention to the reports, she began reading again. She had to read them over and over before they began to make sense, but finally she managed to focus enough attention on them to understand what she was reading.

In the end, it was one line that totally grabbed her attention.

We buried the dead in the tomb they'd dug for themselves and moved to the secondary location to start the new mine shaft.

She stared at the words, read them again and finally, slowly, it sank in. They hadn't found any sign of whatever it was the miners had unearthed, because they'd been looking in the wrong place.

* * * *

Quelling the temptation to race up to main operations and take the place apart until she discovered the surveys, Victoria focused on the logs once more, searching for other possible clues.

The company had issued orders that the senior officer was to induct as many of the construction workers as possible as miners to replace the men they'd lost. The senior officer had offered pay raises and bonuses, but no amount of money could convince the construction workers to go back and work the mine that had collapsed. With great reluctance, because the original mine had had such a rich vein of ore, the senior officer had decided to excavate a new mine. Apparently, he had originally intended to leave the first mine open though.

The surviving miners had nixed that idea, insisting that the mine was haunted by some sort of 'evil' spirits and that the mine should be used as a tomb for the miners who'd died. The senior officer had finally agreed because it looked as if they might have rioting on their hands if he didn't.

Victoria frowned, wondering what could've aroused so much superstition. In general, miners tended to nurse a few antiquated superstitions, maybe more than the average person, but they were minor things--the bad luck of the number thirteen, lucky seven, or tossing spilled salt over their shoulder to appease the 'little folk'. No one she'd ever met even bore a serious paranoia about such things, though, quoting them more for amusement than anything else.

Either they'd been exposed to some sort of hallucinogen, or their fears had had nothing to do with superstition and the senior officers had simply ignored their complaints and put them down to absurd folk lore.

The more she thought about it, the more certain she became that that had to be the case. The miners were afraid of something that was really down there, but they hadn't been able to convince the officers that there was a threat.

She still couldn't see how anything they might have aroused below the surface of the ocean bed might have presented the threat from topside, but the senior officer had mentioned the threat of rioting. Maybe the threat became so great and fears rose to such heights that there *had* been rioting?

She frowned, realizing that wouldn't explain the lack of any bodies.

She decided to shelve it. Later, when she'd found every little puzzle piece that she could find, she would sit down and try to put them all together and see if they fit.

She scanned the remaining logs.

Apparently, problems escalated rapidly after that. The workers were somewhat appeased by the decision to seal the original mine, but tempers were still short and discipline became an increasing problem. There were an alarming number of accidents on the new project, which management put down to the lack of skills of the trainees. Missing men were considered AWOL. There were fifteen men and women on the list.

"Jesus!" Had Johnson been completely incompetent? Insane? Kay was totally uninhabited. No one in their right mind would just 'quit the company and walk off the job', not here.

She realized quite suddenly that the logs had been doctored. Management had expected the probability of a full investigation and had been trying to cover the company's culpability here. And either they'd had no imagination, or things had gotten so bad they hadn't been able to come up with a more believable lie to use as a cover up.

Setting the files aside, she doodled absently on a piece of paper while she tried to sort the useful information from obvious lies.

Mine collapse: accident? Or 'evil' spirits? Was there any chance, she wondered, that it had been deliberate? She decided she couldn't rule it out. It seemed outrageous, to say the least, to consider that anyone would have blown it, risking so many lives--causing so many deaths, but she didn't think it was completely impossible. She found, however, that she was leaning more in the direction of an accident caused by whatever it was they'd found down there ... by workers stampeding away from it, or by the creatures chasing them.

Frowning, she wrote: *Intelligent?* She decided she could rule out a higher intelligence than animal. There'd been no sign of any sort of weapons or tools, other than their own. But if it was a predator by nature, then it was a hunter, and it would have to be more intelligent than the grazers. Hunters were usually territorial, though, and worked alone, and she couldn't believe the loss of life here could be put down to a single creature.

They uncovered something. Unless she considered the possibility that all of the activity below had drawn the interest of a scouting predator, that seemed indisputable. All the problems had started after the first excavation. Moreover, the mention of the 'evil' spirits seemed to indicate that the miners, at least, figured the danger came from the excavation. The problem was, she had not found one single mention of anyone having been attacked by anything or having seen anything.

She thought about it for some time and was finally forced to conclude that management, for reasons unknown, had either decided to omit mention of hostile/dangerous life forms, or those who'd encountered these life forms hadn't lived to tell about it.

Deaths, accidents, disappearances. There'd been thirty men and women caught in the collapse, which in itself was criminal negligence. There should never have been so many miners down in the tunnels, even if they had four tunnels going at once. Counting the construction worker who'd died during construction of the habitat--which predated the problem--and the ten that were killed outright or fatally injured during their attempt to excavate a new mine, that accounted for well over half of the missing workers. When she eliminated all those listed as missing, that left maybe a couple of dozen who'd retreated into the habitat for their last stand.

It seemed irrefutable that the alien life form, or forms, had been picking them off almost from the time the mining crew had arrived. Something had triggered a massive attack, though.

What? Try as she might, she couldn't think of anything the crew might have done. Maybe it had been planetary conditions? Something had happened to drive away their normal food source and hunger had driven the creatures to take the next available thing--the crew.

The habitat looked as if it had been through one hell of a storm when they arrived. Maybe the storm had not been recent, but had occurred before the attack on the habit? She'd made it a point to question the workers below about any life forms. None had caught more than a glimpse of a few, small swimming things. She'd assumed the activity must have driven the indigenous life further away, but what if it was a combination of the storm and the creatures higher on the food chain hunting their food out?

Dropping her pen to the desk, she rubbed her eyes and then massaged her temples. The headache was back, probably as much from lack of food as from the hours she'd spent pouring over the reports. She was tempted to walk up to sickbay and beg a painkiller from Tuttle.

That thought prompted another possibility--that the information she was searching for regarding encounters, or sightings, of the creature might be in the medical reports.

Bringing up the computer, she began scanning the list of files, wondering if Raphael had broken the system security completely, allowing her access to everything, or if he'd merely unlocked the log-on.

She stopped when she reached MANAGEMENT studying it, wondering if she dared access it. Clearly, it was Johnson's files, but she could always argue, if it came into question, that she was higher management on site. Brushing aside her sudden nerves, she opened the file and scanned the files inside. One stood out. Like the button marked 'do not push' its title alone was enough to draw her in.

EXTREMELY SENSITIVE MATERIAL!

She opened the file and read:

Glitch regarding geneoid construction 18945: Further tests have led us to conclude that the particular combination of traits implanted in the crew are not reversible at this time. Since this violates penal law, this is a situation that must be handled with utmost delicacy. The attempt to terminate the experiment en-route failed.

Recommendation: The crew must be kept on Kay until and unless we are able to unravel the problem. Use whatever means necessary. Geneoids expendable.

Further to the defect in geneoid construction: The accelerated growth hormones have failed to level out per expectations. Expected limitations regarding their ability to withstand normal human conditions are exceeded. Prolonged exposure to breathing air expected to result in serious health complications. Calculations of maximum exposure narrowing from 12 hours maximum to 10 within the first month of release. However, if the growth hormone continues to accelerate maturity, this time frame will be further limited as it progresses. It is considered a strong likelihood that the geneoids will progress beyond the point of being able to tolerate normal human conditions, which will render them useless except as miners on KAY2581.

It was her second shock of the day and by far more stunning. Victoria stared at the screen in dawning horror as the meaning began to slowly sink into her sluggish thought processes. Black specks gathered and began to swim before her eyes as she struggled to force herself to breathe.

Something, some sound or movement, drew her attention toward the door and she turned. Raphael was standing in the opening, watching her.

Moments passed while she struggled to force herself to speak. "I didn't know," she finally said faintly. "I swear to you I didn't know."

He studied her for a long moment. "In the end, does it matter?"

Victoria swallowed with an effort, unable to think clearly. One thought, or perhaps emotion, emerged, however. "It matters to me that you know that I didn't ... wouldn't have anything to do with this ... this...." Words failed her.

"Glitch?"

Shame and guilt brought the blood that had rushed away from her head at the discovery flooding back in a hot tide. She realized it was useless to try to explain that it was shame and guilt by association, not because of anything she'd done directly, but because she worked for a company guilty of such an atrocity. It wouldn't matter to him. All that mattered was that he'd discovered they had been betrayed by the people who had created them and they were to be abandoned on this rock as if they were nothing but an embarrassment, to be swept under the rug.

Before she could think of anything to say, he was gone.

* * * *

Victoria stared at the door for several moments. The urge was nearly overpowering to go after him and try to explain, to try to make him understand that she would never have betrayed anyone in such a way, and him least of all. Her pride held her where she was.

He had to know how she felt. He must. If it made no difference to him, how could it make a difference if she swallowed her pride and went to him? What could she say, or do, that would make him feel differently?

What if she swallowed her pride only to have him trample it by refusing even to listen?

She thought about it for some moments and finally realized that she'd recover even if he did. She wasn't so certain she would ever be able to forgive herself if she didn't even try.

Rising, she left her room before she could change her mind, entered his without knocking. He looked up when she entered, his expression guarded. "Did you need something?"

She nodded. "You."

He didn't move, but she sensed his withdrawal. "Leave it."

"I tried. I discovered I couldn't. You told me something. I want to know if it was true, or just pretty words you thought would please me."

Something flickered in his eyes, but his expression hardened. "Don't."

"Why?" she cried. "You have to know I knew nothing at all about that. You have to! As many times as you've entered my thoughts, wouldn't you have learned it?"

He stood abruptly and moved away from her. "I never thought you did."

"Why then? Why have you withdrawn? Why are you so cold?"

"Because nothing I believed I could have can be mine!" he said angrily. "Not you. Not the life I wanted. It's pointless to pursue something you know you can never have!"

"You said you loved me," Victoria said quietly.

"I will always love you, Victoria." He said, almost tiredly as his anger subsided, then smiled wryly. "But always will not be nearly as long as I thought."

"You don't know that!"

"You read it. We've become a glitch, not human, geneoids."

Victoria thought for several moments that she would cry. She mastered the impulse with an effort. "You are not a glitch--none of you are. You're just as human as the rest of us, and I don't give a damn what it said. They were wrong before! What makes you so certain they're right now? I've seen nothing, in any of you, to lead me to believe they know what they're talking about."

"The whole point is, they don't know. What if the acceleration ages us ten years for every month of life? Or twenty? And even if they're wrong about that, what if we reach a point where we can no longer even leave the sea? I will not be human then, even if the aging stops. I can not have a life with a human woman when I must live in the sea. And if none of it is true, and they're wrong, we will never leave this place. The company would terminate us first." Raphael scrubbed his hands over his face, dragged in a deep breath. "I'm sorry. I suppose I'm a coward, but, knowing what I know now, I thought it would be best for you if I left you alone. Before it mattered to you. Before you could be hurt."

Victoria smiled with an effort. "Too late."

She moved toward him, stopping only when she was toe to toe with him. He stiffened, but he didn't pull away. "Aren't you going to ask why?"

He shook his head. "You should have just left it alone, Victoria. You should go now."

"If you love me as you say you do, don't do this to me. Don't push me away. Stay with me now."

He stared at her a long moment. "If you cared for me, you wouldn't want to give me more pain than I can bear."

It was an inarguable truth. It would, ultimately, be nothing but selfishness to take all he offered, perhaps to make it that much harder for him, knowing that she would be taken away from him when and if a ship came, and that he would be left behind. And still she felt the selfish urge to insist until he gave in. It took an effort to turn and leave.

Chapter Thirteen

Slowly, inexorably, rage filtered through Victoria. She wasn't going to let the board of directors get away with it. They'd gotten away with too much, too long. They had grown so wealthy and powerful they believed they were beyond the reach of the law.

It was no accident that Johnson had left the file. He'd hoped it would be found and used to give those who'd lost their lives justice. She knew very well that he would've been given standing orders to destroy any file marked EXTREMELY SENSITIVE once he'd accessed the information.

Rifling through the drawers of the desk, she found a recording chip, deleted the information from it and began reading through Johnson's files, selecting any that contained information regarding the company's efforts to cover up the disaster on Kay and recording them on the chip.

It was almost three AM by the time she was satisfied that she'd collected as much evidence as there was to be had. Rising, she strode from her living quarters and made her way up to Tuttle's quarters, rousing her. "I need you to implant this for me."

Tuttle, still fuddled with sleep, merely stared at her blankly. "What is it?"

"Something I can't afford to loose. Can you do it?"

"Now?"

"Right now."

Nodding, Tuttle stumbled from her bed and into the bathroom. She looked far more alert when she emerged some minutes later and the two of them went down to medical. "Mind telling me what this all about?"

Victoria stared at her a long moment. "Criminal negligence and conspiracy among the company's board of directors."

Tuttle looked as if she might faint for several moments. She moved closer. "If what you say is true, it's worth more than your life to them," she whispered, glancing nervously around as if she expected security to leap out at them at any moment.

"I know. That's why I asked you. You're one of the few people I'd trust with my life."

Tuttle gulped, nodded jerkily. "Where do you want it implanted?"

Victoria thought about all of the more usual places and discarded them. She removed her tunic. "Here, above my heart."

Tuttle blinked, and then a slow smile curled her lips. "Like a heart monitor, or a neuron chip?"

"Exactly."

Tuttle was frowning as she worked, however. "It won't fool the company. They have your records."

"Security won't have access to my medical records. All I need to do is get it past them."

"All," Tuttle said faintly. She shook her head as she finished sealing the edges of the incision with the laser. "Is it really worth the risk?"

Victoria thought it over, but decided she couldn't give Tuttle any more information. The mining crew was telepathic. They probably knew too much already. Otherwise, Tuttle couldn't divulge information she didn't have. "It's worth it," she said simply, climbing off the table and pulling her tunic on once more. She stopped Tuttle as she turned to go back to her quarters. "Promise me something."

Tuttle looked terrified, but she nodded.

"If you make it and I don't, promise me you'll retrieve the chip if you can and hand it over to someone you trust to do the right thing."

Tuttle swallowed with some difficulty. "Raphael?"

The name sent agony flooding through her. She shook her head. "Raphael will never leave this planet."

* * * *

Returning to her quarters, Victoria ripped the work schedule from the board and posted a meeting the following morning. She slept little. The murmur of voices woke her a few hours later. Rising, she showered, dressed and went out to face them.

They began pelting her with questions the moment she emerged. She held up her hand for silence. "Is everyone here?"

Everyone looked around. "Pretty much," one of the miners volunteered.

"Pretty much isn't everyone. Round them up while I grab a half gallon of coffee."

Tuttle, looking tired and anxious, was the last to arrive. "Roach is awake and demanding to talk to you."

"Later," Victoria said shortly.

"He said it was important," Tuttle said hesitantly.

"He thinks everything that concerns him is important. I'll talk to him later. Has he been moved to the brig?"

Tuttle nodded. "Late yesterday."

"Good. He won't be going anywhere until I've had a chance to talk to him."

She looked out over the assembly. "I called everyone here because I've finally had the chance to review all of the information we gathered regarding the incident that preceded our arrival. I've determined that the threat is ongoing."

"What kind of threat?"

"What is it?"

"What are we going to do?"

Victoria held up her hand. "I don't know *what* it is."

That comment stunned everyone to silence for about five seconds.

"I thought you said you'd determined there was a threat?"

"How could you know there was a threat and not know what it is?"

Victoria pounded her hand on the table. "If you'd rather just discuss this among yourselves, I'll leave you to it! If you want to hear what I know, or think, shut up, damn it, because I'm not going to try to shout over you!"

At that, an almost deafening silence fell. Victoria studied them a long moment before she tried again. "I know it's ongoing, because there wasn't a living soul here when we arrived. If they'd even managed to fight whatever it is off, there would have been some survivors. I knew this from the start.

"Unfortunately, I can't find any reference to whatever it is, nothing to identify it because it seems no one who saw it survived to talk about it."

Tuttle raised her hand. "I don't think I follow."

"There's nothing in the reports. They were picked off, one by one, while everyone decided those who went missing had just had an accident, or wandered off, which means those left had no warning."

"You think it's some kind of animal?"

"Some kind of predator, yes. Probably something territorial that was stirred up by the activity here. From everything I've gathered, it looks like the miners might have dug it up. The disappearances began after they'd sunk the first mine shaft."

"So what's your assessment?" Raphael asked.

Victoria glanced at him and then looked away. "It's fast. It's either small, and travels in numbers, or it's big and has some sort of natural camouflage that makes it hard to see. Red maybe. Everything on this godforsaken place seems to be red. Visibility is poor and very limited. It blends extremely well with its surroundings, moves fast, and attacks swiftly--fast enough nobody seems to have been able even to cry out and alarm anyone near enough to hear."

Brown was frowning thoughtfully. "What about something like a jelly fish? Kinda clear?"

Victoria's brows rose. "Maybe--certainly something that would be very difficult to see."

Brown looked as if he might say more, but he was interrupted by one of the miners. "What are we going to do?"

Victoria looked at them for a long moment. "We're going to hunt it down and kill it."

The comment caused an uproar. Victoria studied them for a moment and finally sat down to wait them out, listening to the arguments as she drank her coffee. When they finally subsided, she addressed them again. "This isn't up for debate, or a vote. We can wait for it to come and get us as it did the others, or we can go out and find it first."

"But we don't even know what we're looking for."

Victoria shrugged. "So we kill everything that moves."

Everyone gaped at her in stunned silence. It was Tuttle who finally spoke, however. "It's against the law to ... to maliciously destroy indigenous life on any world."

Victoria gave her a look. "Would you prefer to be the alien life form the indigenous life form wipes out? This is survival, people. We don't have a choice. We're stranded. We have the right to protect ourselves, with malicious force if we deem it necessary. Everyone goes out on this hunt ... everyone. Nobody's going to sit back in the habitat and straddle the fence, just so they can claim innocence while everybody else risks their lives to protect them. We'll take motion sensors and every weapon available. Once we've cleared the area, we'll set up a grid of motion detectors all the way around the habitat in case another predator decides to claim the territory.

"Air breathers, suit up. You won't be any good to us in the Cat." She turned to look at the cooks, who'd been listening from a position inside the kitchen. "This includes the four of you. Short shifts--I know none of you are familiar with underwater gear, but no one is excluded, for any reason."

As everyone began filing out of the room, Brown approached her. Victoria looked at him questioningly. "What is it, Brown?"

"I don't know, but I thought I ought to mention it."

Victoria nodded, trying to contain her impatience. "And?"

He shook his head. "When we started processing the ore, we found something. I didn't think much about it at the time ... thought it was like sea weed or something. Now I'm not so sure."

Victoria got up abruptly. "What did you do with it?"

"Scraped the shit off and kept working."

"Show me." She looked around the room and finally spied the person she was looking for. "Tuttle, you're coming with us."

* * * *

Despite the vast number of lights that crisscrossed the ceiling, the bins containing the raw and processed ore, and the equipment, combined to block out a great deal of light, leaving heavy shadows. It was chilly and damp in the room, far cooler than on any of the living levels, primarily because the company hadn't seen fit to consider the comfort zone of the workers. As long as it was adequate to keep them from freezing to death, it was sufficient.

The refuse bins were full of the slimy material. It had the appearance of mucus. Revolted, Victoria merely stared at it for some moments, finally she reached to touch it. Brown grabbed her hand, stopping her. "Don't!"

Victoria looked at him in surprise. "Why not?"

"Makes you go numb where ever it touches bare skin. But it burns like a son-of-a-bitch, too. That's why I asked about the jellyfish. I got stung by one when I was a kid. I've never forgotten it. This stuff even looks a lot like one."

Victoria felt a jolt of both excitement and fear as she studied the glutinous mass again. Finally, she looked around for something to use to collect a sample of it from the trash bin. Finding nothing ready to hand, she stepped out of her shoe and used it to scoop up a specimen. "Take this to the lab, Tuttle. See if you can figure out what the hell it is, and, more importantly, what's in it that causes the numbness and what might counteract its paralyzing characteristics. I've got a feeling this is how the creature managed to snatch so many people when there were others close enough they would have heard them cry out.

"It would also explain how it is that these things seem to have managed to get in despite of all the efforts to stop them. They're invertebrates. They could probably slip through the crevices under the door."

Brown frowned. "But ... how would they have gotten the bodies out?"

"The access pool. Let's just suppose they have some means of reaching the top of the habitat--maybe they were able to climb, maybe they have the ability to fly, or soar, or even leap to great heights. They attack the habitat from above, driving the crew down to the lowest level, and there the majority of the pack are waiting."

Tuttle shivered. "Wouldn't that mean they'd have to be a higher life form? Intelligent?"

Victoria shrugged. "Only in the sense that some creatures on Earth do much the same thing--surround their prey and use their greater numbers to overpower it, like a pack of wolves or a pride of lions.

"This would also explain why no one's ever seen it. As poor as the visibility is down there, being virtually transparent would make them almost impossible to spot.

"When Raphael and I escaped the collapse of the mine, some force struck us. Raphael assumed it was a shock wave, at first. If it wasn't ... if it was one of these things, then they're huge ... probably at least the size of a grown man, maybe even bigger."

"Are we still going out to hunt it?" Brown asked.

Victoria thought about it. "Tell Raphael there's been a delay. I want everybody to make a sweep of the immediate area, though, and set up the motion grid. Tuttle, take that specimen and let us know what you can find out as soon as possible. I'm going to have a talk with Roach."

Chapter Fourteen

Victoria stared at Roach through the bars for a full five minutes before she finally unlocked the door and entered. If she'd hadn't known it was Roach, she wasn't certain she would have recognized him. He was curled up in a tight knot on the bunk, rocking, staring into space with haunted eyes.

"You wanted to talk?" Victoria prompted, subduing a welling of pity with an effort.

Roach looked at her for several moments as if he'd never seen her before.

Victoria might not be a psychologist, but she recognized pure terror when she saw it. Roach had almost certainly seen their monster.

"Roach! I don't have time for any of your games. Do you want to talk or not?"

Roach blinked. "I s-saw s-something."

"What?"

"D-don't know."

Victoria sighed. Pity was very rapidly giving way to irritation. "That's not much help, Roach. Where? What did it look like? How big? What was it doing?"

He stared at her for so long she thought he wouldn't answer. "Kichens."

The single word was like a punch in the solar plexus. "You're sure?" She knew the moment she said it that it was a stupid question. They were the only humans on the planet. If it looked like Kichens, it must have been. She just couldn't seem to accept it.

She frowned. "They must have found her body...."

She saw that Roach was shaking his head.

"You think it wasn't an accident? That one of them got her while she was up top?"

"I don't know. I don't know! But ... there was something about the expression on her face, you know?" He shuddered and began rocking again.

Victoria knelt before him. "I've got to know everything you know, Roach."

He seemed to make an effort to pull himself together. "I figured, long as I was out, I'd have a look around. So I waited till nobody was paying any attention and headed out."

"Which direction?"

"The other side of the habitat from the mine ... straight out, I think. That was what I meant to do, anyway, so I couldn't get lost. I thought I saw something once I got on the other side, though. I was trying to get a better look at it. I wasn't paying too much attention to where I was going.

"The habitat ... I mean it's huge ... lights all over it. It never occurred to me I wouldn't be able to see it for miles. I wandered around ten minutes, maybe fifteen tops. Never got any closer to whatever it was, but then I got to looking around and I couldn't see the habitat. Scared the shit out of me. I panicked. I was going in first one direction then another. Next thing I know I hit something, or something hit me. I flip over, ass over appetite and then I'm falling ... it must have been a hard down draft, pulling me down. That must've been when I broke my ankle, 'cause I couldn't get up for a minute or two.

"You fell into a hole? Like a cave?"

Roach frowned, scratched his head. "Could've been, I guess. If it was, it was huge. Looked a lot more like a valley, only deep. The sides sloped. Finally, I got up, but my ankle was hurting like a son-of-a-bitch. I couldn't swim. Couldn't walk either. I didn't want to go any further down. I wanted to find my way back to the habitat, but I couldn't fight the current, so I decided to just go with it and see if it'd sweep me up the other side.

"Then I got to noticing these little shallow ... like pits. And I thought, weird, 'cause they looked like little craters. I wasn't really interested, though. I was hurting like hell, scared shitless. But then I saw ... movement. That's about the only way to describe it. I couldn't see any *thing,* not really, not at first. But the movement caught my attention and I got to looking real hard at the spot.

"The current carried me away before I could get a good look at it, but I was focusing on the pits then. That's when I caught a look at Kichens ... what was left of her."

Victoria frowned, remembering the 'nightmare' Raphael had had. "You think maybe it just got lodged there?"

He shook his head, looked for several moments as if he was going to throw up. "Whatever it was, it was eating her."

A shiver went through Victoria. She stood up abruptly. "You'll have to show us where it is."

He gaped at her as if she'd lost her mind. "No way am I going back out there!"

Victoria grabbed the front of his tunic, jerking him toward her until they were almost nose to nose. "They'll come in here, moron!" she said through gritted teeth. "What do you think happened to the others?"

She thought for several moments that he was going to cry. His chin wobbled. "But ... we could barricade ourselves in. Wait for the next ship."

Victoria released him, stepping back. "That's been tried already. It didn't work for them. And, as for waiting, it could be six months, maybe never. What do you think is most likely, Roach? The company finds out they've sent nearly a hundred people down on an uncharted world that they've only half-assed checked out, most of them are killed and they rush to save the last survivors? Or they cook up a shipping disaster, blame it on the captain and sweep it under the rug as missing, presumed dead?"

Roach whimpered. "They wouldn't just leave us here! Look at all the money they've sunk into this project!"

"Think of all the money it's going to cost them if we get out of here and there's an investigation. The penalties and settlements are likely to cost them more than they've already shelled out. I'm thinking they'll decide it's better just to cut their losses."

Roach sniffed. "I told you I was lost. I don't know if I can find it again."

"You found your way back," Victoria said tightly.

Roach gaped at her a long moment and finally got off the cot.

* * * *

Victoria summoned Raphael as soon as they were in the water. When he arrived, she told him Roach was going to lead them to the creatures. *He's been there. He should be able to find it again.*

Raphael looked at Roach questioningly. After a moment, Roach nodded a little jerkily.

He says he's pretty sure he can find it again. Raphael told her. His tone was skeptical.

He's been there. That increases our chances. He also said they were everywhere. No idea what sort of count we're talking about, but I think we need to leave a detail here to act as back up if we discover we have to retreat. I'd also like your input as to which level you think would be most defensible if we have to retreat into the habitat. I don't won't a repeat of what happened to the last crew.

Raphael frowned, considering it. *The habitat is wide open up through the warehousing levels. The lift has the elevator shaft pretty well blocked already. I'd say the officer's deck would be best, if we had to manage a prolonged siege, the crew level if we can't make it that far.*

Victoria nodded. *Good. Pick your detail and see what you can do to make it as secure as possible. Use whatever you can find to block the elevator shaft on both levels and make sure there's plenty ready to hand to block the door once we're in. From what I've heard, I'm thinking they're invertebrates. I've heard an octopus can squeeze itself through the neck of a bottle ... so if water will flow through it, block it ... the ventilation system too. And put motion detectors anywhere you think there's even a possibility of these things getting in.*

Tuttle's on your crew. Tell her to make sure there are plenty of medical supplies on both levels, just in case--and food and water. Caroline and Barbara are up in main operations. Tell them to rig up an automatic distress call if they can and get down here with everyone else.

She stopped, wondering if she'd covered everything.

You stay. I'll take the hunting party out, he said.

No.

Then I'll go with you.

I need you here, damn it!

I need to be with you! he said.

Despite the fact that her nerves were on edge, Victoria felt a smile tug at her lips. *What?*

Raphael gave her a narrow eyed look. *I need to be with you.*

And this is because?

I'll go out of my mind waiting here.

Victoria smiled. *Close enough. Pick the team and relay the message I just gave you to Brown and Quinton. I want Brown up top, Quinton leading our backup.*

Raphael's brows rose. *Roach is third in rank.*

Victoria gave him a wry look. *You really want Roach watching our backs?*

You have a point.

Exactly. Besides which, he's the closest thing we have to a guide. Brown's a good man, but he'd be hampered by his suit. Quinton won't and Quinton is telepathic. He'll be able to communicate with everyone. The com units don't work worth a damn in these conditions.

When Raphael returned nearly fifteen minutes later, Barbara was with him. *We made contact.*

Hope surged through Victoria. *Who? Are they coming?*

Barbara looked distressed. *We couldn't make it out. The signal's too weak. But they responded to the distress call.*

The disappointment was acute, following so closely upon the heels of the surge of hope. *We don't know if they're coming, though, do we?*

Maybe we should just go back to the habitat and wait? Raphael said.

Victoria considered it. She wasn't particularly happy about the task at hand. Finally, however, she shook her head. *If we knew for sure that they were coming, or even had some idea of when, I could see taking a chance that they might get here before we lose anyone else. As it stands, they might never come. We need to at least try to eradicate the threat. Otherwise, they'll be picking us off one by one until there's nobody left.*

Raphael nodded. *Let's do it, then.*

* * * *

To Victoria's surprise, the 'valley' was just as Roach had described it, right down to the current. Despite the fact that she'd more than half expected it, she was very nearly carried over the edge. They paused, looking down.

Ask Roach which direction, Victoria told Raphael.

Raphael glanced at Roach and Roach pointed.

How far?

He's not sure. He says the first he noticed were about a half a mile down slope, maybe a mile.

Check your weapons. No wild shots. No squandering fire power. Keep an eye on the man next to you and make damn sure you don't cut across our line with fire. If your weapon drops below 75% firepower, yell out. Retreat on my orders and not before. Got it? Victoria said, glancing down the row of men and women. They nodded as her gaze touched them.

Form a line, no more than an arm's length between anyone. We're going to do a sweep. You're responsible for the man next to you. Anyone goes down, grab them.

They formed a ragged line and started down the slope at an angle, watching the surface for any sign of the depressions Roach had described.

Victoria halted abruptly when she spotted the first pit, scanning the area around it. At first, she could see nothing. Then, slowly, as she concentrated, her eyes focused on the faintest of movements. It was the general shape of a manta ray, flattened, almost saucer shaped, but so nearly transparent, or so well camouflaged, that it appeared as nothing more than the ocean bed around it.

Her heart skipped several beats as she stared at it, then she slowly moved her gaze across the landscape. As far as she could see there were identical pits, approximately a meter in diameter and probably no more than three meters between them. She didn't need to see them to know a creature lay in each one.

Oh my God! It's a nesting ground!

The thoughts had scarcely formed in her mind when the creature nearest her turned bright red, rising menacingly from its nest.

Fire! Fire!

* * * *

There was no sweep. The moment they stepped within the territorial range of the creatures, they rose like a swarm of bees and attacked aggressively. Victoria pulled her group into a turtle formation, only vaguely aware of the two men on either side of her and those at her back. The color the animals turned when threatened made them marginally easier to see and they were not proof against the fire power of the lasers. She cut five in half in two seconds.

The problem was, there were hundreds of them. As quickly as she killed five, ten more swarmed toward her. She realized very quickly that they didn't have nearly enough firepower.

Fall back! Keep the circle tight!

With the current flowing against them and the creatures swarming, it took them almost twice as long to reach the summit once more as it had taken to move down it.

Once they'd cleared it, Victoria halted for a head count and discovered they had three men down ... which translated to six because the injured had to be carried.

Raphael, try to reach Quinton and warn him we're coming his way.

Albert, check our heading. I don't want to waste time looking for the habitat.

I can't reach him, Raphael told her after a moment.

Keep trying. I'd like to be sure they know we're between them and these things when the censors go off.

They began moving once more, covering as much ground as possible before they were forced to halt again by the circling creatures. Once they moved beyond the tug of the current that dipped into the valley, the water around them turned murky with the fluids of the animals they killed and Victoria couldn't decide whether she was having difficulty breathing because of the effort of fighting and retreating, or because the creatures had released their poisons into the water at death.

I'm down to 20%, the man beside her said, then yelped as one of the creatures brushed against him. Victoria shot it as it arched away, grabbing for the man as he sank slowly toward the ocean floor. Tugging him behind her, she kept moving, kept firing.

It was with a great deal of relief that she saw the habitat come into view once more, for she'd begun to realize that she was almost certainly sucking poisons inside her with every gasping breath. It was becoming harder and harder to breathe. They'd been cut nearly in half, and the few still able to move were each carrying a man as well as fighting.

To her relief, their backup swam out to meet them, helping to pull the downed fighters to the habitat and up through the access pool.

It was all Victoria could do to pull herself up to the edge of the access pool. She hadn't the energy to climb out. Raphael grabbed her, pushing her up onto the lip of the pool before following her up.

"Head count," Victoria gasped.

Quinton took the count. "All present and accounted for."

Victoria nodded. "Seal the access pool. Raphael, did you get any kind of count?"

He shook his head. "Maybe a couple of dozen were still with us when backup arrived.

She smiled wryly. "That's what I thought. I was hoping it wasn't just wishful thinking."

Roach glared at her. "You stupid bitch! You just had to go out and stir them up! Now we're all going to die on this shit hole planet!"

It took more of an effort to get on her feet than she would've thought possible, but Victoria managed it. When she'd steadied herself, she kicked Roach squarely in the jaw. His eyes rolled back in his head.

Satisfied, she turned to look at the rest of the group. "Let's get these people up to medical."

* * * *

Guilt swamped Victoria as she stared out over the eight sheet draped figures lying perfectly still on the floor of the sickbay. "Are they ... comatose?"

"Not in the strictest sense of the word," Tuttle said grimly. "These Kaymons produce some sort of poison similar to some species of wasps. They paralyze their prey, but the paralysis doesn't seem to affect the internal organs to a great degree ... at least it hasn't caused death at this point. They're still alive, quite possibly aware of their surroundings, but unable to move or speak. The problem is, I don't know *if* they'll come out of it, or when."

Victoria glanced at her sharply. "Kaymons? You've identified them?"

Tuttle gave her a wry look. "No. These monsters are exclusive to Kay. I was calling them Kay Monsters, but Kaymons is easier."

Victoria nodded, but a look of revulsion crossed her features. "They looked very much as if they were nesting. There were little pits all over the sides of the 'hills' of that valley. And in each one, one of these ... Kaymons. There were hundreds. We probably killed a couple of hundred, but I doubt we diminished them by half. It was impossible to get a very good look at them, but they looked almost disk shaped, and they moved like manta rays. I'm guessing they can move through the air the same way they move through water--One thing I don't really understand, though, is that they attacked us without provocation."

"They were nesting," Raphael said grimly. "It's mating season."

Chapter Fifteen

Victoria glanced at him sharply. "You saw young?"

Raphael shook his head. "Remember the sleeping vision I had? You said it was a nightmare? It wasn't a nightmare. He reached out to me telepathically. I wasn't certain at the time. I took your word for it, because it was easier to accept that it was a disturbing dream than something that was actually happening.

"But, when Tuttle explained the way the poison works, I knew. They paralyze their prey and leave them in their 'nests' to feed the hatchlings when they emerge. It's to preserve the 'meat', to make sure it's still fresh for their young. Apparently, food is scarce ordinarily and, in the past, they had to hunt over a wide area to find enough food--which is why they developed the ability to paralyze and preserve the food.

"But then the company set a smorgasbord right in their backyard.

"That's why there's so many. Last season, they had more than enough to feed their young. This season, we're on the menu."

Roach, who'd been nursing his head on a cot nearby, made a sound that was somewhere between a whimper and a laugh. "You're just guessing!" he said angrily. "You're just trying to help cover her ass because she screwed up!"

Raphael turned and glared at him. "Let's have your theory."

Roach gaped at him, looked around at the rest of the crew, who were watching him. "I don't know. And neither do you!"

"We all know that's why the last crew went missing," Raphael pointed out grimly. "You saw Kichens. You said...."

"No!" Roach covered his face. "Don't! I don't want to think about it."

"It's not going to do any of us any good to pretend it isn't happening. But I don't think anybody here is qualified to question Victoria's judgment on how she handled the threat. Those things *are* a threat to our survival. I'm guessing, whether we'd gone out or not, they would've been coming for us ... just like they came for the others.

"At least going after them gave us the chance to increase the odds in our favor a little bit. We know where they are now. We can identify the threat and we know what they'll be using against us."

Victoria studied him, wondering if he *had* said it to make her seem less negligent, but the more she thought about it, the more it made sense. "We upset the eco-system," she said thoughtfully. "They'd almost hunted out the area--that's why we didn't see anything else, not because they'd moved further away because we'd invaded their territory, but because there was next to nothing to begin with. These things--Kaymons--must have been on the verge of extinction ... until the company provided a new food source for them."

Raphael shrugged. "That's my guess."

Victoria frowned. "So why weren't they hunting us from the time we arrived?"

"If we accept the theory we've developed so far, they would have had to survive on very little food. Maybe you were on track before. Maybe they hibernate for long periods of time--or something like it. Maybe that's how they were stirred up by the first crew ... maybe that's how we got them stirred up."

Victoria looked around. "Anybody else want to volunteer any theories here? Remember anything you saw, but didn't think much about it at the time?"

"I'm more interested in what we're going to do about it," Sylvia said. "You've got everything you need to survive, assuming we can keep them out--but from what Raphael has told us, we'll die if we're out of water more than twelve hours and we might not even have that long."

Victoria blushed. "I didn't consider that we might be trapped here indefinitely."

"I'm not accusing you of anything," Sylvia said quietly. "You've always looked out for us. I'm just saying, regardless of what Roach seems to think, *we* never had the option of just hiding and hoping we wouldn't be one of the hunted. Caroline said they'd made contact--somebody may or may not be coming to rescue you and the others, but nobody's coming for us."

Brown leapt to his feet. "What does she mean by that?"

Victoria glanced at Raphael and then away. "The company...."

"Fucked up," Raphael finished. "We were supposed to be primarily human, with aquatic traits that would allow us to work the mines for extended periods of time ... traits that could be reversed per the law. Instead, they've found the traits aren't reversible, and the accelerated growth hormone seems to have upset the delicate balance they thought they'd achieved. We're becoming progressively more aquatic and less human. Which means we wouldn't be able to leave, because we can't survive the conditions you require to live."

Brown stared at Sylvia a long moment before his face contorted with rage. "Those fucking bastards! You're not going to go along with this shit, are you Anderson?"

Victoria's lips tightened. "We don't leave our people behind. You shouldn't have felt you had to ask. You know me better than that!"

Sylvia got up. "Stop it! This isn't going to help anyone. Let's just focus on right now or there might not be a later for anybody!"

As if her outburst were their cue, the alarms connected to the motion detectors went off.

"They're back!"

Victoria raced to the command station they'd rigged up, which had a feed from the security videos. At first, she didn't see anything at all. When she used the control to zoom in for a closer shot, however, she could see the cover to the access pool was moving ever so slightly. After a moment, she realized it wasn't the cover that was moving. "Shit! They're slipping through the cracks!"

"I thought you said the damn things were as big as a grown man?" Brown snapped. "How could they get through without breaking the cover?"

"They've done it!" Victoria snapped. "You, you and you," she snapped, pointing. "Grab your weapons and get over to the elevator shaft. Raphael, Quinton, we've got the door. And set the lasers on low!" she added as an afterthought. "We don't want to burn anymore holes for them to slip through."

They waited tensely, watching the clothing that had been stuffed under the door, hardly daring to blink. Quite suddenly, the door latch rattled. Victoria's heart seemed to stand still. Her eye lenses seemed to focus in on the latch, like the zoom on a camera. It was then she saw to her horror that it hadn't been locked. She leapt forward, throwing her shoulder against the door just as something bumped the door and it widened a sliver.

Something was wedged in the door. She couldn't get it closed. She pounded the door with her shoulder a couple of times, trying to force it closed. Next to her, Raphael threw his shoulder against it, as well. The obstruction cleared and the door slammed to. Victoria flipped the lock and looked around. Quinton was aiming toward the ceiling, following something with the site on his rifle.

Grabbing up the rifle she'd dropped, Victoria squinted her eyes, searching. The overhead lights glinted off their still damp bodies and she spotted three swooping, dipping closer and closer to the crew members huddled near the floor. She fired. Around her she heard the high pitched whines of several other lasers as Quinton and Raphael fired. The Kaymon she'd fired on dropped on Tuttle. She screamed, threw it off and dashed for cover, scrambling under a table. Victoria leapt toward the downed Kaymon, blasting it twice more for good measure, then kicked it. When it didn't move, she turned to look for another target. To her relief, she saw that Quinton and Raphael had taken down the other two.

"I think we've got them on the run," Brown said, watching the screens.

Victoria moved to stand beside him. "More likely they had to go back. They probably can't survive out of the water long."

She turned away from the video screens. "Who left the god damned door unlocked?"

Everyone stared at her wide eyed, but no one spoke up. After a moment, she set her rifle down and scrubbed her hands over her face. "We'd probably have to weld the doors shut to keep those damned things out." Her shoulders slumped.

"What now?"

Victoria massaged her tense neck muscles and glanced at her watch. It was mid afternoon. "It'd be nice if the kitchen staff would round us up something to eat," she said, smiling wearily at the kitchen staff.

Clarence, the head cook, perked up at once and scrambled to his feet. "You heard the boss," he said to his three man staff. "Let's get to work."

Victoria looked around and finally spotted Barbara. "Anything else from the contact?"

Barbara shook her head. "It's gone dead. Something must have happened to the lead. You want me and Caroline to run up and check on it?"

Victoria thought about it for several moments but finally shook her head. "Too risky right now. Later maybe.

"Quinton?" She turned to look for him. "It looks like it's clear right now. Get these carcasses out of here. I'm not completely satisfied they're dead--and if they're anything like jellyfish, they could still sting after death, so don't touch them with your hands. Brown, take a couple of people and see if you can come up with something better to seal the doors with."

Brown looked at her a little doubtfully. "You want us to weld the doors?"

Victoria was on the point of shaking her head, but it occurred to her that the elevator shaft could be welded. They couldn't use that anyway and it would eliminate one point of entry. Of course it was also leave them with only one escape route. On the other hand, there didn't seem to be much point in having two exits when they were likely to be besieged at both. "You know where an arc gouge is?"

Brown looked surprised, but he nodded.

"Get it. Then weld the elevator shaft only. If we have to get out that way, we'll have the arc gouge handy to cut a new exit. But find something else for the door. I'd rather not be completely shut in until and unless we find it necessary."

When they'd left, she slung her rifle over her shoulder and went into sickbay. Tuttle was checking the vitals on one of her patients. "Any change?"

Tuttle shook her head. "If this works anything like wasp venom, though, they might begin to come out of it in a day or two."

Victoria looked at Tuttle, then glanced down at the young man she was standing by. She'd named him Richard. It was odd how young he looked, caught in the unnatural sleep. As the others did, he'd appeared to be in his late twenties or early thirties. She'd supposed that was their physiological age. It certainly wasn't their chronological age. If he'd been allowed to develop naturally, he would not even have been born yet. She brushed his hair from his forehead, then looked up at Tuttle self-consciously. "They might not have that long. You'll have to watch them for tissue degeneration due to prolonged exposure."

Tuttle bit her lip. "What'll I do if I see it?"

Victoria rubbed her neck. "I don't know. I'll have to think of something."

Sylvia poked her head in at the door. "Chow's ready."

"You go," Victoria said, looking at Tuttle. "I'll keep an eye on them while you eat."

She didn't realize Sylvia was still standing in the doorway until she looked up as Tuttle left. "It's a habit with you, isn't it?"

Victoria lifted her brows questioningly.

"Watching over us."

Victoria wasn't certain how to take the comment. "I'm senior officer," she said noncommittally.

"It wasn't that, though, that made you feel the need to name us, to check our progress, was it? You do realize we're only here because of you? If you hadn't been so determined to make sure nothing went wrong, they would have terminated us en-route."

Victoria bit her lip. "I guess you all hate me for that."

"You'd be guessing wrong," Sylvia said, smiling faintly. "Don't get me wrong, I think most of us, when we first found out, thought we would've been better off if we'd died before 'birth', but then we realized we were angry because we wanted to live and we were afraid that would be taken away from us. So, why be angry with you for working so hard to give it to us?"

"You don't ... hate me, then? None of you?"

Sylvia's smile widened. "Raphael loves you, we all do." She thought about it for several moments. "Not the way he does, of course. Sort of ... like you were our mother."

Victoria was taken aback. She didn't know how she felt about that comment.

"It makes you uncomfortable."

Victoria smiled wryly. "No. Yes. It makes me feel a little strange, that's all. You're all ... grown, physiologically around my own age."

Sylvia frowned thoughtfully. "The care giver. The one who nurtures and guides. Isn't that what mother means?"

Victoria looked at her in surprise. "I'd never thought about it."

Sylvia nodded. "I just wanted you to know ... well, just in case I don't get another chance. Thank you."

A hard knot formed unexpectedly in Victoria's throat, making it difficult to swallow. "We're going to get out of this."

Sylvia nodded. "If anyone can do it, I know you can."

Victoria stopped her before she could leave. "You're sure Raphael doesn't think of me as ... uh ... as his mother?"

Sylvia laughed. "Does he act like it?"

Victoria blushed. "No!"

"He'll kill me for putting that idea in your head," Sylvia said.

"I'll have to keep him from finding it, then, won't I?" Victoria responded, both relieved and amused.

Sylvia shook her head. "You didn't really understand when Raphael told you he'd mind-melded with you, did you? You are as two halves of a whole, together in mind, body and spirit. He's been trying to release you. That's why he withdrew. That's why he seems so distant. He's trying to sever the tie so that when you go you'll not feel as if you're no longer whole."

"Strangely enough, that's not what I want," Victoria said, controlling the urge to burst into tears with an effort.

"But it's what's best for you," Sylvia said gently. "That's what you do when you love someone, isn't it? You try to do what's best for them?"

Chapter Sixteen

Victoria was thoughtful as she ate, trying to push personal considerations to the back of her mind so that she could concentrate on the problems at hand. It was not something she had ever had to do before. In general, she was completely focused on her job.

She'd cleaned her plate before anything useful occurred to her. "Brown, do we have any kind of explosives?"

Brown looked at her in surprise. "I don't know. The construction crew might have. We use the laser cannon on the mines. What're you thinking?"

"The CAT's air tight. I'm thinking it's doubtful those things could get inside of it."

"The seals are rubber," he reminded her. "They might be able to push past them."

"It's worth a try though."

"What's worth a try?" Raphael asked.

"Using the CAT to get close enough to blow the damned things to hell," Victoria said. "The construction crew would've had explosives to blast out enough rock to set the foundation for the habitat. The laser cannon is great for precision work, but slow. If there's enough left, we can use the CAT to plant a row of explosive on either side of that valley and blow it. Between the explosions and the cave in, we should be able to take care of most of the damned things."

Brown frowned. "Sounds like a plan, but we'd have to go outside to get the Cat, rig it outside, too."

"They keep retreating, though. I'm thinking they don't want to leave their young, or their eggs, for very long. They chased us all the way back to the habitat, then withdrew. They didn't try again for several hours. I think we'll be able to count on at least a small window of opportunity after the next attack. Have we got anyone who knows anything about explosives?"

She looked around.

"I could probably figure out how to wire it if I had a manual," Xavier volunteered.

"See what you can find in the computer. Brown, take a half dozen volunteers and scour the habitat. See if you can locate the explosives."

He looked at her a little sheepishly. "They're in the warehouse. Level three." At the look she gave him, he stammered, "I just figured you'd give up on the idea if we couldn't find explosives."

"You don't think it'll work?"

He shrugged. "Maybe, maybe not. I'm not sure it's worth the risks involved, that's all. What if the seals on the CAT don't keep those things out?"

"That's a chance I'm willing to take."

Brown glared at Raphael. "That's exactly what I figured you'd say. Tell her she can't do it."

Victoria looked from one man to the other, then frowned. "What're you talking about?"

Raphael shrugged. "If I say no, she'll do it in spite of hell."

Victoria glared at him before returning her attention to Brown. "Get the explosives. We'll worry about who's going if and when we get the CAT rigged. Xavier's already volunteered. The CAT holds four."

Brown and his group managed to retrieve the explosives, but they had to fight a running battle to get back as the Kaymons came at them in a fresh wave. By the time the second battle was finished, Victoria had to concede that the possibility of getting to the CAT and setting it up was about nil considering night was falling.

When she'd caught her breath, she walked around the room and tapped four on the shoulder. "First watch, second, third, fourth. Everybody else, find a room and get some rest. You'll have to double up. There are only six suites on this level."

* * * *

Victoria was standing under pelting hot water when she sensed she was no longer alone. She opened her eyes slowly and met Raphael's gaze for a long moment, then, without a word, she stepped toward him. Placing her palms on the ripple of muscles that formed his abdomen, she slid them slowly up his chest, over his shoulders and finally locked her fingers behind his head, swaying closer as she did so until her skin brushed his. Lowering her head, she kissed his shoulder, his throat and then brushed her lips lightly against his.

His arms came around her, tightened almost painfully a moment and then relaxed fractionally as he opened his mouth, covering hers, plunging his tongue into her mouth. The heat of his mouth warmed her. His taste and scent were as heady as strong wine, sending a wave of languor through her. The caress of his tongue along her own, the brush of his flesh against her flesh, made moisture gather in her sex.

She broke the kiss at last, wanting to taste and touch him everywhere at once, to feel him inside of her, to feel him wrapped around her. He lifted her, carrying her in the room, laying her on the bed and following her down. She shivered at the chill of the air on her wet skin, but his lips and hands chased the chill away, quickly replacing it with heat.

Spreading her thighs, she welcomed him. "Now," she whispered. "I want you inside of me."

She moaned as she felt the head of his cock nudging the flesh of her sex, parting her slowly, slipping through the hot moisture that had gathered there to ease his way inside of her. He went still when he had embedded his rock hard cock to the hilt inside of her, pulling away from her so that he could look down at her as he slowly withdrew and then pushed into her once more. She lifted her hands to his shoulders, gazing up at him as she countered his rhythm, then looked down, between them to the point where their bodies joined. Raphael followed her gaze, moving slowly as he watched their flesh meld, separate and join.

A shudder went through him. He hesitated a long moment, groaned and began moving again, faster, plunging deeply inside of her. Victoria dug her heels into the mattress, meeting each hard thrust of his cock with one of her own, clutching his shoulders more tightly until he lowered himself so that her breasts rubbed against his chest with each thrust of his body. The stimulation sent a flood of heat through her, sent her careening toward fulfillment. She pulled his head down and thrust her tongue into his mouth. When he closed his mouth around it and sucked, her body convulsed, the muscles in her belly clenching around his cock, milking him of his seed. He groaned into her mouth, and finally pulled away, gasping, spent.

Victoria tightened her arms around him, wrapping her legs around his thighs and holding him to her. She didn't want to let go. She realized she never wanted to let go.

Finally, gently, he disentangled himself from her and lay beside her, pulling the covers up over them.

The sheets were damp, but she found she didn't care. She moved against him, demanding silently that he hold her close. He slipped his arm around her, stroking her back. She was half asleep when he spoke. "I shouldn't have come."

She nuzzled against him and kissed his chest. "I'm glad you did."

"I wanted to ask you to do something for me."

Victoria pulled away and looked up at him. "What?"

He frowned. "I understand that it was never part of your plans and it's a lot to ask, but I'd like for you to keep this." He caressed her belly.

Victoria stared down at his hand for a long moment before she realized what he was talking about. "Raphael...."

He put a finger to her lips. "Shhh. I know you need to think about it, that you haven't decided. I just wanted you to consider it. It would ... please me to think that my son was with you."

Victoria flipped over, putting her back to him. "Don't talk like that. I can't accept that nothing can be done."

He placed his hand on her arm, leaned down and kissed her shoulder. "Stubborn. I've always loved that about you."

Victoria sniffed. "I find that hard to believe."

She felt him smile against her shoulder. "That's because you never understood that I love everything about you."

She swallowed with some difficulty. "We still have the containment. We could retrieve it, use it to transport everyone."

Raphael sighed. "It was specially designed for the ship that brought us. You know as well as I do that the odds are astronomical that it would fit in the hold of another ship, even assuming they would be willing to jettison their cargo to accommodate us. And what is the likelihood that the ship would be equipped with a pulley system that would work to hoist it? If you think I want to accept this, you're mistaken. I'd like nothing more than to go with you."

Victoria sighed and turned over. "I don't want to talk about it. I want you to make love to me until I can't think of anything at all."

* * * *

The Kaymons attacked again just before dawn. They were caught off guard, for this time the creatures found their way through the ventilation system. A half a dozen managed to slip in before the motion censors went off and Quinton, Caroline and Sylvia were struck down as they ran from their sleeping quarters.

Roach managed to shoot Brown in the leg with the laser rifle before the last of the Kaymons were brought down. Roach threw his rifle down when he saw what he'd done and rushed to see how seriously he'd injured his coworker, whereupon Brown did his utmost to choke the life out of him.

When Tuttle and Albert finally managed to separate the two, both men were in need of medical attention.

Gasping, as much from the adrenaline rush as the expenditure of energy, Victoria rushed to the monitors, watching closely until she was certain the surviving Kaymons had retreated from the general area. "Let's move it! Now people!" she yelled at the group that had been hand picked to outfit the CAT.

Grabbing up weapons and equipment, everyone raced for the door, paused to check the stairwell, and then pounded down the stairs. They arrived at the lowest level somewhat winded, checked it cautiously, and waited while Victoria checked with Barbara to make certain the Kaymons were still in retreat.

At the all clear, the cover was lifted from the access pool and they dove, swimming toward the mines, where the CAT had been parked. Victoria had reckoned without the effects the water would have on their speed. It took them nearly twice as long to outfit the CAT as she'd calculated.

She kept a close watch of the time, alternating by checking the long range sensors.

Raphael swam to her, gripping her arms. *We're ready. Donna and Carol have volunteered to go with me and Xavier. Don't fight me on this, Victoria. You're needed here.*

Victoria studied him a long moment and finally nodded. She looked at her watch. *They're liable to be swarming again before you're done. Be careful.*

He pressed his lips to hers briefly. *I'll see you when I get back,* he said when he pulled away.

She nodded, watching as he and the others climbed into the CAT and started it up. When the CAT had vanished in the murky depths, she called the workers together and returned to the habitat to pace and wait.

Minutes ticked into hours. Victoria kept glancing at her watch, wondering if they'd reached the site in the time calculated, and then, if they had managed to set the charges in the time they'd calculated. Periodically, she checked the video feed and the censors. Finally, she realized she was making everyone jittery with her display of nerves and retreated into her quarters.

The projected time of detonation came and went. Victoria discovered that she'd chewed her nails down to the quick and began pacing again.

Suddenly, all hell broke loose. A noise, like a deep moan echoed hollowly through the habitat. It shivered. In a moment, the faint waver had become hard shaking and every proximity monitor went wild.

Victoria snatched the door open and raced into the rec room. The video feed from beneath the habitat showed billowing clouds of silt. Tumbling through it, Victoria could see a dozen or more Kaymons. "They were too late," she said as the proximity censors topside let out a sharp cry of warning. Dimly, she saw the outline of the CAT as it rolled to a halt beneath the habitat. "Stay put," she muttered. "Just stay put."

To her horror, she saw the doors opening.

"Shit! They're coming in! I need four people, now!" She yelled, grabbing up her rifle and heading for the door without waiting to see who would follow.

Reaching the access level, she started hauling on the wench to lift the top from the access pool. As soon as it had risen a foot, Raphael, Donna, Carol, and Xavier squeezed through and rolled from the lip of the pool. She released the wench and grabbed her rifle up. "The sensors are going crazy. They must be everywhere," she said as she turned and led the way back to the stairwell.

Raphael fell into step beside her, then pushed ahead of her, grasping the door first and pulling it open. They scanned the stairwell and started up. They were nearing the third level when they heard the distinct sound of a door opening.

"Hello the habitat!"

Victoria exchanged a glance with Raphael, hardly daring to believe someone had come for them. "We're here!" she yelled. "Coming up!"

"Make it fast! There's a hell of a storm blowing up here! We need to get off this rig before the ship's damaged by flying debris."

"We've got wounded," she yelled back. "Give us ten!"

She pounded on the door of the officer's level when she reached it. "Our ride's arrived," she said when the door opened and Brown looked at her in surprise. "Grab a stretcher. Let's get these people up there."

Brown grinned. "I think I can make it under my own steam even if I have to crawl."

Victoria grinned back at him, feeling giddy with relief. "I'll give you a hand. You might crawl too slow to suit them."

The wind snatched the door from her grip when she opened it onto the lower deck, slamming it back against the wall. She staggered, almost falling with Brown. Regaining their balance, they leaned into the wind and struggled to climb the exposed stairs that led to the upper deck.

Finally, they reached the upper deck, however, and staggered toward the open bay doors of the ship that awaited them. Victoria was on the gang plank before she recognized it. Looking around, and then up, she met Captain Huggin's gaze. "You're a sight for sore eyes."

He smiled wryly. "I hope you can properly appreciate the fact that I just threw away a forty year career," he said as she came even with him.

She studied him a long moment. "We'll see. After I get through with them, you might find they're anxious to do the right thing."

His brows rose, but he dismissed whatever questions rose to mind. "We need to get everyone in here as quickly as we can. We're not going to be able to take off if the wind gets much harder.

Victoria nodded and released Brown. Turning, she waved the others up, urging them to hurry. Roach brushed past her and kept going. Tuttle scrambled up the gangplank behind him, nearly falling twice. Behind her, Clarence and his kitchen help struggled to make their way into the hold, leaning against the pelting wind.

It was then that Victoria discovered none of the injured had been brought up. Raphael, Xavier and Barbara stood near the stairwell, watching, but unmoving. She stared at Raphael with a mixture of surprise and anger. Placing her hands around her mouth, she shouted at him to bring the injured.

Captain Huggins gripped her shoulder. "We can't bring them."

She glanced at him. "You're out of your fucking mind if you think I'm leaving any of my people on this hell hole of a planet!" she said furiously.

"We can't take them! We don't have the containment!"

"We'll retrieve it!" Victoria said furiously.

"We can't! Not in this." He paused, saw she wouldn't listen and added, "I'm under orders not to bring them off planet for any reason," he said angrily. "If I did, you can be damn sure we'd never make it back to any port."

"They won't know if you don't tell them," she said through gritted teeth.

"Victoria!"

She turned, saw that Raphael had come to stand behind her. "Bring everyone up. We're leaving."

He shook his head slowly, smiling faintly. "I know you think you can do anything, but you can't fight this."

"I'm not leaving you!"

"No. You're being taken away," he said and pulled her close, pressing his lips to hers. Victoria threw her arm around his neck, holding him tightly.

"We can do this," she said. "I've got the weapon I need."

He caressed her cheek, touched her neck. Something shot through her, like a static charge. It was the last thing she remembered as darkness claimed her.

Chapter Seventeen

Victoria felt herself shaking. She frowned, then realized that she was being shaken. With an effort, she opened her eyes. Brown was standing over her.

She blinked. "Where am I?"

"We're on the ship. Leaving our people, that's where we are. What're you going to do about it?"

Victoria jackknifed into a sitting position. The sudden motion made her head swim. "What the hell was I hit with?"

"Damned if I know. Raphael touched you on the neck and the next thing I know, you're falling into a limp pile in his arms. Captain Huggins dragged you up the gang plank and pulled it."

Victoria got up. "I need a weapon. How long was I out?"

Brown produced two pistols, handing her one of them. "Too long."

Huggins glanced around when Brown and Victoria entered the cockpit, then returned his attention to the controls. "I'm sorry, Anderson. I would've done something if I could, but my hands are tied." His heart skipped a beat when a cold, round metal object settled on his temple. He didn't have to look to know what it was.

"I'm sorry, too, Huggins. I want you to know I will deeply regret splattering your brains all over Grant over there, but I'll do it anyway if you don't turn this ship around--right now."

Huggins slid a sideways glance at her. "You're bluffing."

"Are you willing to bet your life on it?"

"You're not qualified to pilot this ship."

"You really think I'm going to worry about a little thing like a license after I've murdered you?"

He paled. "What I meant was, you don't know how."

"I'm a fast learner. But I don't have a lot of patience right now. I'm going to give you to the count of five."

Huggins hesitated.

"One."

"All right!"

"You're going to set it down right where you dropped the containment."

He threw her a startled glance. "That's over the water. I can't hold it there in this weather!"

"I've got confidence in you." She turned to Brown. "I'm going below to get everything situated. Let me know when to open the bay. If either of these two try anything, shoot them." She thought about it several moments. "On second thought, I believe I'll take Grant with me. She might decide to play with the transmitter."

Grant threw a frightened look in her direction. "I won't. I swear I won't."

"She's my navigator. I need her."

"You'll get by without her," Victoria said, grabbing a fistful of Grant's tunic and hauling her out of the seat.

"You'll get life for this," Huggins muttered.

Victoria ignored him, shoving Grant toward the exit. They headed for the brig once they'd gained the corridor. Victoria shoved Grant into a cell and locked it.

"We came back for you!" Grant yelled.

Victoria studied her a moment, then moved closer. "We lost three people because you and Huggins abandoned us on that rock, knowing something had wiped out the entire crew that was supposed to be there to meet us," she said through gritted teeth. "Do you honestly think I believe you came back out of the goodness of your hearts? You came back because we were bouncing that distress signal across the universe and you got to worrying that your boss might not cover your ass if we were rescued and got the chance to tell what happened. In fact, you realized that the company would most likely throw you to the wolves as the perfect scapegoat."

Grant's eyes widened. She licked her lips. "That wasn't it! We realized you were in real trouble."

Victoria gave her a look. "How far did you get before it occurred to you that we 'were in real trouble'?"

Grant looked away. As Victoria opened the door to leave, she said, "You're not going to get away with this."

Victoria patted her chest. "I believe, in my heart, that I will."

* * * *

The storm had abated somewhat Victoria saw when she opened the bay doors. Whitecaps still peaked in excess of six feet, but the wind was not gusting nearly as hard as it had been. Victoria hit the com unit. "Brown?"

"Yeah?"

"I'm going down to hook up. Tell him to hold it steady."

"Are you going to be able to handle it by yourself?" Tuttle asked worriedly.

Victoria glanced down at the waves. "I'll manage. Just watch the wench."

Tuttle gave her a thumbs up. "See you when you get back."

Victoria nodded, grabbed the heavy chain and held tightly while Tuttle lowered her. As she reached the water, she expelled the air from her lungs and began breathing through her artificial gill without even thinking about it.

She spotted the containment less than four meters from where she touched down. That was one thing she could say for Huggins. He was a hell of a pilot, with a memory like an elephant. She cupped her hands around the com unit. "Found it. Give me some slack."

The words were garbled because of the water. She had to repeat the words over and over, slowly, tugging on the chain before, finally, Tuttle gave her the slack she needed.

She was securing the last chain when she became aware that she was no longer alone. Grabbing her rifle, she whirled.

Raphael treaded water near by. Surrounding him were the other miners.

We came back to retrieve the injured.

Victoria stared at him a long moment and finally gestured toward the containment with the rifle. *I came back for my people. Get in ... now. Or I'll throw the lot of you in the brig for insubordination.*

Epilogue

Victoria sighed. Dropping her chin to her hand, she stared
dreamily out of the porthole at the view. The company had been
right about some things, but not everything. Raphael had continued
to mature, not at an accelerated rate, and not to a degree where he
was less human than sea creature. But he was a beautiful merman
and sometimes when she studied him, or when she looked at her
beautiful castle in the sea, she felt as if she was living a fairy tale.

A tap on the other side of the glass brought her out of her state of
meditation. She blinked and then smiled at the two faces on the
other side of the glass.

I thought you were working?

I am ... was. I finished.

*Good, because Dante is hungry and I think he's going to start
eating me if you don't feed him soon.*

Victoria laughed. *You should bring him in then. It's time for his
nap anyway.*

She was waiting for them when they emerged from the access
pool. Raphael handed her the wailing infant and climbed out. She
tossed him a towel and wrapped her son in one, crooning to him as
she climbed the stairs to their apartment. She was curled up in the
middle of the bed with the baby at her breast when Raphael reached
the second floor.

He studied her for a long moment and finally strode across the
room and climbed on the bed as well, sprawling on his side behind
her and propping his head in his hand. He stroked the baby's cheek.

Dante frowned, his hand waving a little wildly. Finally, he gripped
Raphael's finger. Raphael chuckled.

"Shhh!" Victoria admonished him. "He's almost asleep."

Raphael retrieved his finger and sat up. Pulling her back against
him, he lowered his head and sucked a love bite on the side of her
neck. Victoria closed her eyes, savoring his nearness. "Where is it?"
he whispered in her ear.

She gave him a look, but pointed toward the ceiling. Taking the
hint, he left her and went up to her studio.

She joined him when she'd settled the baby. "What do you
think?"

He held out a hand to her and pulled her into his arms. "Aren't you tired of doing me?"

Victoria let out a gurgle of laughter and turned in his arms, putting her arms around his neck. "Not yet. Maybe in a hundred years."

He reddened slightly. "I meant the sculpture."

"I know what you meant," she said, still chuckling. "And the answer is, no. And neither are my customers. They love the figurines I do of you. Of course, I'm not stupid enough to think they buy them because they're so good. They buy them because they can't have you."

Raphael's blush deepened, but he smiled, shaking his head. "Your sculptures are beautiful. That's why they buy them. And we don't need the money ... What're you going to call this one?"

Victoria turned to study the figure. It depicted a merman seated on an outcropping of coral, studying the face of the child in his arms, his magnificent tail fin curled around the base of the outcropping for balance. "The merman and his son."

EXILED

Chapter One

Danica Hearn felt her heart rhythm bump up a notch as she spied a dark shadow moving sinuously along the seabed. Her mind instantly broadcast a shark alarm. She was slightly relieved when she saw it was only a baby and wasn't even one of the 'man eaters', but not much. To her way of thinking, sharks were like snakes or spiders--the world wasn't big enough for her and them.

She checked her watch again for the fifth time in as many minutes and sighed. *Why in God's name am I doing this?*

The water was beautiful, and the tropical fish stunning, but the plain truth was scuba diving just wasn't for her. The ocean gave her the creeps. She didn't know why she'd persisted in taking the damned lessons.

Some vacation!

The really stupid part was that she'd had this half-baked notion that it would be a good way to meet men and make herself more desirable- to them. Sports minded gals seemed to have men flocking around them all the time, but learning to scuba dive wasn't going to make her like sports any better. She hated sports.

Disgusted, she looked around for her diving partner to let her know she was going back up to the boat.

Her heart, which had only just regained its natural rhythm, commenced to thudding in dismay once more when she'd done a 360 and hadn't seen a sign of her partner--whatshername.

Calm down, Danica. The nitwit's got to be around here somewhere.

Slowly, she did another turn. Dimly, in the distance and fading fast, she *saw the moron.* Diving might not have been quite as nerve wracking if she hadn't been paired with a woman who had no fear-- because she was too stupid to have any imagination, had no sense of direction, and topped that off by being as easily distracted by a flash of color as a six month old child.

She'd probably gotten a glimpse of a school of tropical fish and was following them to take another hundred pictures or so.

Danica stared at the retreating form with a mixture of dismay, irritation and indecision.

Indecision wasn't something she was accustomed to. Ordinarily, she had no trouble at all assessing a situation and making a sound judgment call. In this particular case, however, she was torn between the diver's rules which stated diving buddies were supposed to stick together, a completely natural reluctance to take a chance on getting lost, and an irrational sense of responsibility for a woman whose name she couldn't even remember.

Glancing up, she could see the bottom of the boat bobbing on the surface of the water above her. After another moment's hesitancy, she started after the nitwit, deciding to make an honest effort to retrieve her before she was permanently lost at sea. She'd be safe enough as long as she kept her eye on the boat.

She began swimming, stopping occasionally to look up and locate the boat. She could not tell that she was gaining any headway on the vanishing woman, however, and finally stopped and looked for the boat once more.

It was much further away than she liked.

She checked her watch and saw that she'd used fifteen minutes of her air already.

Looking around once more for the woman, she started back, ascending gradually as she headed toward the now distant boat. She'd just begun to breathe a sigh of relief when a strange sensation swept over her. Confused, she stopped and glanced around. The water around her seemed to be swirling. Her heart jerked uncomfortably in her chest as she felt the pull.

Fighting off a sense of panic, Danica began to swim harder, struggling to free herself from the whirlpool. Within moments, she was totally disoriented and realized that she was moving with the circular current, not across it. She struggled harder, unable to see beyond the swirling water now but uncaring where she exited so long as she managed to swim through it.

It wasn't until she began to tire that she noticed something she hadn't noticed before. Her stomach wasn't just tight with fear. A sensation of weightlessness gripped her.

It stopped abruptly. The water settled. Too frightened by now to consider the advisability of surfacing too fast, Danica took a moment to orient herself and began swimming upward as fast as she could propel herself.

She drove her head into something so hard she felt a bone in her spine creak ominously. For several moments, darkness encroached. Completely disoriented, Danica put one hand on her pounding head and reached upward with the other. Her hand met something solid. The boat?

But how could it be the boat? She'd still been a long way from the boat when the whirlpool had caught her.

Slowly, the pain and confusion began to subside. The darkness didn't and Danica realized it wasn't just the crack on the head that had brought it about. It wasn't imminent unconsciousness, or at least not entirely. It *was* dark, suddenly, for no apparent reason.

She wondered with a touch of panic if it was possible that it was night time, that she'd knocked herself unconscious and lost hours. It didn't take much thought in that direction to supply her with a vision of a search party, calling, unanswered, the search party giving up and departing…. It didn't 'feel' like natural dark, though. Wouldn't the water be lit with moonlight? Or starlight, at least, if her fear was a reality?

Flipping her legs, she swam upward once more, cautiously, with one arm extended above her head. Her hand broke the surface of the water and touched something cold and metallic.

The hull of the boat would be in the water, not above it.

She began to follow it, feeling her way along the surface. It was perfectly smooth, and although she felt around for some time, she could find no end to it. The hard surface seemed to go on forever.

Fear crept its way up her spine. Try though she might to block the ticking minutes from her mind it hammered as insistently in her brain as her heart pounded in her chest.

She was going to run out of air.

Balling her hand into a fist, she began pounding on the solid panel above her. She pounded until she was tired and had to stop to rest, then began hammering again. She'd just begun to wonder if she could somehow manage to fit her nose and mouth in the tiny space between the panel and the water and suck in air when light suddenly flooded the area around her.

Blinded, Danica covered her face mask with her hand, closing her eyes. When she finally lowered her hand and opened her eyes a small crack, a wave of shock and horror washed through her.

She wasn't in the ocean anymore.

She was in a tank. It wasn't people staring at her through the windows along the sides, however.

Chapter Two

Mindlessly, Danica fled from the inhuman faces pressed against the glass, staring at her. She nearly slammed into the shark that occupied the tank with her. It whipped around, circled.

Danica stared blankly at the thing as it switched directions again and headed for her. Bits and pieces of memory blinked through her brain. Like the voice on a radio full of static, she caught a thought here and there.

She was not really conscious of cognition, however. She remained as perfectly still as possible, her eyes glued to the large predator as it moved closer and closer. The moment she saw its eyes roll back in its head, she swung her fist at its snout and kicked as hard as she could to propel herself out of its path.

She missed, but so did the shark.

It was difficult to say whether she was more terrified of the shark or the alien creatures, who seemed completely disinterested in her predicament beyond the entertainment value of watching a joust to the death between a human and a shark that was half again her size and had a mouth big enough to swallow half of her whole.

She discovered fairly quickly that the devil she knew completely absorbed her attention.

With an effort, she dragged her gaze from the shark long enough to look around for any possibility of saving herself.

The tank was not a particularly large one, and there was nothing in it beyond sea water, her, the shark, and a smattering of other sea creatures that had had the misfortune to get in the way of whatever the hell the aliens had used to scoop them from the sea.

There was no place to hide.

There didn't seem to be a lot of point in remaining perfectly still either. The shark knew she was there. She struck out toward the windows where the aliens watched, keeping one eye on the predator that was stalking her. He made another swoop at her before she reached the side of the tank. This time, although she managed to avoid his jaws, he caught her with his fins as she dodged him.

She headed for the viewing windows the moment the thing swam away again, plastering her back against it, waiting. The shark made another circuit of the tank and headed for her again. She braced her palms against the window behind her. At the last minute, when it began its roll, she pushed herself away.

The shark smacked into the glass so hard she was a little surprised it didn't rupture.

She dragged her gaze from the shark long enough to see how the aliens had reacted.

Two of them were on the floor. The third was plastered against the wall on the opposite side of the tank. She shot them a bird and moved in front of the window again.

The second time the shark plowed into the observation window, a hatch opened in the smooth panel above the tank.

Danica stared at it as a ladder was slowly lowered, wondering if she could trust the bastards.

She didn't have a lot of options. She could try it, wait until she ran out of air, or wait till the shark figured out her game and caught her.

Pushing away from the wall, she swam toward the hatch.

The shark seemed confused by her sudden movement toward him. He veered away, made another circuit.

Reaching the ladder, Danica grabbed the bottom rung and looked around for the shark, trying to decide if she could make it up before the thing got close enough to bite her. Deciding she had as much time as she was likely to get, she began climbing for all she was worth.

The shark caught her flipper as she levered herself over the lip of the hatch, tearing it from her foot, but she managed to get all of her body parts out. Collapsing on the deck, she closed her eyes, trying to still her racing heart. When she opened her eyes again, four of the alien things were standing around her, staring down at her.

They were humanoid only in the sense that they had the general body shape, two arms, two legs, one head. They were long, skinny and disproportionate in human terms--very long, bug-like arms, legs and torso, big head. She thought at first that their skin was gray, but realized after a moment that it was some sort of form fitting uniform. Their skin, at least in the artificial light, was a nasty yellow/green color.

It made her felt queasy herself, just looking at them, but that might also be because she'd experienced so many levels of terror in the last fifteen or twenty minutes that her stomach, heart, and asshole seemed permanently clenched.

Deciding to ignore them, she sat up, pulling her face mask and the hood of her wet suit off. She was on the point of dropping her mouth piece when it occurred to her that breathable air to them might not be breathable to her. She checked her watch. At the most, she had ten minutes of air left in her tank.

She was surprised she had that much the way she'd been breathing.

Wait till she ran out? Or test the air now?

She took a cautious whiff through her nostrils. A strange, almost sweet taste filled her mouth. A wave of dizziness followed.

She sucked air from her tank, trying to calm herself enough to think it over.

The taste and smell reminded her a lot of the 'laughing gas' her dentist used to calm terrified patients. Nitrous oxide?

Maybe, but even if it was she was no chemistry whiz. If she was right, and it was, a little might make her high, but it shouldn't kill her. The question was, just what was the ratio?

She took the mouth piece out and looked up at the aliens. "Look, you! I'm not a fucking fish, so how about putting me back?" She plugged the mouthpiece back in when she'd finished and took a drag of air.

The discussion that met that demand was completely incomprehensible to her, but she got the impression they were arguing. After a moment, they seized her and dragged her to her feet. She didn't like the aggressiveness they displayed and began struggling. They were surprisingly strong, however, for creatures that looked like walking skeletons with an ounce or two of skin and meat stretched over it.

Obviously, they came from a world where the insects had won the toss up on the evolutionary ladder.

Dragging her from the room, they started down a narrow corridor. She tripped on the one flipper she still wore, but they didn't pause long enough for her to get the flopping thing off her foot so she had to propel herself along, one normal step, one high step to keep from tripping again.

Observation windows lined the corridor they followed and Danica twisted her head from side to side, trying to peer through the windows as they passed. She glimpsed a number of creatures, most of which were like nothing she'd ever seen before. As they moved a along the corridor, however, she began to catch glimpses of animals that did seem to be of Earth origins.

She would've liked to be certain, but she was surrounded by the aliens, and they were pulling her along too fast to catch more than an occasional glimpse.

It became obvious, however, that this was some sort of expedition to collect various species of lower life forms--either for scientific study, or a menagerie.

She tried to decide if the things hauling her along the corridor seemed more like scientists or hunters. The air in her tank gave out about that time, however, and she reached her moment of truth.

By the time she'd dragged in a few breaths of their air, they weren't dragging her resisting any longer. They were half carrying her. It took an effort to hold her head upright. Her thoughts quickly became disjointed and random.

Finally, they stopped before a door. Air gushed from the opening as the door slid back into the wall. The aliens gave her a shove through the portal and the door closed again.

Danica sprawled on the floor, gasping. Slowly, the fog in her brain began to clear. She realized after a few minutes that she was breathing a mixture of gases that closely approximated Earth's atmosphere.

They'd thrown her into one of the specimen cages. The moment that thought filtered through her disoriented mind, her head popped up and she looked around. The small room was empty--completely vacant of anything except her. Shivering, she rolled over, sat up and released the empty air tanks. She pulled her utility belt off too, dropping it to the floor beside her and finally reached down and removed the lone flipper.

She stared at the pile of scuba diving equipment for some moments, trying to decide if there was anything at all useful there for her current situation. The set of tanks were empty, and too heavy for her to launch at her captors with any accuracy or impact. Once out of the water, it took an effort even to lift them.

The belt had a flashlight hooked to it, but nothing else.

The belt was weighted though. Grabbing the belt, she moved to the back corner, drew her knees up and waited. She was cold and knew it was from shock. The wetsuit helped to hold in her body heat. She was wearing tropical gear, however, and it was little more than a bathing suit, covering her torso and nothing else. Her arms, legs and feet were bare, but the decking beneath her felt warm to the touch. It warmed her feet and slowly began to work its way through her shivering body.

Laying her belt close at hand, Danica wrapped her arms around her knees and lay her cheek on the tops of her knees, wondering if she was to become a display in a menagerie or a lab rat.

Chapter Three

Danica had begun to think she was going to be forced to the indignity of relieving herself on the floor when the door to her cell opened. One alien stood in the doorway, blocking any attempts to escape--and what would be the point?--Two others rushed in and out with a number of canisters of varying size and shape, and a pad she had to suppose was for sleeping.

When they'd left again, she examined the canisters. One contained a clear liquid she thought must be water. A second had something horrible in it that vaguely resembled baby food. The third was empty.

She looked it over and finally decided it was supposed to be her potty. Revulsion filled her. She glanced toward the window.

One of the aliens was standing at it, peering at her.

She shot him a bird.

An urge toward violence rose in her breast. It wasn't often that she felt more than a mild urge to become physically violent, but she felt a powerful one just then, considering, with a good deal of satisfaction, wringing their scrawny necks one by one and pissing on their twitching carcasses for good measure.

When the face disappeared, she gathered up the pad and moved to one corner with her potty.

The things a person had to do just to get a little damned privacy!

Except for the fact that she had to drip dry, which offended her sense of fastidiousness, she felt better. The canister was as far as they'd gone toward sanitation. Securing the top, she set it down, fastened the crotch of her wetsuit and tossed the thin pad toward the far wall. Opening the container that appeared to have water, she tipped a small amount into her palm and sniffed it, then rubbed the liquid over her hands, assuring herself that the salt from the water probably purified them enough that a little water was all she really needed to clean them again.

Right!

If she was going to eat, she was going to have to do it with her fingers.

She wasn't hungry anyway, she decided.

* * * *

There was no sense of movement around her. Danica felt the walls and the floor but couldn't detect so much as a slight vibration. It seemed a great deal of time passed, but she didn't know if her watch was still working right or not. The hands seemed to be moving with agonizing slowness.

Exhaustion overcame her after a while. She dozed. After she'd nearly fallen over two or three times, she crawled onto the thin pallet and curled into a tight ball. She was so hungry when she woke, she decided to try a few bites of the baby food. If she didn't start puking or running off, she could eat a little more later.

She discovered it *was* something like baby food. It didn't have much of a taste at all. It was easily digested, though.

By her calculations, two days passed.

On the third, four aliens came, grabbed her and dragged her from her cell. It might have been the same four that had put her there. She couldn't tell a great deal of difference in their features.

They didn't give her air to breathe. Within a few moments of leaving the cell, her head was swimming and she was too disoriented to figure out what was going on. The took her to a room that looked like some sort of machine. The walls were rounded, and covered in electronics. After placing her in the center, one of the aliens tossed a bag-like object on the floor next to her and the four departed.

With an effort, Danica sat up, looking around her and trying to figure out what was going on.

The walls around her began to hum, but even fear failed to pierce the drugged confusion of her brain. Abruptly, her body felt as if it was vibrating. A sensation flowed over her that felt like fire ants were crawling all over her, stinging her. She squeezed her eyes closed, began brushing drunkenly and completely ineffectually at her skin.

Blackness suddenly engulfed her. A few moments later, it vanished.

The stinging sensation had disappeared, as well. She drew in a ragged breath, choked, coughed and finally dragged in a decent breath. It tasted strange on her tongue, but didn't have the sweet taste of the alien atmosphere.

Opening her eyes, she stared up at a brilliant blue sky.

She jerked upright and looked around.

She wasn't on the alien ship anymore, but she had no clue of where the hell she was. The landscape around her was rocky, the vegetation sparse and completely unrecognizable.

She had a very bad feeling this wasn't home.

She wasn't entirely sure why she felt that way. It looked like it *could* be Earth, but something just didn't seem right … maybe the fact that they'd been traveling, she knew, for days.

Shakily, she got to her feet and looked around. The sun was dipping toward the horizon. It looked a lot closer than it should have, and a lot redder.

There was something very strange besides that.

She felt--lighter. She thought at first that her slightly uncoordinated movements were the aftereffect of whatever she'd been breathing.

She was still trying to convince herself she was suffering from paranoia and the effects of the gases of the alien atmosphere she'd been breathing in the ship when a distant sound caught her attention. Instinctively, she turned to look.

Something huge was coming in her direction. It looked to be roughly the size of a small, single engine plane, but it was flapping its wings.

"Son-of-a-bitch! Those dirty, rotten, low down, fucking bastards!" Looking wildly around for cover, Danica saw that the nearest thing where she might hide was a patch of scrubby looking brush. She hit for it--literally.

There might not be much difference in the gravity, but it was enough her muscles were having a little difficulty adjusting. She scrambled most of the way on her hands and knees. She'd barely collapsed in the thicket when a shadow fell over her hiding place.

She froze, holding her breath, expecting any moment to feel sharp talons biting into her. A gust of wind ruffled the brush around her and passed on, along with the shadow. Cautiously, Danica lifted her head and peered through the leaves.

There was something on the bird's back that looked a lot like a person. Long, golden hair streamed around the thing, but she could only see bare patches of what looked like skin and the hair.

The bird banked and headed back in her direction.

"Shit!" Either it had seen her scrambling into the brush or she wasn't nearly as well concealed by the vegetation as she'd thought. She crouched lower, pulling herself into a tight little ball. Her hair was dark and hung half way down her back and the wetsuit was black, but she had a bad feeling there was a lot more pale skin exposed than hidden by hair and wetsuit and that it didn't blend particularly well with her surroundings.

She was certain of it when she heard a flurry of wings and the distinct sound of something heavy settling on the ground close by.

Cautiously, she lifted her head and peered through the web of hair over her face.

A wave of something strongly akin to awe went through her. The creature staring at her through the brush he'd parted looked a lot like a human male, except for the fact that she'd never in her entire life seen one that looked so completely flawless. He reminded her strongly of a Greek statute of a god, except that his face was far more perfectly symmetrical than the most talented artist could manage.

His hair was almost perfectly straight and fell nearly to his waist.

It was practically the only thing he was wearing. Except for some sort of harness thing that crisscrossed his chest, and something that looked more like a jock strap than a loincloth, he was completely and utterly naked, displaying a body that many a weight lifter would envy.

And then there were the eyes. Even from three feet away, she could see they weren't the color of any natural human eye. They were a brilliant aquamarine and surrounded by very dark, very long, curling lashes.

He made a summoning gesture with his hand, but since he accompanied that very recognizable motion with a completely unrecognizable verbal command, Danica began to scramble backwards.

He looked human.

He wasn't.

He came to his feet as she reached the limits of her 'hiding' spot. Danica scrambled to her feet, as well, and whirled to flee. Behind her she heard the man emit a strange warbling noise. She wasn't certain what the significance of it was until the bird dropped into her path.

Skidding to a halt, Danica stared at the thing.

It looked like something that had escaped from an old 'attack of the giants' horror movie, much like a typical Earth bird of prey, except that she had to look up to look it in the eye.

Danica swerved, heading off at a tangent. The bird hopped into her path once more and she skidded to a halt. She feinted to the left, waited until the bird hopped in that direction to cut her off, then shifted her weight and took off in the opposite direction.

She heard the rustle of great wings a moment before something struck her in the middle of the back hard enough it knocked her off her feet.

Chapter Four

Talons curled around one of Danica's ankles. She dug her fingers into the scrubby grass-like vegetation and came away with two handfuls as the bird began dragging her by her ankle.

With an effort, she rolled onto her back and hurled the clods of dirt and grass at the bird. One dirt bomb caught him in the eye. He let out a war whoop. A ruff of feathers around his neck stood out threateningly. Releasing his grip on her leg, the bird jumped into the air and landed on her leg. Danica screamed in rage as much as pain, grabbing up handfuls of rocks and dirt and throwing them at the bird as hard and fast as she could.

From behind her, she heard the warbling noise, or something similar, and the bird abruptly backed off. He made it clear, however, that he was only doing so reluctantly. Opening his beak and stretching his neck toward her, he emitted a shrill screech, then began to pace around her, flicking dirt at her with his talons.

Covering her face to protect her eyes from the debris the bird was flinging at her, Danica had managed to get to her knees when a hand clamped around her upper arm like a vice. She was jerked to her feet as if she weighed no more than a child.

Turning, she gaped at the furious face of the blond god, who promptly pelted her with a barrage of gibberish, gesturing toward the bird.

She didn't need to understand the words to realize he was cussing her for all she was worth, however, and her own anger surged forth. "I hope I did blind the damned thing!" she shouted at him. "If I had a butter knife, I'd saw his damned head off! That son-of-a-bitch attacked me, and *you* siced him on me!" she ended, jabbing him in the chest with one index finger.

He looked down at the finger she'd jabbed him with, then back at her face, his eyes narrowing dangerously.

Danica felt a knee weakening rush of fear as she realized she'd allowed her temper to deprive her of common sense. This being might look human, but she knew damned well he wasn't. What she didn't know was what he might be capable of.

She did know, however, that he was a good head taller than her and strong enough he'd just jerked a one hundred twenty pound woman up by one arm as if she weighed less than fifty. After a moment, to her relief, he merely turned and began dragging her with him as he marched back toward the spot where she'd been deposited by the aliens.

Releasing her arm, he pointed to a spot on the ground imperiously. Danica stared at him a moment and finally decided he was commanding her to sit. It went against the grain to simply drop meekly, but as strong willed as she was, she was not stupid. She could do it, or he could make her do it.

Resentfully, she settled, glaring at him, but the moment he fixed her with his frowning gaze, she wiped all expression from her face and merely looked back at him blankly.

Apparently satisfied that he'd cowed her, he picked up the bag the alien had thrown at her just before they'd dumped her on this godforsaken rock, opened it and poured the contents onto the ground, rifling through it. Danica studied the various things the bag held. Nothing looked familiar to her, but, as she studied it, she began to realize that it was a survival pack--at least the alien's notion of a survival pack.

She supposed that was salve to their conscience. They'd stolen her from her home, dropped her god only knew where, but they'd left her a fucking knapsack with enough in it to survive for a day or two--which was now in the hands of the alien whose world she'd been dumped on.

After a moment, he picked up a tiny bullet looking object from among the things on the ground. Lifting it, he studied it for a moment, blew the dirt off of it and moved toward her.

Danica immediately scrambled back. Catching her by one thigh, he dragged her toward him. She planted the foot of her free leg in the middle of his chest and gave him a shove. Since he had crouched to grab her, the push was enough to throw him off balance. He let out a roar of fury as he landed on his back in the middle of the spoils from her pack.

Danica rolled onto her knees. Before she'd managed to lever herself to her feet, however, he landed on her back, flattening her against the ground and knocking the wind from her. She grabbed two handfuls of dirt as he rolled her to her back, but he'd gotten that trick down pat. He grabbed both wrists with his hands, squeezing until her hand went numb and the debris she held began to rain down on her face. Squeezing her eyes shut, spluttering, Danica wrestled him blindly, trying to pull her hands free. She managed to get one knee between them. He shoved it aside with his elbow and landed on top of her again, driving something long, very hard and cylindrical in shape against her pubic bone so hard it brought tears to her eyes.

She ceased struggling instantly, panting for breath, trying to blink the dirt from her eyes so that she could see his expression and decide whether what she thought she felt was what she was actually feeling digging into her belly.

When she stopped fighting, he placed a knee on the ground on either side of her hips and sat up. Pulling her upright, he twisted her arms behind her back, caught both of her wrists in one very large hand and then looked around. Locating the object he'd dropped, he rubbed it against his chest, blew on it and leaned toward her with it.

Danica didn't know what the fuck the thing was, but she sure as hell wasn't going to just sit still and let him shove it into any of her orifices. She jerked at her arms, trying to pull her wrists free, leaning away from him. He bellowed something at her angrily, but she ignored him and continued to struggle to avoid him.

Releasing her arms, he shoved her against the ground once more, brought her arms to her sides and pinned her hands to the dirt with his knees. Grasping her face with one hand, he twisted her head to one side and shoved the thing in her ear.

Danica screamed, expecting any second to feel her brain explode.

He twisted her face so that she was looking at him, covering her mouth with one hand.

"You understand now?"

Danica blinked at him. Slowly, chagrin enveloped her as it dawned upon her that she'd been fighting him tooth and nail when all he, apparently, intended to do was to insert some sort of translator in her ear. She nodded.

"Good. You slave of Taj."

Danica felt her jaw go slack. Obviously the translator wasn't working that well. In the first place, it seemed to skip words here and there, making it really difficult to follow what he was saying. In the second, it seemed to substitute the untranslatable rather freely. "Excuse me, but I don't think I caught that last."

He frowned. "Woman own Taj now."

Somehow, she had the feeling that hadn't come out just as he'd intended, but clearly he thought just because he'd caught her like some caveman that she belonged to him.

"Look. I don't belong to anybody. Aliens kidnapped me and dumped me here. I'm aware I'm probably trespassing, but if you'll just point me in the right direction, I'll be on my way," she said reasonably.

"Dump all time. Sometime good things, sometime bad."

Releasing her hands, he got to his feet, then reached down and yanked her up. Danica flexed her throbbing hands, rubbing them. "You're going to let me go then?"

"No."

"Look! I'm a person, a free person. You can't just capture me and decide you own me."

"Have," he said indifferently, tightening his hand around her arm and leading her toward the bird.

Danica gaped at the scowling bird as he dragged her toward it. "You don't expect me to get on that thing!"

"Yes. Carry both."

"I'd just as soon he didn't carry both, thank you!" she snapped. "I'm not getting on that thing!"

His lips tightened. Moving to the bird, he held her with one hand and dug around in the pack on the animal's back with the other. Producing a long strip of some sort of hide, he caught both of her hands, pulled her arms together in front of her and bound her wrists together, then grasped her around the waist and hoisted her atop the bird.

As terrified as she was at the thought of riding the thing, it had an attitude toward her already, and she couldn't quite work up the nerve to start kicking at it. She stared at the head of the bird wide eyed as the barbarian that had captured her climbed up behind her. Grasping the reins attached to the bird's hood, he uttered one of those strange, warbling commands and the bird launched itself into the air.

For several moments, she suffered the hope that the bird actually wouldn't manage to become airborne with the two of them on its back. Sluggishly, flapping its wings in long, hard movements, it rose. Danica caught two hands full of feathers, trying hard not to think about how easily the feathers might part from the bird's hide. If he hadn't bound her wrists, she would've wrapped her arms around its neck.

After several terrifying minutes, Taj grasped her around the waist and dragged her back against his chest, holding her securely. It was almost enough to make her feel safe.

Chapter Five

Danica was far too frightened to look down. For the first twenty minutes or so, she couldn't even bring herself to open her eyes. When she finally did nerve herself to crack her eyelids enough to peek, she saw trees directly beneath them. She closed her eyes again, gripping the feathers even tighter as she felt the bird dip and her stomach went weightless.

She quickly discovered it wasn't just a 'bump'. The bird made a slow, spiraling descent. Her head swam sickeningly and she squeezed her eyes more tightly, promising herself that if she had to go up on the bird again she was going to be nice so that Taj didn't tie her wrists next time. At least then she could hold onto something more substantial than a wad of fucking feathers.

A squeak of fear tore from her throat as she felt a sharp jolt, but the cessation of movement was sufficient enticement to open her eyes. To her relief, she saw that they'd landed in a clearing near a tiny brook.

Sliding from the bird, Taj turned, caught her around the waist and swung her down. The moment he let go of her, her knees buckled and she landed in a heap. He plunked his hands on his hips, frowning down at her. "No rest now. Make camp."

With an effort, Danica struggled to her feet and looked around. "This doesn't look like any camp ground I've ever seen," she muttered, but then she'd only actually seen them in pictures before. She wasn't really 'in' to nature. It was rather a lot like sports--way too physical, uncomfortable, and unhygienic for her taste.

He caught her face in one hand, forcing her to look at him. "Make camp," he said slowly. "I hunt food."

Danica blinked at him. "How am I supposed to do that?"

He studied her for several moments and finally rolled his eyes. Obviously irritated, he untied her wrists, then gripped her around one arm. After looking around for a moment, he dragged her to a spot that was nearly bare of vegetation and pointed at the ground. "Here fire." He pointed to the area around it. "There sleep."

"On the ground!" Danica demanded, outraged.

He gave her a look. "See bed?"

"Has anyone ever told you that sarcasm is very unattractive in a man?"

Ignoring her, he strode to the bird and pulled the packs from it's back, dropped them on the ground and removed the hood and the saddle. Danica studied him speculatively, but decided he was just too close to try to make a break for it. He'd said he was going to hunt for food. He'd have to leave her alone to do that. She decided just to wait and see which direction he took and flee in the other direction.

When he glanced at her, she trained her eyes on the ground and began a search for anything that might burn. She discovered when she straightened from picking up a small piece of wood that he was studying her in much the same way she had him only moments before.

Taking the leather thong he'd used to bind her wrists, he tied his hair back. When he did, she saw that the straps that crisscrossed his chest were there to secure a scabbard along his back--a scabbard that held a really big sword. She returned her attention to searching halfheartedly for wood when he crouched beside his pack and began looking through it. When she glanced at him again, she saw he was standing beside the bird, talking to it. Slung over his shoulder was a quiver full of arrows and a long bow.

She had a bad feeling about the conversation he was having with that damned bird, especially when he lifted his arm and gestured around the clearing.

Spying another piece of wood, she made her way to it carefully and bent to pick it up. Straightening, she turned to carry the pieces she'd found back to the area he'd ordered her to build a fire and discovered he'd closed the distance between them. She jumped, dropping all three limbs.

He stared down at the three branches, frowning. When he looked up at her again, his eyes were narrowed with suspicion. "Expect cook with that? Keep warm?"

Danica studied the twigs wryly and finally shrugged. "There aren't any trees here. And even if I could find anything bigger, and move it, how would I cut it?"

He caught her jaw and bent his head towards her until they were practically nose to nose. "Have fire when Taj return ... or have regret."

Danica stared at him blankly while the words slowly sank in. Fortunately, just about the time comprehension hit her, and anger surged through her, another realization did also.

She was alone on an alien world with a man who held her life in his hands. He could do anything he pleased to her and there was no one to stop him. This was no boy friend that she could manipulate by refusing to put out if he pissed her off, or pitching him out of her apartment. This was a primitive being whose culture she knew absolutely nothing about.

She swallowed the knot of fear in her throat. "I don't know how to make a fire," she said weakly.

He frowned, studying her in patent disbelief for several moments. "How woman cook?"

Danica's lips twisted wryly. "Uh … microwave. Actually, I don't know how to cook either. I usually just buy stuff already cooked and warm it up."

Releasing her jaw, he looked her over from the top of her head to her toes. Finally, he grabbed a handful of breast and gave it an experimental squeeze. Danica was still gasping over that when he slipped his hand between her legs and examined her genitals. "Are woman?"

Rational thought went out the window. Danica glared at him. "Do you see a damned spatula growing out of my pussy? I fail to see why it should be automatic that a person born with tits and a cunt has to know how to cook to be a woman!"

Something suspiciously like humor gleamed in his eyes for about two seconds before he banished it. "Evil tongued woman."

Danica gave him the evil eye, but she'd remembered her situation by that time and refrained from giving him another taste of her malevolent tongue. "Actually," she said placatingly, "I don't imagine you'll find me very useful as a slave at all, because I'm not used to this sort of thing and … I'm very good at my job, but I can't imagine you'd have much use for an office manager, so you might just as well let me go."

"No!"

Danica sighed. "But … it's not at all like this where I'm from and I don't know how to do anything you're bound to want me to do."

His gaze slid down her length in a slow, thorough appraisal. When he met her gaze once more, his eyes gleamed with humor and something else she couldn't quite identify. "I teach. You learn."

Danica stared after him slack jawed as he turned and strode away. If she hadn't known better, she would've strongly suspected he'd just made a suggestive remark to her!

She frowned, thinking it over and finally decided she was probably wrong.

In the first place, he'd not only wallowed all over her when he'd first caught her, he'd felt her up, and he hadn't seemed to have that much interest in her in that direction. Of course, she was fairly sure he'd had an erection when they were wrestling over the translator, but then that didn't necessarily mean anything, particularly since he hadn't made any attempt at all to have sex with her. She certainly wasn't hot every time her nipples got hard.

Besides that, from what she'd seen so far, on the scale of civilization, he seemed to be on a level with the wild Indians of the old west. In fact, except for that blond hair and those blue eyes--and the sword--he reminded her of an Indian, or at least Hollywood's interpretation of an Indian.

If he'd wanted to fuck, he probably wouldn't use a lot of finesse. He'd just throw her on the ground and hump her. He wouldn't be making sexual innuendoes.

Of course, the translator could be responsible for the strange way he talked. It seemed to skip words at random, as if they weren't translatable. It was also possible, indeed likely, that the sentence structure of his native tongue was completely different and that accounted for a good bit of the strangeness.

She wondered if her speech sounded as strange to him as vice versa.

Even though it had been obvious he was familiar with the devise and knew its use, she'd wondered how it was that he could understand her, until she'd noticed he was wearing one of the devices in his ear.

Evidently those alien bastards made a habit of discarding whatever they decided they didn't want on this planet.

It occurred to her then that she might not be the first human to find themselves exiled on this primitive world, light years from home. Briefly, hope surged through her, but it died a quick death. Even if there were others, and even if the aliens habitually used the same spot for dumping, what were the chances she'd manage to find them?

Dismissing the thoughts finally, she looked down at the sticks she'd dropped, then over at the bird speculatively. Picking them up, she moved to the collection spot and dropped them, then began to work her way toward the woods, picking up a branch here and there.

The bird met her at the edge of the clearing.

Pretending she hadn't noticed the damned thing was blocking her path, she turned and carried the wood she'd gathered back to the camp area. She discovered, though, that no matter how casually she wandered toward the woods, the bird always managed to block any chance of slipping away.

She would've tried to make a dash for it except that the bird had already attacked her once and she didn't want to know what it might do if Taj wasn't around to call it off.

Accepting defeat, she finally realized that she'd been so intent on trying to escape that she hadn't gathered more than a handful of branches in all the time Taj had been gone. She wasn't exactly sure of what he'd promised her if she didn't do as she was told, but she was sure she didn't want to find out. She set to work then with a will, combing the area for anything small enough to drag. Finally, when she decided she had a pile big enough to appease the savage, she looked the ground over carefully and sat down to wait for him to return.

Chapter Six

It was nearly dark by the time Taj returned. Danica had begun to grow increasingly uneasy as the sunset and the clearing where she sat grew dimmer and dimmer. Taj had dumped the things out of the pack the aliens had given her and then left it. She had no idea whether there'd been anything in it to provide light, but if there had been she certainly didn't have it now.

There were animals in the woods. As soon as the light began to fade all sorts of hidden, unknown denizens of the forest began to make noises. Every time something new added its voice to the growing chorus Danica jumped and whirled, peering into the deepening gloom to make certain it wasn't as close as it sounded like it was.

She didn't know why it hadn't occurred to her when she was working so hard to slip through Taj's grasp that, without him, she was completely alone in an alien, and probably hostile, untamed wilderness.

She supposed it was only that she was so used to depending upon herself and muddling through just fine. In the back of her mind, she really hadn't accepted that there was no civilization out there waiting for her to find it, that she would not make her way through the woods and stumble upon a highway, a gas station--a country residence.

Even acknowledging it, trying to wrap her mind around the inconceivability of no civilization to run to was like trying to grasp infinity.

When she finally heard a rustle of movement in the brush that indicated something large was coming toward her, she leapt to her feet, poised for flight. She felt like bursting into tears of relief when Taj stepped into view, carrying a couple of limp, dead things. It took an effort to restrain herself from rushing over to him and throwing her arms around him.

He threw her a curious look as he dropped his bow and quiver by his pack. Turning to her once more, he made a 'come here' gesture and headed for the creek. Still feeling a little weak in the knees, Danica followed him, standing over him as he squatted beside a stone and lay the dead things on it. He looked up at her after a moment. "Kneel here."

Slightly miffed at the command, Danica crouched beside him. Without another word, he pulled a knife from his belt and cut the animals from neck to groin. Danica felt a wave of blackness rush over her. When she finally managed to fend it off, she discovered she'd gripped Taj's arm.

He was frowning at her disapprovingly. "No close the eyes. You watch, you learn. Can't watch eyes closed."

Danica swallowed with an effort. "You want me to learn how to do that?" she asked a little sickly as she watched him remove the innards and toss them aside.

He studied her assessingly for several moments. "You eat, you work. You no work, you no eat."

That was certainly to the point.

It wasn't that she minded working. She worked, or had worked, on Earth for food, shelter--vacations, beautiful clothes. Sniffing at the wave of self-pity those thoughts evoked, she focused on what he was doing, mentally kicking herself in the ass.

Whether she was with Taj or managed to escape, she damned well better learn it if she didn't want to starve to death--which she didn't. It wasn't like there was take-out around here, or even a good old grocery store that had the meat cleaned, chopped and neatly packaged.

Despite her certainty that he was giving her a lesson in survival, however, she thought for several moments that she was going to puke when he stuck the other animal at her and indicated that she was to do what he'd just done. Closing her eyes, she ripped the guts out, trying not to think about the fact that the inside of the carcass felt warm and sticky and that her hands were now covered in blood and probably even worse stuff that she'd rather not think about.

When she thought she'd probably got most of it, she peered at the thing through her lashes, her lips curled in revulsion. Taj, shaking his head, took the thing from her and hacked its head off. She almost did throw up then.

Instead, when he took the knife and began peeling the skin off, she felt backwards on her ass, wavered for several moments while darkness closed in on her and finally drifted down toward the ground. A cold splash of water brought her around. She sat up, gasping, brushing at the water.

It wasn't until she tasted something disgusting on her lips that she remembered the blood and guts all over her hands. She stared down at her hands and the reddish water dripping off her face, then looked up at Taj, horrified.

He was grinning.

With a growl of fury, she came up off the ground swinging. Surprise flickered over his face briefly. He leapt out of range and Danica missed him.

She was far more interested in getting the goo off her face, at the moment, however, than cutting his heart out. After swinging at him halfheartedly several times, she stalked to the little creek and scrubbed her hands, then her face.

She would've liked some antibacterial soap. Even after she'd scrubbed until her face and hands felt numb, she felt contaminated.

Finally, dripping, she turned to look for Taj.

He'd moved to the pile of wood she'd dragged up and was breaking the longer pieces into shorter ones and arranging them. As she watched, he picked up something he'd lain on the ground next to him while he broke the wood up and began stroking it with his thumb. Abruptly, fire erupted from the tip.

Danica shot to her feet, forgetting her anger in that instant. "That's a lighter!"

Taj glanced at her sharply. Frowning, he returned his attention to the wad of dry grass he held in one hand. When the grass had caught fire, he dropped it on the wood, watching it smolder and finally catch.

Danica stalked over to him. "Let me see it!" she demanded.

He gave her a long look and finally stood, towering over her. Very deliberately, he shoved it into the pouch that held his cods, then folded his arms over his chest with a look of smug satisfaction.

Danica glared at him, but at the moment, she wouldn't have cared if he'd stuffed it in the crack of his ass. Without hesitation, she stepped up to him, shoved her hand down his 'marble bag', and retrieved the lighter.

He jerked, stiffening all over when she rammed her hand into his pants.

Danica examined the object she'd retrieved with an indescribable mixture of emotions. It was a BIC lighter! From home! "You total asshole! You were going to let me try to light a fire rubbing sticks or something and you've got a damned lighter!"

Glaring at her, he grabbed her wrist, squeezing until her grip loosened. Scooping the lighter from her hand, he shoved it into his loincloth once more and gave her a look that dared her to go after it again.

Danica watched the lighter disappear, then looked up at him

again, remembering, belatedly, that she was a captive and feeling her first taste of uneasiness.

She couldn't help but notice he still held her wrist in a tight grip. "It's from my world! That means there are others like me here, from Earth. Can't you just take me to them?"

His brows drew together in an angry frown. "No," he growled, releasing her wrist abruptly and returning his attention to building the fire.

Danica stared down at his stiff back for several moments, torn between the urge to pick up a rock or branch and knock him over the head with it, and an equal urge to simply flop down on the ground and cry like a baby.

"I want to go home," she said childishly, feeling her chin wobble ominously.

He glanced up at her, studied her a moment and looked away again. "Are home."

Danica dragged in a ragged breath. She knew he was right. It was stupid to cry about it and wouldn't do the least bit of good. She doubted it would even help her feelings, all things considered. After a moment, she moved to the other side of the fire from Taj and sat down. Drawing her knees up to her chin, she fought the urge to cry, trying to turn her mind to something more useful--like what in the world she was going to do now that nothing she knew was of any use to her.

She sensed Taj's gaze on her several times, but ignored him. She didn't doubt, as slave, she was supposed to be making herself useful, but she couldn't cook on a damned stove with a recipe book in front of her. She didn't have a clue of how to cook over an open fire, without pots, pans, utensils, herbal seasonings.

He cleared his throat. "Sky gods leave offerings. Never take."

Danica glanced at him, studied him a long moment, and then returned her attention to the sky, wondering just how far from Earth she was. Not in the same system, of course. She might not know a hell of a lot outside her field, but she knew that much.

"Sky gods, my ass," she muttered.

"No say that. Dangerous."

Danica glanced at him in surprise. "Why?"

"My people worship sky gods."

Danica resisted the urge to roll her eyes. "You really think they're gods?"

He frowned, looked around uneasily. "No," he said finally. "Others do. They worship. Kill any who don't believe."

She thought it over for several moments and finally shrugged. "Sounds a lot like where I came from … except not so much anymore. They used to, though, from what I've heard."

"Best no talk of this."

"Just between the two of us, I've seen them. They're just people from another place, intelligent, I suppose, but they're still irresponsible assholes. Evidently, they think it's all right to go around stealing things from other worlds and then just dumping what they don't want on the first planet they pass."

He frowned. "Never speak this again. In my village, dangerous to think these things."

His uneasiness communicated itself to her and banished the thoughts of home from her mind.

If she was going to survive here, she was going to have to get her head on straight and focus. "They would understand me?"

He shook is head. "Maybe. Probably not. Need this," he added, pulling his translator out and showing it to her. "But your face tells your thoughts," he added when he'd put it in his ear once more.

Danica studied him thoughtfully for several moments. "You've captured others like me, haven't you?"

He got up abruptly, moving down to the stream. After a moment, she followed him. He was kneeling at the edge of the water cleaning the meat when she caught up with him. "It's how you got the lighter. It must be," she persisted.

"Not like you," he said shortly, rising and heading back to the fire with the meat.

She followed him again, watching as he skewered the meat on sticks and carefully set it over the fire. "But … the lighter! It's from Earth. From my country!"

"Not like you," he repeated. "Man."

Danica blinked. Slowly a smile curled her lips. "An Earth man?" she said excitedly. As if she cared what gender, race, or whatever! The only thing that mattered was that is was a fellow human being! "There's an Earth man here? In your village?"

"No."

His expression was hard now, uncompromising, but Danica found she couldn't just let it go. "But you said…."

"Man is dead."

Chapter Seven

As accustomed as Danica was to rising early so that she could be in the office when the personnel began trickling in for work, she wasn't used to waking up with leaves stuck to her face and the smell of dirt in her nostrils. Disoriented, she sat up, brushing absently at the debris she'd collected over night.

Taj, and his blanket, were gone.

She stared blankly at the spot where he'd slept the night before, across the fire from her, wondering why it was important to her where Taj was.

Her bladder reminded her.

The frigging bird wouldn't let her leave the clearing. She'd finally had to ask Taj to let her go the night before. Rather than have to ask again, she disentangled herself from the blanket and went in search of a little privacy.

A little was all she was likely to get.

She managed, however, and had already headed for the creek to wash up when Taj appeared. As she splashed water over her face and scrubbed her teeth with one finger, she thought longingly of all the toiletries in her suitcase back at the hotel in the Bahamas. If she'd even been wearing clothes instead of a damned wetsuit, she would've been worlds better off.

She was pretty sure she hadn't missed a single sharp object in the entire clearing with her bare feet. Bugs had gnawed on her all night, despite her best efforts to form a cocoon with the blanket Taj had tossed at her. She could tell from her reflection in the water that her hair looked like a fright wig. And she didn't have so much as a scrap of cloth to wipe her face and hands on, brush her teeth with, or … anything else.

She would almost have welcomed the notion that she was as miserable as she could get, but she was very much afraid that this was only the beginning.

How did people survive camping trips?

Why in god's name did they want to?

She had always been distantly appalled by the notion of 'roughing' it in the woods and wondered why there seemed to be so many people who considered it 'fun recreation'. Now that she had a better idea of what camping was actually like, she realized exactly why they liked it. They were insane.

When she'd finished scrubbing at her teeth, she washed her hands, flung as much water off as she could and took a stab at finger combing her hair. It wasn't exactly a rousing success, but she thought she managed to get most of the sticks and leaves out of it. Giving up on it finally, she trudged back to the blanket and picked it up to shake it. When she did, something slithered out from under it.

She screamed. Instantly wide awake, she flung the blanket as far as she could throw it and tore off in the other direction. Taj caught her around the waist as she sailed past him. Her momentum swung them both in a short circle. When he set her on her feet again, she tried to climb up him, peering around him to see if the thing she'd spotted was headed in her direction.

It didn't help her feelings at all that Taj was shaking.

It royalty pissed her off, however, when she discovered he was shaking because he was trying not to laugh.

"Kank," he managed finally. "Got cold, crawl under for warm."

"Don't tell me I slept with that thing!"

"Gone now. You scare it."

"*I* scared it!"

"Jump this high when scream," he said holding his hands up. "Run that way." Peeling her loose, he set her away from him. His eyes were still dancing with suppressed laughter, however. "Harmless."

Danica shuddered, rubbing her arms. "You're sure it's gone?"

Shaking his head, he went to retrieve the blanket and tossed it at her. She caught it and held it away from her to examine it. Once she'd assured herself there was nothing clinging to it, she shook as much ground debris from the cloth as she could and carefully folded it.

She'd managed to achieve a nicely precise quarter fold when Taj strode toward her and snatched the blanket from her hands. Rolling it tightly, he moved to his packs and began stuffing everything into it.

Irritated that he didn't seem to appreciate her effort, Danica merely watched him, wondering if she should try to help or just stay out of the way. It pretty much looked like a one person job, so she turned to survey the area to make certain nothing had been missed. Taj caught her arm and led her to the bird and she felt her stomach tighten.

She'd promised herself she wouldn't do anything again that might prompt him to tie her wrists, however, and she went willingly enough. Her stomach clenched a notch tighter as he lifted her up onto the thing's back. As soon as Taj had climbed on and settled himself, he pulled her back snugly against him and wrapped an arm around her waist to steady her. She dug her fingers into the bird's ruff as Taj spoke to it and the bird took several hopping steps, then launched itself into the air with a horrendous flapping of wings.

Danica's heart was in her throat as it climbed sluggishly, struggling, it seemed to her, under the added burden of a second rider. She squeezed her eyes closed.

"Woman lucky."

It took several moments to decipher that comment. "What?"

"Kank no lay eggs … probably."

"Eggs? What do you mean probably? They like to lay their eggs under people?" she asked, totally perplexed and revolted at the idea.

She felt him shrug. "Like warm, dark hole."

Danica thought that over for several minutes before her eyes widened and she looked down at the crotch of her wetsuit, wondering if there was any way that thing could possibly have burrowed in while she was sleeping.

He chuckled.

It was a rather pleasant sound, but Danica wasn't presently in the mood to appreciate it. She gritted her teeth. "You have a sick sense of humor," she muttered.

* * * *

It could not be said that Danica lost her fear of soaring and dipping on the back of the bird. She was highly suspicious, in fact, that Taj and the frigging bird rose and dipped and swerved merely for the pleasure of hearing the occasional squeak of fright that erupted from her whenever the bird made an abrupt drop of several feet or suddenly banked into a turn. After a while, however, she reached maximum tension and there wasn't anything else on her body that could be clenched any tighter and once she reached that point, she couldn't maintain it indefinitely. As the hours passed, some of the tension began to ebb from her.

The sun reached its zenith and began to slide down toward the horizon. They hadn't stopped to eat, or relieve themselves and Danica's mind slowly began to focus more and more on her discomfort and less and less on her fear of death.

She'd been fighting the urge to ask Taj to stop for the better part of an hour, partly because it embarrassed her to have to ask to relieve herself and partly because, as bad as she hated flying period, she hated the take off and landing even worse. Just when she thought she'd reached the limit of her endurance, the bird began a slow descent. She dared a glance downward and caught a glimpse of manmade structures.

Her heart executed a strange little dance of absolute delight.

Civilization!

Ignoring the flutters of fear in her stomach, she craned her neck to get a better look as they dropped a little lower.

Doubt surfaced. It *was* dwellings--of a sort--and she supposed since they were clustered fairly closely together the place would have to be termed a village, but it looked as if she'd been right before. There was no civilization, at least as she knew it, on the whole damned planet.

Chapter Eight

There were perhaps two dozen birds like the one they rode strutting about the field where they landed, pecking at the bright orange blossoms of the flowers that grew in profusion all over the cleared area.

It wasn't natural. It had been cleared. Here and there burned tree stumps of varying heights protruded from the vast bed of flowers. As soon as Taj slid from the back of the bird, he reached for her and pulled her down. It was a relief to get off the back of the bird, but she still had to go and wondered if it would be worth waiting to see if there was any chance the village had anything remotely resembling a bathroom.

She finally decided it was. Besides, they were too close to the village for her comfort. It would be just her damned luck that the moment she squatted, one of the villagers would come up on her.

Dismissing her discomfort from her mind, she took the pack Taj shoved at her, clutching it to her and looking around as he finished removing the tack from the bird. Slinging it over his shoulder, he grasped her arm and guided her toward the dwellings she could see a short distance away.

As they neared the first dwelling, curious villagers began to gather and stare at the two of them.

More accurately, she supposed, to stare at her.

Within five minutes one thing was patently obvious. Blond was the rule, not the exception. The hair of everyone they passed varied from almost white blond to very nearly brown, but she didn't see a single person from infant to adult that wasn't fair. Their skin tones were the same golden brown as Taj's, their eyes ranging from an unnerving blue-white to the same aquamarine as his. In fact, the blue-white seemed to be the most dominate color and Danica was reminded of a very old science fiction movie she'd watched where the children had all been born blond with scary eyes and had powers of mind control.

A shiver skated along her spine and she inched a little closer to Taj, wishing suddenly that she'd given in to the temptation when she was getting ready for her vacation to go blond to see if blondes really did have more fun.

Except for the very small children who didn't seem to wear anything at all, the men all wore loincloths much like the one Taj did and the women wore something that looked like a knee length, sleeveless tunic that was belted at the waist.

With an effort, she ignored the people staring at her and studied the dwellings they passed. A tiny spark of hope welled inside of her. The houses looked pretty solid. They had that 'rustic' look of log homes, not quite as refined looking as the log homes she'd seen, but they were certainly made out of tree trunks. Something had been daubed in the crevices between the trees.

There were strange looking shutters over the window openings-- no glass, or even anything similar. The roofs looked like they'd merely heaped piles of long grass on top.

They'd passed perhaps a half a dozen similar buildings of varying sizes when a feminine shriek drew Danica's attention. She whirled toward the sound in time to see a blond goddess rushing toward them. The girl launched herself a Taj so hard he took a step back when they collided.

Danica gaped at Taj and the girl in stunned surprise. Taj's face had darkened with color, but his expression was a mixture of surprise, pleasure and dismay as he disentangled her from around his neck, not anger. The girl favored him with a provocative pouting of full, luscious lips as he set her away from him and admonished her about her lack of decorum.

At his tone, her expression changed abruptly from provocative to irritated. "Been gone long time. Not miss me?"

He sighed, looked around uncomfortably and finally forced a smile. "Missed."

Smiling, she slipped a possessive arm around his waist and turned to look Danica over, her expression hardening. "Where you find this ugly?"

Taj frowned. For a moment, his lips tightened. Removing her arm from his waist, he caught her hand and began to move determinedly toward whatever destination he had in mind. "She is gift from sky gods."

The girl glanced back at Danica, who'd fallen into step behind them, and sniffed. "Certain is female?"

Danica studied her feet, trying to shield the indignation that went through her at that comment. She damned well wasn't built like a man! She might not be as voluptuous as the blond goddess hanging all over Taj, but she wasn't by any means flat-chested and she'd always prided herself on her small waist.

Of course the girl had youth--and blond--and a voluptuous figure on her side.

She must be at least twenty, though, Danica decided, despite the fact that she acted like she was more in the neighborhood of sixteen or seventeen.

Spoiled brat!

"Not need her. Have Kara."

"When we wed, she help you."

"Looks stupid. Think female can be trained?"

Danica surreptitiously pulled the translator from her ear, palming it. She had a feeling that, if she heard any more, she was going to do something rash. When she looked up once more, she discovered that Taj had turned to glance at her over his shoulder.

To make sure she was still following like a good little slave, she didn't doubt.

At least this answered the question of why he hadn't shown any interest in her as a sex object.

Not that she cared. In fact, she was actually very relieved, she assured herself.

The mixture of hurt and anger she felt was because she'd lost all chance of having anything like that for herself. She'd focused since college on developing her career. It wasn't until her twenty eighth birthday, almost a year ago now, that it had suddenly dawned on her that she was running out of time for the other half of the future she'd planned for herself--the husband and one point two kids.

She was solid. She had a good job, a great apartment, and a very respectable income. She wasn't beautiful, but she was certainly no dog--whatever that empty headed twit thought.

For the past year and a half, she'd been on the hunt for a likely partner to settle down with. Actually, she'd been halfheartedly looking for more than two years. She hadn't gotten serious about it, though, until the sense of running out of time had begun to creep into her. Then, in desperation, when nothing else seemed to be working, she'd joined the gym and begun taking the sort of classes where she could be certain to find men; taekwando; karate; kick boxing--scuba diving. She'd even managed to find a couple that had looked fairly promising until she'd discovered they were already taken and just happened to be the sort who removed their wedding ring when they went out.

She supposed it was just as well she hadn't had any luck, but it didn't help her feelings to have to watch the two lovebirds coo at each other.

Ignoring the chatter she could no longer understand, Danica turned her attention to studying the village, deciding, maybe, that they were a little more advanced than Indians. At least they didn't seem to be nomadic. Most of the dwellings looked as if they'd been there for a number of years.

Although they'd passed several large, planted fields on their way into the village, a sizable, neatly kept garden was also planted around each dwelling and each had a couple of small outbuildings and a pen where they kept animals of some kind. Not very surprisingly, the animals didn't look like anything Danica had ever seen, but they were roughly the size of a large dog and had horns. She decided they must be something like cows, or maybe goats-- some sort of herd animal, anyway.

She almost plowed in to Taj when he stopped. Realizing they had undoubtedly arrived at his home, Danica looked around curiously. Dismay filled her.

Unlike the places they'd passed, she saw nothing but a garden, a tiny, ramshackle structure that looked to be about the size of a child's playhouse, and a stack of timbers that were perhaps waist high and had been formed into a large square. The girl, who'd called herself Kara, skipped over the unfinished threshold and twirled in a wide circle, almost like a ballerina, her arms spread wide.

Taj was studying the construction with a mixture of pride and resignation.

Hoping she was wrong and this wasn't their final destination, Danica shoved the translator back into her ear as Taj strode toward the small building and hung his tack on pegs sticking out of the side of the wall beneath a lean to roof that extended out to one side.

Kara had her hands on her hips now, studying the partially finished structure critically. "Should make bigger," she finally decided. "Will have many little ones."

Taj moved to the wall closest to him and leaned on it, his expression unreadable.

"Big enough," he said finally.

Kara frowned at him and finally moved toward him, placing a palm against his bare chest. "Kara want bigger. Want biggest in village."

His lips tightened for a moment, but finally he took her hand. "Show."

She gestured toward the dirt floor. "This and half more."

Sighing, Danica looked around for a place to park herself. It looked like they were going to be discussing their little love nest a while. She wished now that she'd asked to relieve herself earlier. The urgency had passed, but she still needed to go.

Finally, she decided to check out the tiny building.

She discovered once she was inside and her eyes had adjusted to the gloom that it was actually bigger than she'd thought it would be. It looked to be roughly twice the size of her walk-in closet and contained a narrow bunk built into the wall and a small, crudely built table and chair. There was a circle of rocks in the center that held ash and a few pieces of charred wood. Above it, like a spot light, was a hole that let in the little light that brightened the small room.

Spying a door in the back wall, she went to it and opened it. Discovering it let out onto something like a porch and that there was another structure attached to the back side, she crossed it and opened that door.

The smell told her at once what it was--an outhouse.

On the other hand, she'd been in public restrooms that didn't smell any better and, as crude as it was, it was so close to 'civilized' when compared to squatting in the woods that she felt an instant leap of pleasure.

There was no lock on the door.

She used it anyway, checking the perimeter first to assure herself there was nothing crawling near where she planned to plant her ass.

When she left the outhouse, she could hear Kara's high pitched voice. Obviously they were still planning their future, she thought wryly, and went back into the small cabin. Moving to the bunk, she studied it suspiciously for several moments and finally tested it with one hand. Discovering it felt surprisingly comfortable, and even better, smelled reasonably clean, she climbed into it and lay down.

She was fairly certain she shouldn't, but she had hardly slept the night before and she was almost as exhausted emotionally as she was physically. Pulling the blanket up over herself, she curled into a tight ball and decided she'd get up when Taj dragged her out of it.

Chapter Nine

The opening door woke Danica. Groggily, she sat up, peering through the gloom at the figure that stood just inside.

"Not make fire," Taj observed irritably.

Danica stumbled out of the bunk. "I'll get wood."

He dropped an armload on the floor beside the fire pit. "Too dark now."

Nodding, Danica stumbled back to the bunk, crawled in and rolled onto her belly, pulling the cover over her head. She was just drifting away when the cover was snatched off of her and a large hand smacked her on the ass. She came up on her hands and knees, twisting her head around to look at Taj with a mixture of surprise and irritation.

"Lazy. You cook."

She stumbled out of the bed again. "Cook what?"

He tossed a limp carcass at her. Danica caught it without thinking, then looked down at it in revulsion. It took an effort to refrain from snarling at him, but one look at his face in the flickering light of the fire he'd started was enough to convince her that now was not a good time to give vent to her own temper.

He was definitely in a nasty mood.

She looked down at the bloody thing again. It was pretty unrecognizable now, but looked a lot like the headless things they'd eaten the night before--which had actually tasted a lot better than she'd expected, most likely because she'd felt like her stomach was going to cave in.

It felt pretty much the same way now.

"Water?" she asked a little weakly.

He gestured toward the back of the cabin. Since she hadn't seen anything that looked even remotely like a faucet, she decided he must mean somewhere outside and in that general direction. Clutching the piece of meat, she went out the back door and looked around.

It wasn't completely dark, but the next thing to it. Dimly, however, she saw something that looked like a culvert sticking up out of the ground a few yards from the cabin. Moving toward it, she looked inside and caught her reflection in the water below.

It took her a few minutes to figure out how she was supposed to get the water up, but she finally found something vaguely resembling a bucket, but made out of what appeared to be animal skin that had been made to form a pouch. When she'd hauled it up, she discovered it only held water after a fashion. Water sprouted in little trickles all the way around the seam where it had been sewn together.

After studying it for several moments, she washed the meat and carefully perched it on the rim, then dipped up another skin full of water and held the pouch up with one hand, allowing the water to trickle over her.

The water was chilly, but the closest she'd come to a shower in days. She just wished she had something to hang the thing on so she could use both hands to scrub herself.

What she really wished for, though, was a real shower, soap, a nice thick washcloth, or bath sponge.

Sighing, she determinedly dismissed the whining thoughts and bathed her face, her arms and legs the best she could with what she had--her hand and cold trickles of water. After glancing around, she unsnapped the crotch of her wetsuit and bathed the nether regions and finally unzipped the front of her wetsuit.

Feeling slightly refreshed, she fastened the crotch of her wetsuit once more, zipped the front closed and then rinsed the meat off once last time.

Taj looked her over speculatively when she came in, dripping water. "Next time, use bucket," he said dryly.

It took her a couple of moments to realize he was suggesting she'd dove in. She refrained from glaring at him with an effort. Crouching on the opposite side of the fire pit from him, she used the rod he handed her to skewer the meat and carefully set it in the brackets that had been made to hold it above the fire.

Frowning thoughtfully as she watched the water drip from the meat and sizzle on the fire below it, she studied the rod. It was metal. So, too, was the sword Taj only removed from his back when he slept and never allowed more than a few feet from his hand even then.

She didn't know a hell of a lot about primitive cultures, but the metal seemed inconsistent with the level of sophistication she'd seen since she'd arrived. She supposed it was possible that both the rod and the sword had originated off world, just as she had, but it just didn't seem likely.

It wasn't as if she'd really had much of a chance to study the village or the people, so it was possible, she supposed, that she just hadn't noticed other evidence that they knew something about metal working, but she didn't think so.

Somewhere on this planet, there must be a race that was more advanced than the one where she'd found herself.

She cleared her throat. "Where did you get this?" she asked, tapping the end of the rod.

He gave her a long look. "Find."

"It wasn't made here, then?" she persisted.

He shrugged.

"In the village, I mean."

Instead of responding, he merely studied her speculatively. Finally, he stretched out on the hard packed dirt on the opposite side of the fire. "What called?"

Danica looked at him in surprise, then frowned. "I guess it's just a rod."

He snorted impatiently. "You."

She felt her face reddening. "Danica."

He tested it on his tongue a couple of times. "Strange name."

Compared with what? Taj? Kara? Inwardly, she shrugged, but refrained from comment.

Her legs were beginning to cramp from squatting. She didn't really want to sit on the dirt, but she had to turn the meat every few minutes to keep it from burning up. Finally, with a long suffering sigh, she sat down.

"Clothes strange also. Woman dress like this all time?"

"No. It's for swimming … scuba diving, actually. I was in the ocean when the aliens picked me up."

He looked perplexed. She didn't really feel like trying to explain it, however.

"Sky gods?"

She rolled her eyes. "Yeah, them."

"How look--sky gods?"

She shrugged. "Tall, skinny, long arms and legs, big heads, no hair--pretty scary, actually."

"Scare Danica?"

"Not nearly as much as the damned shark that was in the tank with me."

"What shark?"

"A big fish with a lot of sharp teeth that eats people."

He looked skeptical.

"Considering the size of your bird, I don't see why that's so hard to accept," she said tartly.

He was silent for a while. "Danica's world look like Glaxo?" he asked curiously.

She had to suppose Glaxo was what they called their world. She glanced around the cabin. "Not even close," she muttered glumly.

She saw when she glanced at him again that he was looking more than a little affronted.

"How different?"

Danica stared at him a long moment, thinking of all the things she'd taken for granted, all the things that had made life easy, comfortable, enjoyable. "Infinitely," she said and promptly burst into tears. "My apartment had a floor, with carpet, a big bed, sheets, towels--a bathroom with running water. A refrigerator to keep food cold and a stove and microwave to cook. Plates to eat on and forks to eat with instead of my fingers. I had a closet full of beautiful clothes and shoes for my feet."

"Things," he said with a touch of contempt. "Women!"

"Yes, things!" she snapped. "All sorts of things to keep me warm, and dry, and not too hot--and clean! I hate being dirty and I hate having to cook over a fire and I hate eating meat that's burned on the outside and half raw in the middle--and not having salt!"

Taj rose abruptly, strode to the door and went out, slamming it behind him.

Danica stared at the vibrating panel for a moment, then burst into tears again.

As tempted as she was to crawl in the bed and indulge herself in a marathon of self-pity, however, Taj had left. The meat was going to burn if somebody didn't stand over it and turn it every few minutes.

Sniffing, she mopped the tears from her cheeks and turned the meat again.

She didn't even have tissue to blow her nose.

"Or toilet paper!" she wailed on a fresh sob.

Drawing in a shuddering breath after a moment, she wiped her cheeks with her palms again and sat staring at the fire, sniffing every few minutes. The urge to cry finally subsided.

As it did, it occurred to her that dwelling on everything she didn't have was only going to make the rest of her life miserable. She'd always considered herself a realist, and moreover, fully capable of adapting to change.

Of course, in the life she'd had before change mostly meant a turnover of personnel who had to be trained, new software, new equipment, making adjustments to the fluctuating economy.

She looked around the cabin again. It was awful, really awful, but then obviously no one had lived in it before but Taj, who seemed to spend most of his time outside, and even Earth bachelors tended to be pretty indifferent of their surroundings. Surely, if she set her mind to it, she could figure out a way to make it more comfortable?

The bed was really only big enough for one and there wasn't a lot of space on the floor.

She would've liked to think she'd be getting the bed, but somehow she doubted it.

She'd been 'rescued' to supply labor in a world where hard labor was obviously the rule, not the exception.

She pushed those thoughts to the back of her mind. The cabin was dry. It probably wouldn't be when it rained, not with the smoke hole in the roof, but it was shelter and beat the hell out of being on the ground completely exposed to the elements.

The toilet was a horror, but that, too, was still better than having to relieve herself in the woods.

The truth was, no matter how much she hated admitting it, or how insulting and demeaning it was to be called a slave, she was fortunate Taj had found her and decided to keep her. She doubted she could survive on her own in his world.

If she was going to live here, and there certainly didn't seem to be an alternative, then she would just have to adjust and work to make life a little better.

It wasn't like she had anything else to do with her time.

Rising finally, she dragged the blanket off the bed and used that to grasp the rod and remove the meat from the fire. After looking around helplessly for a moment, she laid the meat directly on the wooden surface of the table, tossed the blanket back on the bed and went to the door.

"Taj?"

She could see his silhouette in the darkness beyond the door. He was staring up at the stars.

"The meat's done," she said tentatively.

When he continued to ignore her, she went back inside, stared at the meat for several moments and finally pulled off a piece and went to sit in one corner to eat. There was only one chair. She didn't want to piss Taj off any more than she already had by taking his chair like she thought she was entitled to help herself to whatever was his.

Chapter Ten

After nodding off a couple of times, Danica finally lay down on the floor, wiggled until she was reasonably comfortable and dozed off. She roused when Taj finally came in, but when he neither approached her nor spoke, she went back to sleep.

When she woke, she saw a thin stream of light coming through the smoke hole. From somewhere outside, she could hear a rhythmic thud, as if someone was hammering on something. Stretching, she staggered around the room a moment and finally found her way to the door that led to the outhouse.

She headed for the well when she came out again, gasping as she splashed the cold water over herself. The rhythmic pounding stopped as she placed one foot on the lip of the well and washed the dirt off her leg. Curious, she looked around.

Taj was standing over a log, the ax he'd been using to hack the limbs from it resting on the ground now.

His gaze was on her.

She couldn't tell anything about his expression, but when he said nothing, she turned her back to him and continued, washing the other leg and finally unzipping the suit and cleaning as much of her body as she could reach. After a couple of moments, the chopping started up again.

When she'd finished, she zipped the suit up again, replaced the water bag and, after slinging as much water off her skin as she could, turned and headed toward Taj to see what she was supposed to do today to earn her food. He stopped chopping when she started toward him, leaning on the handle.

His gaze, she realized when she reached him, was on her wetsuit. Instinctively, she looked down at herself. It really was wet now, but the styrene suit was a long way from being revealing. Except for the fact that, beginning at her breasts, the suit was now darker all the way to her crotch, she couldn't see what there was about it to arrest his attention.

When she looked up once more, he was studying the blade of his ax frowningly.

It was a stone ax, and almost certainly as dull as a butter knife. Small wonder he was so muscular. "What do you want me to do?"

He nodded toward the branches he'd cut off and pointed to a small pile near the cabin. Danica grasped the end of one of the branches and began dragging it to the pile he'd started. She discovered when she released it that the tree sap was thick and sticky. Lifting her hand to her nose, she sniffed it.

It was some sort of conifer. The smell was pleasant, not as sharp as the pines from home, but so strongly reminiscent, it sent a pang of homesickness through her.

The sap wasn't nearly as pleasant.

Scrubbing her hand on her suit, she headed back for another limb. None of the limbs were very big around, but they were long and had many smaller branches, which made them heavy and hard to drag.

By the time she'd cleared the branches away, she had pitch in sticky patches all over her hands, arms and even her legs.

Pines were just about the biggest 'crop' in her native state, and used for all sorts of things, she knew, jogging her mind to try to think what those purposes were as she moved the pile from one spot to another.

It wasn't recommended for fireplaces because the pitch built up in the chimney and could catch fire.

Not that that information was going to do her a lot of good. She couldn't even cook food and make it come out eatable. Trying to tackle cooking up some kind of burnable fluid was way out of her league.

It smelled like cleaner, though. She decided to put some of the smaller branches around the outhouse and the cabin and 'pretend' she'd disinfected the place. If nothing else, it smelled good.

By the time she'd finished dragging the limbs from the first tree, Taj was working on his third. She stopped for a few moments to rest, watching him.

Either he was in a hell of a hurry to finish his house for his bride, or he was working off steam. He moved from branch to branch with hardly a pause. Sweat glistened on his skin, emphasizing the fluid movements of his muscles beneath the smooth surface. The bunching and flexing of his muscles was mesmerizing, so much so that Danica realized she'd been standing stock still, staring at him as if hypnotized for several minutes after he stopped and turned to look at her.

Reddening profusely when she saw he'd caught her staring, she hurried toward the next pile of limbs and began moving them. When she dared another glance in his direction, it was just as he glanced at her again to see if she was standing in the yard like an idiot gaping at him.

She found that it was really hard to focus on what she was doing after that. The temptation to stop and watch him was nearly overpowering. It took an effort of will just to keep from glancing at him.

Her stomach redirected her attention after a while, however. She hadn't eaten anything since the night before and realized it was nearing midday.

Almost as if the thought had conjured her, Kara appeared on the road leading up to Taj's place, a basket over one arm. Danica's stomach immediately set up a demand for whatever was in it.

"Shut up, stupid," Danica snarled back at the growling beast. "Little miss big tit sure as hell didn't bring it for you."

Seeing that Taj had stopped to take the basket, Danica was on the point of slinking off when Taj lifted his hand and summoned her. Hoping against hope that her stomach wouldn't growl loud enough for both on them to hear it, she moved toward him, stopping a couple of yards away. He held out the basket and told her to take it inside.

Danica took it and headed for the door. Setting the basket on the table, she went straight through the one room cabin and out the back again, making for the well. Once she'd downed enough cold water that her stomach had begun to gargle instead of growling, she focused on trying to rub some of the pitch off of her hands. She was so intent on her useless attempts to remove the sticky sap, Taj caught her unaware. The moment he touched her shoulder, she nearly jumped out of her skin.

Clutching her pounding heart, she looked up at him questioningly.

He nodded toward the cabin. "Come. Eat."

A mixture of emotions flooded her, relief that he'd remembered she hadn't had anything to eat, reluctance to eat anything big tit had cooked, and an immense desire to put something into her stomach before it caved in against her backbone.

She had always worked out regularly, but she wasn't used to such physical labor. She'd had no idea it could make her so hungry she felt like she could gnaw the leg off a cow if it wandered close enough.

His lips twisted wryly. "Mother sent."

"Your mother? Oh!" She followed him back into the cabin, watching hopefully as he unpacked the contents and set it out on the table.

"Sit."

She glanced at him. "Oh no! I couldn't take your chair."

"Sit!"

Frowning, she moved to the chair and sat down. Setting an earthen ware dish on the table in front of her, he pulled a wooden spoon from the basket and lay it beside the plate, then turned his attention to unwrapping the food.

There was a dark piece of meat that looked and smelled like roast beef. She knew it wasn't but it was enough that it looked and smelled like it could be. Pulling his knife, he began carefully slicing the meat until he'd sliced the entire piece. When he'd finished, he took what looked like a rounded loaf of bread and carved a couple of pieces off. Grabbing a piece of meat in one hand and the bread in the other, he moved over to the bunk and settled on the edge.

After a moment, Danica took a little bit of everything and placed it on her plate.

It tasted like heaven. She was certain she'd never tasted anything so wonderful in her life. The feeling was almost orgasmic. "Your mother is *such* a good cook!"

When she glanced at him, she saw he was grinning. "Danica hungry."

"Yes, but it's still fabulous. Do you think she'd teach me how to cook?"

He looked at her skeptically for a moment and finally merely shrugged.

Danica felt a mixture of hurt and irritation dull her enjoyment. She knew what he was thinking. She would've learned how already if she could.

She hadn't desperately needed to know how before, though. Besides, her mother hadn't even tried to teach her, because her mother could barely cook, and what she did cook was hardly edible.

Maybe he hadn't intended it as a slight, though? Maybe he just figured his mother wouldn't want to be bothered with trying to teach her?

She wished she believed that, but the truth was she was pretty useless in her current situation and she knew it. She hadn't even really had any homemaker skills in her own world. It hadn't seemed to her that she was any more ignorant than the next woman, though. She didn't know anybody that could cook a full meal, or sew, or even do laundry.

Not that knowing how to use a washing machine was likely to do her any good here.

She was suddenly deeply regretful, though, that she hadn't had an interest in learning any sort of handicrafts that might have been useful to her now. She would've been a hell of a lot better off taking something like gourmet cooking, or weaving, or making pottery, than kick boxing or taekwando.

It would've been nice to know how to make something like the plate she was eating out of, or the containers that held the food. Obviously, these people only had what they could make and, if you couldn't make it, you did without.

They would almost certainly have some kind of barter system, though, wouldn't they? Everybody here couldn't possibly know everything. Some would be good at one thing and others at another thing.

She didn't have anything to barter with, unfortunately.

She might not be allowed to own anything anyway. Taj had never actually explained the rules of enslavement as his people saw them.

She had a feeling, though, that she'd already gone way out of bounds a lot of times.

When they'd finished eating, she wrapped everything back up very carefully and repacked the basket, then went out to the well to clean the pottery dish and the spoon.

Taj was already busy hacking at tree limbs again by the time she'd finished.

It was just as well.

She rather thought, all things considered, that it might be best if she kept her distance as much as possible. Irritating and uncivilized he might well be, but he was also cute as hell when he teased her, the most handsome man she'd ever seen in the flesh, and she was way too fascinated by Taj's mostly naked body when he was chopping wood. Big tit was liable to claw her eyes out if she caught her drooling.

Chapter Eleven

By late in the afternoon, Danica had lost all awareness of, or interest in, Taj's beautiful body. She was way too tried to think about anything but moving. Finally, when she thought she couldn't move another step or lift another branch, he called a halt.

Danica merely wilted to the ground, too exhausted to consider moving for a while.

Finally, she rose with an effort and trudged toward the well to bathe as much of the grime off as she could. Her arms were shaking with effort by the time she managed to haul the first skin of water up, however, and she was seriously considering just giving up on the bathing thing when Taj came out of the cabin with a bundle under one arm. Catching her around her upper arm, he started tugging her toward the woods behind his cabin.

She didn't bother to ask him where they were going. She wasn't certain she could've summoned the energy to ask even if it had occurred to her.

Once they'd stepped into the woods, they followed a narrow path for perhaps ten or fifteen minutes and came at last upon what looked like steps set into the dirt. Danica stared down at the half covered slab of stone in surprise, nearly stumbling as Taj urged her forward.

She saw as they began to descend that it was a fairly deep depression--not a depression, she mentally corrected. She could see the remains of stone walls here and there, mostly covered in vines. At the bottom, large stones formed a courtyard. In the center of the courtyard was some sort of sculpture. On either side, she saw the gutted remains of what must once have been rooms.

Leading her across it, Taj entered an arched opening at the opposite end.

When Danica's eyes adjusted to the gloom, she saw a pool perhaps ten feet square in the center of the room.

Steam wafted off of it in the cooling evening air.

She stared at the pool blankly as Taj released her and strode toward it. Slowly, it sank in to her mind that the pool, although obviously manmade, must be fed by a hot spring.

Setting the pack he carried down on the stone beside it, Taj removed his loincloth and stepped into the pool.

He submerged himself completely. Sloughing the water from his face as he came up again, he took something from the bundle he'd brought and began to lather his hair.

Momentarily distracted by the flash of a really impressive package and the firm buttocks she'd just gotten a really good look at, Danica's mind went back to the desperate desire to feel hot water--soap.

Doubt flickered through her briefly. She wasn't particularly modest, or uncomfortable with her own nakedness. She wasn't concerned that Taj would be so overcome with lust that he'd forget all about his fiancée, particularly since she wasn't at all sure she'd mind if he did. She *was* worried that big tit might just decide to drop by about the time she decided to get naked and climb into the pool with Taj. She was pretty sure she could hold her own even if the woman did attack, but she didn't particularly want to.

Finally, she dismissed it. She wasn't about to pass up a chance of a hot bath even if she ended up having to defend herself from a wild cat.

And she damned well wasn't going to try to bathe in a wetsuit when she finally had the chance of a really good bath with soap and hot water.

Taj was busy with his own bath anyway.

Unsnapping the crotch of her suit, she slid the zipper to the bottom and peeled the suit off. She hadn't been completely out of it in days and removing it felt almost like peeling skin. Discarding it, she moved to the edge of the pool and looked down.

There were stairs!

Feeling almost like a little girl at Christmas, she practically danced down the steps, closing her eyes as the warm water lapped over her.

She almost hated getting soap in it, the water felt so wonderful to her sore, aching muscles.

When she glanced over at Taj to see if he was done with the soap, she saw that he'd stopped scrubbing and was staring at her. Feeling a little self-conscious, she took the soap when he finally held it out to her and moved to the opposite end of the pool from him. She lathered her hair and rinsed it twice, deciding, whether she could completely rinse the soap from it or not, it couldn't feel any worse than the dirt that had clogged the pores of her scalp before.

No amount of scrubbing could remove the tree sap completely. She scraped off as much as she could with her nails and finally moved to one of the steps to work on her legs.

She was pleased with the smooth, silkiness of her skin. It might be a sad epitaph to the civilization that she'd lost that the only thing she really had to remind her of it was the laser hair removal she'd had done before heading down to the Bahamas on vacation, but she certainly didn't regret it, especially now that she was stuck in this uncivilized place. At least she didn't have to walk around in a swim suit all day looking like a gorilla with the mange.

That was the one thing she hated most about having dark hair instead of blond. Even the fuzz on her body was dark and body waxing had just gotten to be too much to bear.

She was almost sorry, though, that she hadn't had her pubic bush tamed a little more while she was at it, she thought as she studied the thatch of hair between her legs.

She was still working on the patches of sap on her thighs when Taj stalked up the steps on his way out of the pool. Sighing, she realized her reprieve from the world was over. Setting the soap Taj had given her aside, she slipped into the water to rinse off.

By the time she emerged, he'd finished drying. He tossed the damp cloth at her and dug a clean loin cloth from his bundle.

It was cloth, she discovered when she caught it. Like the blankets they used, it had been woven and for the first time Danica wondered if this was something his people made or if she'd been right before and there was another race on his world more advanced than his people, perhaps, traded with for the things they couldn't make themselves.

She glanced at Taj to ask, but his expression wasn't at all welcoming. Shrugging inwardly, she finished drying and, very reluctantly, retrieved her suit from the floor. To her surprise, Taj took it from her and shoved a wad of something else into her hands.

She saw when she'd untangled it that it was one of the tunic like dresses like the women of the village wore. Unlike the towel, it looked and felt as if it had been made from some thin leather, but it was surprising soft.

She looked up at Taj, flicking a smile of gratitude at him.

To her surprise, he stepped toward her. His hands closed around her upper arms and he dragged her close, so close she felt her pubic mound butt up against the hard ridge in his loincloth, felt the rake of her distended nipples along his bulging pecs. Tipping her head back, Danica gaped at Taj in surprise and a little dismay, too stunned to think what she might have done to provoke his wrath.

He seemed angry. His expression was stony.

"Taj not Earth man. Still man. Think stinking savage? Think

animal? Man. Not stone. Not post. Next time, bathe, not tempt Taj forget vows."

Obviously, he'd had a close and very nasty encounter with a human before, but she couldn't remember *saying* she thought of him as a savage. "I didn't," she gasped, feeling the beginnings of anger at being falsely accused when she finally realized exactly what he was accusing her of. He'd acted as if it was perfectly acceptable for them to bathe together. How was she supposed to know it wasn't?

He looked down between them, where her breasts, heaving with her gasping breaths, trembling with the force of her pounding heart beats, brushed his chest.

"Did," he said thickly.

"I didn't intend to. I just didn't think…."

"Taj man?" he finished for her. "Not Earth man, so not matter? Feel nothing, stupid animal?"

She gaped at him.

He released his grip on her arms, repositioning them so that one arm curled around her back, holding her tightly against him. He slid his other hand to her buttocks, pressing her hips against his lower body. "Feel much same, yes?"

She merely stared at him, feeling her surprise give way to burgeoning desire as she felt his erection digging into her lower belly, nudging her mound.

He moved against her, setting off jolts of heat inside of her as she felt his cock begin to nestle its way into her cleft with his movements, teasing the sensitive flesh around her clit.

"Yes? No?"

She gulped, too flustered to even understand what he was asking her. Before she realized his intention, he'd bent her backwards over his arm and lowered his mouth to one of her breasts. The strength left her knees as the heat of his mouth covered the sensitive tip and an electric current of desire charged through her.

Her head swam. She'd begun to feel as if she was going to faint when he released her abruptly and set her away from him almost roughly.

She wavered, locking her knees to keep from wilting to the stone floor.

He pointed to the dress she was still clutching. "Clothe yourself."

Danica stared down at wad of clothing stupidly and finally began struggling into it.

When she had managed to wiggle her head and arms through, she saw that he was already striding away from her.

She stared at his stiff back, too bemused to really understand what had just happened. Shakily, she looked down at herself, smoothing the dress absently, trying not to think about the dull, aching throb in her breasts and her femininity.

There was no belt, but it didn't matter. The dress he'd given her smelled clean. It felt wonderfully unrestrictive after having worn the wetsuit so long.

The lack of anything beneath it only seemed to make her more aware of her body, however, not less.

Looking around a little blankly, she saw that Taj had left the bundle he'd brought lying beside the pool. She went to gather everything up. When she rose and turned, she saw Taj had paused to wait for her just outside the chamber.

Still more than a little shaky, she approached him cautiously, studying him more than a little uneasily and trying to decide if he was still angry with her.

He'd been angry. There was no doubt about that, and as broken as his English was, there was also no doubt that he'd seen her behavior not as an attempt to tempt him, but as a disregard for him as a human being, a man. She shouldn't have been surprised or dismayed that she'd managed to get her revulsion of this place across, her loathing of it as primitive and savage, or that he'd taken it personally, but she was. She really hadn't intended, or realized, that the words and actions she'd flung at him had given him the impression that she considered him little more than an animal.

The truth was, she was having a hard time not thinking of him as a man, a human man, but somehow she didn't think he'd believe that at the moment, particularly when she'd managed to be completely oblivious to him while she was bathing. And it hadn't just *seemed* so. She *had* put him from her mind when she decided he had no interest in her.

He studied her face for several moments and then looked away. When she stopped a few feet from him, he turned and started back the way they'd come. She followed him, feeling her uneasiness begin to abate when it seemed he had no intention of pursuing their little misunderstanding any further.

Relieved, that he seemed to have gotten a grip on his temper, she studied the ruins as they passed through them again, peering through the deepening gloom at the chamber as they left it, and the chambers along either side as they passed them.

"Did your people build this?" she asked tentatively as she trotted along behind him, trying to keep up.

"No."

She felt silent. There was just enough bite in the one word to prove he wasn't entirely over his anger. Besides, she figured he probably didn't know who'd built it. She could tell just from looking at it that it must be ancient. Whoever had built it, however, had been damned good at construction for so much of it to still be standing after so long.

And they'd been smart enough to harness nature, building the pool around a natural hot spring.

She wondered what other 'civilized marvels' they might have been capable of and what had happened to them.

They were almost back to the cabin before it dawned on her that Taj was still stewing.

It occurred to her for the first time to wonder if she'd actually been invited to partake of the pool. Maybe he'd only meant for her to assist him with his bath? Maybe that was part of why he was angry? Aside from having mortally insulted him, maybe she'd overstepped the bounds of slavedom again?

But surely he'd meant for her to or he wouldn't have shown it to her at all? Obviously, it was where he bathed. She hadn't seen him at the well, but he was always clean and fresh smelling.

Maybe his little 'lesson' had bothered him more than he'd thought it would?

She tried, hard, not to feel vindictive about it, but her own body was still thrumming and she didn't believe for one moment that she'd tormented him nearly as badly as he had her.

"Did I do something wrong? Else, I mean?"

He threw her a speculative glance. "No," he said finally, his voice tight with suppressed violence.

Danica's brows rose, but she decided it might be wiser not to pursue it.

It was dark inside the cabin. Danica plowed into Taj, who apparently was on his way out again. They 'waltzed' briefly, trying to get around one another and finally Taj grasped her shoulders, set her to one side and left again. When he came back, he had wood for a fire and squatted by the fire pit to stack the pieces and get a fire going.

Danica wasn't certain of where to put the bundle he'd given her to carry, but finally decided to push it under the bunk, out of the way. Removing the damp towel from the bundle, she looked around for a place to hang it and finally settled on the back of the chair.

Taj was busy emptying the basket and examining the contents, sampling them as he went. Wordlessly, she took the dish from the basket and held it out to him. He ignored it. "Temperamental," Danica muttered under her breath as he grabbed up a hunk of bread and meat and moved across the room to the bunk.

Maybe he was just tired and hungry? She felt pretty damned irritable herself, despite the fact that the hot bath had done wonders for her, soothing all her aching muscles. After helping herself to a portion of the food, she sat and ate. By the time she'd finished, she was almost ready to nod off in the chair.

With an effort, she got up and put everything away, then went out to wash the dish and spoon.

Taj was sprawled on the bunk when she returned, one arm across his face. On the floor, she saw the bedrolls they'd used to sleep on when they'd camped. Untying them, she spread one on the floor and then stretched out on top, covering herself with the other blanket.

A deep sigh of contentment escaped her as she curled onto her side. It was actually pretty amazing when she thought about it, that it took so little to bring happiness when a person had had to do without for just a little while--a full stomach, a hot bath, clean clothes and a blanket between her and the dirt floor and she felt almost pampered.

Stifling the urge to chuckle, she stretched, and yawned. "Taj?" she asked quietly, not wanting to wake him if he was already asleep.

"What?" His voice sounded gruff.

"I'm sorry. I didn't mean to piss you off. I was just glad to get the chance of a hot bath. Thank you!"

Instead of responding, he rolled onto his side, facing the wall.

Chapter Twelve

Danica woke to pain. Despite the hot soak the night before, every single muscle in her body protested at the slightest move. It took three tries to get up off the floor. When she finally managed it, she hobbled out to the 'necessary' and then to the well. She was creeping painfully toward the cabin again when it occurred to her that she didn't hear or see Taj. Walking between the cabins, she looked over the construction site.

Finally, deciding he must have either gone to the pool to bathe, or off to hunt, she went back into the cabin and finished off the food remaining in the basket. It tasted all right. She hoped it hadn't set out so long it would kill her.

When she'd finished, she took the basket outside and cleaned each container carefully, setting it to dry before she returned it to the basket. There was still no sign of Taj when she'd finished.

After looking around the area uncertainly for a few minutes, she studied the pile of limbs. She really didn't feel like moving them. Finally, she decided to gather up some of the smaller branches and take them inside to freshen the place up. Starting with the necessary, she piled a few branches inside and tossed a couple down the hole. After some thought, she decided to leave the door open to let it air and went to gather more branches for the main cabin.

As tiny as it was, there wasn't a lot to clean. She dragged the mattress off of the bunk and took it outside, thinking the sun and wind would freshen it. The blankets weren't in dire need of washing, and she didn't have anything to wash them with anyway except water since she discovered she'd left the soap the night before, but she carefully hung them over branches to blow in the breeze.

Leaving the front door wide, she moved around to the side of the cabin and stared at the branches again. Finally, with a sigh of resignation, she set to work moving them to the growing pile near the cabin. She supposed Taj meant to chop up what was useable for firewood, which meant she was going to have to move the smaller branches yet again once he was done.

Near midday, she looked up and saw one of the village women coming toward her. As the woman neared, she saw that it was a mature woman, though she found it difficult to pinpoint her age. She finally decided the woman probably wasn't much older than her, maybe mid thirties.

The woman walked right up to her and looked her over frankly.

Danica stared back at the woman warily.

"Kara lie," she said after a moment, looking strangely satisfied. "Not ugly."

Taken aback, Danica merely stared at her. After a moment, the woman leaned forward and flicked Danica's hair behind her shoulder. "No let others see this," she said, touching the translator in Danica's ear. "Bad thing for Taj."

Danica smoothed her hair over her ear again. "Why?" she asked uneasily.

The woman frowned. Obviously, she didn't have a translator. She shook her head and tapped her ear. "No have."

Wonderful. This was going to be interesting.

"Where Taj?"

Since she knew the woman wouldn't understand anything she said, and she didn't know anyway, she shrugged.

Apparently, that gesture was universal. The woman nodded, looking around. "Came for basket."

Enlightenment finally dawned, but Danica could hardly believe it. The woman must be his mother, but she looked so young! She thought about it really hard and finally remembered the word Taj had used and repeated it haltingly.

The woman smiled. "Smart."

Danica blushed at the compliment. "Thank you. I'm Danica."

The woman's brows rose questioningly. Danica touched her chest and repeated her name.

The woman imitated her. "Sheena."

Nodding that she'd understood, Danica turned and gestured toward the well. Leading the way, she took the pieces she'd washed and returned them to the basket carefully before she handed it to the woman.

"Enjoy?"

Danica didn't know whether she was asking if Taj had enjoyed it or her, but she nodded enthusiastically.

"You come my house. I teach."

"Really?" Danica asked, surprised but pleased that she'd offered.

Apparently the woman got the gist of it. Smiling, she nodded. "You learn feed my Taj. Taj no good cook. Kara no good cook. He starve."

Danica bit her lip, fighting the urge to smile. Obviously, his mother didn't particularly approve of his choice.

Amusement flared in the woman's bright blue eyes for a moment but was quickly quelled. "Bad thing. Taj no want. No choice. Chosen one." She gestured toward the partially finished house. "Work long time now, he no finish. Finish, Kara move in. Need finish. Bad thing, not finish. Much trouble. Maybe more than keep forbidden things," she ended, pointing toward Danica's ear.

Danica stared at her in confusion, wondering if she'd understood anything at all. It sounded to her as if she was saying Kara had been chosen for Taj, but if Taj didn't chose her and his mother hadn't, then who had? And why would Taj allow anyone to tell him whom he had to marry?

She finally decided she must have misunderstood.

Maybe his mother didn't know him as well as she thought she did?

It seemed certain, however, that Taj's fascination with alien technology was something forbidden, and liable to land him in trouble, but, again, she couldn't figure out who it was that posed a threat.

The followers of the sky gods? The priests, maybe?

She remembered that Taj had warned her it was dangerous to be an unbeliever. Uneasiness shivered through her. Despite what he'd said, she'd simply found it impossible to grasp that his people might be subjugated by some sort of religious fanatics that controlled their lives.

She still found it hard to believe, and yet it seemed to her that his mother was confirming it.

The woman motioned at her. "Come now. First lesson."

Danica glanced around uneasily. "Taj won't know where I am. He'll be angry."

The woman shook her head, either because she got the gist of it and considered it unimportant, or because she didn't understand but was determined to have her way. Danica went with her without further protest, hoping, if Taj did get pissed off, his mother would smooth things over for her.

The house Sheena led her to was one of the larger ones in the village. When the woman had led her inside, Danica stopped in the middle of the room and stared around her in amazement. In her other life, she very likely would have dubbed it quaintly rustic and shuddered inwardly at the unrefined furnishings. She'd learned an appreciation for anything remotely civilized, however.

The floor was made from something that closely resembled cement, but might only have been very well packed white clay. In any case, it felt solid, and looked solid. Brightly colored rugs that looked as if they'd been braided were scattered here and there around the floor. The furniture looked nearly as crude and rough as that in Taj's cabin, but cushions and pillows had been made for them and softened the overall effect. There was no glass in the window openings, only the shutters, which were opened wide to let in the light and Danica saw what looked like pottery lamps here and there about the room.

Sheena led her through the main room and into a second, much smaller room, which Danica realized must be the kitchen that had produced the wonderful food. Handing her a large, earthenware pitcher, Sheena pointed to a door. "Get water."

When Danica returned from the well, lugging the filled pitcher, she saw Sheena emerging from a hole in the floor, carrying a chunk of meat. Setting the meat down, she climbed down the steep, ladder-like stairs again and returned a few moments later carrying something that looked like vegetable roots.

Once she'd placed those on the table beside the meat, she led Danica out into the back yard to something that looked a lot like a kiln. Taking the wood stacked beside it, Sheena built a fire and then returned to the kitchen and put Danica to work cutting the meat into small pieces with a stone knife while she prepared the vegetables, tossing them into a shallow earthenware dish as she finished and indicating that Danica was to do the same with the meat.

Once they'd filled the dish, Sheena showed Danica the herbs she used to season the food and how much to add, then they took it back into the yard. Using the hem of her dress, Sheena opened the door and pushed the dish inside to cook.

Danica crossed her arms, staring at the oven.

Sheena studied her for several moments and finally laughed. "Cook slow, long time." She pointed at the position of the sun, which was almost directly overhead, and then to a point just above the tree line.

Danica studied it over for several moments and realized Sheena was telling her hours. She thought that was what she was telling her anyway. She was horrified to think it was going to take hours cook, and dismayed at the thought that she was going to have to figure out the timing by watch when Sheena used the sun--or figure out how to guess by the sun's position. Either way, it seemed much more complicated than she'd thought it would be. Preparing the dish for cooking had seemed pretty simple, except that Sheena didn't seem to have actually measured anything. She'd simply thrown meat and vegetables into the cooking dish until she decided it was enough and then thrown in a pinch of this and measure of that to season it.

Besides that, she'd had the impression that she was going to be allowed to take it with her. She'd spent much of the time while she was working envisioning the look of surprise on Taj's face when she proved to him she actually could learn how to cook.

Now it looked as if she was going to have to go back empty handed and try to convince Taj she hadn't merely wandered off, or tried to escape.

Disappointed, she followed Sheena back into the house.

She quickly discovered, however, that Sheena planned to make good use of the time while they waited. She ushered Danica to one corner of the main room and bade her sit on the floor, then dragged a large basket out, setting it beside the stool she apparently meant to use herself and picked up a strange looking tool.

Danica wasn't completely certain what it was in the basket, but it looked a lot like some kind of hair. Settling on the stool, Sheena took a small amount of the fiber from the basket and began rolling it between her palms until she'd produced something that looked like a skinny caterpillar. Attaching one end to the tool, she began twirling the tool and pulling on the caterpillar until it got longer and thinner.

Thread! Danica thought triumphantly, and then it hit her. This was how the blankets started. A sense of doom descended over her as she finally grasped the enormity of the labor it took to produce something that seemed so simple.

Small wonder they used animal hide to make their clothing!

Danica looked around the comfortable room through new eyes, realizing just how much work had gone into every single thing it held and feeling more ashamed than she'd ever felt in her life that she had considered it with a healthy dose of contempt. She'd appreciated it, especially after doing without everything for so long, but she had only appreciated it in that sense, not as a tremendous accomplishment but 'better than nothing'.

She hadn't said anything derogatory, and Sheena wouldn't have understood if she had, but she wondered uneasily if Sheena might have seen her thoughts in her expression. Taj had said he could read all her thoughts in her face.

It took an effort to push the thoughts to the back of her mind and concentrate on what Sheena was trying to teach her. Finally, Sheena handed the spinner to her and watched and directed her until she was sure Danica had the idea of it. Leaving it with her, she rose and took threads she'd already spun and dyed and began smoothing them and sorting them while she watched Danica.

Danica was pleased that it went fairly smoothly after she'd finally gotten used to using both hands independently. Just about the time she relaxed, however, she managed to catch a wad of her own hair in the damned thing. She was busy trying to untangle it when Taj arrived looking for her.

Chapter Thirteen

The moment Taj saw Danica sitting on the floor beside his mother very happily toying with his mother's spinner and a hank of yarn, his anxiety was instantly transformed into rage. For the past hour and more mindless fear had driven him while he had searched for her frantically, envisioning everything from finding her torn, bloodied body half eaten by some predator, to discovering she'd run off with one of the men of her own kind, to finding that the priests had taken her as a sacrifice. As relieved as he was to discover she was perfectly all right, the desire to beat her senseless was so strong for several moments that he felt dizzy with it.

One look at his mother's face stopped him cold in his tracks, however. Without uttering a single word, she chastised him for his lack of self control and dared him even to consider punishing Danica for his own failings.

With an effort, he tamped his urge to do violence, realizing the accusation in her eyes was completely justified. He'd risen before day and left Danica to her own devises, completely at the mercy of all those things he'd feared had happened to her--except he hadn't considered the jeopardy he was leaving her in until he'd returned and found her gone.

She had no more idea of the dangers that surrounded her here than a child. He knew, from the way she behaved and the things she said, that she had come from a world where there was little danger and little expectation of encountering it. She wasn't so stupid she didn't recognize a threat when she saw it. She was simply ignorant of his world, had no fear because she didn't know there was danger around every turn and because he had shielded her from it and she trusted that he would keep her safe.

Instead, he had been so mindless with lust after his lapse in judgment in trying to please her by making a foray to the forbidden ruins with her the night before, and so tormented by desires he didn't dare assuage, that he had fled the cabin like a green boy, seeking to distance himself to cool his blood.

He reddened with shame under his mother's hard stare, feeling suddenly as if he *was* a child again, rebellious, unreasonable, undeserving of respect as a man. He had to tamp the urge then to slink away in shame and that made him angry all over again.

He watched her in fuming silence as she caught Danica's face and tipped it up to her, then pulled the translator from her ear and dropped it into her lap, knowing the moment she did that that she meant to treat him to a dressing down as she had when he was a boy. Returning her attention to him, she said pointedly, "I have been teaching Danica to cook. She is not from our world and she knows none of the things a daughter of Glaxo would know. I have decided to make her my daughter."

Taj gaped at his mother in dismay, the one thought running through his mind the fact that if his mother acknowledged her as her adopted daughter, he would be forbidden to touch her as his sister. "She is no child! She is a woman full grown. You can not take her as your daughter!"

His mother shrugged. "I have no daughter. I will persuade the council."

"But … mother! She is mine! I found her," Taj growled angrily, reddening even more when he realized how much his very reasonable response sounded like his complaints to her when he had been a child and she had been determined to thwart him from keeping the treasures he had found. "I am high chieftain!" he reminded her.

Again his mother shrugged. "Kara told me she did not want the woman as her servant, and, in any case, she is right. Danica does not know enough to be a good servant. I will teach her and then I will have a daughter to help me … until she is wed."

"You will not!"

"Do not take that tone with me in my house!"

Taj ground his teeth. "I apologize, my mother."

She looked only slightly mollified, most likely because his tone wasn't particularly apologetic.

"I have need of her."

His mother waved that away. "You should train a nyatt to drag those limbs for you. They are better suited to it."

Taj glanced at Danica then back at his mother. "She has come to no harm. You know very well that I would not allow her to do, or tell her to do, anything she is not capable of doing."

"Kara does not want you to keep her."

"It is not Kara's decision," he ground out.

"There will be no harmony between you with the dark one there."

His lips tightened. "Perhaps Kara will not be there."

Sheena whitened. "Do not speak that aloud! *They* will learn of it."

"*They* will learn of it soon enough if I refuse to take her to wife."

"You were eager enough to take her before."

Taj's gaze flickered to Danica before he sent his mother an uncomfortable glance. "I was never eager to be guided by the priests in decisions that I am capable of making for myself. I am a man, not a child who must be told what is good for him because he does not have the experience to judge for himself."

"This is sacrilege!"

"It is reason, mother."

Sheena bit her lip, her face full of anxiety now. "You want this woman. I see it in your face and it will bring disaster to our house. Leave her with me. I will care for her and teach her what she must learn and she will not be there to tempt you to loose your head and do something foolish."

Taj swallowed with an effort against the thickness in his throat. "No."

"Why?"

"Because it is already too late for that, mother."

He could tell from the look of horror on his mother's face that she had immediately concluded that he had acted on his desires. He reddened. "I have not broken my vow of chastity mother. I only meant that taking her into your home will spare me nothing."

Sheena shook her head. "I was wrong to allow you to keep the forbidden things that have always fascinated you. I see what has come of it now. You think you can rebel against them and have your way, but you can not."

Taj scrubbed his hands over his face tiredly. "I am not planning rebellion, mother." He studied her a long moment. "Teach her. She knows nothing that she needs to know and she must learn for her own sake. But I will not allow you to take her."

Sheena sighed, but she knew defeat when she saw it. At least he had agreed to allow Danica to spend a part of her days with her. That would remove temptation from Taj's path some of the time and perhaps that would be enough to prevent him from doing anything dangerous. Reluctantly, she accepted the compromise, nodding her agreement.

* * * *

Danica had a burning desire to know what Taj and his mother had argued about, but it seemed likely it was going to be one of those desperate itches that would never get scratched. Taj certainly wasn't going to tell her and it seemed obvious since his mother had taken the damned translator from her that she wasn't going to be sharing either.

She'd thought at first that it was just an argument about her leaving without permission, but it had seemed just a little too heated for something that minor. After all, even though she hadn't actually asked if she could leave, she had been with his mother. He couldn't object to that, surely?

When he seemed to cool down a little, she decided to prod him for information. "Are you angry with me? Or your mother? Or both of us?"

He slid a glance down at her. Finally, his lips twisted wryly. "Me … I think."

"Oh." She thought it over for a few minutes and finally decided that if he wasn't mad she would point out that they'd left their supper at his mother's house. "I helped her make … uh … something with meat and vegetables. I think she was going to let me bring it back with me."

"Are thinking of stomach?" he asked, obviously irritated all over again.

Danica felt a blush rise to her cheeks. "I suppose you never think of yours," she said tartly.

"Brought meat," he said shortly.

"Yum," Danica muttered, ignoring the dark look he sent her as disappointment settled in, "blackened meat tonight."

Chapter Fourteen

Regardless of the fact that Taj had said he wasn't angry, he had continued to act irritated long after they'd returned to the cabin. Maybe she hadn't been around him long enough to figure him out as well as she'd thought, but she had gotten the distinct impression that he was really easy going. Despite the battle between them when he'd captured her, he hadn't seemed to hold a grudge about it. He'd ordered her around, but when he'd made her angry enough she'd lost her temper, he had taken it in good part.

He'd begun to brood, however, almost as soon as they'd gotten to his village, she finally realized.

In fact, now that she thought about it, he'd seemed to be in a pretty good humor right up until they'd met up with Kara.

She supposed Kara must be what had put him in such an unpredictable state.

It irritated the hell out of her.

Men! How was it, she wondered, that some women could just lead men around by their dicks? All that big tit blond bimbo had had to do was rub herself all over him and she had him working like a maniac to get her house finished!

It made her even madder to realize that it was probably that that been behind the incident at the damned pool. All this time she'd been toying with the idea that he was tense because of her, when he probably wouldn't have done anything to start with if Kara hadn't already teased him.

And he was too blind to see Kara was a total witch with a capitol B, self centered, spiteful, narcissistic and avaricious. It wasn't enough to have a big, nice house. She had to have the biggest house in the village.

And he wouldn't even take *her* to the pool now.

He'd said it was forbidden. If it was forbidden, why had he taken her the night before? Even if it was forbidden, he'd already taken her once. Why not do it again?

She supposed she could see his point, if it was against the rules to go. The more they went, the greater the chance of getting caught.

He still hadn't told her who had forbidden it, or why it was forbidden.

Sighing, Danica got up from the table to clean up from their meal.

Truth be told, she was looking forward to the time when Taj had the house finished herself. She figured he would probably build it like his mother's house, which meant it would have a cool place for storing food, and probably one of those oven things his mother cooked with. There'd be room for a bed, too, hopefully one she could sleep in.

She supposed by that time she'd be used to sleeping on the floor, but it wasn't something she wanted to accustom herself to. She knew the life she had had was a thing of the past. She knew the things she'd had were luxuries, even though she hadn't really realized it when she'd had them, and that she would never have anything like it again. Regardless of how backward this world was, however, there was still the possibility of having some comforts and she meant to see that she had them no matter how much work it took to get them.

When she'd wrapped the meat, cleaned the table and added a couple of pieces of wood to the dying fire, she went outside to the well. The moon had risen, lighting the way. Pulling her shift off, she carefully placed it where she wouldn't get it wet and began hauling up water to bathe with, shivering as she splashed the cool water over her warm skin.

She'd washed her hair the night before, but she'd hadn't managed to get all of the tangles out of it and she had decided enough was enough. She'd 'borrowed' the knife Taj used to cut the meat. She just hoped it was sharp enough to cut her hair with.

She jumped guiltily when she heard the door of the cabin open. Resisting the urge to turn around, she focused on her bath, deciding to wait until she heard Taj go back into the cabin before she tried cutting her hair.

He might not like it if he saw she had the knife.

She didn't hear him go back in, however. Wondering if he had and she just hadn't heard the door, she glanced around. She jumped when she discovered Taj was leaning against the cabin, watching her.

Had he seen her palm the knife? Or was he merely bored and looking for entertainment? And if the latter was the case, what sort of entertainment?

The kind that popped into her mind sent a rush of heat through her. Resolutely, she ignored it. She had no intention of acting as stand in for his bimbo until he could get his hands on what he really wanted.

She turned away when he pushed away from the wall and started toward her, feeling a moment of panic.

Why hadn't she just pretended she hadn't noticed him?

Had he taken her surprised gape as an invitation?

He took the water bag from her nerveless fingers and dropped it down the well, hauling up a skin full for her. She stared at him blankly for a moment as he held it up, but finally moved beneath the trickling water, raking her fingers through her hair as the water made it more manageable.

Keenly aware of the knife she'd lain on the edge of the well, she did her best not to look at it. When the water ceased to flow, she grabbed up the cloth she'd used to dry off with the night before and began drying herself briskly.

"Why have this?"

Danica felt a sinking sensation in the pit of her stomach even before she turned to see what it was he was asking her about. She stared at the knife in his hand for a long moment and finally looked up at him, trying to jog her panicked brain into supplying her with an acceptable answer.

She was suddenly very certain that he wouldn't be at all pleased with her decision to whack her hair off.

Maybe because there wasn't a soul in the village, man, woman, or child, that had short hair?

The realization of just how reluctant she was to displease him, irritated her. "I'm going to cut my hair off. I don't have a comb and I'm tired of it getting in my way. Half the thread I spun today was made with my hair," she retorted tartly.

He studied her hair a moment, his lips flattening disapprovingly. Without surprise, she watched him slip the knife into the sheath at his waist.

She wanted to argue about it, but decided that would only make him more determined to prevent her from cutting her hair. Instead, she pretended to dismiss it with a shrug and turned to pull her shift on before he could accuse her of trying to tease him again. He was certainly unreasonable enough to be a human male!

When she'd struggled into the shift, she stalked back to the cabin, leaving him standing beside the well.

Naturally, he followed her, keeping step until they reached the door of the cabin once more. She went in, grabbed the blankets she used for a pallet and began unrolling them.

He surprised her when he came up behind her. Catching one arm, he guided her to the bunk and urged her to sit. Confused and a little unnerved, Danica perched on the edge, studying him uneasily as he settled behind her, stretching one leg along the bunk and shifting closer so that she was settled between his spread legs.

She thought, at first, that it was the knife he pulled from the waist of his loincloth and flinched when he grasped a lock of hair. To her surprise, she saw it was a comb carved from what looked like bone.

"You've got a comb!" she exclaimed, reaching for it. She didn't know why she hadn't realized he must. His hair was usually neat and it was longer than hers. It was fine, though, and very straight, like her mother's hair had been, which meant it resisted tangling much better than hair like hers. Her mother had hated her own hair, couldn't get it to hold so much as a crimp for more than five minutes, but she had envied the sleekness of it and the fact that it always looked neat when her own hair tended toward unmanageable much of the time, even with all the things she'd had before to tame the soft curls.

He held the comb out of her reach. "I comb."

Danica gaped at him a moment in surprise, but finally sighed. She knew it was useless to argue with him. It hadn't taken a full week with him to figure that out. Once he made up his mind to do something, he was stubborn as hell.

She'd come to realize though, that even something seemingly as simple as a comb was hard to get on Glaxo, precious, and therefore guarded like gold. He probably didn't trust her not to break it.

It was fine by her if he wanted to do the honors. At least it would get combed, and that was what mattered.

About five seconds into it, however, she began to feel uncomfortably aware of his nearness, his hands in her hair, the occasional brush of his skin against hers as he worked his way through the snarls.

An all too familiar warmth began to spread through her. She closed her eyes, trying to pretend it was someone else combing her hair. Instead, closing her eyes only seemed to focus her more surely on his warmth, his touch, the faint, enticingly male scent of his skin.

Her mind instantly supplied her with the memories she'd been trying so hard to shelve of the night beside the hot pool.

She'd done her utmost to convince herself she was no more physically attracted to Taj than he was her. In a distant sort of way, she'd admired his purely masculine beauty.

She'd tried hard to believe it was distant. She had to suppose now that it hadn't been blatantly obvious because, except for that one incident, she hadn't been this close to him before that she hadn't had something else dominating her mind to overshadow her attraction.

She felt an urgent desire to put some distance between them, acutely conscious of the heat of his body penetrating the fabric that covered her back, the leg he'd stretched out on the bunk beside her grazing her hip, his bare knee near her elbow. She swallowed with an effort, trying to regulate her pounding heart, hoping he wouldn't notice her sudden breathlessness, or recognize it for what it was if the did.

She was so caught up in the heated desire flooding her, and her desperation to keep him from noticing, several moments passed before she realized that he'd ceased to comb her hair and merely sat behind her, unmoving. Swallowing against the dryness of her mouth and throat, she nerved herself to glance back at him over her shoulder. In the flickering light of the fire, she saw that his expression was taut.

He lifted his hand, smoothing his palm over the dark hair.

His gaze met hers. For several heartbeats, they merely stared at one another while Danica tried to decide whether she saw desire in his eyes or only his awareness of her own, while she considered closing the short distance between them and brushing her lips against his in mute invitation.

Realizing finally that his body was rigid with tension, she looked away. His hand settled on her waist. Her belly jumped, tightened reflexively. She sat as still as a stone, waiting breathlessly to see if he would do anything else--touch her, pull her close, push her away. His fingers tightened and then, almost reluctantly, it seemed, he removed his hand. His fingers grazed her back as she got up and moved to retrieve her bedroll, sending a shiver of keen awareness skating down her spine.

With an effort, she ignored it. There was little doubt in her mind that he'd noticed her desire, but more than she liked as to whether or not he'd felt anything similar. It seemed certain, either way, that she'd misjudged him. Quite obviously, he would not settle for her to ease his needs as she'd hoped and feared when she saw that he'd come out to watch her bathe.

Abruptly, she was angered by it.

The anger was unreasonable and she knew it. Only moments before, when she had thought that was what he had in mind, she'd been indignant at the thought of being used as a substitute for what he couldn't have. She should be relieved that he had enough self restraint to control himself.

She supposed, though, as she smoothed the blankets and settled at last, that what was really bothering her was that he was *able* to control himself.

She couldn't convince herself that he had that much moral fortitude. The alternative was that it simply didn't take that much effort.

Chapter Fifteen

Taj was back to hacking at the trees the following morning as if his life depended upon denuding the forest around his small farm. He stopped when Danica presented herself for work. Leaning the handle of the ax against a log, he motioned for her to follow him and set out toward town.

Danica had mixed feelings about it. As hard as the work was that his mother had shown her, it was still far less physically demanding than pulling limbs. She was also anxious to learn the skills to cook a decent meal.

It was ironic that she'd spent so much time back on Earth worrying about gaining weight and working determinedly to preserve her youthful appearance by staying physically fit. Now she was sorry that she hadn't had a few more pounds to shed than the ten or fifteen she'd been constantly battling.

The Atkins diet certainly worked. She'd had little besides meat since she'd arrived and she could see the difference in her body already.

She was certainly not happy about it, however. She'd hadn't realized she had such a craving for starches.

The problem was Taj and his mother had argued rather heatedly about her the day before and she wasn't certain what taking her to his mother meant. Was she in training? Or was it only that he didn't want her around?

Had she been too obvious about lusting over his body?

It was an embarrassing thought.

She found when he'd left her that she didn't have quite the enthusiasm she'd had the day before, which was when it occurred to her that her objective wasn't just to have the skills she needed for her own sake. She'd hoped to impress Taj.

He and his mother had another disagreement when they arrived, this time about the translator. The moment Taj removed his and held it out to his mother, she turned as white as a sheet and looked absolutely terrified.

"No!" she said emphatically, holding her hand up. "Is forbidden use machine. No want evil thing my house."

Taj frowned. "How teach when you not understand Danica?"

"Danica understand me. Is enough."

"Can not ask question."

"No care. Take away that thing. Danica must learn our speak she stay."

"Priests not know you have," Taj said reasonably.

"Always know everything," she said stubbornly.

Shrugging, obviously irritated, he replaced it in his ear and left without another word.

Distracted by the disagreement, Danica puzzled over it, trying to make sense of it.

The only part of it that did make sense to her was that, apparently, the priests controlled every aspect of their lives.

They wanted them ignorant, she realized finally. As long as they kept Taj's people ignorant, they could retain control of the villagers. Enlightenment would almost certainly bring about a lessening of superstition and make controlling them more difficult.

She still couldn't figure out how the priests were supposed to 'know' everything, though. She was pretty sure she hadn't seen one of them since she arrived and electronic listening devices would be light years from their grasp.

She was reasonably certain she didn't want to either if they terrorized the villagers, who, as a whole, were quite possibly the finest specimens she'd ever seen. All of the men were tall and muscular. All of the women voluptuous, but certainly not fat. In fact, she'd be willing to bet even Sheena was stronger than she was, despite being her elder by a number of years.

They had nothing to defend themselves with, however, except crude, primitive weapons. Taj was the only one she'd seen with a metal sword. The others seemed to have nothing but spears and bows.

Maybe that was it. What technology there was, the priests reserved for themselves?

She discovered the project of the day was mattress making. They spent much of the morning preparing something that looked like rounded loaves of bread, but once they'd placed them in the oven, Sheena took her inside once more, produced two lengths of cloth, a needle and thread, and set her to making tiny stitches along three edges. The fourth was only sewn about halfway across.

Mystified, Danica struggled with the cumbersome thing, leaving tiny dots of blood along the seams since she stabbed her fingers with the sharp piece of bone almost as regularly as she managed to poke it through the fabric. She hoped it wouldn't be noticeable.

Sheena tsked, shaking her head, but seemed to take it in stride.

When they'd removed the baking from the oven, they took the bag Danica had put blood, sweat and tears into making and left the house, heading for the shed. There, Danica discovered a veritable mountain of bird feathers of every color. She spent the remainder of the day sorting the feathers that still had quills attached, stripping them and stuffing the bag. By the time Sheena returned to check her progress, the light was already fading, Danica's fingers throbbed incessantly and her back and neck were killing her from the hours she'd spent hunched over.

She was also itching from the down that had coated her from head to toe, clinging to her skin, and she had sneezed and rubbed her nose until it felt raw.

The bag was finally stuffed, although she was far too miserable to feel a great deal of triumph over having finished it.

Sheena helped her to lug the filled bag back inside the house then showed her how to seal the open end. She was still stitching on it when Taj arrived.

One look at his face was enough to assure her she hadn't imagined the down. She probably looked as if she'd been rolled in it. Glaring at him for smiling, she focused on finishing the seam and knotted the thread, biting the thread to break it when she was done.

She was rewarded by a loaf of the bread she'd helped Sheena to bake … which almost made up for the hours she'd spent torturing herself over whatever it was she'd made.

To her surprise, Taj took the cushion from her when she'd finished. Tossing it over his shoulder, he headed out the door once more. Shaking her head, Danica took the loaf Sheena held out, thanked her, and followed. He led the way, assuming she was behind him, which would've irritated her more if she'd had enough energy left after the day she'd spent to feel much besides tired.

When she reached the cabin and went in, she saw that Taj had arranged the mattress she'd made. Hearing her, he stepped back so that she could see he'd added a bunk above the one he had been sleeping on. He'd moved the old mattress to the top and placed the one she'd made on the bottom.

Danica stared at the double decker for several moments before it actually sank in that he'd spent the day building a bed for her. She thought for several moments that she would burst into tears. It took an effort to keep from rushing over to him and hugging him. Somehow, though, she had a feeling he wouldn't welcome such a display of gratitude.

He frowned at the tears swimming in her eyes. "No like?"

Her chin wobbled. Afraid to open her mouth for fear she'd squall, she nodded instead, sniffing. Finally, she moved toward it and sat on it very carefully.

She discovered a quill she'd missed almost immediately, but overall it felt better than anything she'd sat on in a long time. She looked up at Taj. "Thank you. This was just so sweet!"

As she'd known she would, she started crying the moment she tried to speak.

Frowning, Taj knelt in front of her. "Something wrong," he said with certainty.

Sniffing, she shook her head. "No. It's just … I'm so overwhelmed that you and your mother have been so kind to me."

"So cry?" he demanded, obviously considerably outdone at her reaction.

Danica uttered a sound midway between a laugh and a sob. "It doesn't make sense, does it?"

"Miss home," he said intuitively.

She did, so badly it didn't bear thinking on, but for all that Taj had informed her that she was his slave, he didn't treat her like one and his mother certainly didn't. She doubted seriously that her own mother would have shown even half as much concern for a complete stranger as they had her. "Not so much now," she lied.

He tapped the bottom of her chin so that she looked up at him. "Will be better."

Sniffing back her tears, she mopped her eyes with her hands. "I know."

After a moment, he smiled faintly. "Danica look like beautiful, strange bird."

She blinked, confused at the abrupt change in conversation and tone of it, though she realized he was trying to divert her.

He pulled a feather from her hair and showed it to her, and she was torn between embarrassment and amusement. Chuckling self-consciously, she raked her fingers through her hair and extracted several more. "I think I got more on me than in the thing. Poked holes in my fingers, too," she added, showing him her abused fingers.

He grasped her hands, lifting them to study the punctures more closely. "Should sew cloth, not fingers," he said finally, his eyes teasing as he looked up at her.

"Why didn't I think of that?" Danica said dryly, trying to pull her hands from his grip.

His hold tightened. Lifting her hands, he brushed his lips lightly over the injured tips. Danica's stomach clenched. A rush of warmth washed through her.

Uncomfortable, she tugged against his hold once more.

Frowning, he released her. "Cook now," he said gruffly.

Danica chuckled. "Thinking of your stomach?"

Amusement flickered in his eyes. "Work hard. Build strong bed so plump woman no break."

"Plump!" Danica gasped indignantly. "I am *not* fat!"

He looked her over critically. "Thinking food all time. Get fat."

Danica shook her head, torn between amusement and indignation. "Men! You are such an ass!"

He frowned. "What ass?"

She chuckled. "A stubborn animal with long ears that says hee haw."

His eyes narrowed.

"Of course some people mean this when they call somebody an ass," she said, patting her butt saucily.

He swatted it soundly and chuckled at the look of shock that came over her face. "No respect. Taj high chieftain here. Should respect."

Rubbing her butt, she moved away from him, putting the fire pit between them as she studied him doubtfully, trying to figure out if he really was angry about her calling him an ass.

He shook his head, smiling faintly. "Taj not believe. Danica never fear Taj. Greatest warrior in all Glaxo. Men shake. Woman swoon. Danica poke with finger and growl."

Danica bit her lip to quell a smile. It occurred to her to wonder, though, if he really was joking about the comment about his prowess as a warrior. He hadn't said it was if he was serious, but now that he mentioned it, she'd noticed the other villagers tended to give him a wide berth and those who acknowledged him did so respectfully.

If she'd considered it at all before, she would've thought the way they behaved around him must have to do with his tendency to ignore the 'forbidden' whenever it suited him, that he made them nervous, or maybe that it was just the custom of these people, not particular to Taj. Sheena certainly wasn't timid, and yet she was terrified of being discovered using any forbidden technology.

Unfortunately, she couldn't ask Sheena about it since she could understand what Sheena said, but not vice versa. Her curiosity couldn't be completely appeased by merely observing. Besides, she knew Sheena was right. If she was going to live among them, she couldn't expect them to learn her language. She would have to learn theirs. Once she'd made up her mind that she had to learn their language, she stopped wearing the translator except when absolutely necessary, knowing that as long as she had it to rely on she would use it as a crutch.

It wasn't easy. Even though she spent most of every day with Sheena, after nearly three weeks, she'd only managed to accumulate a vocabulary of about a hundred words, and she still didn't know how to make them into sentences, much less carry on a conversation.

It didn't help that Taj, apparently, had a warped sense of humor. As soon as he saw she was struggling to master his language, he began to coach her, and when she repeated it to Sheena, she would either laugh, or look horrified and give Taj a tongue lashing when he came to collect her.

She couldn't trust her own judgment, either. Sometimes he'd coach her with perfect seriousness and it would turn out that he'd taught her something naughty. The next time, his eyes would gleam with amusement and she'd find out that the words meant exactly what he'd told her they meant. When she, or his mother, fussed about it, he would behave for just long enough she would let her guard down, and then he would teach her something else outrageous. She'd been telling him 'I like your ass' for almost a week before she discovered that it didn't mean 'Light the fire'. She wouldn't have tumbled to it then, since she'd grown wary of asking Sheena the meanings of words Taj had taught her, except that he finally burst out laughing.

After that, she went back to wearing the translator.

Taj waited until she was sound asleep, removed it from her ear and refused to give it back to her.

When Danica had searched the cabin thoroughly, she turned to study him suspiciously, her gaze resting speculatively on his loincloth. Grinning, Taj lay back on his bunk, crossed his arms behind his head and invited her to search.

She had to suppose he was accustomed to retiring females. He just couldn't seem to get it through his head that she wasn't the least bit shy. After studying the challenge in his eyes several moments, she crawled onto the bunk, straddled his thighs, and patted him down.

That was when she discovered that he hadn't underestimated her. She'd underestimated him. He'd known she wouldn't be able to resist the challenge. The moment she settled, he caught her and rolled over on top of her.

Chapter Sixteen

Danica blinked at Taj in breathless surprise as he levered himself up and stared down at her, all traces of amusement gone from his face. With deliberation, he caught her hand and guided it to the waist of his loincloth.

She hesitated in uncertainty then. It was one thing to search him with purely clinical detachment, another entirely to deliberately touch him intimately. She wanted to. She could see that he wanted her to.

Reason was fading fast into the sunset as the heat of desire welled upward and flowed through her veins. She knew that as small as the village was, though, that there was no way she could be intimate with Taj without everyone figuring it out fairly quickly and god only knew what sort of repercussions there could be in such a society.

Pregnancy was also a risk. Never having had to worry overmuch about it in her adult life, the realization that that was no longer the case sent a chilling jolt through her.

And yet, her mind argued, the villagers must know how to prevent unwanted pregnancies. There were not nearly as many children as one would expect in a primitive society like theirs. In all the time she'd been there, she hadn't seen any couple who had more than two children.

He'd already stiffened to pull away from her when need finally subjugated reason.

She slipped her hand beneath the waist of his loincloth and cupped his turgid cock.

He gasped, the breath rushing from his chest as if she'd punched him. His features contorted as if he were in agony. His arms began to tremble. Slowly, he lowered himself against her, resting his forehead against the crook of her neck and shoulder.

Doubt swarmed up inside of her again. Every reason why she should not be doing what she was doing surfaced.

Ignoring the warning voice inside her head, she massaged his length experimentally. He groaned, gasping as if she was torturing him, his tumescent flesh jerking against her hand. Finally, he reached between them and very carefully pulled her hand away from his heated flesh. For several moments afterward, he merely lay tautly against her, struggling with whatever inner demons were riding him.

Abruptly, he rolled off of her, hesitated and then got off the bunk. "Can not do this," he said, his voice hoarse. With that, he strode from the cabin, slamming the door behind him.

Danica was too stunned by his abrupt departure to move for several moments. The sudden loss of heat sent a shiver through her, but her mind simply refused to grasp that he'd abandoned her.

Why? Her mind couldn't seem to move far from the question, couldn't supply any palatable answers. Discomfited by her unrequited needs, inexplicably hurt, she rolled onto her side, but it was a long time before she slept.

Taj didn't look as if he'd slept at all as he walked her to his mother's house the following day. He looked like a bear that had been woken from hibernation--dangerous.

She felt about the same way, however, and was in no mood to either care that he was disgruntled, or to attempt to draw him out of his mood.

When they arrived, he drew his mother outside to speak to her in low tones, breaking through her self-absorption for the first time. Her curiosity went as unappeased as her needs had the night before, though, since, try as she might, she couldn't hear what was under discussion.

She didn't discover precisely what Taj had said to his mother, but she had her first hint when she found out she would be staying the night with his mother. By the time another day and night had passed, she was less angry than confused and hurt.

Had she completely read the signals wrong? Done something that had thoroughly disgusted Taj?

She'd thought he was enjoying it, but he'd certainly left abruptly if he was. Had she been so focused on what she'd wanted that she'd missed subtle hints that her efforts weren't appreciated?

He'd accused her before of teasing him, but she hadn't instigated what had happened between them the night before. He had. It almost reminded her of when she'd been a teenager and desperate to find some pleasure even while fearing that going too far would bring disaster down upon her, the urge to try a little fondling, and then the discovery that, while it certainly brought pleasure, it also brought a lot more misery.

She and Taj were both adults, though, certainly old enough to make the wrong decision and figure out how to fix it later.

It seemed that there must be some really serious sexual taboos among his people, but she had an uneasy feeling it was even more than that.

As peaceful as the community seemed, there was something going on that was completely beyond her understanding, and it had begun to look like she wasn't going to be able to figure it out until she could understand the language a little better.

Desperation finally drove her to struggle through a half mime half verbal inquisition of his mother one day when they were coming back from collecting herbs in the woods. "Not many," she said, pointing to one of the children she saw playing. "Why?"

Sheena glanced from Danica to the child. An indecipherable expression crossed her features. "Same," she said. "In village, 200 male, 200 female. Match," she added, putting her two index fingers together.

Danica frowned. She was pretty sure she'd gotten the question across, however. It seemed to her that Sheena was determined to pretend she didn't understand. "Much sick?" she prodded.

Sheena pretended not to grasp the question. Danica was certain of it that time. She was determined to have some answers, however. Once they were in Sheena's kitchen, she tried again. "How not many? Have way not have many?"

Sheena sent her an amused glance. "Not sex. Not have."

Danica felt a blush rising. If not having sex was their way of birth control, it might be effective, but it sure as hell sucked. She realized, dimly, that she'd hoped they had some kind of herb they used.

She had to say one thing for these people, they weren't the sort that didn't practice what they preached. She had never seen such carefully controlled reproduction, even in her own society, and she knew for a fact that the more backwards countries on Earth didn't practice birth control of any kind, unless one counted starvation. Abstinence didn't seem to be a word any of them were familiar with.

Not that she could blame them. There wasn't much that was more torturous than wanting and not being able to have.

She should have known, just from the fact that Taj clearly needed release and just as clearly wasn't going to take it that he must have a powerful motivation for denying himself. It was certainly balm to her wounded ego, but she wasn't certain of just how much faith she could put in it. Why had he initiated it to start with if he hadn't meant to go through with it? Testing his control?

It would be nice to think he'd considered he could enjoy a little fooling around without letting it get out of hand and then realized he didn't have as much control as he'd thought.

There hadn't been a lot of that, though, and as much as she'd like to think it was because she turned him on so much, if they lived celibate lives, unless they ingested something to inhibit their libido, it probably didn't take a whole lot to get their engines revved.

Maybe that was why she never saw any of them hugging, or kissing, or even just holding hands?

Something didn't feel entirely right about her reasoning. After a while, she realized that the reason it didn't was because of Sheena's reaction to her questions and her pretense of having misunderstood. Even though she'd carefully kept her thoughts on the subject concealed, Danica sensed that she'd been afraid.

It was also damned strange, now that she thought about it, that there was exactly the same number of males to females. How often did that happen naturally?

And what had Sheena meant by 'match'?

They were paired?

A faint uneasiness wafted through her. Taj's wife had been chosen for him and it sounded as if Sheena was saying this was typical practice, but it wasn't *their* custom, *their* choice. The choices were made by the priests.

They were being bred.

Danica dismissed the idea almost the moment it occurred to her. It was just too wild. Why would they be bred? Except for such decisions being made for them, she couldn't see that they were enslaved, used as labor or anything like that. She supposed it was possible that the priests gathered a portion of everything they grew and manufactured and that would, in a sense, make them slaves. But why breed them so carefully, if, in fact, that was what they were doing?

The village constituted a fairly small gene pool. Maybe that was all there was to it? The priests were advanced enough to know that indiscriminate breeding would weaken the Glaxons, produce sickly, perhaps defective, offspring?

She wasn't completely easy with that conclusion either. It would explain why they didn't go around screwing whatever struck their fancy. It didn't explain why they were so careful to produce only one or two children, and she was almost positive that Sheena had said that was something they were careful to control themselves, not another edict from the priests.

Shortly before midday, four days after he'd left her, Taj returned, leading that damn bird she hated. Tied across the bird's back were two large animals that resembled something from the deer family on Earth.

Sheen didn't seem the least surprised, so she supposed Sheen had been told about the hunting trip.

Taj seemed almost like his old self, except that he was coolly distant.

They spent most of the remainder of the day processing and preserving the meat. They were still hard at work when Danica heard something that sounded like a horn.

Lifting her head curiously, she saw that both Taj and Sheena were as pale as ghosts and standing as rigidly alert as an animal caught in the cross-hairs of a hunter's gun.

Without a word, almost as if they'd ceased to be aware of anything else around them, they stopped what they were doing and began to move around toward the front of Sheena's house.

Stunned, Danica merely stared at them for several moments. Finally, she followed them.

When they reached the road that ran in front of Sheena's house, Danica saw that all of the villagers had gathered along the main road that bisected the village. All of them were staring into the distance, waiting.

Following the direction of their gaze, Danica saw dust rising in the distance. The horn sounded again, louder this time. In a few moments, she heard a pounding sound, as of many feet on packed dirt.

A 'herd' of the giant birds appeared in the distance, closing fast. Danica's heart slammed into her chest wall. For several moments, she thought it was a stampede.

She saw the riders then. More specifically, she saw dark cloaks flying behind them like waving flags.

"What is it? What's happening?" she asked in a frightened whisper.

Taj glanced at her sharply as if realizing for the first time that she was standing beside him. "Go inside. Now!"

Danica merely gaped at him. "Why?"

He seized her arms in a bruising grip, giving her a shake. "No question. Go!" he said furiously.

"Priests see Danica," Sheena whispered fearfully. "Bad happen."

Suddenly as fearful as the rest of the villagers, Danica stumbled away when Taj released her with a hard push in the direction of the house. Too confused to think straight, she did as she was told and scurried inside. Once she'd closed the door, she realized she was shaking, more because of the urgency in Taj's voice and the fear in Sheena's than anything else.

She knew Taj would be livid if he caught her peering through one of the windows, but she'd had enough of wondering what cloud hung over this place. She had to know what sort of threat it was.

The riders slowed as they reached the edge of the village. Danica moved from one window to the next, peering through the crevice between the shutters. She could see little even as the riders came nearer.

Their heads were swathed in something that looked like turbans, the lower portion of their faces covered. She could see that they were big, however, at least as big as the Glaxon's, possibly bigger. Each wore a sword strapped at their side. Beneath the cloaks, she saw the glint of metal and decided it must be something like armor.

She thought at first that they were wearing some sort of dark leather gauntlets. As they passed, riding in formation three abreast, she stared hard at the wedge of face visible above the cloths that covered the lower portion of their faces, however, and finally realized it wasn't leather of any sort. It was their skin.

They weren't anything at all like the villagers. They looked … reptilian.

Chapter Seventeen

Disbelief was Danica's first reaction. The longer she studied the 'priests', however, the more certain she was that she was right. Even with the distance that separated her from them, she could see their eyes-- a dull, merciless yellow with slitted pupils that sent shivers racing up and down her spine. There was no bridge to their nose. The cloths covering their lower faces hung straight down, without the protrusion of lips or nostrils.

As they passed along the road, they turned to study the villagers, almost as if they were counting them.

When they'd passed out of sight, Danica realized that she'd been counting the priests. In all, there were fifty, including the two who had led the group, all armed to the teeth.

Come to collect the rent, she wondered?

The villagers remained where they were, standing rigidly at attention long after the 'priests' had passed from Danica's view. She decided they could not be merely passing through.

Danica stood away from the window, wondering if she dared try one of those that were open. The shutters on the front of the house had been closed against the afternoon sun, but those on the shaded side were still wide. She might be able to see what was going on if she tried one of those windows.

Sheena had been afraid that they would be in trouble if the priests spotted her, though. If there was a chance she might bring danger to them, she couldn't risk it just to appease her curiosity.

She forgot all about her resolve, however, when she heard the screams.

Running to the window, she peered in the direction the priests had disappeared. They were too far away, though, and there were houses and trees blocking her view, preventing her from seeing more than some sort of commotion. As they seemed to form up and turn toward her once more, she collected herself sufficiently to realize she couldn't remain in plain view. Ducking down, she moved to the front windows again, moving from one to the next until she had the longest view.

The screams became mournful sobs as the group returned. When they came abreast of the house once more, Danica saw that one of the village men, his hands tied, was astride one of the birds now, riding with one of the priests. The riders gained speed as they headed out of town once more. Behind them, a young woman and an older woman followed, wailing, their arms outstretched in supplication.

It was only after the dust cloud of their passing had settled that anyone moved. The women of the village crowded around the two who'd collapsed in the road.

Suddenly discovering her knees felt like limp noodles, Danica wilted onto the floor, covering her face with her hands.

It didn't take a great deal of intelligence to figure out they would not be seeing that young man again.

"Come. We go home."

Danica looked up at Taj in surprise, having been too wrapped up in shock to notice he'd come in. She stared at him for several moments questioningly and finally got to her feet. When he led her outside, she saw that the villagers had disappeared.

She glanced at Taj several times as they traversed the distance between his mother's house and his farm. His face looked as if it had been carved from stone.

"What happened?" she demanded once they were inside the cabin.

Taj merely stared at her for several moments. Finally, without a word, he turned and strode toward the door. Fury washed through Danica. She followed him outside. "Tell me, damn it!" she demanded, grabbing his arm.

He halted, staring at her so coldly it was almost as if she was looking at a complete stranger. "Priests take sacrifice," he said harshly.

Danica felt her jaw drop as a wave of shocked disbelief and terror went through her. It was several moments before she roused herself sufficiently to realize Taj had pulled free and walked off again.

She chased after him, moving in front of him to block his path, feeling the fury of pure terror pumping through her. "Jesus fucking Christ! You mean to say they took that man to kill him while everybody just stood around like a fucking stone and did nothing?"

Rage suffused Taj's face. "Try, priests kill all!" he roared furiously.

At any other time, Danica would have been cowed by such violence of temper. She was running on adrenaline, however. She didn't even flinch. "It looks to me like they'll kill *all* one by one if nothing is done! Is that why there are so few children?"

"Yes! No one want bear child for priests to take."

Danica studied him for several moments. "But they have to, don't they? How many are the villagers required to produce? Two? Three? How many of Sheena's sons have they taken?"

Taj grasped her upper arms bruisingly. For several moments, she thought he was going to shove her away. To her surprise, he pulled her tightly against him. "Next time, take woman," he said hoarsely.

Danica thought she was going to be sick. "Jesus!"

Evenly matched. They kept them paired. Now she knew why Taj was so reluctant to marry Kara. Now she knew why Sheena was so anxious for him to do as he'd been told.

She was suddenly sorry she knew. Ignorance was bliss.

Wrapping her arms around Taj, she tried to communicate her sympathy, stroking his back soothingly. When he pulled away at last, she lifted a hand to his cheek. "I'm so sorry, Taj! I just didn't underst…."

He cut her off, covering her mouth almost bruisingly with his own. Anger, fear, and need came together in a fierce ravishment of her mouth with his lips and tongue that sent keen desire pouring through Danica's veins with the corrosive fire of acid. She slipped her hand from his cheek to his neck, to hold herself closer to his hard strength, to steady herself, as an inferno of desire decimated every thought and sent her senses reeling.

When he finally released her, she was gasping for breath. Glancing around, he pushed her backwards and she felt her back come up against the trunk of a tree. Briefly, the certainty that he'd thrust her away washed through her. In the next moment, however, he pressed tightly against her from chest to groin, grinding his erection against her lower belly. Feeling the moisture of want flood her femininity, Danica came up on her tiptoes, tipping her hips up to meet his thrusts, frustrated as much as pleasured by the pressure that teased as much as it assuaged her need to feel him intimately.

Catching her beneath the arms, he lifted her up. Danica tightened her arms around his neck and wrapped her legs around him, making a sound of pleasure in her throat as he cock settled more surely against her cleft, sending wild jolts of exquisite sensation through her. Groaning, he sought her lips once more with more hunger than before, stroking his tongue along hers and the keenly sensitive inner surfaces of her mouth with something akin to desperation.

Danica's heart was pounding so savagely against her chest wall and at every pulse point of her body that darkness warred with the heat of desire filling her as she felt the weeks of sexual tension winding rapidly toward an explosive culmination. Dissatisfaction filled her. She wanted him inside of her, wanted to feel every hard inch of him caressing her passage.

She could not stay her body's determination to find release, and began to tremble as the first, faint palpitations gripped her. As ecstasy seemed to consume her, she tore her lips from his, gasping keenly. He groaned hoarsely, shuddering as his body jerked with his own release.

For many moments they remained still, struggling to regulate their erratic hearts and breaths. Finally, Taj released his grip on her legs and allowed her to slide down until her feet touched the ground. He did not move away from her, however, instead pressing himself tightly against her as he nibbled at the exposed flesh along her neck and throat. "Danica make Taj crazy," he murmured hoarsely.

Finally, almost reluctantly, he pulled away from her. "Not follow no more. Go. Before do something both regret."

Danica stared at him shakily, belatedly aware of the fact that they were standing in clear view of anyone who might pass along the road. Both guilt and uneasiness swamped her then. Numbly, thoroughly confused over how she felt about what had just happened between them, she fled back to the cabin.

Guilt began to take clear precedence as she went to the well and drew water to cool her heated face, guilt that she'd succumbed to lust in the very midst of a horrific calamity that had thrown the entire village into mourning. The timing was as insensitive and disgraceful as laughing in the middle of a wake.

She wasn't even entirely sure of how it had come about that fear and an honest attempt to offer comfort had translated into mindless lust, but it had left an unpleasant taste of self-loathing in her mouth.

Chapter Eighteen

A dark cloud had appeared on Danica's horizon and nothing she could do would shake it. From what she could see, as devastated as the Glaxon's were about loosing their loved ones, everyone, basically, accepted that it was something that couldn't be changed. She'd never considered herself a rebel, but then she'd never been in such a situation, never even conceived of anything like it.

Taj refused to discuss it with her at all, turning stony faced with anger each time she tried to broach the subject. Balked, Danica turned her determination on Sheena, refusing to allow her to pretend she didn't know what Danica was talking about.

"Something has to be done. You can't just stand by and allow this to happen. Surely there's some way to stop this?"

Sheena finally turned on her angrily. "No can stop. Tried many times. When Sheena child, first see priests. Not many then. Stay far from my people. In time, the great temple of many towers rise and with it, power of priests. Sheena father great chieftain. Call warriors, make war to drive them from our lands. Priests slay half my people. Glaxon people become slave. Many years pass, husband of Sheena take sons, call men to war once more. Husband die, eldest son die, many die. Taj almost die too. Taj great chieftain now, but no can bring people together. Not many seasons ago, in village once near here, man talk people to fight when priests come. They kill all, man, woman, child … even tiny babies. Drag them through every village to show. Villagers see what happened other village. No will fight. No will try. They are too many, and our warriors too few now. Have weapons much superior Glaxon weapons. This way, some live."

Danica felt sick to her stomach at the image that rose in her mind's eye. Fear quickly followed when she thought of what the priests would do if they learned that Taj had tried to instigate a rebellion. She had come to care about Taj and his mother. She couldn't bear the thought of anything happening to either one of them.

And yet, despite everything Sheena had said, and her own fears, she couldn't imagine carrying on with life with something like this hanging over them.

"Is there no one you can turn to for help?"

Sheena shook her head. "Sky gods favor priests. No help people of Glaxon."

Danica's lips tightened. "I'm sure you're right, but they sure as hell aren't gods if you're talking about the same assholes that dumped me here. I wouldn't be at all surprised to discover it was the so called 'sky gods' that dumped the 'priests' here. They sure as hell don't look like they belong on this planet."

Sheena looked horrified and refused to speak to her the rest of the day.

Danica backed off, but she had no intention of simply caving in if there was any way to get the Glaxon's to realize that they had no choice but to save themselves. The following day, when Sheena took her to the river with baskets to find the clay she used to make her pottery, Danica tried again. "How many priests are there?"

Sheena shrugged.

"You told me there were 200 men in the village. More than that?"

"Not need 200. Killed all villagers other village."

"Because they are farmers and hunters now, not really warriors. I saw the priests. They march like soldiers, in formation, with discipline. If anyone could organize the villagers, teach them how to fight together, they could win. Especially if everyone in all the villages got together. When you were talking about not many warriors, you didn't count the women, did you?"

Sheena gaped at her as if she'd lost her mind. "Women not warriors. Not can fight."

"Why not?"

"Women keep hearth, bear child. Not fight."

Danica studied her for several moments. "There were women warriors on the world I come from. There have been women who were warriors throughout the history of my world. Maybe women aren't inclined to enjoy fighting like a lot of men, but they're just as capable of defending their homes and families."

"Glaxon different. Women afraid."

"Do you think the men aren't?" Danica demanded in exasperation. "Sometimes you just have to do whatever it takes to live, whether you're scared or not."

Sheena still looked doubtful, but she also looked thoughtful.

"From what you told me, it sounded as if Taj was trying to organize an army and the people of the other village acted alone-- which is why they failed. The lizard people *are* an army. Nothing but another army could defeat them. How many villages are there?"

Sheena shook her head. "Dangerous talk. Priests will hear."

"We're in the woods. How could they hear?"

"Have watcher every village."

Danica's heart skipped a beat. "Do you have any idea who?"

"Kara."

Danica stopped abruptly. "The Kara that's supposed to marry Taj?"

Sheena nodded. "Priests choose Kara watch Taj."

"Does he know this?"

"Yes."

For several moments fear for Taj overrode every other thought. Everything she'd seen him do, and say, that his mother had fussed about suddenly crystallized in her mind as a constant, ongoing challenge of the priests' authority. "That man is crazy!" she snapped angrily.

Sheena shook her head, not in disagreement, but worriedly. "Take chances. Too many. Not marry Kara spring. Not marry Kara summer. Priests will do terrible thing if Taj not marry by winter."

Danica stared at Sheena in horror. "What terrible thing?"

"Make ... not man. Then no have wife."

It took several moments for that to sink in. "You're not saying…. You can't mean what I think you mean." She knew from the look on Sheena's face, though, that she hadn't misunderstood.

"But…. It doesn't make any sense. Taj is no fool. He must know he can't defy them alone and get away with it. Why would he take such a chance?"

Sheena stopped on the trail, studying her for several moments in silence. "You."

If Sheena had suddenly slapped her she couldn't have been more stunned. Denial sprang immediately to her lips. "I haven't even been here two months," she snapped indignantly.

Sheena shook her head. "Delay before. Not want watcher in his home. Not want take woman not of his choosing. Now, say will not have. Want Danica."

It would've been an understatement to say it was a stunning revelation. It effectively silenced Danica for the remainder of the walk, throwing her into such utter turmoil that she merely followed Sheena like a sleepwalker. As the shock wore off, though, a mixture of emotions that was nearly as confusing pelted her.

Uppermost, though, was fear and the sudden realization that she was not merely looking on here as an observer. She'd become a part of the community. Her fate was entwined with theirs.

When she finally came out of her state of meditation, she saw that

Sheena had knelt near a small stream. With a stone scraper, she was very carefully separating the bluish colored soil from the soil around it. After studying her for several moments, Danica set her own basket down, took the scraper from it and began filling her basket.

"That was why you argued with him, wasn't it?"

Sheena glanced up at her. "Your welfare not unimportant. Taj my son."

"I know that. It's just…. I thought he didn't like me at all."

Sheena rolled her eyes. "Taj fool. You big fool."

Danica didn't know whether to be insulted or laugh. She realized, though, that there was a part of her that was thrilled, disbelieving still, but certainly welcoming the thought.

The rest of the revelation was hardly news for celebration. Only a few weeks ago, she would not have been able to accept what Sheena had said without a good deal of skepticism. She'd seen the priests take the man from the village, however. They weren't just a scary story anymore. "I couldn't bear it if he was hurt because of me," she muttered finally.

Sheena glanced up at that. Whatever she'd been about to say, however, froze on her lips. The fine hairs on the back of Danica's neck lifted at the look on her face. With dread, she slowly turned to see what it was that threatened them.

At first, she merely stared disbelievingly at the two unkempt creatures that had stepped from the woods not far from them. Slowly, as her gaze moved over them and her brain sluggishly assimilated the details, something more strongly akin to joy flooded her than fear.

As ragged as their clothing was, there was no mistaking the two men for men of Earth. The biggest of the two looked rather like a scarecrow, as if his flesh had shrunken rapidly from the massive skeletal system that must once have supported an extraordinarily large specimen. Much of his clothing was missing, or torn and hanging about him, but the faded denim was as unmistakable as the faded red plaid of his shirt. A nasty, matted beard that was mostly red, but streaked with gray, hung down from his chin to his chest. The hair on his head, by sharp contract, was nearly black, but it might only have seemed so because of the grease slicking it to his scalp.

The other man was even thinner. Undoubtedly, he'd had far less flesh to lose to begin with. His hair was almost as greasy and stringy, and hung down even longer than the other man's, but it was closer to blond than brown. He, too, had a beard, though his was not nearly as thick, sprouting from his face in patches like a dog with the mange. The tatters of his clothes looked as if it might once have been a suit.

They were still a sight for sore eyes, something Danica had never thought to see again in her lifetime.

"You're from Earth!" she gasped as the two men approached.

The two men exchanged a glance. "Not anymore," the bigger of the two muttered.

Uneasiness touched Danica. Firmly, she dismissed it. She knew very well she would've given two men who looked as they did a very wide berth if she'd come up upon them on Earth, but the situation was radically different. "How long have you been here?"

The men stopped when they were only a few feet away. "I've been here almost a year," the thinner man said. "Gus has been here almost two."

"I'm Danica. Danica Hearn. I guess the aliens took you, too?"

"Good guess," Gus muttered sarcastically.

All right. So it was a totally inane question, but she was trying to be friendly. They were acting as if they'd come upon a wild animal … or maybe as if they were?

Her uneasiness grew despite her best efforts to tamp it. "Do you live near here?"

The thin man, who hadn't identified himself, snickered. "Yeah. Wanna see?"

"We have to get back. We're expected," Danica said sharply as she noticed that Gus had been sidling around her while she spoke to the thin one. She took a step back, so she could keep an eye on both.

Uttering a shriek, as if she'd just been released from the trance-like state of her fear, Sheena took off at a run. The moment she did, the men reacted like the predators Danica finally realized they were. Gus tore out after her, tackling her and slamming her to the ground. The thin man reached for her. The moment he did, Danica acted instinctively with the training she'd never in her life thought she'd have any use for. Grasping his arm, she gave it a yank to pull him off balance and threw her hip sideways.

It worked like a piece of art. The man flipped, landing in the dirt at her feet flat of his back. Instead of doing her follow through and stomping his ribs, or in fact anything to incapacitate him, Danica whirled and rushed to help Sheena. Drawing her leg back as she reached the two on the ground, she kicked Gus in the ribs as hard as she could. The kick sent pain shooting up her leg, but it made Gus lose his grip.

Sheena scrambled to her feet and ran. Danica turned to follow her, but she was caught from behind before she'd managed to put much distance between herself and their attackers. Uttering a shriek, she whirled, slamming her elbow into the man who'd caught her. He grunted in pain, his grip slackening, but he recovered faster than Danica expected. Belatedly, she realized she shouldn't have hesitated. She should have hit him again while she could. Grabbing her by her hair, he slung her to the ground, stunning her for several moments. Before she could push herself to her feet, he grabbed her hair again, lifting her by it.

She caught a glimpse of Sheena, who'd paused, uncertain of whether to keep running or return to help. "Run!" Danica screamed at her. "Get Taj!"

The moment she shouted, the man released her and started after Sheena. She launched herself at him, slamming into him hard enough she knocked him to the ground. His head hit a stone with a sickening crack.

Danica rolled off of him, wondering where Gus was. She found out before she could get to her feet. He caught her in the ribs with his foot, flipping her twice before she hit the dirt.

"Pay backs are hell, bitch!"

She felt a rib crack at the impact. Nausea swarmed through her, and blackness. She lay still when she hit the ground, fighting both. Before she'd mastered either, she was caught by the hair, dragged to her feet and shaken so hard she thought her neck would snap.

A groan from the man on the ground distracted Gus from shaking her brains out of her ears.

He stopped. "You OK, Slim Jim?"

"No, I'm not fucking OK," Slim Jim muttered. "I hit my head. Did the other one get away?"

"Yeah."

"We'd better get out of here, then."

"She ain't one of them. Why would they come after her?"

"Don't be a fucking idiot, Gus. They figure she's theirs. They'll come lookin'."

Gus chuckled with an effort. "She's ours now, though, ain't she?"

"Only if they don't catch up to us," Slim muttered, stumbling to his feet and looking around to get his bearings.

"You don't look to me like you're in any shape to do any running," Gus muttered, not with concern, but more as if he was wondering if the man would slow him down.

"I'll keep up, asshole."

Chapter Nineteen

It wasn't part of Danica's plan to slow the men down by stumbling and falling every few minutes. In point of fact, she was too disoriented to formulate any sort of plan and, fortunately, too stunned to feel much fear or pain. Her body seemed wildly uncoordinated, however, her knees wobbly and insubstantial. Her legs kept giving way beneath her. Every time she fell, Gus snatched her up and slapped her, or shook her, growling at her that he was going to choke the life out of her if she didn't quit trying to slow them down.

She put forth a strenuous effort to keep from falling after the second time.

"Gus! You moron. Quit slapping her around. It ain't helping her to keep up."

Gus stopped long enough to glare at him. "If you'd caught the one you was supposed to catch, it wouldn't be a problem."

"I might've caught her if you hadn't been laying on the ground whining about your ribs."

"You wouldn't have had to catch me if you hadn't attacked us," Danica muttered.

"Shut up!"

"All I'm saying is, I'm from Earth, too."

Slim Jim eyed her speculatively. "You looked pretty chummy with that Glaxon woman to me."

"Exactly what was I supposed to do? They captured me. It wasn't like I had anywhere else to go, anyway."

"You told her to get Taj," Gus growled.

Danica shrugged. "I like Sheena. I didn't want her to get hurt, but she can't get Taj because he's gone off hunting again," she lied.

"She's bound to bring somebody, though," Slim Jim said, glancing around them worriedly. "Better get moving."

Danica had recovered in the time they'd been standing still sufficiently that much of the dizziness had abated. Her ribs still hurt like hell. She was pretty sure Gus had cracked one. It was hard to breathe. "Where are we going?"

"We built us a camp deep in the woods."

From the looks of them, it wasn't anywhere near water. Gus

looked like a lumberjack, or maybe a hunter, but it didn't necessarily follow that he had been, or that he'd known the first thing about surviving in the woods. Slim Jim had probably been a business exec type, which meant he might have had a little knowledge from books, but it was obvious whatever either of them knew hadn't helped them a lot.

A month or so ago, right after she'd arrived, she would have wanted to go with them regardless of what they looked like, only because they were familiar. Now she had only to look at them to see that they weren't fairing a lot better than she could've done on her own.

Besides, it wasn't 'better the devil you knew' in this case. These two men had descended down the evolutionary scale into something not much better than beasts. Maybe they'd always been dangerous and maybe not, but they certainly were now.

She kept her thoughts to herself as they hauled her deeper and deeper into the woods, trying to keep up to keep from angering them any more than necessary.

She didn't think her chances of overcoming two men were very good. One on one, she might have had some chance, especially if she caught them off guard, but neither man was so distracted by fear of pursuit to give her much advantage.

She didn't particularly want to think about what they had in mind, but it didn't take a genius to figure it out. As revolting as the thought was, it occurred to her after a while that at least seeming to be relieved that they'd 'rescued' her might be her only chance.

By the time they had reached their campsite, Danica decided she needed to try for something midway between friendly and hostile. Being too friendly was bound to arouse their suspicions, but acting like a captive might make them more inclined to treat her like one.

She collapsed on the ground when they finally released her, hoping they wouldn't think it necessary to tie her up. When she finally thought it safe to look around with some curiosity, she saw that both men had taken up a watchful position. Obviously, they still thought there was a chance they would have to fend off an attack, which meant, hopefully, that it could be a while before they got around to deciding to sample their spoils. "Where were you when you got caught?"

Gus glanced at her, his expression surly. "The girly fag with the long blond hair caught me the minute the aliens dropped me here," Gus growled.

"Me too."

Not exactly mental giants either. And, despite the cutting remark about Taj, neither one of them had managed to best him, obviously, or they wouldn't be near the village. This had to be the 'man' Taj had said was dead--the one that had called him a stinking savage and an animal. He hadn't told her there'd been two men, or that they'd escaped. Apparently, he'd thought she had too much interest in finding others of her kind. "I meant, the aliens that brought you here."

"Lousy bastards. I was fishing," Gus growled.

"Guess they didn't beam your fishing gear up with you," Danica said.

"Blondy got it," Gus snorted. "As if that savage would know how to use a rod and reel."

The remark angered her, but Danica ignored it. She glanced at Slim Jim. "Wall Street?"

"Huh?"

"The suit."

"I was ... uh ... meeting some colleagues about a sale."

Gus snorted. "Arms deal. The spics took his cargo and tossed him in the drink."

"Shut up, Gus."

She wondered what Gus had been fishing for. He didn't seem like an upstanding citizen himself. "So ... we were all somewhere around the triangle?"

Gus looked at her blankly. "What triangle?"

"Bermuda?"

"I was deep sea fishing in the gulf."

She dropped the subject. She'd just been curious. It wasn't important, except that it suggested the aliens 'fished' there often, and also that humans who were in the wrong place at the wrong time could find themselves in a world of shit.

It also suggested, unfortunately, that she was in very bad company.

An hour dragged by. The sun dipped below the tops of the trees.

Danica discovered she had to pee, but she didn't want to ask when it was liable to lead to something else. "Should I build a fire?"

Gus and Slim Jim both eyed her speculatively.

"If I don't gather wood now, it'll be too dark to see."

"You think it'd be safe, Gus?"

Gus frowned. "I think we better forget it for tonight. If they're out looking, the fire would sure as hell help them find us."

"Sheena might not even have told them," Danica said after several moments.

"Why wouldn't she?"

Danica sighed. "I think she wanted me gone. She figured her son would get into trouble with the priests if they found me there." She wished she could convince herself that it was a lie, but she had a strong feeling that relief would be uppermost in Sheena's mind if Danica wasn't around to cause trouble.

Slim Jim and Gus exchanged a look. "Even if you ain't lying, that don't mean they wouldn't come looking," Gus said finally.

"All I'm saying is they probably won't try that hard to find me."

"What do you think?" Slim Jim asked.

Apparently, he consulted with the mental giant about everything.

Gus shrugged. "I don't think I trust her any further than I could spit."

Danica felt the little bit of headway she'd made slipping away from her. "Look, except for being total assholes, I wouldn't have had a problem leaving with you two. I don't appreciate being slapped around, but I'd rather be with my own kind than with the natives. If you two could just bring yourselves to act a little more civilized, I could handle this. And Sheena taught me a lot about surviving around here," she added as a rider, hoping they'd see she had some potential value above and beyond a dark hole to poke with their sticks.

The idea of having sex with either one of her made her nauseous, but she could always hold her breath and close her eyes. She doubted either one of them had a clue about finesse, which meant that it probably wouldn't take more than three minutes of slobbering and humping and they'd be done.

She could handle it. Maybe she could even manage a few convincing groans.

They were bound to let their guard down sooner or later.

And maybe it *was* for the best, all the way around. Not that she had any intention of staying with the two stooges, but she did think she might manage to survive on her own now, and being alone seemed preferable to what was liable to happen to Taj if she went back. If Gus and Jim hadn't caught her and dragged her off, maybe she would've stayed, maybe she wouldn't even have considered that there was an alternative.

She wasn't completely certain that she believed Sheena was right about her clouding Taj's judgment, but if there was a chance of it, then she didn't want to be responsible for something horrible happening to him.

Besides that, she didn't think she could live with the dread of having the priests swoop down upon them. Sheena hadn't suggested it, but she knew damned well that sooner or later her name would be entered in the pot if she continued to live with them. And even if she hadn't had to worry about it, she didn't want to stay knowing anybody could be taken off and killed at any time, people she cared about, or might come to care about.

Gus studied her for several moments. Finally, a slow grin curled his lips. "Hear that, Slim Jim? I think she's offering to take care of us." He returned his attention to Danica. "It wasn't cooking and cleaning we had in mind, sweetheart."

"Duh," Danica said dryly. "Two men, no woman, what *could* be on your mind?

"You got a smart mouth. I'd've figured blondy would've beat that outta you by now."

"Apparently, he feels secure in his manhood."

"What do you mean by that?" Gus growled threateningly.

Danica bit her tongue, resisting the effort to taunt him even more, or worse, inform him that she had every intention of giving as good as she got if he tried anything else. It was stupid to goad him into attacking her, and obvious that it wouldn't take much to do it. After a moment, she forced a slight smile. "I figured you guys were looking for a fuck partner. I was just pointing out I can do other things besides."

"We don't need no pottery," Gus snickered. "How are you at giving head?"

Bile rose in her throat at the thought of their unwashed bodies. It was bad enough to think of being poked with the nasty things. She smiled with an effort. "All of my boyfriends said I was really good at it."

She had his full attention now. "All?"

She forced a chuckle. "You didn't ask me what I did before," she said provocatively.

Jim looked excited. "You were a call girl?"

It was better than being called a hooker, she supposed, and probably more flattering. At least they thought she looked like an expensive whore. Instead of answering, she gave them an 'I'm not telling' smile.

It was enough for Gus. He, too, left his watch post. "How about giving us a tour?"

It was for certain she wouldn't have been able to put this moment off indefinitely, but she hadn't intend to bring it to a head quite so soon either. Of the two, Jim looked the least repulsive. He also didn't look like he'd ever had much luck so she thought the chances of him being diseased was slighter.

Gus was another matter, but then he'd been here, according to them, almost two years. Surely if he'd brought anything with him he'd be dead by now?

"I think I'll start with Jim."

"I think you'll start with me," Gus growled.

She looked at Jim, but whatever hope she'd nursed that she could draw them into a fight over firsts died a quick death. Jim was obviously a total pussy.

"Whatever," she said, trying not to panic. A voice in the back of her mind was screaming 'I'd rather die! I'd rather die!', but the voice of reason kept telling her being beat senseless and *then* raped wasn't going to make it any better. She was hurt already. Her chances of getting away at all, and especially in one piece, went down drastically if she provoked them into beating the shit out of her.

"Doggy style's my favorite," she said hopefully, figuring it would be easier if she just didn't have to look at him.

Gus looked like he was going to cum before he could get his pants down. Apparently, it was his favorite position.

She turned her back on him, getting on her hands and knees as she repeated the mantra 'I'm not going to throw up' in her head.

Gus hit the ground on his knees behind her so hard she wasn't surprised at the strange noise he made, but it drew her attention. Just as she turned to look back at him, however, he slammed down on top of her so hard she hit the ground. Something sharp dug painfully into her back.

Stunned, confused, Danica was still trying to figure out why he was lying on top of her like a log when Taj landed in the clearing with a yell uncannily like an Indian war whoop. It made the hair on her neck and head stand on end. The sound galvanized Jim, who'd been staring down at her and Gus blankly, as if a bolt of electricity had been shoved up his ass. He came off the ground almost two feet and tore out of the clearing so fast his feet churned up dirt and debris into the air.

It sank into her stunned mind as Taj charged after him that Gus was lying on her like a log because he was dead as a doornail. More repulsed, if possible, by dead Gus than she had been by the living, breathing skunk, she struggled harder to shove him off of her, feeling her flesh cringe.

A high pitched scream, abruptly cut off, told her Jim hadn't run nearly as fast as he appeared to be moving. The jolt that went through her at the sound lent her enough strength to roll Gus off. She saw then that he had an arrow head sprouting from the middle of his chest.

Shuddering, she tried to struggle to her feet. Her back was on fire, however, and so were her ribs.

Taj reappeared. Grasping her arm, he hauled her to her feet.

"I thought you said the Earth man was dead."

"Is now."

Danica glanced up at him then. The look on his face made her mouth go dry.

Chapter Twenty

If she hadn't been running on adrenaline, Danica thought she probably wouldn't have made it back to Sheena's on her own steam.

She thought, at first, that Taj was still in the grips of his killer instincts and that was why he treated her with such little consideration for the possibility that she might've been hurt. She realized after a time, however, that although that might have been a part of it, he was in a rage, and it was directed at her.

It didn't take long after that to figure out that it was either because she had appeared to be offering herself to the two men willingly, or he'd heard enough of the conversation to jump to that conclusion, or both.

Her first instinct was to try to explain herself. Pride lodged the words in her throat. He must have a very low opinion of her if he believed such a thing when anyone with any sense would've realized she was using what she had to fight for her life.

Jealousy had the tendency to deprive people of sense, of course, and it was possible that that was what made him so unreasonable, but she couldn't get past the insult, whatever his reasons for it.

By the time she realized he was so furious that he was taking her to his mother's house, she was too angry herself to consider trying to explain. She'd also begun to realize that, maybe, she shouldn't even try.

Sheena took one look at her face and turned to stare at Taj in disbelief. "What happen?"

"Earth mans dead. Slave no run no more."

Sheena gaped at him. "Danica no run! I tell you!"

Danica grabbed her arm, giving it a squeeze, and shook her head slightly.

Sheena frowned, her lips tightening into a thin line. "Act fool, then!" she yelled at Taj as he turned and left. "Jealous make him stupid," she apologized, leading Danica inside. "Scared stupid, too. Think them hurt Danica. Never mind."

"Do you think I could just lie down for a while?" Danica asked weakly. As much as she appreciated Sheena's angry support, she felt vaguely ill and more than a little wobbly in the aftermath of her ordeal.

"Hurt?"

She rubbed her ribs. "He kicked me."

Nodding, Sheena led her to the pallet she'd used before when Taj had left her with his mother. "Sit. I get medicines."

As badly as Danica had wanted to lie down, she discovered very quickly that there was no position that didn't make her hurt worse. Sheena brought a basin filled with water and some cloths. "Bathe, feel better."

Danica nodded. She didn't doubt she was filthy from rolling around on the ground, but even more than that she felt the need to scrub the distaste from herself. She felt nasty from just being around those two. She shuddered to think how she would've felt if they'd forced her into having sex with them.

Dragging her dirty dress off, she dropped it beside the pallet and began scrubbing herself. Sheena returned a few minutes later with one of her own gowns. Setting it on the mattress beside Danica, she picked up the discarded dress and examined it. "What this?"

Danica shuddered as she stared at the blood on the back of the dress. "The guy fell on me after Taj shot him."

Frowning, Sheena grasped her shoulder and turned her slightly. "Danica blood."

Surprised, Danica twisted, trying to look at the wound. "It hurts like hell, but I thought it was just my ribs. Is it bad?"

Sheena examined it thoroughly. "Hit rib. Bone stop it."

"What luck!" Danica said dryly.

Sheena shook her head at her. "Was luck. Be dead now, too, probably."

At any other time, the bald statement might have scared her. She found, however, that she was in too much pain to worry overmuch about something that hadn't happened.

"Need stitch together skin."

That comment got a rise out of her since it meant more pain. Groaning, she gave in to Sheena's insistence and lay down on her stomach on the pallet. Sheena poured something over the cut that burned like fire. She wasn't certain if the burning distracted her from the stitching, or it was the fact that her ribs were killing her, but the ordeal of being sewn up wasn't quite the trial she'd expected.

When she'd finished, Sheena had her sit up and wrapped her ribs tightly. She couldn't breathe any better, but she didn't hurt nearly as badly as she had. She was half asleep when Sheena roused her and made her drink something truly horrible to 'help her sleep'.

Whatever it was, worked, because she was out like a light almost before her head hit the pallet once more.

She woke feeling worse than she had the day before, primarily because every muscle in her body now hurt from the unaccustomed exertion.

Sheena fussed over her as if she was a sick child. It was balm to her soul after the way Taj had behaved, but it made her uncomfortable, too. Her mother hadn't coddled her like that even when she *was* a child.

"I'm not really hurt that badly," she said when Sheena insisted on bringing food to her and tried to feed her.

"Are hurt."

"I'm mostly sore."

Sheena was silent for a few moments. "Man do strange thing when worry."

Danica thought about just ignoring the comment. "It doesn't matter," she said finally.

"Does. Misunderstand. Not good to leave that way."

Danica sighed tiredly. "Not if two people expect to make a future together, but there *is* no future for me and Taj. As hurt as I was at first, I know what it must have looked like. It would be hard for anybody *not* to jump to the wrong conclusion. I expect if I'd found him like that, I would've believed the worst, too.

"Let's just forget it, ok? I'll live, and Taj will live better if he does what he was told to do and marries Kara."

Sheena frowned, obviously torn. Finally, after looking around nervously, she settled on the side of the pallet. "Sheena think about warrior woman from your land," she said quietly. "You teach, I fight."

Danica blinked at her in surprise. "I can't teach you," she said, aghast. "I've never been in the military."

"Know how fight. Sheena see."

Danica frowned, trying to remember exactly what had happened in the woods. Finally, she smiled wryly. "It's really embarrassing to admit it, but I just took some classes because I was hoping to meet cute guys. Actually, any guy that might be a reasonable prospect for a husband. You would not believe how hard it is to meet men where I'm from, especially if you don't grab one in college. The first thing you know, all the ones worth taking have already been taken. Then you have to wait for the next turn over … when the divorces start and everybody decides to change partners."

Sheena dismissed it. "Still learn. Fight men."

It was a scary thought, realizing she might have instigated a rebellion, particularly since she didn't feel at all confident that she could teach anyone how to be a real warrior. It was true she'd learned the basics of a lot of different martial arts, but she very much feared it was just enough to get a lot of people killed.

"I get some really stupid ideas sometimes, Sheena. You ought not to listen to me. Anyway, you said the men wouldn't fight. It would take everybody, and even then the lizard people might still win."

Sheena's face hardened. "We die one by one, or we die trying take home back. Worth risk. Men fight when they see women will do without them," she added slyly.

Danica felt a smile tug at her lips. She knew Sheena was right. Anyway, the main reason the men wouldn't fight was because they were trying to protect their women and children. Once they saw that the women could fight their own fight…. "I shouldn't have said anything. This is a really bad idea," she said guiltily.

"You teach. I decide."

Danica gnawed her lip. "You think you could talk the other women into it?"

"They like me. Tired watch priests take son, daughter, mother, father. I know I talk, they listen. My father great chieftain. My son great chieftain. They listen."

"Kara could be a problem. And we'd have to figure out a way to get with the women in the other villages. If there are a lot of these creatures, it'll take everyone and that'll take planning."

Sheena patted her hand and got to her feet. "Rest. Teach when better. Sheena talk to others. Start here, go to next village."

It was hard to rest after such a conversation. Instead, Danica decided to get up. She couldn't make her cracked rib mend any faster, or the gash on her back, but she could work the soreness from her muscles.

Danica was stunned at how readily the women accepted the idea, until she remembered that the recent visit by the priests was still fresh in everyone's mind. Before she was really able to get around, the women of the village began coming. The unaccustomed activity worried her, too, because she knew Kara was bound to notice and come to investigate.

Sheena, she discovered, was way ahead of her. The day Kara finally showed up, Sheena merely smiled at her without concern. "Plan celebrate. Good harvest this year."

To Danica's relief, Kara was so excited at the prospect of entertainment, she was instantly diverted from her suspicions. "Oh!

Not have that since Kara small! Should invite other villagers. Make big celebration."

Sheena nodded in satisfaction. "Good thought. Kara talk chieftain daughters, send to Sheena. We make big plan. Ask all villages."

When she'd gone, Danica was torn between excitement, amusement, and horror. "You think it's a good idea, sending her?"

"Best. Priests no suspect. Kara good watcher."

Taj was deeply suspicious of the sudden activity, as well, and not nearly as easy to fool.

Danica and Sheena were so deeply involved in their discussion that it was several moments before either woman noticed him standing in the door. Danica had heart palpitations, but it wasn't only because she was afraid of what he might have overheard.

It had been nearly a week since the incident and she hadn't seen him in all that time. It would've been stretching it to say she hadn't thought about him at all, but she hadn't had the chance to dwell too deeply on her misery. Sheena kept her thoroughly occupied.

"What are you planning, my mother?"

Sheena lifted her brows. "Kara did not tell you?"

Taj frowned. He had not once so much as glanced in her direction and after a moment, Danica got up and went outside, settling on the back steps.

"You were wrong," Sheena said quietly, drawing Taj's attention back to her when Danica had shut the door behind her.

His lips tightened. "You know nothing of it. You were not there. You did not see what I saw, or hear what I heard."

"Then tell me."

"I would not sully your ears with it, my mother."

"They attacked her as they did the woman from the village?"

"They did not have to," he said harshly. "She offered herself to them."

Sheena felt a prick of doubt, but quickly banished it. "Whatever you believed you saw, or heard, Danica protected me from harm. She was only trying to protect herself."

"She told you this?"

"I didn't ask her. I didn't have to. I know Danica."

Taj frowned. "Why do you defend her to me?"

"Because it's only right. She won't defend herself. She knows that I'm afraid for you to defy the priests as you do. To be honest, I don't think it's even entirely for me, or for you. It wounded her pride that you thought such things of her. She won't explain because she hasn't forgiven you for it."

"Forgiven me!" Taj roared indignantly. "It was not *I* who was offering my favors!"

"Jealousy has eaten up your brains!" Sheena snapped.

Taj reddened. He could not bring himself to tell his mother, however, that he suspected her motives because she had been so willing when he had accosted her that he knew very well she was no stranger to congress between a man and a woman. After a moment, his eyes narrowed on a new thought. "I did not come to discuss the female," he said stiffly.

Sheena sniffed. "You need not think I am fooled by such talk … 'the female' 'the slave'. You said that to wound Danica, and I am sure you succeeded, but I am not such a fool as to believe you consider her of so little worth. If you did, you would not behave like a beast with a thorn in his paw."

Taj ground his teeth. "Tell me what that Earth woman has talked you into doing!" he snapped angrily.

Sheena returned her attention to the spinning forgotten in her lap. "Nothing."

"You are not planning a celebration, whatever you have led Kara to believe."

"Yes, we are."

"And this requires that every female in the village come to your home daily?"

Sheena shrugged. "It was Kara's idea to invite the folk from the other villages. I thought it would be a good thing, for we have need of something to improve the spirits. And if others are to come, then it will take a good deal of work and planning."

Taj studied her for several moments. Finally, he knelt beside her. "You are not planning anything foolish?"

Sheena lifted her gaze to meet her son's. "What might I be planning that would be foolish?"

Taj frowned. "I am not certain of anything except that I am uneasy. The women of the village behave … strangely, almost secretive."

Sheena smiled and patted his cheek. "We *are* planning a surprise, but I will not tell. You must wait and see like everyone else."

Chapter Twenty One

Danica had dredged up every fight move she'd ever learned, everything she'd ever heard and every movie she'd ever seen, and she still felt less than confident that what they were planning was going to work. She shook her head dejectedly at Sheena. "Do you really think they'll be willing to kill? It's not going to be enough just to beat the hell out of them. You do know that, don't you?"

"I know." She thought it over. "When we go to fight, I will remind them of all who have been taken to die. They will be willing to kill."

"They're getting very good, but I'd feel a lot better if we had better weapons."

Sheena nodded. "It is easier now that you have learned our language better and you can explain the things they must do, but I think you are right. They are not very good with the weapons and we do not have enough."

Danica smiled wryly. "It would be really nice if the aliens would decide to drop a few automatic weapons … maybe a cannon or two."

"What are these?"

Danica shook her head. "Something we don't have and aren't likely to get. The good news is the lizards don't have them either."

"Why do you call them lizards?"

"Because they're not human like me and you. Haven't you seen their skin? It's like…." She trailed off, trying to think of something she'd seen since she'd been on Glaxon that looked reptilian. "The Kank."

Sheena frowned. "I was always afraid to look," she confessed finally. "Their eyes … there is no feeling there at all. The way they look at us…."

Danica shrugged. "Well, it is certainly an advantage in one sense. There won't be any mistake about who's the enemy and who isn't. I just wish I could think of something that would really even the odds." She rubbed her throbbing head. "I took chemistry in school and it was a total waste of time. I don't remember a damned thing."

Shrugging it off finally, she concentrated for a time on grinding the grain the Glaxons used to make their bread. Typically, the moment she stopped struggling to think, an idea popped into her mind that sent a jolt of excitement through her. "Grain explodes!"

Sheena stared at her in confusion. "Explodes?"

"Yes! Horrendously! There was a factory near where I grew up that processed grain. You couldn't take a match or cigarette within a mile of it because all it would take was a spark and the whole place would explode." She grabbed Sheena's arm. "Tell me the priests collect and store grain!"

It was obvious Sheena still didn't understand. "I don't know," she said slowly. "The temple is in the center of a great lake. No one who has gone in has ever come out again."

"We'll have to figure out a way to get someone in for a look and then out again."

"In where?"

Danica felt all the strength go out of her knees at the voice. Whirling, she stared at Taj in dismay, wondering how long he'd been listening. "I wish you wouldn't sneak up like that!" she snapped as anger quickly overtook her start of fear.

His face tightened with anger at her tone. "You might have heard me if you had not been so busy planning mayhem."

Danica glanced at Sheena guiltily. "I think I'll go get more grain," she said stiffly, plunking her grinding stone down on the table and stalking toward the back door. To her dismay, Taj followed her to the shed, closing the door behind him and blocking her exit.

"What have you done?" he demanded.

Danica turned to face him, plunking her hands on her hips. "Something somebody should have done a long time ago."

He seemed surprised to discover she could speak his language without difficulty, as well he might be since he hadn't spoken to her in almost a month. He was only briefly diverted, however. "You will get our women killed," he growled furiously.

"It's better to die for something than for nothing!" she retorted shortly. "They're tired of waiting to see who will be taken next!"

He was silent for several moments. "How many are involved in this crazy scheme of yours?"

"Every woman in every village who is not too old or too young," she responded tightly. "Six hundred, give or take a few."

She could tell from his expression that she'd stunned him. "You did this?"

"We did this," Sheena said, entering the shed and closing the door behind her.

Taj whirled on her. "Mother! You told me you were not planning anything foolish!"

"I told you we were planning a surprise. We have. We have built an army."

"Women!"

The contempt in his voice goaded Danica into saying something she almost instantly regretted. "Sometimes it takes a woman to see that something is done right!"

Taj paled at the insult, which was when it dawned on Danica that he could hardly construe the remark as anything but a direct attack since it was he who had tried to stir up the last failed rebellion. "I'm sorry!" she said quickly. "I didn't mean that the way you took it, but we have worked hard and we're good. You've got no right to dismiss us as if we were children, incapable to doing anything on our own."

"This has nothing to do with you!" he roared furiously. "You are not one of the people. You are not even from our world!"

"Oh! You ass! How the hell can it have nothing to do with me when I live here too?"

Sheena glanced from one to the other and finally left quietly the way she'd come, deciding Danica wasn't in need of her defense. Perhaps Taj was, but Sheena figured he had it coming.

"You are still an outsider," Taj growled. "You do not understand our ways, and I will not have you … corrupting our females with your strange ways!"

"You won't have…," Danica gasped in outrage.

"I am chieftain."

"Well, why don't you go discuss it with the other men, then? Maybe they'll find their balls."

She thought for several moments that she'd gone just a little too far. Taj looked like he might explode. After several moments, he seemed to come to grips with his temper and ceased flexing and unflexing his fingers. Glancing around the small building, he moved to a work bench and perched on the edge, folding his arms over his chest as he studied her. "What am I to tell them?" he asked after a moment.

Danica looked at him doubtfully for a moment. "Tell them that we have decided that we will take Glaxon back from the priests. If they don't want to stand with us, they can stay home and tend the children."

His lips trembled on the verge of a smile. "Will you lead them?"

Impulsively, Danica moved toward him. "We need you. I don't know anything about war or strategy … except for marketing, which isn't really a lot of help here. I've taught them what I learned myself in self defense classes, but they need to learn how to use weapons. We need a plan of attack."

The humor left him. "I will not lead them to their deaths. You must stop this, Danica."

Danica shook her head. "You don't understand at all. I didn't start it, and I can't stop it."

"They have listened thus far. They will listen if you tell them that they can not do this."

Danica's lips tightened with exasperation. "They listen to what they want to hear and they do what they want to do. I didn't make up their minds for them. I didn't convince them they could do this. I told them the women on my world could choose to be warriors the same as the men. I taught them what I'd learned. When they realized that it was a matter of skill and determination, not their gender, they knew that they could do this because this is their home, too, their families, and they want to protect them just as much as you do."

She studied him for any sign that he was weakening toward acceptance. Seeing none, she moved away from him once more, returning to the grain bin. "I should have known better than to think you could yield one inch. It must be nice to be so damned certain you are always right."

She thought when he pushed away from the bench that he meant to leave. Instead, he moved up behind her. "Was I wrong before?"

Danica's belly clenched. She swallowed with an effort. He was giving her the chance to explain, hoping, she thought that she would tell him something that he could live with. "No. You weren't," she said honestly.

"My mother said that I was wrong."

Danica fell idle, staring down at her hands. "Not in the sense that you think." She sighed. "I don't suppose there is a right or wrong in such a situation, only the way a person feels."

"And you think you know how I feel?"

She shook her head. "Maybe. I think I understand, anyway. Mostly, it's just the way you made me feel about myself."

He was silent for so long she thought he wouldn't pursue it any further. "How did I make you feel?"

She smiled wryly. "Unworthy." She sifted idly through the grain, watching it flow through her fingers. "I used to think the need to survive changed a person. I realize now that it only strips the lies from them; the lies they've told everyone else; the lies they've told themselves. It reveals who they really are.

"I've spent my entire life trying to be accepted by saying and doing and even thinking the way it seemed everyone expected. I've tried to mould myself into being something I'm not just to find acceptance … because I desperately wanted to be wanted even if it was a lie based on a lie.

"I finally realized that it wouldn't bring me the satisfaction that I'd believed it would, that what I needed was someone who could accept me exactly as I am, even with my flaws.

"I've got a pretty good idea about what you saw, and what you heard in the woods that day. It was me, the real me, doing what I believed was necessary to save my life … and if I'd had to go through with it, I would have. And if I was faced with the same situation again, I would behave exactly the same.

"I was hurt and angry about the way you acted at first, but then I realized that you hadn't misjudged me at all. You'd only seen something you couldn't accept and that I had to respect that, particularly when it's been a real struggle for me to accept it myself. In some ways, I still don't like myself much, but I'm getting used to it."

She turned and faced him finally. "I'm not looking for an apology. I'm not going to apologize to you, and I don't want, nor need, your forgiveness. Let's just leave it at that, OK?"

His gaze flickered over her face. After a moment, he swallowed audibly. "I'm not sure I can."

Danica smiled wryly. "It gets easier with time."

"Does it?" he asked, his expression hardening. He shifted closer.

Awareness swam through Danica's senses in a dizzying rush. She'd hoped she'd overcome her intense physical attraction to Taj and wondered with a touch of despair if she ever would. If he affected her like this without even so much as touching her, even casually, how was she going to get over him?

He leaned down so that his face was only inches from hers, bracing his palms on the bin on either side of her. "In time, it will cease to torment my mind when I taste the scent of your skin on my tongue? I won't feel the longing to taste you in truth? The thirst to place my lips over yours and feel the moist heat of your mouth with my tongue? Or imagine when I do it that I can feel your body enfolding mine in much the same way?"

Danica swallowed with an effort, trying without much luck to control her pounding heart and the little gasps of air she had to struggle to drag into her lungs.

Taj shook his head slowly. "There is only one thing that will give me surcease from my torment, and it is not time."

He studied her for several long moments and finally straightened. "Bring your warriors to the field at the edge of the village tomorrow. I want to see what you have taught them."

Danica glanced up at him, torn between relief and disappointment that he'd given up so easily, feeling hope surge through her that he seemed willing to at least give them a chance to prove themselves. "Bring a dozen men."

His brows rose. "Why?"

Danica's lips curled into a smile. "They'll need dummies to pose as the enemy."

His brows rose. Finally, he nodded and left.

Shaken by the encounter, Danica turned to her task once more, but she only stared at the jar, trying to fight the hope that there had been something more to the promise in Taj's eyes than desire.

Slowly, as her body cooled and her inner turmoil abated, she became aware that she'd been staring fixedly at the pottery jar she'd brought to fill with grain and several errant thoughts collided at once.

She'd been wracking her brain for something that might give them an edge, a fighting chance to win against a superior foe of undetermined numbers, and all the time the possibility of a solution had been right in front of her.

She studied the jar, trying to tamp her rising excitement. She didn't know if it would work. She needed to do a lot of thinking, and then a little experimenting before she allowed herself to get too hopeful.

* * * *

Sheena dragged Kara with her to the clay pit to make certain that she was far enough away that she would see nothing that she might report to the priests. They had arranged to meet in the pasture where the birds were kept. The women were naturally nervous, but they were also filled with determination. This would be their first real test, they knew. If they couldn't prove beyond a shadow of a doubt that they were fully capable of taking their men down they would never convince them that they were just as capable of taking the priests out.

Danica was annoyed when they arrived to discover that Taj had arrived with most of the townsmen. They began to snicker and make lewd comments the moment they saw how the women were garbed. To Danica's relief, however, the women refused to acknowledge the taunts, focusing as they'd been taught. She had them form up at the opposite end of the field from the heckling men.

"Hold your ground. Wait until they charge. Take them down and execute a simulated knife thrust to the throat. Remember, the lizards wear armor. Your knives won't penetrate it. Concentrate on the throat, but if you don't see the access you need, or the knives fail to penetrate their hide, go for the eyes."

They waited. Finally, Taj pointed to a dozen men. Separating themselves from the crowd, they swaggered across the field, stopping a few yards away from the women. The taunting continued for a full five minutes. Slowly, however, as the women continued to wait, unmoving, their expressions impassive, the humor began to leave their faces and Danica saw a touch of uneasiness take it's place. One of the men stomped his foot and made a shooing motion.

The men laughed uproariously. The women didn't move.

Finally, the men looked at each other. Several turned away, as if they intended to abandon the exercise altogether. Abruptly, they rushed the women. "NOW!" Danica shouted.

The women leapt to their feet in an almost perfectly fluidly, perfectly synchronized motion. Uttering screams of challenge, they met the men. Executing the hip throw, they flipped the men into the air, landing in the middle of their chests with their knees when the men hit the ground, stunned, and executing a quick feint with the knives in their hands.

Danica looked down at the stunned men. "My warriors have just sliced your throats or stabbed their blades through your eyes into your brain. You're dead," she said with satisfaction. When she looked up, she saw Taj and several dozen townsmen moving toward them.

"Form up!"

The women left their 'victims' and assumed their ready stance once more.

Taj stopped when he reached them, glaring at the men on the ground. "You have forgotten how to be warriors. You shame me! Get up!"

The men crawled to their feet, glared at the women and limped off the field.

Taj surveyed the women, his hands on his hips. "Why are they dressed like this?"

"They have bound their hair beneath the caps to make certain the enemy has nothing to grab to control them. The tunics and breeches offer some protection while allowing them to move freely. The sandals protect their feet."

"Why do you have them stand like this?"

"We will choose the best place to fight and stand our ground while the enemy uses his energy to come to us. When they see we don't move, they will suffer doubt because they can not frighten us away and begin to worry that they are racing into a trap, which they will be. We will dig pits in front of our position, line them with spears planted into the ground and cover them over with brush so that the lizards fall into them before they realize they are there. We will fight those who make it across in hand to hand combat, killing as many as possible, and then retreat to make another stand."

Taj frowned, walked slowly around the women and finally stopped in front of Danica again. "Are they all this good, or are these the best?"

Reluctantly, Danica admitted that they were the best in the village. "But the others are nearly as good, and with more practice will be better. And there are many in the other villages as good as these or better."

He nodded. "The priests will attack on their war birds."

"Which is why we need to learn to use the weapons. We need archers to bring them down. More archers to shoot the birds from under them if they form a mounted ground assault ... or bigger trenches to take out the birds."

"How do you plan to summon them from their temple?"

"I'm working on that."

Taj studied her for several moments and finally smiled. "Somehow I feel confident that you will think of something."

Turning to the women, he gestured for them to follow him. They marched across the field to where the men still watched. Taj surveyed the men for several moments, his hands on his hips. "I will lead your wives and daughters who have decided that they will buy peace with war, that they will take back what was stolen from us, protect their homes and families. You may stand beside them and fight for the same, or stay home and tend your fields and your children."

Naturally enough, the men were outraged, both at the assumption that they were too cowardly to fight, and that they would allow the women to go off at all. They cursed and blustered, but, although the women glanced uneasily from their men to Danica, they did not follow when their men turned and stalked from the group.

After a moment, Danica dismissed them. Slowly, the crowd began to dissipate.

Taj's expression was a mixture of amusement and irritation as he turned to study Danica. "There will be no peace in any household now."

Danica shrugged. "They'll get used to it."

Taj shook his head. "It is the women who make peace."

Danica chuckled. "We will make peace, but on our own terms. We'll kill the lizards, or drive them from these lands, and then we will have peace."

"The price will be great."

"We know that."

"But still you think it's worth it?"

Danica frowned. "There was a war on my world many years ago. One race decided to wipe out another. No one did anything because they were afraid, because they couldn't accept that these people were being systematically killed, because they didn't know how to fight back, because they thought the enemy would only come for their neighbors, not for them. I don't know all of the reasons. I don't know how the Germans managed it. All I know is that more people died than even I can grasp and nothing was done until it was too late.

"These 'priests' think they have the right to take your lives whenever they please. They will not stop unless someone stops them. I don't want to wait until they come for me."

Taj was silent for a long while. "What is this idea that you believe will bring the priests to us so that we can slay them?"

Chapter Twenty Two

Taj was right about the battles within the households. It was waged for three days. On the fourth, the priests came again, took a young woman from the village and departed.

Before the dust of their passing had settled, the decision was made.

Taj took Danica with him to settle on the battle ground. They decided upon a field that was fairly centrally located among the villages. It was a large field, and used to corral their birds. The trees were felled beyond the field and a low split rail fence built. Just beyond the fence, they began to dig the trenches, the idea being that the priests would land the birds in the field and charge them at the edge of the trees, which would require them to leap the fence and should cause greater damage when they landed in the pits with the spears.

Once they'd engaged the lizards and killed as many as they could, they could retreat through the trees to a second stand at the crest of a short hill. Here they built a retaining wall and began stacking stones and boulders to be released upon the lizards as they tried to charge up the hill.

The 'bombs' Danica came up with were dangerously unstable and unpredictable. They worked most of the time, however, and it was certainly better than having nothing of any substance at all to throw at the superior force.

The day Danica decided she was ready to test them, she and Taj strapped two pottery bombs to his bird and flew to the place where the aliens had left her. Tethering his war bird, Taj took both jars and set them on the ground. Danica studied them for several moments and decided to move them further away. Shrugging, more than a little amused, Taj took the other jar and followed her. When she decided she'd placed the jars far enough away from the position she planned to use to watch for her comfort, Danica set the one she was carrying down carefully.

She winced when Taj plunked his down beside hers. "Let me hold the lighter."

His eyes narrowed. After a moment, he handed it to her. She held it up to the light, seeing with dismay that most of the fluid had already been used. "This isn't going to last much longer. We'll have to carry torches."

It took several tries to get the fuses lit. Once she had, however, Danica discovered that they burned much faster than she'd expected. "Run!" she said, leaping to her feet.

She glanced back when she saw Taj wasn't following her. "Run, damn it!" she screamed at him. Waiting only long enough to be sure he was following her, she tore off toward the rocks and dove behind them. A few minutes later, Taj joined her.

Danica plugged her fingers in her ears, squeezing her eyes shut.

"We're making bread now?" Taj asked humorously.

Danica opened her eyes wide enough to glare at him. "No we're not making bread," she snarled at him.

Nothing happened. Danica waited a little longer and finally stuck her head up to peer toward the two jars. The wicks had burned down to the lids and disappeared. She studied them with the beginnings of disappointment.

"How long do we wait?"

Danica gave him a look. "Look, smartass, I haven't made any bombs before, OK? I told you it would take some trial and error to figure it out. Maybe the jars aren't tight enough? Or maybe I didn't put enough grain in them? Maybe they just didn't set up long enough?"

"What is supposed to happen?" Taj asked, irritation lacing his voice.

"A big boom."

"Noise?"

"All right. Maybe a little boom. I told you I didn't know...."

The explosion was loud enough Danica nearly had a heart attack. She tackled Taj before he could shoot to his feet to see what had happened. Shards of pottery flew over their heads and peppered the rocks around them. The bird let out a whoop and tried to fly off.

Danica sneezed at the cloud of grain dust and dirt that settled over them. Finally realizing that she was still sprawled on top of Taj, she scrambled to her feet and looked toward the place where they'd left the jars. "Yes!" she exclaimed triumphantly, leaping into the air.

Taj, she saw, was studying the burned area around where the pottery had been with a mixture of amazement, uncertainty, and dawning excitement. "How did you do that?"

"The fire makes the grain expand--a lot like when it's being cooked. In the jar, though, it has no where to go so it builds up pressure. When it builds up enough pressure, it explodes." Striding toward the experiment, Danica knelt to study it. She'd filled one only about half full and the other about two thirds. She looked up at Taj as he squatted next to her. "We'll have to experiment to see how long it takes so we know just how much time we have to get away. But I was thinking that you could have people fly over the temple and drop them. When the priests come after them, they could lead them to the field. We could put rocks or sharp pieces of bone in the jars and it would make them even more deadly because when it exploded, it would throw the shrapnel out in every direction."

Taj studied her a long moment. Abruptly, he grabbed her upper arms, yanked her toward him and kissed her soundly on the mouth. Before Danica could even get her wits about her to begin to enjoy it, he thrust her away again. He was grinning. After a moment, he sobered. "You *are* a gift from gods."

Danica blushed, both pleased and embarrassed by the compliment. Uncomfortable, she directed his attention back to the plan. "The best would be if the priests keep large granaries. If they do, and we could set those on fire, it would blow the entire temple down."

Taj frowned. "You think?"

"I know. Believe me. I saw a granary that had blown up on TV one time. It killed everybody in the place and the whole building and everything around it looked like this jar. The more grain, the bigger the container, the bigger the explosion." She studied the pieces of pottery. "These would do the trick, though, I think. They'd be easy enough to carry on the birds. They could be lit and then dropped. They might not cause that much damage, but a few dozen of these exploding all over the place would definitely get them riled up and throw them into just enough confusion, I think, they'd ride into the trap without even realizing it was a trap."

The closer they came to completing their preparations, the shorter everyone's temper and the more difficult it was to exert control. The time was approaching when everyone knew that the priests would come again and take yet another sacrifice from each village. No one wanted to stand idly by and watch them taken away. Taj was no happier about it than anyone else, but to act before they were ready would only make the risk of failure greater. They still had no clear idea of how many they would face. If anyone jumped the gun, it could bring the entire plan collapsing around them and they might not get another chance.

It was almost inevitable that the priests would begin to suspect something, despite their efforts to keep the watchers from learning of their plans. The tension alone was enough to alert anyone with any powers of observation that something was going on.

In Kara's case, Danica doubted she could see much beyond her nose, but she discovered one thing she hadn't taken into consideration and should have. Kara knew that Taj was spending a great deal of time in Danica's company.

When the priests came again, the formation halted before Sheena's house. Six dismounted, marched inside and seized Danica, dragging her from the house. As frightened as she was, she found that she was far more afraid that it might provoke Sheena into doing something rash. She caught Sheena's gaze as the priests marched her from the house, shaking her head fractionally. As they came abreast of her, she muttered, "Don't even think it!"

A commotion at the edge of the crowd drew her attention as she was placed before one of the riders. When she turned to look, she saw that a half dozen villagers had surrounded Taj, restraining him with an effort.

She shook her head at him and looked away. They weren't ready. It might take weeks more before they were. Despair threatened to overwhelm her as the priests rode out once more. With an effort, she quelled it.

She'd wanted a look inside the temple. It appeared that she would get her wish.

* * * *

Despite the fear that was gnawing steadily at her calm, her first sight of the temple to the sky gods completely diverted her from her anxieties. In the light of the great moon's rising, the water surrounding it gleamed like jewels. The temple seemed to rise up from the water. What appeared to be hundreds of spiny turrets covered the outside of the pyramid shaped building, rather like the bristled quills of a porcupine. Four towers, taller even that the temple itself, were evenly spaced around its base. At the peak of the pyramid, a larger, taller spire reached up toward the heavens.

She saw as they drew nearer that the temple was perched on a tiny island, covering the majority of it, which was what gave it the appearance from a distance of merely floating on top of the water's surface.

Telling herself she was gathering recognizance that the Glaxon's would actually get the chance to use, she had noted everything that had happened from the moment she was taken, mentally calculating the time between stops.

The village where she lived was the largest and apparently their first stop. They'd proceeded from there to each of the other villages, taking a sacrifice at from each.

She was the only female among the prisoners. They'd taken women the time before. The only conclusion she could draw from it was that Kara had reported her as a trouble maker and they had decided to remove her … permanently.

Dismissing that thought, she focused once more on her observations as the birds settled along the narrow strip of beach outside the temple and formed up. Two abreast, they passed through the gate at the base of the largest tower and into a small courtyard.

They dismounted there, and for the first time, Danica heard the priests speak.

She was sorry she'd long since discarded the translator, but it had inhibited her ability to learn the language of the villagers as much as it had helped and she had finally reached the point where she hadn't felt that she needed it anymore.

It would've been helpful, though, to know what was being said.

Upon reflection, she thought it might have been useless anyway. The sounds they were making at one another must be language of some kind, but it was more a series of clicks and hisses and guttural noises than identifiable speech patterns.

Balked of learning anything that way, she studied the building, trying to decide what area they might use for storing their food. She had little time to consider it. Almost at once, they began to herd her and the others through a wide doorway and into the building itself.

The birds, she saw as she was taken inside, were led off to a series of stalls along the outer wall. She guesstimated fifty along the wall she could see and wondered if it was the same around the entire perimeter. If so, she didn't think they could have more than two hundred total, but then they might keep as many as two to three birds in each stall. It was too dim within the walls to pierce the gloom inside those areas.

Once they were led inside, they were herded toward a set of stairs that led down from the main level. Despite every effort to hold her fear back, Danica felt it swarm over her in a chilling wash as they began to descend into the bowels of the earth. Torches were set into the walls every ten or twelve feet, throwing a flickering light across the stairs in patches. Shadows spilled between them, making it treacherous to negotiate the treads.

A stench laced the air and grew more overpowering as they descended, the mixture of smells difficult to separate and identify.

The sight that greeted them when they reached the base of the stairs didn't defy identification so much as it so stunned Danica that it was many moments before her brain could accept what she saw.

The pit near the foot of the stairs was filled nearly to the brim with refuse from the temple. Light from the torches spilled across the debris, illuminating the clutter of bones and rotting vegetation from the tables of the priests.

Rotting meat still clung to some of the gnawed bones, which accounted for a good deal of the stench, but most of the bones had been crushed by powerful jaws that had left them splintered.

The skulls would've been recognizable even without the flesh that still clung to them.

Bile rose in Danica's throat. For several moments she teetered between fainting dead away and emptying her stomach on the stones beneath her feet.

They weren't sacrifices to the gods! They were food!

Chapter Twenty Three

If she hadn't been too shocked even to jog her sluggish brain into functioning, the lizards would've had to drag Danica kicking and screaming into the cell they locked her in.

The guards had marched away again before the shell of shock began to crack and open her awareness to her surroundings. She'd been locked into a small cell, she saw, with the men who'd been taken with her. In the cell across from theirs were the women who'd been taken the time before.

Many of them were weeping loudly, asking the men about their families, if they knew what was going on, what would happen.

Obviously, they hadn't gotten a good look at the pit as she had or they wouldn't need to ask.

The surprising thing was that they were still around to be asking.

They were cattle to these damn things!

Sluggishly, her brain began to tally the clues she'd failed to put together--the careful breeding, for one, the way they culled the 'herd' monthly. Apparently, they held them in these holding pens for at least a month before they butchered them.

Her mind almost shut down again at the horror of that thought. With an effort, she redirected her thoughts along another channel. Moving to the front of the cell, she examined the bars and the lock. They were primitive by Earth standards, but on the other hand workmanship in the modern world wasn't quite what it had been in the old days according to everybody over the age of fifty.

Primitive, but effective, she finally decided, glancing toward the women in the next cell after a few moments. "The guards--how often do they come down?"

The women ignored her. After a few moments, the girl from her village pushed her way to the front. "They only come once a day, unless they're bringing in new ones, but they bring plenty of food and water when they come."

She just bet they did. The girls had spent a month here crowded into one small cell where they could move around very little. "Bread and water?"

The girl blinked in surprise. "Yes. How did you know?"

Danica felt a little nauseated. 'Grain fed' popped into her mind, but she dismissed it. "They'd have a granary then. Did you see anything like that when they brought you in?"

The girl frowned. "I don't know. I was too scared to look around much. We might have passed storage. Why?"

Because I want to blow this place off the fucking map, Danica thought. She shook her head. "It'd be useful to know if there was any chance of getting out. I don't suppose any of you've tried?"

Several of the women exchanged glances, which told its own tale. Danica restrained herself from uttering anything she might regret later, but she found it damn hard to stomach the thought that, knowing they'd been brought here to die, they hadn't even tried.

Finally, she left the bars and found a space on the floor large enough to sit down and prop her back against the wall. She wasn't at all sure she felt more revulsion at the thought of dying than she did about having to go potty in a cell full of men. She wasn't particularly self-conscious about nudity, but some things just damn well required privacy.

If they killed her, if she had to gnaw through the fucking bars with her teeth, she wasn't going to stay penned up for a fucking month like a damned cow being fattened up for slaughter. Pulling her knees up to her chin, she stared at the bars that formed the pen, studying every square inch of them, looking for anything that appeared to be a weak spot.

After a while, she realized that the bars weren't set into the stone. They were resting against it. There were crosspieces spaced about a foot apart, but she thought if even one of the bars was bent she might be able to wiggle out. If she could get out of the cell, she might be able to find something to use to jimmy the lock.

There was nothing in the cell. The men, like Taj, wore next to nothing at all and they had no kind of metal.

Shrugging inwardly, she placed both feet on the bottom edge of one of the bars and began pushing. The muscles all over her body began to burn with the exertion. Finally, she relaxed and sat forward to examine the bar. Triumph surged through her when she saw she'd moved it, not much, but she'd bent it enough to encourage her that there was a chance that she could push it far enough to create an opening.

After studying her for some time, one of the men squatted beside her. "Let me try it."

Nodding, she moved so that he could brace his back against the wall and push.

"What are we going to do if we manage to get out?" one of the younger men asked.

Danica glanced at him and then looked around at the others. That was when she realized everyone was waiting for her to produce a solution. Irritation surfaced. When the hell had it gotten to be *her* job to figure every damned thing out? "I hadn't thought that far ahead," she confessed.

When nobody else was forthcoming, she began searching her mind for possible solutions. "Did anybody see any guards on the walls when we came in?"

"I think I saw one in the tower," one of the men volunteered.

She should've realized that was what the towers were for. "That makes sense, but they're probably watching for a threat from outside, not the inner courtyard, which means if we could get that far without being seen we probably wouldn't have a problem until we were outside the temple. What're the chances of us getting the birds?"

"Not good. They only know one master. They're trained war birds. They would attack anyone who wasn't their master, or handler. Even if we didn't approach them, they would alert the guards if they heard us, or saw us, and they see very well in the dark."

"Does anybody here know how to…." She realized there wasn't a word for swimming in the Glaxon vocabulary she'd accumulated, which gave her a bad feeling. She resorted to mimicking the action. Everyone merely stared at her blankly.

They might get out of the cell, but of all of them, she was the only one that had any chance at all of getting off the island and making it back to shore, and she wasn't completely confident about her chances.

They were a very long way from shore.

And God only knew what lived in the lake.

"All right. We came in by bird, we're going out the same way."

"They're war birds…."

"I don't give a fuck what they are! They're animals and if we have to tie ourselves to them and beat the living shit out of them, they're flying us off this fucking rock!" Danica snarled furiously. They couldn't think up anything useful themselves, but they were hell bent and determined to shoot down any idea that occurred to her.

Everyone merely stared at her for several moments and Danica finally realized she'd reverted to her own language. "How many do you think each bird could carry? Two? Three? As many as four?"

The men scratched their heads over that a while. Finally one of them volunteered the information that he'd killed two dalops and carried them on his bird. This time, she gaped blankly until he explained it was a grazing animal that was about the size and weight of a grown man.

"All right, then three, possibly four if we're talking about smaller people. So ... if we get out, we head for the stalls furthest from the towers as quietly as possible and hope the birds won't set up an alarm, or that they won't be heard at once from that distance. We can use our dresses to blind the things long enough to get on. Hopefully with three of us piled on their backs, they won't be able to give us too much trouble. Once we're on the other side of the lake, we can ditch the birds and lose ourselves in the woods."

The women immediately began to protest.

"All right. Anybody that doesn't want to volunteer her dress to catch one of the fucking birds can stay here."

Both the men and the women looked at her reproachfully, but they shut up.

After about an hour of working on the bar, between them, they'd managed to push one bar almost completely out of the way. It was still a very, very small whole. From what the women had said, though, the guards would be coming back by morning. She didn't think they could spare the time to try to push another one out of the way and they might not be able to anyway since they wouldn't be able to use the wall as leverage.

Shrugging, Danica lay down on the filthy floor. She didn't know if she could squeeze through or not, but she was the smallest person in the cell and their best hope.

Working her head and shoulders through was going to be the trick. She didn't doubt that she'd have trouble with her ass, too, but that was fleshy and would give. Her head and shoulders wouldn't.

She almost wedged herself in twice before she managed to get her head and one arm through. She was still working on her other shoulder when she heard the distinctive scrape of feet on stone. Freezing instantly, she jerked her head toward the sound.

Three cloaked figures were moving rapidly toward her along the passage.

Danica's heart seemed to stand still in her chest.

There was no way they could fail to see her and no way she was going to be able to wiggle out, or back in, before they reached her. She opted for out. As she'd feared, however, the one in the lead reached her before she managed to free herself.

She flinched when he knelt beside her, pulling the cloth from his lower face, then stared up at him disbelievingly. "Taj?"

His smile was grim. "I had thought you would meet me outside the gates. Instead, we were forced to climb the tower and slit the throats of the guards. Their clothing is useful, however."

It took Danica several moments to realize he was teasing her.

He surveyed her dilemma and finally grasped her shoulders, helping her to extricate herself while the two men who'd come with him worked on the locks. When he'd helped her to her feet, he pulled her tightly against him. "I'd feared I would be too late," he muttered against her hair.

Weak with relief, Danica hugged him back. "Fortunately, they wanted to fatten us up a bit first."

His arms tightened even more. Finally, he released her. "Don't speak of it now," he said quietly. "Did you find the granary?"

Danica gave him a disbelieving look, but then frowned. "No, but this seems to be where they store their food."

He nodded, then glanced to see how the men were progressing on the locks. "Progress?"

"I'll have it in a minute ... I think," one of them muttered.

"Junt?"

The faint creak of the door answered for him.

"Not a word. Not a sound," Taj cautioned the women as they scurried out of their cell. "Take them to the stairs and wait, unless you hear the alarm. Danica and I will look for the granary."

Danica's heart skipped several beats. "Now? But ... we're not ready."

Taj's face hardened. "We strike now."

"You should have waited. You shouldn't have come."

He caught her face between his palms. "There is every reason. The only reason for me."

Releasing her, he caught her hand and pulled her along the passage. The end lay in darkness. Stopping, Taj pulled a torch from the wall. Danica grabbed another and they set off once more.

Danica sniffed, realizing she could smell the grain and that the scent of ripe, and molding grain was growing stronger as they progressed. They came at last to a stout wooden hatch. Handing his torch to Danica, Taj wrestled with the latch for a moment and finally opened it.

When they peered inside, they saw it was a chamber perhaps twelve feet square and ten high. Grain filled it almost halfway up the walls on the sides and mounded higher still in the center beneath a hole in the ceiling of the room.

Taj glanced at her. "Do you think it will work?"

"We can only try. There's no predicting how well, or how long it would take to blow even if it does."

Taj took both torches and tossed them inside, then closed the hatch tightly once more.

"We'll find out," he muttered, grabbing her hand and heading swiftly back the way they'd come.

Danica stumbled, disoriented by the thick darkness that surrounded them, trying to focus on the torches that lit the other end of the passage.

They'd only traversed a little more than half the distance when Danica heard a sound like thunder. "Oh God! It's going to blow!"

Taj glanced upward, as if he could see through the stone. "It's the bombardment." He muttered a curse under his breath. "I'd hope we could get out before they started."

They increased their speed until they were running. As they reached the antechamber where the stairs were located, they saw the others racing up them toward the exit.

Taj and Danica followed. They reached the top to discover it bottlenecked as the others froze indecisively. "Move!" Taj roared.

The temple and courtyard were in chaos. Cloaked figures ran in every direction, obviously driven more by panic than purpose as the pottery bombs rained down around them, some exploding before they hit the ground. They'd managed to make it almost all the way across the courtyard before it apparently dawned on the priests that the three escorting the villagers were not priests. Taj and the two men he'd brought with them, armed with swords as the priests were, placed themselves in the forefront and engaged the enemy, trying to cover the retreat of the others.

"Don't you dare slither out of here like whipped dogs!" Danica screamed at the other prisoners as she saw more and more priests racing toward them, knowing there was no way three men could hold them all off. "Arm yourselves and fight or I'll kill you myself!"

Without waiting to see if they'd listened, she raced to the first body on the ground and snatched up the sword he'd dropped, wishing she'd taken it into her head to try fencing lessons while she was so busy taking everything else. Even with the adrenaline pumping through her, the blade felt heavy. Resolutely, she decided speed and ferocity was going to have to make up for lack of skill and turned to face the creature racing toward her with his sword raised above his head like a hatchet. Leaping to one side seconds before he reached her, she swung at him as his momentum took him past her. The blade she held slammed into his back and vibrated as metal met metal. Numbness invaded her hand, wrist and elbow.

Tightening her grip, she whirled to face her opponent and discovered that the blow and his momentum had combined to throw him off balance. Even as he sprawled in the dirt, she leapt at him, hacking at his head and neck.

Someone grasped her arm, jerking her away from her victim and giving her a shake. "He's not going to get any deader," Taj ground out.

Gasping for breath, Danica stared at him blankly, stumbling as he dragged her toward the gate. Finally, she surfaced sufficiently from her shock to look around. Sounds seemed muted, movements slowed as if she was watching a movie in slow motion. Around her, the others were fighting, some limping, some dragging others as they fought their way to the gate and then through it.

The moment they emerged on the other side, Taj let out a high pitched whistle that pierced her shock. Around her, the other men made similar sounds. Breaking off the fight, they ran along the beach.

In the distance, Danica saw a dark cloud rise from the ground into the brightening dawn sky. Within moments, it resolved itself into a flock of war birds. Taj's bird landed almost on top of them. Grabbing Danica around the waist, he tossed her up before climbing up behind her. A war bird dove toward them even as their bird tried to lift into the air once more. Danica heard Taj's blade slice the air above her head. The bird screamed as the blade made contact and veered away.

Quarreling, Taj's war bird launched itself into the air. A brief struggle ensued as the bird tried to turn and fight. Taj uttered a warbled command and slammed his fist down on the crown of the bird's head. The bird whipped its head around and screamed at him, but it ceased fighting him and headed for the beach, racing the other war birds around them, some of which belonged to the villagers, and some to the priests. They'd barely cleared the stretch of sand at the edge of the temple when they heard an ominous rumble.

Chapter Twenty Four

Danica stiffened, twisting to look back at the temple. It looked as if the entire structure was vibrating. "The granary."

"I know," Taj said grimly. Pushing her down over the bird's neck, he leaned over her, commanding the bird to more speed. The other villagers had managed to catch up, surrounding them in a ragged formation.

The explosion was more horrendous than anything Danica could have imagined. The concussion hit them about two heartbeats before deadly debris began to pepper the air. Taj's bird plowed into the beach, throwing off. Screams from more than a dozen human throats, screeches from the birds and bellows of pain and surprise from the lizards added to the cacophony of noise as the blast rolled over them and passed on. Taj recovered first. Scrambling toward her, he turned her over, searching her frantically for injuries.

"Are you hurt?"

He was shouting, but she could barely hear him. Sluggishly, she tried doing a mental inventory, but she was too stunned to feel anything if she was hurt. "I don't think so," she finally managed to get out.

He looked her over again and finally lifted his head to survey the damage. Some of the other birds had made it to the beach with them. Some had plunged into the lake.

Around them, men, women and birds were struggling to their feet, staggering around drunkenly or simply staring stupidly at the mound of debris that the temple had become.

"Move!" Taj yelled abruptly. "They're regrouping."

Everyone who was able, jumped to their feet and fought a round with their terrified birds. When they were finally airborne once more, Danica glanced around for a count. They'd lost a third of their people.

She couldn't see behind them, but she didn't need to know that far more of the priests had made it out of the temple than she'd hoped. She'd seen the dark mass that Taj had spotted. Most of their birds were in no better shape, however--she hoped.

Relief flooded her when she saw they were nearing the

rendezvous. Taj urged his bird into a slow dive. "Get ready to jump."

Danica nodded, trying to gather herself for a controlled fall. Her mind and body were still responding sluggishly to her commands, though, and pain shot through her wrists as she hit the ground and rolled.

Taj was limping as he moved to help her to her feet.

She didn't realize until she was on her feet once more that she'd lost the sword she'd captured. Trying to shake her state of semi-stupor, she looked around a little vaguely. Taj grasped her arm and hauled her toward the line of trees, shouting for the archers.

The archers moved from the trees and formed a line, kneeling and notching their arrows.

Within moments, the sky above them was thick with war birds. Taj gave the signal to fire and hundreds of arrows filled the air with their whine even as the birds wheeled to land at the opposite end of the field. Chaos followed as wounded and dead birds collided in the air or plowed head first into the field.

As Danica had feared, however, the priests were disciplined soldiers for all that they could not have much battle experience. Within twenty minutes, they'd already begun to bring order and begin to form up.

She studied them, feeling a surge of hope as she realized that the blast of the explosion and the marksmanship of the archers had cut them down to a more manageable size.

As the soldiers began to advance, Taj lifted his hand and the Glaxons began pouring from the woods. Unintimidated by the size of the force they were facing, the priests let out a furious challenge of eerie bellows and spurred their war birds to more speed. Taj grabbed Danica's arm when she started toward the warriors lining up to meet them.

"You're hurt. Stay back."

Danica looked at him, fighting the urge to simply accept the order. "You're hurt, too."

"I am chieftain. My place is at the front."

"Do you think it won't undermine the women's confidence if I slink to the back?" Danica demanded.

Taj shook his head angrily, but they both knew he didn't have time to argue. "Stay beside me then."

"I lost my sword."

Taj handed her the one he held and drew his own sword. They moved to wait with others.

It became evident that some of the priests sensed they were riding into a trap. Moments before they reached the pit, they pulled back sharply. Many were carried onward by the wave behind them, however. Even as the first of them fell into the pits, impaled on the spears, those who rode behind checked only briefly before charging forward again, leaping the ditch.

The two armies collided. The priests who'd managed to jump the ditch were mounted, however, putting the Glaxons at a distinct disadvantage. Within a very short length of time, Taj could see they'd lost the advantage of the field and ordered everyone back.

Almost as one, the Glaxons turned and fled toward the trees, most of them so disordered after being told to break off so quickly that they completely forgot that they were supposed to fight and fall back. The priests cut many of them down as they ran.

Taj yelled instructions, but they were either deaf to them or the noise was such that it drowned him out. By the time Taj and Danica had made it to the tree line, hundreds lay dead or dying.

The trees would either force the enemy to dismount, however, or take flight once more.

Danica hoped for the latter. She discovered when they reached the next field that the other army had split, half taking to the air, the other half plunging through the woods behind them.

They were surrounded, open and vulnerable to those in the air if they tried to cross the field and about to face those charging through the woods.

Taj assessed the situation and lifted his head to call his war bird. Realizing his intention, the others followed suit. Within moments the Glaxon war birds filled the air above the trees. As they wheeled through the air, dipping toward the ground, the Glaxons called out the attack command. Instantly, the birds changed course and shot upward, meeting the war birds of the priests.

Catching Danica's hand, Taj raced across the clearing to the second stand. They were both breathless by the time they reached the gathering point and pulled back into the tree line to recover and wait for the warriors to regroup. As they waited, they watched the birds. Slowly but surely, the Glaxon war birds were forcing the mounted priests toward the ground. As their own men emerged from the trees, the priests' war birds yielded to the pressure, landing and the priests began forming up for another assault.

Danica glanced at Taj as he handed her a skin of water. "If we don't beat them back this time….."

"Can you find your way to the ruins of the old ones from here?"

he asked, studying the oncoming army through narrowed eyes.

"I think so … yes."

"Then, if we get separated, I will meet you there and we will decide what to do next." He fell silent for a moment. "If I do not come …."

"Don't say it! Don't even think it!" Danica said fiercely.

His gaze flickered over her face. A faint, tired smile curled his lips. "They are half our number now. We will not fail. This time, we will slay them all."

* * * *

There was not one Glaxon who was not aware that this battle, win or lose, would very likely be last. When the priests who survived the rock slide met them on the field, they met warriors grimly determined to take back what was theirs.

The sun had passed its zenith before the ragged remains of the lizard army finally accepted defeat and began to retreat. It was not allowed. The Glaxons pursued them, cutting them down as they ran, and when they'd finished, they scoured each battlefield and dispatched any that still breathed, and when they had swept the battlefields, they took to their war birds and scoured every inch of land between the fields and the temple, and the temple itself, until they were absolutely certain not one still lived.

Of the villagers, those who'd been deemed unfit for battle were set the task of tending the wounded. The watchers, who'd been seized and imprisoned so that they could not give away the surprise attack, were released and put to work hauling the bodies of the priests to the pyres.

The pits that had been dug to defend their first pitched battle were cleared and became the burial mound for the Glaxons who'd fallen in battle.

It was nearing dusk, and Danica had collapsed to rest for a while when she saw Taj and Sheena coming toward her across the field. She studied them for injuries and was relieved to see that neither seemed greatly hurt, although both wore bandages. For herself, she was scraped and cut and battered from head to toe, and felt as if she were the victim of a car crash, but she'd managed to come through two battles with only one wound that needed stitching.

Taj and Sheena collapsed on either side of her. "I have never smelled a sweeter stench," Sheena said gustily.

Danica looked at her, torn between revulsion and amusement.

"That is because you are a blood thirsty wench," Taj retorted.

"Be glad I am too tired to get up and beat you for your insolence to your mother," Sheena shot back at him with amusement.

Taj chuckled. "It was a compliment, my mother. This one is as blood thirsty as you. Twice I had to pull her off priests who had been long since dead and immune to her sword."

"Don't start!" Danica snapped, embarrassed. "I've never killed anything bigger than a spider. I just wanted to be sure."

"When do you think you would have been certain?"

"When it was dismembered and none of the parts were crawling. If you'd seen any of the damned horror flicks I had, you'd know they always get up again."

Taj studied her curiously. "What is this flick?"

Danica sighed. "Hard to explain. Let's just say it's something from a land far, far away, and a culture with more time to play and seek entertainment than they realize or properly appreciate."

"You miss your home world and your people?" Sheena asked.

Danica thought it over. "I miss some people, some things. I'd rather not think about it, though."

The three fell silent for a while. Danica was almost tired enough to sprawl out and sleep where she was, but as the light faded she sat up. "The stench of the burning is beginning to make me feel ill."

"It smells like freedom to me."

Both Taj and Danica turned to look at Sheena.

When Danica looked at Taj, she saw that his eyes were lit with promise.

Chapter Twenty Five

Danica had not thought it was possible to feel any worse than she did after the day of the battles, but she discovered the following day that she'd been wrong. Shock and adrenaline had kept her going the day before, dulling her pain, numbing her senses. She discovered the next morning that she could not rise from her pallet without a struggle.

Sheena was in no better shape. The burial rites for those who had died had to be performed, however, and everyone gathered to celebrate their lives, to honor their courage and to bid them a final farewell.

Almost a week passed before the Glaxons even began to pick up their lives and begin again.

On the morning of the fifth day, Taj appeared at Sheena's door. He did not enter, to Danica's surprise.

Smiling, Sheena summoned her to the door.

Puzzled, Danica glanced from Sheena's beaming face to Taj's pale, drawn one. He looked tense, almost fierce. "I have built a house for you, Danica. I have come to ask if you will make it into a home for me."

Danica stared at him blankly. "You built a house for me?"

Sheena pinched her, hard.

"Ouch! What did you do that for?"

"You must accept his proposal or decline," Sheena said in a fierce whisper. "It is our custom."

"What proposal?" Danica whispered back, thoroughly confused by now. "I thought he was building the house for Kara."

Taj reddened. "I began the house for the wife I hoped to bring to it. I finished the house for the woman I wish to fill it with my children."

Danica felt a little faint. "Fill?"

Sheena snickered

Taj's lips twitched. "We need not fill it at once. We will practice first."

Danica turned red, but it finally dawned on her that Taj was asking her to be his wife. A smile started inside of her and blossomed on her face. "Yes!"

Taj uttered a triumphant war whoop, grabbed her and tossed her over his shoulder, all before she could do more than squeak in surprise. Sheena raced ahead of them down the steps and stopped at the road. "My son has taken a wife!" she called out loudly.

Every door and shutter up and down the road banged open. Within moments, the road was lined with the villagers, shouting well wishes, laughing and clapping as Taj trotted down the road with Danica over his shoulder.

"What are you doing?" Danica demanded, torn between amusement and mortification.

"All have come to witness the capture of my bride!" Taj said with a laugh.

When they'd run the gauntlet, Taj set her on her feet, pulled her into his arms and kissed her until her toes curled and she went weak all over. He chuckled at the look on her face. "Come. I will show you your house and you will tell me what you want me to make different."

The comment startled a chuckle out of her. "You're so certain I'll want you to make it different?"

"My father spent many seasons changing my mother's house until she was satisfied."

To Danica's surprise, the logs that had once formed the beginning of the house Taj had been building for Kara were gone. She glanced at Taj questioningly, but he only smiled and shook his head, leading her toward the path through the woods.

He'd widened it, she saw, clearing the brush well back from the edges. She stopped as they reached the stairs to the place of the old ones, staring speechlessly at the roof that now covered it. After a moment, he caught her hand and tugged her into motion once more and they descended the stone stairs.

The ruins had been transformed, meticulously cleaned and restored. The courtyard had become the main living area. Whole trees had been used to form the columns to support the roof above it. The walls of the rooms on either side had been carefully rebuilt and Danica moved from one to the next, saving the bath, her favorite, for last.

She grew misty eyed with pleasure as the realization sank in that Taj had built this house especially for her. "It's … beautiful!" she exclaimed, rushing to him and hugging him. "Let's try the bath!"

His eyes gleamed with both amusement and desire as he stared down at her. Suddenly feeling strangely shy, Danica pulled away from him and moved toward the pool. When she'd discarded her dress, she turned and smiled at him over her shoulder before she walked down the steps.

Taj glanced toward the door, shrugged, and followed her to the pool. Discarding his loincloth, he descended the steps and advanced on her, crowding her against one side.

Mine! She thought as she lifted her hands from the water and skated them up his chest, enjoying the feel of hard muscle and slick skin along the way. Finally, she slipped her arms around his neck, pressing her breasts against him as she nibbled a path across his upper chest, along his neck and nipped at his earlobe before sucking it between her lips.

A shudder went through him. He slid his cheek along hers, sucked at the crook of her neck and shoulder, then sought her lips. Heat curled in Danica's belly as his lips brushed hers, melded with her own briefly, and then opened over hers. She parted her lips, sucking in a shaky breath as he thrust his tongue into her mouth in a bold, intoxicating exploration that built heady desire in both of them rapidly.

She slid a hand down his back and gripped one firm buttock, pulling him tightly against her.

The outer door banged open abruptly, sending a jolt through both of them. They jerked away from one another guiltily.

"We bring gifts!" several voices shouted happily.

"Oh hell!" Taj growled, both amusement and irritation in his voice.

"Who is it? What are they doing here?" Danica whispered frantically.

Taj chuckled, kissing her briefly on the lips before he pulled away. "Our wedding guests."

"Jesus fucking Christ!" Danica gasped in a horrified whisper. "You couldn't have told me to expect company?"

His lips trembled on the verge of laughter. "I could've … but then you wouldn't have lured me into the bath to ravish me. I was rather hoping we could get in a little practice before they got here."

Resisting the urge to smile, Danica popped him on the arm lightly. Unfortunately, the water created a loud smacking noise that echoed through the chamber.

"There you are!" Sheena called gaily, stepping into the doorway. "You'll have plenty of time for that later. You must come now and greet your guests."

She disappeared again after a moment. Danica dropped her head against Taj's shoulder. "I will die of mortification!"

Chuckling, he waded from the pool, but then frowned. "We did not bring a cloth for drying. Wait here. I will bring one."

"I swear to God, Taj, if you walk out of this room looking like that I will … drown you in this pool!" she hissed at him.

He turned back to look at her questioningly.

She gave him a look. "You might at least wait until *it* isn't standing straight up!" she said testily.

Shaking his head, he pulled his loincloth on, struggling to straighten it over his damp body. "*It* has been standing at attention from the first day it met you. *It* is tired of being teased and *it* isn't going anywhere until it finds what it's looking for," he said with a mixture of teasing amusement and hard won patience.

He left the room. Sheena brought the towel and a clean dress.

Danica was embarrassed when she finally left the bath and discovered that a goodly portion of the villagers were crowded into the main living area. Her discomfort vanished, however, when she saw that all of them had indeed come bearing gifts, bountiful gifts. The room was overflowing with them.

Everyone had brought gifts of food to offer for a wedding feast, and more besides to fill their larder. Sheena had brought pottery plates and mugs, jars to store food, and baking dishes. Someone had brought a table, and someone else chairs. Others had brought baskets, and pillows, and blankets, and other woven goods.

Overwhelmed by their generosity, Danica admired everything, held it up so everyone could see it, and thanked the gift givers. They feasted. When they had eaten their fill, everything was moved back against the wall, musical instruments were produced, and everyone else gathered to dance until the shadows of night began to creep into the house and the torches were lit.

Finally, the revelers began to depart and Taj and Danica climbed the stairs and waved them off. Sheena was the last to leave. Smiling, she leaned forward and embraced Danica. "Now I have the daughter I always wished for." When she pulled away at last, she patted Taj on the cheek affectionately. "I will expect some little ones soon."

Taj and Danica exchanged a look and laughed.

When she'd disappeared from sight, they entered the house once more. Taj studied her a little uncertainly as they reached the main living area again, and she turned to face him, moving closer until there was less than a hand span between them. Leaning toward him, she kissed the spot on his chest level with her mouth, the point between his bulging pecs where his heart thudded strong and hard.

He tensed, and she looked up at him, smiling faintly. Slipping her hand between them, she cupped his sex. "You were telling me this fine, upstanding gentleman here was looking for something in particular. I think I've got just the place he had in mind."

Taj's eyes glittered with a hint of amusement, but there was something far more elemental in his eyes, almost savage. Catching her hand, he thrust it aside, slid one arm around her waist and the other beneath her knees, lifting her against his chest. Without a word, he strode to their room, placed her on the mattress, and fell upon her with startling
ferocity.

Danica was torn between delight, uneasiness, and unadulterated lust as he covered her mouth with his own and kissed her with a ravenous hunger that spoke more of desperation than tenderness. His taste, and touch, and scent called to her own needs, however, her own primal urges, quickly summoning a hunger to match his, each of them striving to explore and caress the body of the other and tangling arms and legs until their mating became more of a frustrating wrestling match than a mutual caress.

Tearing his mouth from hers at last, gasping hoarsely, Taj kissed her neck and throat, trying to push the neck of her gown away to reach more bare skin. The dress thwarted him. Grasping it, he ripped it half way to her waist.

"Taj!" Danica gasped.

Ignoring her complaint, he pushed the dress aside and explored the flesh he'd exposed with open mouthed kisses from her collar bone to the tip of one breast. A sharp jolt of white hot pleasure went through her as the moist heat of his mouth covered the tender, swollen tip. Fire spread rapidly from that teased nub of keen sensation throughout her body. Her belly tensed, clenching almost painfully with need. "Taj!" she gasped in pleasure, wrapping her arms around his shoulders and holding him tightly to her, stroking his back, uttering a sound of complaint as he abandoned his delightful torture of one breast and then groaning in pleasure as he sought its twin.

Her dress had ridden up to her hips with the restless movements of her legs. It remained a frustrating barrier between her and Taj, however, riding just high enough to tease her with the possibility of rubbing her flesh against the hard ridge biting into her belly.

Blindly, she groped for the tie of Taj's loincloth. He was tall, though, and even hunched over her as he was, she couldn't quite reach her goal. Thwarted, she struggled with the tail of her dress. It was pinned beneath her and had risen no higher because of that.

She found she was extremely reluctant to distract Taj from his wholly thorough and welcome caresses, but she needed more. Slipping her hand between them, she stroked his hard belly, searching for the turgid flesh that had done no more than tease her unmercifully thus far. Her questing fingertips touched the rounded head of his shaft.

He broke off suckling at her breast, instantly diverted to explore new territory.

For several moments, he wrestled mindlessly with the tie of his loincloth. Finally, uttering a growl of frustration, he ripped it loose and pressed his distended flesh against her. She dug her heels into the bed, arching up on his downward stroke, so that he plowed along her moist cleft, parting the folds of flesh with his next stroke. His heat, the pressure of his cock as it slid along her clit tore a ragged gasp from her that was part pleasure, part frustration.

Grasping his cock with his next downward pass, she guided the head along her cleft until she'd planted it firmly in her opening.

Gritting his teeth, as if he was in pain, he pushed against her, delving deeper, struggling against the resisting muscles of her passage. Nearly mindless with her own needs by now, she countered his thrust, grasping his buttock and digging her fingers into him when he pulled away slightly to try again.

As wet as she was for his possession, her flesh fought every inch of his possession until they were both slick from effort, gasping hoarsely. He moved with short strokes, gaining a little more ground each time. She dug her heels in and pushed harder each time, wanting all of him, needing to feel the stroke of his heated flesh along the entire length of her passage.

By the time he managed to possess her fully, she felt her body trembling on the verge of release. When he hesitated, struggling to regain control, she continued to move, stroking his back and buttocks, kissing any part of his flesh she could reach. He shuddered, groaning as his body eluded his efforts to exert his will over it and began moving with hard, awkward thrusts at first, and then more purposefully, with hard, deep, aggressive thrusts that broke the tension inside of her explosively. Ecstasy washed through her in a blinding, mind numbing tidal wave, beyond restraint, tearing a ragged cry from her throat that spiraled upwards as the pleasure flowed through her, inundated her for many moments and finally began to dissipate, leaving a warm glow of satisfaction behind.

The convulsing muscles of her crisis tore the last of his control from him. He drove into her with mindless precision until his own body erupted with bliss, his body jerking uncontrollably as it pumped his hot seed deeply inside of her.

Gasping for breath, he sought her mouth with his own, kissing her briefly before he pulled away to drag breath into his lungs, then dipping his head to kiss her neck gustily. His arms began to quake with the effort to hold himself up. He settled against her, their skin melding and clinging with the dampness of their efforts.

Even as their breaths and heart rates began to assume a more normal rhythm, however, he levered himself up until he was hovering just above her once more. She gazed up at him through languid, half closed eyes as he moved his hips slightly, stroking his sated flesh along hers, a faint smile playing about his lips.

His flesh hardened, reclaiming the length of her passage. His strokes became more purposeful as desire bloomed afresh. More slowly this time, with deliberation and new knowledge of one another's bodies, they shared kisses and exploratory caresses until they broached the threshold of control and began striving with abandon toward ultimate bliss.

Their culmination this time, stoked, approached with a leisure that built their passion to a higher level, was more explosive, more enduring, more exquisitely satisfying even than their first joining. Reluctant in the aftermath to part, Taj settled beside her, drawing her leg up over his hip.

"Mmm," Danica murmured as Taj nibbled at her neck. "The wait was worth it."

He chuckled. "No it wasn't. It was a torture devised by the women of this village to drive the men insane."

Laughing, Danica pulled away so that she could study his face. "I never said no."

He sighed gustily. "I know. That was the worst part."

She chuckled again. "I wouldn't have told a soul."

He ran his hand along her body, settling his palm on her belly. "This might have told its own tale." He sobered. "We all agreed that it was the only way we could protect our children. I could not, in good conscience, break my vow, especially with you. I was almost sorry when I realized that you meant far too much to me for me to ignore the vow I'd taken."

"When was that?" she asked, trying to sound casual.

He frowned. "I think it was when we arrived in the village."

Good boy! Danica thought, smiling inwardly. Not that she

believed it, but if she'd ever had any doubt at all that Taj was an extraordinarily perceptive and intelligent man, which she hadn't, his words would certainly have banished it.

"When did you know that you wanted to be my wife?" he asked, nuzzling her neck once more.

Danica tensed. She hadn't anticipated having the tables turned on her, but she somehow thought his question was no more idle than hers had been. He probably wouldn't receive, 'when you asked me' very well. "I'm not sure," she hedged.

He lifted his head to study her.

She smiled.

He frowned.

She searched his eyes for a glint of amusement and failed to find one.

She searched her mind for an answer that he would accept. "You scared the hell out of me when you caught me, but even then I thought you were the most attractive man I'd ever seen."

He disentangled himself and lay back against the mattress, staring at the ceiling. "You have thought of nothing beyond your yearning to return to your people since you have been here," he said gruffly.

Danica bit her lip, shaking her head. Finally, she placed her palm along his cheek, urging him to look at her. "I love you. You're so very wrong if you think I don't. The truth is I never thought about being your wife at all, because I knew you were supposed to marry Kara … not because I didn't care about you, or because I didn't want you. I just didn't see any point in wishing for something that couldn't happen."

Taj swallowed with an effort. "I have thought of nothing beyond how I could have you. Almost from the first moment I saw you, I knew that it would not be enough to claim you. I wanted to see in your eyes what I saw in my mother's eyes when she looked at my father."

Danica brushed her lips along his and lifted her head. "Don't you see it?"

He searched her gaze. Swallowing audibly, he curled his hand along the back of her head and pulled her down for his kiss, making love to her this time with as much sweetness as passion.

Chapter Twenty Six

Taj, Danica thought wryly, either knew her better than she knew herself, or he just understood women very well. He'd been watching her with a mixture of amusement and expectancy as she strolled through the house, studying the walls, the doors, the size of the rooms.

"How old are you anyway?" she asked, turning to him abruptly.

His brows rose. "I have twenty summers."

Danica felt like someone had punched her in the solar plexus. "Twenty?" she echoed in shock.

He frowned, tilting his head curiously. "Why? How many years have you?"

"Twenty ... two," Danica lied promptly, wondering why she'd thought he must be the same age as she was, remembering she'd thought the same thing when she'd first seen Sheena. She'd dismissed it from her mind after that. She'd only asked because she was curious that he was so perceptive, not because she'd expected a shocking revelation.

Not that it mattered, really. It was obviously immaterial to him. They weren't on Earth. It dawned on her then that the rotation of his world was different, the days, weeks and months longer. Their calendar had more months, too. Calculated that way.... The effort at mental calculation defeated her.

There was a gleam in his eyes that told her he suspected she'd hedged.

She frowned at him, directing his attention to the strange looking stone figure in the center of what had once been a courtyard. "This is so curious. It reminds me of ... uh ... pictures I've seen before of the 'modern' freestanding fireplaces that were designed for homes back in the 60's and 70's on Earth."

She knelt beside it. "I thought it was, well, like a potbellied god of some kind, but there's a hole in the back of this 'mouth' that goes through the top. I think it must have been a fireplace, used to heat this, whatever this place was. Or maybe they used it to burn incense or something like that, but I think it'd work as a fire pit."

Taj dutifully joined her and examined it. "Maybe," he said a little doubtfully.

Danica patted his cheek affectionately and straightened. "I'm sure. All you need to do is build the chimney all the way up to the roof and we could keep it nice and cozy in here when the weather gets cold. It gets cold, doesn't?"

Taj chuckled, grabbing her hips and nuzzling his face against the rounded mound of her belly. "You see, little one? Your mother wants her nest made comfortable before you arrive."

"She can't hear you," Danica said, resisting the urge to smile.

He looked up at her, grinning. "He can. I felt him wiggle with delight when he heard his father's voice. He is so excited to meet me."

Straightening, he pulled her against his length, bending his head to nibble her ear. "What else, my warrior woman?"

"I'm still thinking."

He chuckled. "I think I will test this theory of yours and see if this works first. Then, I will figure out how I'm to obey your command."

She smiled at his retreating form as he left to get wood and finally returned her attention to the project at hand.

When Taj returned, several moments passed before she realized that he had only come inside, that he hadn't come down the stairs. She turned to look at him questioningly.

There was such a look of devastation upon his face that it struck terror through her.

"What is it?" she asked breathlessly, moving toward him as she saw how pale he was.

"We have … visitors," he managed finally.

"Taj! You're scaring me. What's wrong?"

He seemed to be struggling with some internal conflict that caused him so much pain that he could barely think or speak. "You must come," he managed finally.

Danica's knees felt so weak, she wasn't certain she could climb the stairs. When she reached him, she grasped his arm. Instead of reassuring her, however, he merely caught her arm to support her and led her outside.

She recognized the 'visitors' instantly, despite the strange looking devices they wore that reminded her strongly of the oxygen tubes hospitals used, except she knew they weren't breathing oxygen. Unconsciously, she moved a little closer to Taj. As if sensing her need for comfort, he slid one arm around her protectively, or perhaps possessively. She was in too much turmoil to really register more than the comfort of his nearness.

"You are the Earth woman?"

Danica stared at the one who'd spoken. He looked like a dubbed movie. His mouth didn't work in sync with the words spoken and she knew he was using a translator.

"Why?"

He spread his hands. "We mean you no harm."

"Somehow I just don't believe you."

He nodded. "We are from the Portanium Coalition. It has come to our attention that raiders have been encroaching upon territories forbidden to them, and practicing unscrupulous acts, which are against our laws. I wish to assure you that they have been brought to justice and we are only here to correct the wrongs that they have done."

"Brought to justice?"

"They have been fined twenty credits and their license to collect species for sale has been suspended."

Danica felt like rolling her eyes. "Slapped their little hands hard, did you?" she asked tightly.

He seemed almost to shrug. "The species that they deposited on this planet represent an imbalance to this world." He lifted his hand. A hologram appeared before him which contained strange symbols. "We have collected most everything that must be returned. There were some reptilian beings left some time ago--a female, two males. Capable of reproducing in great numbers and rapid maturity, these beings represent a substantial danger to this environment...."

"This is so timely! My God! Those things were here for years, bred like fucking roaches, and you're just getting around to trying to do something about it? You can't even begin to imagine what they did to these people."

Again, he seemed to shrug. "The Glaxons appear to be thriving well enough."

"You only think so because you obviously haven't seen the burial mound where we buried everyone who fought and died trying to rid Glaxon of those things!"

"There was war?"

"Yes, and you won't find any of the damned things, because we slaughtered them."

He nodded, produced the hologram once more and raked his finger across it. One line of symbols disappeared. "There remains three higher intelligence life forms from the planet called Earth."

Danica stared at him, her mind frantically scurrying to come to a decision she knew she had little time to make. Remembering the look on Taj's face, she glanced up at him. He looked away, but not before she saw the look in his eyes.

The aliens were offering to take her home. Such yearning rose inside of her for several moments that she felt breathless with it.

Taj expected her to seize the chance and shake him off like yesterday's news.

He loved her. She knew now why he'd looked as if his entire world had just collapsed around him, like he had stared into the face of death. He expected her to go.

If she didn't go, there would never be another chance.

If she went, she would never see Taj again, and Taj would never see his child.

They would not allow her to take Taj, even if he was willing to leave his own world behind and she couldn't do that to him, knowing he would be as out of his depth on her world as she had been on his, probably even more so.

It wasn't fair to be forced to make the most important decision of her life in two seconds! She realized, though, what her heart was telling her, where the worst pain lay. She might always miss home if she didn't go, and she might not. It would tear her apart to leave Taj.

"The Earth people are dead, too. There are only Glaxons here."

The alien studied her for several moments and turned to consult with the two who stood behind him.

"You are an Earth woman, of another species than those here. You will contaminate their gene pool."

Insulted, Danica gave him a look. "Too late."

"Your species is advanced far beyond the civilization here. You know that this can be … changed."

"Don't even think it!" Danica said with quiet threat. "If I'd had a choice before, I would have stayed with my own people, on my own world. I didn't, but I have a choice now. I will fight to stay if I have to. I'm Taj's wife. I'm carrying his child. I belong here and this is where I will stay."

The alien nodded. "Violence is not necessary. We will monitor your progress."

Danica rolled her eyes. "If you monitor my progress like you did the raiders, I'll be dead with old age before I see you again … which is fine."

Nodding again, the aliens turned, walking toward a beam of light that appeared along the footpath. When they reached it, they vanished.

The tension left Taj as they disappeared. He looked down at her and finally lifted a shaky hand to touch her cheek, as if to reassure himself that she was still there. "You decided to stay?" he asked, his voice hoarse as if with disuse.

"You didn't believe me when I told you I loved you, did you?"

He flushed faintly. "It was enough that I loved you."

Slipping her arms around his waist, she rested her cheek on his chest. "I adore you. I just gave up indoor plumbing for you," she said teasingly, lifting her head to look up at him. "I've been thinking about that, though...."

Taj chuckled shakily. "Did I not tell you my father labored for ten years before he had my mother's house to suit her?"

"You said five seasons."

He looked chagrined. "I was hoping that would be enough to satisfy you."

Danica stroked her hand down his chest and cupped his sex. "You will have to labor much longer than that to satisfy me," she said, chuckling at his expression.

He gathered her close, bending his head to caress her cheek with his lips. "I will do so gladly and with all my heart."

The End

Printed in the United States
53694LVS00010B/1-6

9 781586 087241